Receiver of Many

Receiver of Many

A Novel by

Rachel Alexander

RECEIVER OF MANY
ISBN-13: 978-0-9966447-0-9

for Robert, my muse

Prologue

She looked skyward and blinked back tears, determined not to let them fall on the infant's head. If Demeter shed tears, who knew what terrible consequences her sorrow would have on the newborn child?

The ten-year war was over. Father Kronos was cast into Tartarus along with the other Titans, monsters, and demons of the old order. Her child was safe here at her home in Eleusis. All the Olympians were safe.

Her heart was broken. She had been his first and his love, their child conceived to rule in peace or in war. But as her belly grew, Zeus Kronides turned his attentions elsewhere—first to Metis, then to Hera. Hera had not captured his heart; she'd secured his critical alliance with the priestesses of Samos. She had convinced several of the Titans to join with the rebel god, Zeus. She had ensured their victory and earned herself the title of Queen of Olympus.

And with that, Demeter was forgotten. She had been left to tend the growing things while her brother gods divided the firmament, the waters, and the earth.

The infant was oblivious, happily gumming her breast. Demeter coaxed her child to suck droplets of ambrosia from her finger. She smiled, enjoying the grip of her daughter's tiny hands and staring into her wide, pale eyes.

The soft voice of her servant Cyane interrupted her.

"My Lady," the nymph said, "Th-there is someone here to—"

"Hades Aidoneus," Demeter said to the looming figure behind her. She hid her breast behind her red chiton, brushed back her long blonde hair, and clutched the swaddled infant to her shoulder.

Demeter looked up at him; his dark eyes peered at her through the slits in his golden helm. The black plumes of the crest were stiff and caked, the helm and plate armor stained with the blood of ancient gods and monsters. The edges of his charcoal and crimson tunic were frayed, and his great black cloak was torn and flecked with blood. Cyane bowed and departed quickly.

"Deme," he said informally, removing his helm and shaking out his hair, "Please, I'm Aidon to you. I was— I am your ally, even still. "

"I will have no such familiarity with any of you. Keep your war and your scheming to yourselves. I'll have no part of it."

"But you *did* have a part in it. Just as we all did," Aidoneus said, standing over her. "Deme…"

"Address me by my proper name, my lord."

"Fine. Demeter Anesidora," he said, chewing on the words, "the war is over. I regret that all was not resolved the way you hoped."

She looked away, her green eyes filling with tears again.

He continued, "This war didn't turn out as I wanted either. When we cast lots to divide the cosmos, I received rulership of the Other Side. I, the eldest. Do you really think I fought for the privilege of having Kronos and his pantheon of monsters haunting my doorstep?"

"The Other..." Demeter paled. The third lot was not rulership over the earth as they had all thought, but... ruling the dead. Aidoneus would rule over the *dead*. And if he did... she held her infant daughter closer. "At least you were *given* something. What I have lost—"

"Enough, Demeter. Do you really want to be with him? To marry him? In just the past year he's had many and pursued more women than I can count. Not least among them Themis..."

"Stop."

"Metis..."

"Stop!"

"Hera—"

"*Stop it!*" She screamed, jerking away from Aidon's hardened eyes. "Stop it." The wind howled coldly outside, and the baby squalled, balling her tiny fists. Demeter held her closer, cradling her head with her arm as the gale subsided. "You scared her." She turned back to Aidon, glowering.

He waited silently for her to calm the child. As he listened to her cries, something heavy and unfamiliar settled in his chest. Aidoneus shook his head, and then straightened. "About Persephone—"

"Kore."

"Excuse me?"

"Her name shall be Kore."

"Zeus— the *Fates*— named her Persephone. Given her name, and who she is destined to become..."

Demeter looked away from him. "She is not to marry. And certainly not to someone as hard-hearted as you."

He recoiled, then drew himself up and narrowed his eyes. Demeter wouldn't— *couldn't* do this to him. Too much had already been taken from him today. "When she comes of age—"

"She will remain with me," she said, but her voice wavered as she spoke. Demeter's eyes grew wide and pleading. "Aidon, please; she's all I have left." She looked down at her baby girl, who murmured softly as she drifted to sleep.

"We made a bargain," he said, growing impatient. "I rallied the House of Nyx against the Titans and their servants. The war would have been lost without me. She is part of the oath that both of you swore."

"There is no longer a *both of us,*" Demeter cried. "He has taken that... that... bloodless, brainless, conniving—"

"Careful," he said quietly, his teeth on edge. Love and loss were not his concern. He didn't understand matters of the heart any more than he understood childbirth or the movements of the sea. "His choice of queen has nothing to do with our pact."

"Marriage is now Hera's domain, and I'll have no part of it. Not for me, and not for Kore! I swear off all the Olympian men and *swear on the Styx* that none of them shall have her. No one shall destroy her as *he* destroyed me!"

"I accept," Aidoneus said.

"You accept what?"

"*Your oath.* After today, I am no longer one of them. If you are so eager to keep her from the Olympian men, then I will renounce their company, and with them the sunlit world."

"That doesn't mean you can take her from me! I didn't mean—"

Aidoneus stood resolute. "For my part in the Titanomachy, when Persephone comes of age, she is to be my queen and consort and rule the Underworld by my side. You cannot change that!"

She glared up at him, tears staining her cheeks, saying nothing.

Hades shook his head and turned his back to her, walking to the door. "Do not think to see me again until that time," he called out behind him. "None of you will see me. If you are going to swear off the Olympians for her sake, then so will I."

1.

"KORE!" DEMETER SQUINTED IN THE NOON SUN AND called out again, "Kore?"

"Over here, Mother!" Kore stood amidst the sheaves of barley to wave Demeter over, then crouched again and poked her finger into the soil. Dark green leaves shot out in every direction, and she circled her wrist upward, raising a stalk out of the earth. She stood slowly. The plant crept toward her hand. Kore splayed her fingers wide and a purple blossom sprang from the thorny stalk.

"Oh, Kore, if you grow a thistle in the barley field, someone might prick their finger."

"Wait," Kore said, smiling. "Just watch."

A fiery copper butterfly fluttered on the warm breeze and alighted on the blossom. Demeter smiled.

"You see? I saw her wandering in the barley and made her a home. You don't mind, do you?"

"My sweet, clever girl, of course I don't." Demeter hugged Kore. The butterfly folded its wings, fed and content.

"My thistle won't interfere with the harvest, will it?" Kore knit her brows.

"Not in the slightest."

The butterfly spread its wings, sunlight catching them as they fanned. "I don't think she will be alone for long. Surely a good mate will come looking for her."

"Yes."

"What's wrong, mother?"

Demeter looked north, toward distant Thessaly and Mount Olympus.

Kore leaned on Demeter's shoulder. "I'm sorry. I didn't think before I spoke. The meeting is tomorrow, yes?"

"It is…"

"Why must you go?"

"Because," Demeter smiled and stroked her daughter's shoulder. "Although I don't dwell on Olympus with the rest of them, I am *still* a member of the *Dodekatheon.* I have my responsibilities here, but each full moon, I also have a responsibility to them and to the domain I govern. Just as you have a responsibility to the fields and all that blooms within them. And my going there… keeps us safe."

Kore swallowed. Demeter, she knew, had made Eleusis forbidden ground for the rest of the gods, specifically the *male* gods. She had known little of the Olympians since her childhood in the Fields of Nysa. Artemis and Athena visited infrequently, and she had seen Hermes on the rarest of occasions when he delivered news to her mother. She'd heard about Apollo and Hephaestus, and all the rest of her cousins, only from nymphs and in stories told by the mortals.

"There remains much for me to do before tomorrow. I need to go to Thassos and Crete. And I regret leaving you with Minthe again…"

Kore sighed.

"Daughter, you *know* you're safest here. Eleusis is under my protection, and with it— most importantly— *you.* Don't ever forget what Daphne was forced to do to protect herself from Apollo."

Kore's lips tightened into a line and she looked away. Maybe if she met these gods herself they would see that there was nothing at all tempting about her. Maybe she could convince her mother there was nothing to fear. Kore would wait until tomorrow. "All right," she said. "Perhaps I can accompany you to Crete next time, Mother? Or to… wherever you happen to go?"

Demeter grinned and stretched her hand out, opening up a pathway that would carry her over land and sea to the ripe fields across all of Hellas. "We'll see."

"I'll see you around sunset," Kore called out as Demeter disappeared into the sheaves of barley. She turned back to the thistle, watching the butterfly rest on the thorny stalk before it flew off toward the pasture. Kore danced after it down the pathway.

* * *

Rhadamanthys handed a scroll to Minos, who unrolled it and ran his eyes across it.

"The one before us is Aeolides, son of Aeolus and Enarete, king of Ephyra." He flattened the scroll on the ebony table before him and folded his hands.

Hades nodded to the judges, then leaned back on his throne, regarding the trembling mortal. "Aeolides, known to his people as Sis—"

"Please! You don't understand!" The dead mortal screamed. "I'm not—"

"Silence," Minos said, barely raising his voice. "You dare to interrupt the Receiver of Many? At your own judgment, no less?"

"There's been a mistake," he said, crumbling to his knees and weeping. The man raised his eyes to the inexorable god on his throne and the fearsome winged daimon beside him. "Please… Mercy. Please…"

"You will not speak unless spoken to. There are worse fates than even Tartarus," Rhadamanthys added before addressing Hades. "My lord, this one has been ranting since he arrived that he is not Sisyphus. Should we—"

Aidoneus raised his fingers from the arm of his throne and the brothers fell silent. "Hold, Alekto." The winged daimon relaxed her golden wings and stepped back. The Lord of the Underworld turned to the mortal. "You died three days ago, no? A mighty king leveled by tooth rot."

"No, no I wasn't, I was burned. I was *burned* by him!" The man trembled. "I am not he. I am not Sisyphus!"

"Aren't you now," Aidoneus peered at the mortal, his face a mask. "You know of my other names, do you not?"

"I know, y-your Excellency. You are the Lord of Souls. Please, Merciful One, Righteous One, I *beg* you, look into mine. Look into my soul. My *true* soul," he cried, his words choked out through sobs. "Please. You will see. I am not Sisyphus. He betrayed me. The black henbane… the pyre…"

The barest hint of a smile crossed Minos's face. He snorted. "I've heard this before, my lord. Wealthy mortals, fearing an eternity in Tartarus, pay charlatans to *cleanse* them of their wrongdoings, and will even murder, thinking the sacrificed souls will take their place so they can escape your judgment." He leaned forward to speak to the weeping man. "How many talents of gold did that false trick cost you?"

Alekto snickered and folded her wings.

Aidoneus was not amused.

"Please," the mortal begged again, his voice a hoarse whisper.

"You wish for me to look into your soul, then? A brave request." The Lord of the Underworld narrowed his eyes. "I will tell you what I see."

"You," the mortal's voice shook, "y-you will give me a chance?"

"If your words are true, you will drink the waters of the Lethe. You will forget the suffering of your mortal life, and you will join the souls in the Fields of Asphodel. If, however, your claims prove false…"

"Thank you; thank you my lord. You are wise and just." His shoulders relaxed and he closed his eyes, sighing deeply.

Aidoneus stood, his staff held firmly in his right hand, his gaze affixed to the mortal. "I see one who defied Zeus, the King of the Gods."

The dead king's eyes opened wide. "No…"

"A host who murdered his own house guests."

"No, please!"

"A kinsman who raped his own niece, compelling her to murder her children, then drove his brother to madness and death."

"That's not true. That was *him*! It was *him*!!"

"I see a man who, through his own hubris, tried to elevate himself above the gods."

"Please, no, no, no," the man crumpled forward, sobbing.

Aidoneus had seen the wicked react this way before when the breadth of their sins was laid bare. He had very little patience for it. His staff pounded the floor, the echo resounding through the room. He stood tall, his shoulders drawn back. "Abandon all hope, Sisyphus, son of Aeolus and Enarete. For the murder of your guests, the violation of your niece, for offenses against Zeus and all the gods, you are denied the waters of the Lethe. I, Hades Aidoneus Chthonios, firstborn son of Kronos, sentence you to Tartarus for all eternity. Rhadamanthys and Alekto will escort you to the Phlegethon. You will be cast into the Pit where the Hekatonkheires will exact your punishment."

"No, it's a mistake! Please, Merciful One, *please* have mercy on me! Mercy! Mercy!" The man let out a wail of grief, his voice ringing through the granite halls as golden-winged Alekto dragged him bodily.

Aidoneus sat, exhausted. He rarely sent a soul to Tartarus, and disliked doing so. But it was a necessity. He pinched the bridge of his nose and slumped back into his throne.

"Are you well, my lord?"

"I'm fine, Minos."

"Hypnos tells me you haven't been sleeping."

"A full night's sleep would be worthier of Hypnos's gossip, no?"

Minos chortled.

Aidoneus opened his eyes. "Are there any more today?"

"No my lord. And no coming judgment of any other kings or nobles, either."

"That is good."

"You know, the harvest is on the full moon," the judge said. "Fewer die during this time. I truly believe the sick, weak, and old are filled with enough joy from the harvest festivals to stay alive a little longer than they normally would."

Aidoneus nodded, staring across the dimly lit expanse of the Styx outside the terrace of his throne room, distracted and deep in thought. "Perhaps."

"If you no longer require me, I'll rejoin my brother and Aeacus at the Trivium."

"You may do so. Goodnight, Minos."

The judge nodded to his king and shut the door of the throne room behind him.

* * *

Her every footfall was filled by small flowers, and Kore glanced back to admire the bunches of larkspur climbing toward the sun along the roadside. She skipped, and soft petals grew under her springing feet. She twirled, and left a spray of purple irises all around her.

"My lady!" Kore vaguely heard Minthe call out behind her, the blonde nymph jogging to catch up. "Please, milady, we must stay within these fields."

"What are you afraid of?" Kore brushed her hand across the bare earth. "You needn't worry about straying from your river. What could possibly harm you?" Roses, thorny and thick with pink blossoms, circled them. "I can protect you better than you can protect *me,* Minthe."

"That's not what worries me, milady. Your mother said—"

"She wouldn't object to *this,*" Kore said, rolling her eyes. "We'd have to walk this road for half a day before we left the Thriasian plain, and there is no one for miles around!"

A fan of scattered crocus spread across the field as she ran. The pale naiad picked up her skirts and chased after the maiden goddess. "Wait! Lady Kore! Please!"

"Besides, Minthe, even if we were to see someone, Mother taught me long ago how to make myself—" She stopped cold and staggered back. White lilies crowded around her, perfuming the air, heady and sickly sweet. Kore's breath caught in her throat and her eyes grew wide.

"What's wrong?" Minthe said, catching up with her. A yearling fawn sprawled on the ground before them, bunches of beguiling aconite growing all around it. Its eyes were vacant and its mouth held a half-chewed wad of its last, poisonous meal. Flies swarmed its face. Minthe grasped Kore by the wrist, startling her. "Come, milady, you don't need to see this."

"Why not?" Kore answered distantly, rooted to the earth.

"It's ugly and… it's…" Minthe tugged at Kore's wrist again, encouraging her to continue down the road, to grow more roses, to forget the fallen deer. "Your mother wouldn't like it if she knew you were troubling yourself with such things."

"Why would she care? I've seen this before; it's part of life."

The naiad's mouth went dry. "But I can't… your mother told me to act in her stead. You are an earth goddess of young life and blooming things. She wouldn't want you around anything… a-anything that's…"

Kore gave the nervous nymph a half-smile. "Dead?"

Minthe nodded and wrung her hands.

She giggled. "Please, Minthe. There's dead grass under the plants, and insects, and…" She broke out into full-throated laughter. "Did you think she meant you to keep me away from *all* of that?"

"No," the blonde naiad muttered. "Only the bad things."

"The *bad* things." Kore cocked her head to the side. "Like what?"

Minthe fidgeted.

Kore grasped Minthe's hand and they walked away. Violets peeked out of the earth along their path. She wasn't altogether fond of being escorted through the fields like a little girl, especially by a nymph who was younger than her. But Kore knew that Minthe didn't, *couldn't* discuss certain things with her— that myriad topics were forbidden by her mother or simply made the poor naiad uncomfortable. Mating was off limits, and no topic was more forbidden than the process of decay in the fields behind them. "Alright, Minthe, we'll not talk about it."

"Thank you, milady," she sighed in relief.

"But your mother was *from* the river that flows through the world below, where the dead belong, wasn't she? The place where the spirit of that deer went..."

"I..." Minthe tensed again.

"Let's not talk about the 'bad things', Minthe. But..."

"Yes?"

"What about something *good*? Surely there must be *one* thing. Tell me something else about the world below."

"I-I know very little," she demurred. "I wasn't born there."

"Please?"

Minthe looked to the clouds above them, trying to find something to appease Kore's insatiable curiosity and end this conversation. A butterfly flew overhead, settling on a flower. More followed, clustering around the sweet violets. "Well... my mother told me something once, a very sweet idea. I don't know if it's true, though..."

Kore licked her lips, ready to devour anything Minthe offered.

"She said that sometimes mortal souls get lost on their way to the world below."

"What happens to them?"

"She said they grow little wings and become butterflies. They find their way back faster because their lives are short. But sometimes, if they loved someone deeply, they will find the one they lost, and journey to the Land of the Dead together."

Kore clasped her hands together and grinned. "What a lovely idea! I wonder if that's true of the butterflies who found my thistle today."

"What?"

"I grew a thistle this morning so the little copper butterflies could have a place to rest. Maybe they are wandering souls that needed to find each other and journey to the Other Side together."

Minthe grew pale. "F-forget what I said."

"Why? It's sad, but I think it's lovely, honestly."

"Milady, please! Please don't tell your mother what I said!" She looked horrified.

Kore raised a confused eyebrow. "I won't. I didn't plan to, anyway. But why should my mother be troubled by the Land of the Dead?"

* * *

The antechamber was dark, but Aidoneus didn't bother lighting torches. He strode the familiar path across the room, one he'd trod for millennia, and entered his bedchamber.

He removed his crown, robes, and rings, then drew the bed curtains, shrouding himself in total darkness. Aidoneus pulled up the cool bedclothes and closed his eyes. He slept in fits and starts, just as he always had, but if he lay still and purged his mind of thoughts and cares, sleep would come. Eventually, his body slackened and his breath became slow and measured. In his mind's eye dark and light coalesced and resolved, gaining form.

When he saw narcissus flowers dappled with sunlight, he knew. *Fates,* he thought, *why now?*

The dream, repeated throughout the aeons of his rule, hadn't manifested for centuries. But this past fortnight, every time he shut his eyes, there *she* was— lying entwined with him in a shaded grove, with flowers growing all around them.

Her face was hidden— it was always hidden. He got teasing glimpses: a flash of russet hair, his hand on her flared hips, her flower-trimmed ankles brushing against his shins, her soft fingers dancing across his skin. Her hand brushed across his chest and down his stomach. He closed his eyes, felt her breath on his cheek, and heard her whisper his familiar name into his ear.

Aidon…

He turned and captured her lips in a kiss, tasting distant memories of sunlight and heady new life springing from the earth. He could not see her, but he knew it was *her*— his unknown betrothed— that haunted his dreams. It was her that inexorably drew him to this shaded bed of white and yellow-trumpeted flowers time and time again. Her fingers tangled in his hair and he carefully rolled over her.

Aidon…

His pulse quickened as she encircled him in her arms, drawing him closer and covering her supine body with his. He grew hungry for her, giving in to the delights of skin upon skin, his mouth upon hers. The dream was always like this. He would caress her, she would kiss him, their hands, their mouths demanding more. These motions were familiar— their dance repeated across the aeons.

My lord husband, she said within his very thoughts. *Come to me… Find me, Aidoneus.*

He awoke with a start.

"Persephone…" Her name exploded from his lungs, and he lay back, light headed with the same rampant need he'd had for her in the dream—aching, and unfulfilled. It was always unfulfilled. Every time his body compelled him to complete their union within the dream, he would awaken. But this time was different.

She'd never whispered anything more than his name. Why did she call for him? *Why now?* Aidoneus breathed deeply and wiped the sweat from his face. He closed his eyes, shaking off the heady sensations of the dream world. After the ache subsided, he threw off the sheets and rose. He was grateful for the handful of hours he'd been able to lie still.

He couldn't banish the dream. He was certain the Fates wouldn't *allow* that. Morpheus had told him plainly aeons ago that there was nothing he could do. And any remedy Hypnos offered by way of poppies allowed deeper, darker things to dominate his dreams.

Aidoneus scooped a handful of water from the basin in his room and splashed it across his body before attacking his skin with oil, pumice stone, and a metal *strigil*. After he shaved his neck and upper lip with a razor, he neatly pulled back his long black hair with a golden torc, dressed, and opened the door to the antechamber. A figure stood by the window. He stiffly drew back his shoulders, annoyed.

Hecate turned from the open window, a knowing smile on her face. "Tonight is the full moon, my lord."

"That's hardly worth the intrusion," he said, knowing where this conversation was headed. "The moon waxed and waned before any of us came to be."

"Hermes's sandals alight here today, no? He will ask if you have any message for Olympus…"

"Yes." Aidoneus strode across the room, trying to avoid her next question.

"She danced in your dreams again, didn't she?"

He stopped.

"Were the steps the same as ever?" Hecate asked, walking toward him. "Or different this time?"

"I don't know why you bother with questions to which you already know the answer."

She smiled. "Different, then. What did she whisper?" He thinned his lips and looked at her helplessly. Hecate already knew exactly what she'd said. "It's time, Aidon. The moon is full."

* * *

"And Thassos?"

"Lovely, as always," Demeter said. Kore picked a few violets, weaving them into a crown. Demeter gave her an orange poppy, and Kore smiled, adding the finishing touch. "More importantly, their crops grow thick this year. The harvest will provide for them all."

"I'd love to see Thassos some time." Kore clasped her hands behind her back. "So… the meeting of the Olympians is today…"

"Yes, it is. I will leave shortly. Minthe will keep you company."

" I don't want to be kept company, Mother. I wonder if I could go with you this time." Kore raised her eyebrows and grinned. Demeter's face fell.

"I cannot watch over you there. You've seen what a rage your father can get into," she said, gesturing toward the gathering clouds, "and some of your cousins are… not to be trusted." Zeus's thunder cracked the northern sky, calling the twelve Olympians to court.

"But I'm the first born of the cousins and have only been to the Mount once, Mother," Kore pleaded. "And that was aeons ago, when I was too young to remember it."

Demeter sighed. "Sweet child, I promise you can come with me someday… But not today."

"But, Mother—"

"That is my final word," she said.

Kore folded her arms and turned away. "Fine. Someday."

Demeter squeezed her daughter's shoulders. "Next time the gods assemble, I will take you with me."

Eyes lighting up again, she turned to her mother.

"If," Demeter continued, "and only if, you promise not to speak with Hermes or Apollo."

"Really?" she smiled, knowing she could find a way around Demeter's restrictions.

"Yes, child." Another rumble of thunder rolled through the plain. "I must go. Minthe will meet you by the river."

* * *

"I don't understand why she doesn't join us," Hephaestus said, pouring another glass of nectar for Demeter. "She works far too hard."

Demeter smiled thinly at her nephew. "She's… shy. Kore prefers the fields and flowers. She's remarkably talented. You should see what she created yesterday."

"I'm sure my cousin's flowers are lovely. But she does the job of a nymph, not what she was born to do. Persephone might not feel at ease in court, but I'm here, and… well, look at me!"

Demeter shared a strained laugh with the crippled Blacksmith. She had worked all her life to protect Kore from the advances of the immortals. Zeus had fallen for woman after woman, human and immortal alike, and Queen Hera had fallen into petty jealousy and vengeance. Demeter hated to admit it, but Aidoneus had been right, about that at least. That could have been her.

Zeus sprawled on a cushioned divan, leaning on his elbow toward Apollo. His baritone carried over the chatter that filled the hall. "…as a bull, I tell you!" He grinned and gestured lewdly. Apollo threw his head back and guffawed. Demeter pursed her lips, remembering the lengths Daphne had gone to escape Apollo. The sons of Zeus were worse still— Kore would never suffer at their hands.

In a blur, Hermes flew through the white portico columns that stretched across the hillside of Olympus. The Messenger alighted and strode forward, gripping his caduceus with white knuckles. He whispered in Zeus's ear.

"Impossible! He hasn't left that place since..." The Ruler of the Sky's voice grew irritated. "*Why* would he come here for *that*?"

The king rose from his divan and climbed the steps to the top of his marble dais, settling onto his throne. He motioned to Hera, who obediently took her seat three steps below his. The other immortals hummed with questions.

A vise gripped Demeter's heart. It couldn't be. Aeons had passed— enough time for him to have let go of the matter, or to have forgotten altogether. No one had seen him outside his realm since the end of the war...

The linen chitons of the Olympians fluttered against their sun-kissed bodies as a cool wind blew through the throne room. A river of black smoke flowed into the hall, startling all but one. Demeter stood her ground, fists balled in anger.

Hades walked out of the smoke clad in black robes, his long, curling black hair pulled back with a golden band. He wore a simple crown of poplar leaves and three dark red gems shone on his left hand. His raiment looked austere among the rest of the bejeweled immortals. Aidoneus surveyed the room. *This court is more revelry than rule,* he thought, *a social club in the sky for the deathless ones.*

Hestia drew her veil over her face. Artemis whispered in Athena's ear. Aphrodite sneered and crowded toward Ares, who puffed out his chest. Apollo raised a golden eyebrow. One by one, they bowed their heads to the eldest of the Olympian gods.

Demeter stood imperiously in the middle of the hall, the last to bow to the Lord of the Underworld. Aidoneus could feel wrath flowing from her, and was transported back to the last night any of the Olympians had seen him outside his realm.

He approached the throne and bent to one knee. The room was silent, every eye transfixed. He planted one hand on the white marble floor and bowed his head low.

"Lord Zeus, Queen Hera, I have come to claim what was promised to me during the Titanomach—"

"*No!*" Demeter cried out. The room collectively gasped, then filled with chatter. Aidoneus kept his gaze fixed on the floor.

Hermes slammed his caduceus three times on the floor and Zeus bellowed, "Silence!"

After the roll of thunder subsided, Demeter calmed, her voice wavering. "Lord Hades, you cannot have her. She is sworn only to her worshippers, the fields, and to me." She walked forward and stared up at the dais. "Zeus! Your daughter tends to the young shoots and flowers—"

"Demeter," Zeus sighed. He had loved her once; had intended to make her queen until she had proven her ineptitude during the Olympians' war with the Titans. "Persephone was long ago promised to Hades. She is a woman now and has been of age for centuries. It is past time for her to leave you."

"I will *not* hand over my only daughter to the Lord of the Dead. I will not see her traded like chattel!"

"It's not your decision to make, *my lady*," Zeus replied stonily.

"Why not?! You had nothing to do with nurturing her; you have no right to give her away to someone who has been a stranger to us for aeons."

"It is *not* your responsibility to decide these things," Zeus said. "You did well in raising her, but Persephone is one of my—"

"My lords," she interrupted, raising her voice. If they would not listen, she had to leave now, before it was too late. She had to protect Kore. "Know this. If you so much as touch her," she hissed at Hades, "I will know of it. And rest assured, I will turn the world upside down before I allow her to be taken from me."

"Demeter…"

She bowed curtly to Zeus. A field of barley rose around her and she disappeared into the thick of the blades, her final words on the matter echoing back through the ether. "I have spoken."

Aidoneus rose and looked around the room, insulted and embarrassed. The others stood stock-still. So this was how it was to be— no one would speak up for the oldest and most sacred pact of the Olympians. He wondered why that surprised him. Hades turned on his heel, and a soft rumble emanated from the throne. "Aidoneus…"

He looked back up at Zeus. "You must make Demeter comply."

"Leave us, now. All of you!" Zeus bellowed. "Except you two," he said, motioning to Hermes and Eros. Hades waited while the ten remaining Olympians and their attendants departed, nodding respectfully to Hera. The winged son of Aphrodite thinned his lips. Hermes fidgeted with his caduceus.

"Why them?" Aidoneus growled.

"Witnesses, of course. This *is* a marriage negotiation, is it not?"

"There is *nothing* to negotiate. I kept my end of Deme's bargain. I have been patient long enough. Persephone is due to me."

"Demeter will never agree."

His mouth went dry. "You and her mother swore her to me on the banks of the River Styx. A binding oath *on the Styx*, Zeus. Did either of you think I would forget?"

"I never said I wouldn't honor it."

"What about Demeter?"

"You know she's too stubborn to let her girl go."

"Persephone has been a *woman,* a full-fledged goddess, for nearly a millennium. *Longer,* perhaps."

"That doesn't matter to Deme. Persephone will always be her Kore."

Aidoneus clenched his teeth. "Then what do you suggest?"

"Take her."

"That's it?" He raised an eyebrow.

"I sired her; my consent is all you need to marry her. You want her? It's done. She's yours. Find Persephone and take her."

"I can't just… have her. What do you expect me to do? Turn into a swan? Rain down around her in a shower of light?" he said. "Those are not my ways."

"I know, Aidon," Zeus said, shaking his head. "You are too reserved, too somber. There's no way you can seduce her outright."

"Well, that's reassuring," he said, stung.

"I'm not giving you an impossible task. You command more than just the dead; you can find ways to her that are closed even to me." Zeus shifted on the throne and rested his chin on his hand, knitting his brow. Then he smiled. "I may have something to help you along… Eros!"

The winged youth raised his bow, his arrow already nocked, took aim, and loosed. Aidon caught the golden arrow and winced, his hand clamped around its head, inches from his heart. He opened his fist. Parallel wounds from the razor sharp edges closed themselves. His blood quickened as he held the golden arrow in his shaking hands.

Heart racing, his head grew light, and he shifted his stance to steady his feet underneath him. Flashes of russet hair, a soft female voice, the twirling skirt of a green linen chiton, grass-stained knees, and delicate, flower-trimmed ankles invaded his thoughts. He looked at Zeus with a mixture of bewilderment and fury. "Was that necessary?!"

Zeus laughed. "We shall see."

2.

MOIST SOIL GAVE WAY TO TENDER BLADES OF GRASS and a host of flowers. Kore waved her hand over the barren earth at the banks of a stream and bright green shoots appeared in its wake. A twirl of her fingers drew gentle buds up from the ground.

"Larkspur, milady?" said Minthe, brushing her blonde hair behind one ear. "I doubt your mother would want even more in this field. Why not something else?"

"I'm feeling... uninspired right now," she said, annoyed by Minthe's high-pitched voice. Though Kore was older than Minthe, she looked younger, and her more youthful appearance made the naiad's cosseting chafe all the more.

It would be worse if Athena and Artemis were here. Though older than them by aeons, she still retained the countenance of a youth and they looked so... womanly. She was not alone among the immortals in her youthful appearance. Eros, Demeter would remind her, looked as young as she did and was nearly as ancient as Kore. She sighed. Perhaps that was what her domain would always mean for her. Flowers and budding shoots were young and she was their goddess. Kore frowned. And because of this, she thought—

remembering that her cousins had been elevated to the *Dodekatheon* while she had not— she would *always* be a goddess of little consequence or responsibility.

Kore made short strands of larkspur and wove them about her wrist, then a strand around each of her ankles, contrasting the white blooms against her short, sage green chiton. Kore looked down at her bare legs. Though youthful, she was ages past her flowering and the same as every other woman who had her monthly courses, she wanted to wear the longer belted dresses of an adult, and to wear her russet brown hair braided up in a beautiful chignon.

Kore dropped her gaze, frustrated.

"What's the matter with you?" Minthe asked. "You've been like this all afternoon."

"Nothing…" she lied, looking to the storm raging around Olympus. While she had begged her mother to let her come today, she was now glad that Demeter had refused. The dark clouds and lightning did not lie: there must have been a terrible disagreement today.

The sweet sound of pipes in the distance caught her ear. A plucked string from a lute answered the pipes and grew louder, closer. She heard laughter. Kore started walking toward the music.

"Lady Kore, we mustn't. It's the mortals! Your lady mother forbids us to go near them."

Kore giggled. "The way you talk, they sound like monsters! Honestly, Minthe, we have nothing to fear."

"I really shouldn't stray too far from the river, milady, please…" Minthe implored her. Her immortal spirit was rooted to the riverside, vulnerable anywhere else. Kore rolled her eyes.

"Then stay. I'm going to see what they're doing," she said, quickening her pace.

"But your mother—"

"I won't tell her if you won't!" Kore called out behind her. Minthe nervously wrung her hands before disappearing into the grasses in a flash of green.

Kore ran toward a grove of venerable oaks and peered around the thick trunk of a tree. The villagers from Eleusis were casting white flowers into the wind around a tent they had erected in the clearing. From under a saffron cloth emerged a man and woman smiling at each other, followed by one of her mother's white-cloaked priestesses. They paraded around the tent with other guests, then sat at a small table while the rest gathered around. On the table were two small barley cakes alongside straw effigies of Kore and her mother that were draped with vibrant flowers.

She smiled. It was a wedding party!

The woman wore a long saffron peplos and a crown of laurel and olive. The man, bare shouldered and tanned, fed a cake to the woman. The bride picked up her cake and fed him a bite. They kissed, and the crowd cheered again.

Kore clapped her hands together with the host of friends and family. From her hidden vantage at the edge of the clearing, she felt a tinge of loneliness.

The couple entered the tent at the behest of the Eleusinian priestess, kissing each other, their friends cheering them on lasciviously. A short, red-cheeked man poured barley beer, and the guests passed ceramic cups to the renewed melodies of lute, pipes and tambourine. Kore crept into the clearing, casting a glamour of invisibility over herself as she approached the wedding party.

Through the swirling music and dance she heard a cry from the woman. Was she hurt? She found herself in the middle of the revelers, close enough to see through the fabric of the woven tent. Their saffron nuptial robes lay in a heap on the floor. The man and woman lay beside each other amidst blankets and cushions and strewn flowers, his hand trailing down her neck to her breast. When his fingers reached its apex, he gave her nipple a little pinch. As she cried out, Kore looked at her face. She was smiling, and curled her body against the man. He took the stiffening peak in his mouth and kissed her breast, his hand now sliding downward, fingers gently moving through the thatch of hair between her thighs.

The woman bucked and gasped, her hand caressing the man's chest and shoulders. Kore felt something deep within her start to tighten and coil, making her suddenly, and strangely, very aware of the place between her thighs. The woman turned and grasped at a part of the man, unseen to Kore, the woman's hand moving in long strokes. His face contorted in a strained sigh and he moved over his new wife, kissing her lips and pushing her hand away from his loins.

The woman parted her legs, lifting her knees above the man's waist and staring up into his eyes. Kore looked on, wide-eyed, as he pushed slowly forward. The woman's mouth opened and her eyes squeezed shut, her fingers curling as she grasped her husband's back. The man paused to stroke her forehead.

He leaned down, kissed her, and pushed forward again. The look of agony on the woman's face intensified, then melted away as he brought his hips to rest inside hers. The husband embraced his wife again, moving in a slow rhythm between her thighs, drawing her closer, kissing her, and caressing her breasts. The wife raised her legs higher, slender calves alongside his back, her hands raking his shoulders as she moaned her pleasure.

Her knees lifted to his shoulders, ankles crossed behind his waist, and Kore now saw between their bodies. A hard shaft of flesh protruded from the man and thrust rhythmically into the woman. Kore felt her insides coil tighter and her thighs squeeze together. Her nipples hardened and chafed against her dress.

The woman cried out and moaned, arching toward her husband. The man rose above his wife and his hips thrust faster through her. Kore's heart beat out of her chest, her breathing paced in time with the woman's strained cries, and then the man groaned and collapsed onto his wife.

They unwound together, breathing heavily, skin glowing with sweat. The man pulled out of the woman, his engorged flesh softening as he held her close, kissing her and whispering sweet praises into her ear, thanking the gods that he had her as his.

So this is how these mortals worship each other, she thought. The ache of loneliness grew stronger as she turned away from the tent.

The sky had become golden, small clouds tinted with pink on their undersides as they traversed the sky. She left the wedding party and walked back toward the meadow. Kore felt an unexpected slickness between her legs and blanched. It wasn't her moon cycle; that had ended a week ago. She reached under her dress, and shivered when she touched her nether lips, inexplicably swollen and… wet. Kore looked at her glistening fingers.

She raised an eyebrow. This was new— a fluid that wasn't water or moon blood, but flowed slick and clear between her fingers. Kore bent to wipe it through the grass as she walked. A thick shrub bearing clumps of white, pungent flowers grew from where she trailed her dripping fingers.

Kore sighed, knowing she would have to explain this new hedge to her mother. She made herself a crown of the pretty little flowers. It would be a decent excuse. She walked on, her mind filled with questions and a strange yearning for something unknown and unexpected. She'd felt loneliness before, had felt it painfully since her mother had moved them back to Eleusis from the fields of Nysa a millennium ago, but never this acutely. Oftentimes, it was a loneliness and boredom she could deal with on her own, busying herself with the simple acts of creation her mother taught her— her divine role as the Maiden of the Flowers. But this feeling… this wasn't anything she could possibly solve or satisfy alone. It tormented her— flooding her with a strange ache and curiosity.

The images of the husband and wife in the tent played back and forth in her mind, one to the other. Nature had been a part of her as long as she had existed. She knew what mating was, that most creatures needed to do so to create more of their kind. But what she saw today, the motions made, the things done, the dizzying heights to which the husband had taken his wife and what she had in turn brought to him had little to do with making more humans. If that was what they wanted, the man would have just mated quickly with her to plant his seed at the proper time in her cycle, like deer or rabbits, and that would be the end of it. But he'd taken his time. He'd ensured that she enjoyed it. And the look on the woman's face, the convulsions of her body, confirmed it. To see pleasure and desire and love… she'd only heard whispered stories…

Questions were all she had now, and there was only one person who could answer these riddles for her— one who had loved and had been loved, one who knew what it all meant. Her mother. The sky lit up in a soft flare of reds and purples. Demeter appeared, her emerald-pinned blue peplos echoing the colors of the sky, under a flowing gold mantle that matched the barley fields beyond Eleusis. The wind came in from the sea and whipped her long robes about her. Kore's feet padded through the grass, faster as she grew closer, eager to have her answers before it was time to rest for the night. She wrapped her arms around Demeter. "Mother!"

"Kore!" she caught her daughter and held her close, relieved. Her face was creased with worry. "Where have you been?"

"There was a wedding near Eleusis. I went to watch."

Demeter frowned. "Is that where you got those flowers in your hair?"

"Not exactly…"

"Tell me the truth, Kore. You didn't speak to anyone there, did you?"

"No, I didn't even let anyone see me. And the flowers are new. My creation," she said, turning once on her toes before walking toward the sunset. "I think I'll call them lilacs."

Kore raised her left hand over the fields and gently closed her fingers to her palm. All the flowers followed suit, resting for the night. "Mother?"

"Yes, dear one?"

"Will I ever get married?"

Demeter halted in her tracks and pursed her lips, struggling to hide her distress from Kore. Had he come unseen to visit her? Hades has been unknown and unseen by most of the Olympians since the war. Who knew what tricks he'd learned during all his aeons in the darkness? He could be capable of anything. Demeter quickly schooled her expressions. "Why do you ask?"

"Well, I…" she flushed and looked away from her mother. "The man and woman at the wedding looked so… so happy when they were alone together in their wedding tent. I just wonder if…"

Demeter watched her daughter twist. She smiled, relaxing. He hadn't come to her, and Kore was still innocent. It shone through in every turn of her ankle and her hands clutching at the edges of her chiton. She tried to explain the best she could. "Darling, what you saw wasn't true love, it was just lust. They were pricked by Eros, and their love will die someday. The husband will take a *hetaera* or a lover, and the wife will be shut away in his home to bear his children. The love of men is fleeting. It is the way of things."

"He told her how much he loved her, that he would never leave her," Kore said, walking beside Demeter. She watched her mother shake her head, a disappointed grimace on her face. Kore knew that look well. "And… and he said that he was so very happy the gods had let him find her, Mother. That didn't sound fleeting to me."

Demeter stopped and turned to Kore, trying to keep irritation from creeping into her voice. "Child, you might be aeons old, but you are still young in the ways of the world. The only lasting love is that between a mother and her children. I am sparing you the agony of a husband who lords himself over you, then breaks his oaths and your heart. Please learn from my folly, my bitter experience. This is what's best."

Kore wilted as they resumed their walk through the field. Twilight descended, washing the fields in a pale pink. A tall oak rose over the hill as they crested it. Maybe her mother was right. After all, her father had left Demeter to wed another, and even then had not found his wife's attentions to be enough. The ongoing tales of his philandering had been impossible to avoid. But not all men were Zeus, were they? "Maybe it would be different for me," she muttered under her breath.

Demeter spun about to face her. "No, it most certainly would not. And don't ever believe any man who would tell you otherwise, Kore. Men will say and do anything to have… that."

"Have what?"

"What they all want: a girl's maidenhead. They think to possess and own a woman once they take it, and they will say anything, do anything, to claim it. What you saw the man doing to that woman in the tent was all he wanted or cared to have from her."

"Doing *to* her? But she," her cheeks burned and her voice grew small, "she looked like she enjoyed it."

"Did she now?" Demeter knit her brow. "At first, even?"

Kore recalled the pain on the Eleusinian woman's face, the anguished cry. "No. But—"

"You saw how he hurt her when he took her. Kore, she clung to him out of desperation, not love, through the rest of the act once she realized what he had done— that she was a maiden no more. It is what is expected of wives. They must submit to the demands of their husbands. If she did not, he would have taken it from her anyway and with greater harm to her. When women fall foolishly into the bonds marriage— or worse and more often these days, when they are *sold* by their fathers— then they are obligated to submit their bodies to their husband. The woman you saw today only chose to go along with him to avoid more pain than he had already caused her."

Kore looked at the ground and felt tears sting the corners of her eyes before she willed them away. Ownership. Submission. The loss of her very self, if she were no longer a maiden— no longer Kore. Her wise mother was right. It was foolish to wish for a husband, despite the softness and love and unbounded joy she had witnessed. What if Demeter's prediction was correct and they despised each other later and her husband strayed from her so he could claim another? Perhaps she should be glad that she was to remain a maiden, just like her cousins Athena and Artemis, and would never endure the shame of that.

"And those poor mortals," Demeter went on. "Half the women don't even survive childbirth. Including the woman you saw today."

Kore looked up at her mother in horror. "That can't be true! Please tell me that's not true."

"Kore, you know as well as I do that Eleusis calls on me to bear witness to their marriages. I can foresee their fates and that's the most likely cause of her inevitable death. I cannot stop her from passing to the Other Side."

"Mother, no! Please, these are your people! Surely there is something you can do?"

"It is not my role to decide who lives and who dies. And it is the natural order. All men and women must die, or mankind would overrun the earth."

"But can't you at least save just this one woman, Mother?"

"No, child. Those decisions are for the Realm of the Dead."

The look on her daughter's face made Demeter wish she hadn't let her current worries cloud her words. Even talking about that godsforsaken realm might pique Kore's boundless curiosity. The immortal Olympians shouldn't bother themselves with death anyway, and her little flower didn't need to trouble herself with these things. Kore was panic stricken, and looked helpless. Demeter immediately regretted filling her daughter's mind with such dreadful thoughts right before bed.

"Kore," she said, inclining her head and smiling. "You don't need a husband. On your own, you have a remarkable role to play in this cosmos. Flowers sprout, they live, then they wilt. These people are alive right now, and your gift teaches them to enjoy the fleeting days they do have, and to celebrate it with each other."

They passed under the sweeping branches of the great oak tree and stood outside Kore's bower. The Maiden turned her mouth up in a half smile at her mother's praise, and also remembered that there were others on Olympus she hadn't yet met— Aphrodite, for instance— who might be better able to answer these questions, if only she could find a way to visit them. "When are you next going to Olympus?"

"Not any time soon, dear. Today was... tumultuous. I won't be going for a long time, I expect," she saw disappointment cross Kore's face, remembering the promise she'd made earlier that day. "I'm sure everything will clear up some day. I'll take you then."

"So, I will see you tomorrow morning for the harvest?"

"Of course." She kissed Kore on the cheek before vanishing with a rustle of barley. "Sleep well, darling. You're safe here."

People throughout Hellas had built shrines of wood and living things to Kore and to her mother aeons ago, maintaining them generation after generation. Her private sanctums were always open to the sky, the sunlight, the honeybees and birds that helped her tend to the new shoots and flowers. One of Kore's favorite sacred places lay in this very clearing at the base of the oak tree. Clusters of white larkspur grew up the perfect circle of green willow shoots that served as her walls. Her ceiling was the vaulted branches and the stars wheeling above. The grass beneath her was soft, not wet with dew as it sometimes was, and strewn with rushes and violet petals upon which she made her bed.

As Kore lay on her side, she clasped her hands together and spoke a prayer in her own shrine, quietly pleading to Eileithyia, the goddess of childbirth, to watch over the newly married woman and deliver her from pain and death. Maybe she would get to speak to Eileithyia directly before it was too late.

Marriage. They seemed so happy, so content with one another. Her mother had never had that before and perhaps she was wrong. Demeter was not omniscient, nor was her mother one of the Fates. The wife in the tent could live and thrive with her husband and child, and make many new children. She may have created a child today.

Kore's body grew hot as she imagined making a child, the act of love. She quaked as images from the wedding swirled through her head, casting her into a fitful sleep. Her hands came up around her shoulders, her arms pressing against her breasts under the thin chiton. Kore dreamed. In her mind, she felt the woman's joy again and felt it returned. She was the married woman, and could feel the husband's arms holding her. Except she was still her maiden self lying in the grove and he was—

He was holding her. Kore felt his chest rise behind her and saw that the hands upon her arms were not hers. He was here, and *holding her* and she was leaning back into his embrace. Warm, strong hands rested on her arms, then traced down to the crooks of her elbows. Heat followed their path. The realization startled her— and startled the owner of those hands, she realized belatedly, feeling his fingers tense and relax on her skin when she stirred.

"Shhh… Persephone," a voice whispered in her ear. Persephone; the name her father had given her. It was her *official* name, she always knew, that lay beyond her mother and the nymphs calling her Kore, *maiden*. "You're dreaming; there's no need to be frightened…"

She stayed still, not even daring to breathe. Who— why would he specifically call her this, or even know her true name? His voice had shaken just a bit, as though he were trying to assure himself that what he had said was true, that this *was* just a dream. The hands continued to move, lightly dropping from her elbows to her waist then traveling up her arms to her shoulders with a soft squeeze.

Only when his fingers touched her back did she realize that her chiton was gone. She was naked in front of… him. Kore's hands flew instinctively to shield her mons, her stomach and breasts, but he gently pulled them away by her wrists, unwinding her. His careful, almost cautious movements made her breath catch in her throat, and when he didn't immediately caress what he had revealed, she relaxed. This wasn't real; it was only a dream. And he just felt so…

She knew that he spoke the truth. If this were indeed a dream, then surely she was safe. Wasn't she? Even if he tried to do something… unthinkable, she could wake up and escape him. Couldn't she? But as his hands moved back to her arms, her urge to wake, to leave him in the dream world, to leave the gentle stroking of his fingers, quickly diminished. Wordless answers to her unspoken yearnings after the wedding, as well as a pervasive calm, filled her the longer he touched her. His rich masculine voice rose slightly above the level of a whisper. "Let me look at you."

Kore felt the gentle stranger roll her onto her back, her eyes shut and her face turned away as he ran his hands down her outstretched arms. What was he? Who was he? Was he an *oneiros* from the dream world or some shadowy creature from the Other Side? She'd heard tales of their visits— some benevolent, some terrifying. Did his voice match or mask his true appearance? Would she scream if she saw him? She felt his eyes on her body, but kept hers closed. Fingers brushed through her hair, moving russet waves away from her face and tucking them softly behind her ear before his hand rested on her shoulder, deliberately— *respectfully*— avoiding the parts of her unseen by the sun. Kore felt the same coil form low in her belly, stronger than this afternoon, becoming an ache that made her hips move just to soothe it. No reprieve came.

"Open your eyes," she heard him whisper, his voice catching. Kore did so. She wanted to see who this was, a man who she had either conjured in her dreams or who had deliberately entered them. She needed to see what manner of man he was, but was afraid to look on him directly. With her head faced to the side, she first saw pale fingers brushing over her shoulder with short, smooth nails.

The moonlight danced along the shadows and rough contours of very male hands holding and caressing her. Kore's skin thrilled at the sight, and the ache became a dull, pleasant throb around a strange feeling of emptiness. She could feel the strain in his arms as he fought to keep his hands away from her breasts, fought to ensure that he didn't stray too far into intimacy and frighten her. A faint luminescence played under his skin, the tell tale sign that this was not a mortal man. He wasn't one of the frightful creatures mortals told their children about and swept from their homes at Anthesteria, either. Who was he?

Kore turned slowly toward him, taking in first the smooth defined muscles of his arms and wide shoulders, then the slope of his body pressed to the side of hers. His face loomed into view, a thin smile deepening as he examined her. He tensed, almost imperceptibly. Though his face remained steady, she saw the pronounced lump in his throat bob nervously, knowing that she was now studying him.

She stared up at him with her pale blue eyes, her lips parted in curiosity and wonder at his appearance. He was… she didn't have a word for it; she'd never looked at a man this closely. The sensation coursing through her— the tightening coil within, the quickening of her breath— gave her at least some sort of answer to what she felt today when she'd peered into the wedding tent. This was desire.

The eyes that met hers were wide and deep brown, almost black in the soft light and framed with black brows. Long, black curls of hair framed his moonlit face, falling away down his back. A narrow, trimmed black beard sat below wide soft lips and a regal aquiline nose. She felt the coil inside unwind into a flutter and gasped slightly.

They stayed that way, simply beholding one another before Kore felt his hand gently frame her face. He eclipsed her view, drawing closer. She sensed her whole body pulling toward his. His warm mouth tentatively brushed once over hers before capturing her lower lip between his, drawing her into a kiss. Kore had never been kissed before, and she realized she still hadn't. This was a dream. Wasn't it? He felt so real and warm and sweet. And the jolt his touch sent through her had her returning his kiss, her lips seeking out his and parting to enjoy him. His tongue darted across her teeth before she pulled back to see him.

"I never dreamed you would be this beautiful," he said quietly, trembling slightly, his baritone voice resonating low and intimate as he scanned the length of her body.

"What do you m-m—" she began, her voice swallowed by another kiss. This one was more insistent, and she felt her skin jump. Her hips rocked, her stomach tensed at the firmer press of his mouth against hers. It was only once she leaned into him that she felt something hard and hot pressed against her hip, eliciting a soft groan into her mouth and a shiver that moved like a wave along his entire body. She mewled a wordless question against his lips, wanting to ask who he was. His only response was to skim his tongue across her teeth until they opened, letting him taste her.

Kore heard him sigh as his hand traced up her ribs and settled firmly on her breast. Her nipple instantly tightened under his palm and she cried into his mouth at the unanticipated pleasure of it. He languorously stroked her tongue with his and tasted of ancient groves and deep, warm earth, and the cold, faint sweetness of a foreign flower she knew but couldn't quite place. With a gasp she broke off the kiss to look up at him again, her face and neck flushed, her lips tingling, her heart pounding. The cool night air moved over her hot skin.

He smiled down at her again. "You taste exquisite."

"Who are you?" she said, barely able to hear her own words as her heartbeat thrummed in her ears.

He froze at her question and darted his eyes from her gaze, taking in, *memorizing,* her face and neck, the lines of her collarbone. He reached for a lock of hair that had spilled over her breast. "This is your dream, remember? Tell me who I am," he said smiling, absently coiling the long brown tendril around a finger.

She narrowed her eyes at him, her tone firm. "If this is my dream, *oneiroi,* then answer my question. Who are you?"

He was hearing her true voice— that of a natural ruler. His smile widened at her fearlessness, even though he was twice her size and loomed over her, caging her body with his. "I am not an *oneiroi,* sweet one."

"What are you, then?"

"Deathless," he said simply. "Like you."

"Wh-who are you?" she whispered.

He slowly lowered himself to her, hovering just above her, the heat of his chest making contact with her, making her quiver, making her want to pull the weight of his body down to cover hers. He whispered in her ear. "I am your lord husband."

Her eyes grew wide and he settled his mouth on hers for another kiss. She felt everything tilt, and drop away underneath her as he lifted her at the small of her back, pulling her against him to sit up with him. He grasped her leg with one hand, positioning her in his lap. Her trembling legs splayed around his hips and her body was flush against his. For a moment the heat she'd felt earlier pressed and pulsed against her lower lips as they adjusted. He pulled back, his face filled with caution and longing. Instinctively, her feet locked around his lower back, raising her higher and breaking that brief, intimate contact. His arms supported her upright frame effortlessly. He brought her inches from his face, and his eyes darkened with intensity and heat, midnight black, and Kore suddenly felt very small again. "M-my husband?"

"Yes," he said, feeling her arms rest on either side of his chest and her fingers grip his shoulders. "And you will be my queen, Persephone."

He whispered her name to her and kissed her again, letting her hands move up to his neck and weave through the curls of his hair. She grew curious and snaked her tongue into his mouth. *Did he say 'queen'?* Kore felt him surge against her as she led in kissing him instead of being kissed. He tightened his arms around her, his control starting to slip. It sent a thrill through her, but she realized how dangerous her forwardness could be.

Physically, he could easily overpower her and take whatever he wanted. But he didn't. In her sensual haze she wondered nervously for a moment if he intended to enter her here and now— to make her his queen in the deepest sense. Kore shuddered at this idea, wondering if by just entertaining that thought within the dream, he would do just that. But he didn't. She felt one supporting arm grasp at her shoulder blades and the other move down her back and firmly cup the cheeks of her rear as he lifted them up. Still holding her, he rose up on his knees and laid her back down in the soft rushes, fitting his body over hers.

Kore felt the world tilt back and squeezed her legs tighter around him. She was entirely at his mercy. What would it feel like for him to be within her? Would he go gently, knowing that she was a maiden? If he tried to take her now, he could. But he didn't. He arched above her and carefully fanned out her lilac-strewn hair and stroked his fingers through it, brushing it back from her forehead. He cupped her cheek and made her shiver as his thumb trailed over her lips, her chin and down the column of her neck. He drew closer. Black curls fell from his head and down his back, forming a curtain around them. The oak tree was blotted out. The stars were gone. There was only she and he, her body blanketed by his above her, their tongues mating together in a kiss, the throbbing heat pressed hard against her inner thigh. His hips rocked forward of their own volition and she felt him grind against her skin, his breath hissing through his teeth.

In a bid to salvage his control, he broke away from their kiss and pressed his lips against her neck, lifting his body away from hers, making her shiver in the night air. He planted light kisses across her collarbone, molding a breast with his hand.

The sudden absence of his skin against her made her delirious, her thoughts rapidly shifting back and forth between relief at his restraint and wanting to draw him down again to quench the ache consuming her. Kore's body was on fire. She didn't want him to stop. She needed him to stop. She needed to know who he was. She didn't care who he was as long as he didn't stop. Her frustrations became a moan, the sound surprising her and encouraging him, when his lips wrapped around a taut nipple. The electric sensation of his tongue rasping against the very tip arched her body toward him and shot pleasure through the center of her. Kore's mind snapped into focus as his hand came between them and landed with a massaging squeeze on the nest of curls covering her mound.

"Wait..." she whispered.

He pulled that hand away instantly, his breath shallow. His arms tensed and he stared straight at her, straining between holding himself back and pressing onward, deciding, weighing her single word against their shared desire. He smiled at her before inhaling and letting out a long cool sigh, shutting his eyes. "You're right."

She felt relief tinged with longing, her body cursing her for stopping him. He pulled himself away from her with difficulty, and Kore felt the sudden cool rush of air over her as he settled at her side. He tilted her chin toward him.

"You're right, Persephone. When we have each other, it should be in the proper place— in my own bed, after I've claimed you."

Kore felt herself blush from the bottom of her feet to where he pecked a light kiss on the tip of her nose. She resisted tilting upward to kiss him again, to draw his body back down to her. *Into her,* she thought with a shudder. Was that what she wanted? What she needed? She didn't even know his name. But in every way else she felt him, *knew* him, and knew intuitively that she was his and he was hers. That potent knowledge coursed through her very veins.

"Please…" Kore licked her dry lips and stared up at him, "I need to find you. Tell me your name."

He smiled at her and caressed her cheek, a soft sadness in his eyes. Sighing, he bent down to kiss her in the middle of her forehead.

She jolted awake, sitting up, alone, her heart racing. The grove was empty and cold, but her body felt hot and her inner thighs were slick with liquid warmth. She brought her arms around her and felt only her chiton, the peaks of her breasts chafing against the thin linen. She was dressed as she was before. It *was* a dream. Gasping for air, she looked around for the powerful lover— her husband, he had said—

who had been holding her seconds ago, and then glanced up into the oak tree.

A thin pale figure, wrapped in a cloak and silhouetted against the faint light, turned to meet her gaze before vanishing into mist. She barely had time to register if it was real or imagined before she heard a sparrow chirp. The first flicker of dawn licked the eastern sky. The light grew stronger, revealing that the white larkspur had turned dark crimson overnight. Within her shrine, a new and beautiful light gray flower sprang from the ground, surrounding her.

Asphodel.

3.

KORE TOUCHED THE GENTLE FLOWERS GROWING around her and shifted the coloring of her dress to a soft white, mimicking the color of the blossoms. How beautiful they were… like last night, like *him,* though she knew 'beautiful' was seldom applied to men, and was too soft a word for him anyway.

Asphodel… she was the Maiden of the Flowers and knew that's what these were intuitively, but tried to remember where she had heard the name— and what their significance was.

She had only ever seen asphodel growing as a gnarled dark gray weed. It was one of the few plants her mother would rip out of the fields wherever she had seen it. Kore had always trailed behind her, doing the same. She had never seen asphodel bud and blossom. The white blooms were thin, veined with a centerline of crimson, six petals with bright filaments bursting from the center and ending in deep red anthers. They were beautiful and foreign.

The man in her dream returned to her thoughts. She shivered at the idea of kissing him again, of tangling her fingers in the jet black curls of his hair, and melting into the heat of his body pressed so close to hers. She picked one of the small flowers from its dark stalk and twisted its stem around a lock of hair, her russet waves matching the red veins of the flower. She smiled, studying it, then walked from plant to plant, picking one bloom from each, and expertly weaved them into a crown, placing it atop her head.

And you will be my queen, Persephone.

Queen… he'd said 'queen'. Not wife, but something more. Something greater. What would he think of her now, in her simple linen shift, her hair hanging loosely like a child's? She wanted to change her clothes to something more womanly: lengthen it, cover her knees and legs in sumptuous, fine-spun wool, and drape a soft mantle over her shoulders but resisted the temptation. Demeter wouldn't approve, and would insist that Kore keep her youthful short chiton.

She wondered what he would like to see her wearing. Kore imagined him standing behind her and kissing her neck as she wore a beautiful burgundy peplos held up by bronze fibulae, and a girdle of bronze and polished sard stones, but her imagination quickly turned to him unhooking it from her waist with a flick of his wrist and pushing the gown off her shoulders to hold her against his body, as he had in the dream. Kore blushed, fairly certain that if she asked him what he wanted to see her in, his answer would be 'nothing at all'. She leaned back onto the bark of the great oak tree, remembering his hands stroking her body, both of them as naked as the day they were born, caressing each other under its sprawling branches.

"Persephone," she said quietly, remembering him whispering her true name, his lips grazing her neck. She faintly felt the same coil tighten in her belly she had felt with him last night, the same sensation she felt at the Eleusinian wedding. Kore crossed her arms over her breasts and closed her eyes, wanting him to appear to her again. If she willed it enough, would he come to her as he had last night?

The love of men is fleeting. I am sparing you the agony of a husband who lords himself over you, then breaks his oaths and your heart.

Her mother had said she wasn't to marry. She was just Kore, the Maiden of the Flowers, not a queen, not his queen. These thoughts were dangerous. And it was all just a dream, anyway. But if he were not real, if the dream was just a dream, then why were these flowers here? Had he left them for her?

Maybe it would be different for me. She remembered her words to her mother.

It most certainly would not. And don't ever believe any man who would tell you otherwise, Kore. What a fool she must be to moon over flowers, of all things. Flowers— *her* domain, even! But he hadn't taken anything from her or trespassed on her. He hadn't grown bolder with his touch until she'd wanted it— until he felt her respond to him and ask for it with each gyration of her body against his. Her lips against his…

She felt ice pour over her. Demeter! Her mother was supposed to arrive any minute and they were to spend the morning together preparing the fields of Eleusis for reaping. She heard the familiar rush of barley, and looked around, panicking for a moment, wondering how she would explain the new color of larkspur that had appeared overnight.

"Kore?"

"Coming, Mother!" She blanched and tried to push the dream from her mind before stepping out of her room. Kore would meet her outside. Maybe Demeter wouldn't notice the changed flowers. She pulled herself together, took a deep breath and put on a bright smile.

"Are you ready yet?"

Kore skipped out of the bower. "Good morning!"

Demeter's own smile quickly turned to horror when she saw her daughter.

"Where did you get those?"

"Get what?" Kore said, confused.

"The asphodel! Where did you find these poison weeds?!" she said, snatching at one of the flowers in Kore's hair.

She ducked out of the way as Demeter tried to pull at another. "Mother! What's the matter with you?! They started growing this morning in my—"

Demeter cupped her hands over her mouth with a gasp, not giving Kore time to finish her sentence before she ran into the shrine.

"Mother, why are you— Mother!" Kore stumbled in to find Demeter kneeling in the rushes amidst the newly grown flowers, tearing them out root and stalk.

Demeter turned to look at her daughter, her hands shaking. Her eyes were stained with tears, and her voice became a whisper as she looked around wide-eyed and pale. "He was here."

Kore's face paled as ashen white as the flowers that were withering in her mother's clenched fists. *Gods above, she knows; she knows who he is.* She swallowed hard. "Wh-who was here?"

"Do not lie to me! Did he hurt you?"

Her eyes started to water. "No, Mother, there was no one here. No one hurt me. It was just a dream. I woke up surrounded by these pretty white flowers."

Demeter grew angry, her eyes flashing, her voice low. "If that monster laid a finger on you…"

Kore blushed at the memory of his fingers, then felt her voice and breath catch in her throat, tears spilling from her eyes. "Mother, please! It was just a dream. I saw someone in it, *I think,* and then when I woke up— I told you— I was just surrounded by all these flowers."

Demeter stood up and took her by the wrist and marched out of the sacred place. "Dear child, you are no longer safe here," she panicked, her voice wavering. Kore heard the rushing of barley around them. Her mother prepared to transport both of them away, as she did herself when she visited the great mountain.

"Where are we going? Olympus?" Kore said, following her.

"No, we mustn't. You are in even greater danger there. We are going to the fields of Nysa. Pallas Athena and Artemis, the virgin warriors, will watch over you just as they always promised me they would, if *trouble* came."

"But what about the harvest?"

"It can wait! They all can wait," she turned to Kore, brushing her tears away as the stalks of barley wound into the silver filaments of the ether, opening a pathway over land and sea. "I don't know what I would do if I lost you, my child."

"But nothing is wrong! I'm right here, Mother! And you're sending me away? At the harvest of all times?"

"There will be aeons of harvest for us Kore, but not if we stay here."

Kore clenched her jaw silently and looked down, hiding her anger from Demeter. She wanted to see him again, and hiding in Nysa would make that impossible.

* * *

"Your Excellency, I simply did what you asked of me." Even in the Underworld, the Lord of Dreams stood in shadows, his face hooded, his blind eyes veiled.

"Morpheus, I asked you to send me to Persephone so that I could introduce myself to her as her betrothed. Not to have us meet in the dream world naked and embraced!" Aidoneus felt his frustration rise. White-hot memories of holding Persephone shuddered through him unbidden.

"I manifested what was in your heart of hearts. My world is not the waking world. You just can't walk into it with expectations of—"

"You saw us together!"

"I see *all* in the dream world. Do you really think I just sat there and watched both of you through the night? And honestly, Aidoneus, what I did see was relatively tame. For Fates sake, I have to preside over Thanatos's dreams, and let me tell you—"

Hades narrowed his eyes at him, his silent anger filling the room, palpable enough to be felt by Morpheus.

"Aidon, truthfully—" he said, stepping out of the marble column's shadow, "How you came to her, what you saw, what you did— all of it was of your own making. I am not responsible for the desires of your heart, and I will not be the focus of your anger over it. Those feelings are yours to contend with."

Aidoneus shifted uncomfortably between the wide arms of his ebony throne. He had arrived in the dream unclothed, holding her thin arms, his body pressed against her back. Morpheus had given Aidon the choice of appearing to Persephone in false form, or as himself. But the way he had come to her in the dream, the way he had felt when he was with her, the words he had dared to speak to her, were almost as unfamiliar as she was.

Morpheus felt the Lord of the Underworld's anger relent as Aidon retreated into thought. "If that is all…"

"Yes. Go, my friend. You need to prepare for tonight, and I've kept you long enough."

Morpheus drew out a thin gray arm and wrapped his black cloak around him before disappearing into mist. Aidoneus stood up and descended the stairs of the olivine dais. The room was still, and his footsteps echoed through the empty hall as he made his way to the torch lit terrace outside.

Its view swept out over the river Styx, silently flowing broad and dark across the fields below. He felt the cool air of the Underworld wash over him and sighed, leaning on the balcony edge. Aidoneus dug his fingers into his temples and closed his eyes. Next to the terrace was a waterfall that flowed upward along the cliff, its roaring cascade feeding the rivers of the corporeal world above. The sound of the falls and the cooling mist that fell from it usually gave him some measure of peace, but it couldn't soothe him now. The Lord of Dreams was right.

He took the golden arrow out of his robes and held it in his hand, turning it over. This small thing had only scratched his palm, and now her face was everywhere in his mind, awakening potent and dangerous feelings where there had been none before. He thought only about her flower-strewn hair, her pale arms and small breasts. The gentle curve of her hips. Her legs. The warmth between them.

Aidoneus pulled himself away from the balcony and walked back in, still clutching the arrow. Persephone had been only a name to him— the daughter of Demeter who was to be his queen— but was now made flesh, a woman. He had often wondered about her over the aeons, but had not expected to arrive in the dream world and find himself holding her so intimately, his body readily responding to the closeness of hers. All rational thought had vanished the moment he looked into her eyes. The small, inviting sounds she'd made in response to his touch had driven him mad… and continued to do so…

He would throw this cursed arrow headlong into the river if it weren't so dangerous— if he didn't already know the powerful consequences it had for him, and the unknown feelings it could bestow on others.

"Lord Hades," a rich female voice said. He turned to see Hecate, wrapped in a dark crimson peplos and cloak, her long red hair, cascading down her back. Round selenite beads adorned the crown of her head, sweeping down to hold a silver half moon charm over her forehead. Her bare feet were tucked up underneath her as she sat on the base of a column in the corner of the great chamber.

Aidon's breath hitched. "Have you found her?"

"The field from your dream was Eleusis. Many of Demeter's and Persephone's worshippers reside there."

"I will go to Eleusis tonight, then."

"She's no longer there," Hecate said calmly. "I can see their thoughts… You'd think Demeter would be more careful. If she is traveling through the ether, I can find them."

"Why did they leave?"

Hecate closed her eyes to look into the ether. Within its hidden world: feelings, hopes, curses, the past, the future, the present, all flowing together in a chaos she alone could interpret. Hecate searched for Demeter and Persephone and tried to pluck the first coherency she could grasp. A smile crossed her face. "Did you plant asphodel in her shrine?"

"No," he said, confused, "I— Wait; is that a euphemism for something?"

Hecate opened her eyes and snickered quietly against the back of her hand. "No, my lord. I was being quite literal. I saw asphodel flowers, your own sacred blooms, growing where she sleeps. That made me curious— perhaps you had her, and wanted to make it known? In her dream, are you sure you didn't—"

"Dishonor her? No. I almost…" That part he remembered very clearly. Aidon swallowed, then gritted his teeth together. The need to be with her— *within her*— had bordered on pain. The memory of nearly losing control at her moan of pleasure, right before she stopped him, welled up through him. He turned away. "What is happening to me? I can't stop thinking about her; it's as if she's possessed me."

"Aidon, this is a new sensation for you; do not fear it, or fear the confusion that it brings," she said calmly. "You have only begun to glimpse how powerful these feelings truly are. Love is why most mortals call upon my priestesses. They work magic with my gifts, spells that can swell the desire of men and gods alike, giving them furious passion powerful enough to make them rend their own flesh."

"Zeus's little winged demon poisoned me!"

"And what a sly little monster he is, isn't he? Drawing forth *your* greatest desires with his arrows…" He narrowed his eyes at her, the words ringing true. "I assure you, Aidon, there was no poison on that arrow. The wound Eros made only broke the lock on your heart and set free what was waiting inside."

He put the arrow back into the folds of his robe. *What was waiting inside…* Aidon didn't know which prospect disturbed him more: that this had opened up in the first place, or that these feelings had been roiling under the surface unseen… for aeons, perhaps. "If Eros opened that door, then you need to close it, Hecate."

"So soon, Aidoneus? You've seen this treasure— tasted it, I dare say— and you'd have me shut it away again? I wonder why would you ask me to do this."

"Because this was supposed to be simple. Ordered," he said sharply, pacing the stone floor. "I've received what was due to me for my part in the war. She's already consecrated to me— I was to have my queen, and we would rule together. All I had to do was… take her and be done with it. Now it's been complicated by these… desires… to—"

"To win her? To make her love you?"

He thinned his lips and turned away from Hecate.

"Your influence here is great, but not all souls bend to your will. Not even your own, hmm? Our destinies are mysterious, Aidon; they are woven with threads we do not always expect to see. Even if you don't trust the weavers, you may be certain that they weave with a pattern in mind."

"The Olympians don't have to contend with this! Their adoration lasts only as long as their lust. Where are these 'mysterious weavers' for them?"

"Aidoneus, look…" she said, motioning to the inverted waterfall outside. "The rivers of their world don't flow like ours, or carry as much meaning. Our ways are not their ways. This is Chthonia; the Other Side."

Hecate closed her eyes, her mind prodding and exploring the ether, searching for signs of Persephone.

Aidon thought about the flowers growing where they lay together in the dream. He couldn't have grown a weed from the richest soil if the safety of the living world depended on it; Persephone had brought them to life herself. But why out of all the flowers did she choose his? He had taken great pains to conceal his identity to her.

"Oh, I see," Hecate said, her eyelids fluttering as she followed the trail of thoughts emanating from Persephone. Her silent smile turned into a light laugh. "She grew them while she slept, from the seeds you planted in her dream. Your true nature may yet be shrouded to her eyes, but another part of her knows you very well indeed." Hecate's gaze darted to his face.

Then Hades did something he had never done before in all his ageless years. He blushed.

"And every larkspur in existence, which for all the ages have been white, are now crimson, purple and pink? Hades

Aidoneus, whatever did you do to her?" she said in a sing-song voice, a wide smile on her face.

"Enough!" He looked away from Hecate.

"I daresay you did enough, indeed." Hecate smirked, until she felt confusion wash over him. Her face softened and she spoke gently. "Why feel shame, Aidon?"

"Because I'm not supposed to feel... *alive!* Look around you. These foolish— these *dangerous* passions have no place here!"

"So certain, are you?" Hecate silently walked across the floor to him and reached out a hand to his forehead, which he let rest there. "What you feel for her is not as far outside our world as you think. Open your mind."

Her eyes closed and she spoke to him in the three voices of her aspects, the Maiden, the Woman, and the Crone. He closed his eyes as her fingertips moved to his temples. Aidoneus felt her reach further from where her fingers met his skin, touching the deepest parts of his mind, restoring order to his thoughts, soothing him. He breathed out as the chaos and confusion that had plagued him since he awoke was given shape and form. Feelings gained sigils and signifiers through her intervention. Need. Purpose. Longing. Desire. Rapture. Lust.

"Love," the voice of the Maiden said.

"I never thought that word."

"You didn't have to," the three voices answered.

Hecate watched the maelstrom of thoughts flash through his mind. The past. The feel of her soft skin, the press of her naked flesh, their mutual need. Hands running through hair, lifting, entangling. The present. Cypress and wind; fire and union in the void.

The future. Red flowers clinging to a tree that rose from the field of gray, branches entwining through others' branches. Red, ripe fruit hung on interlocked boughs. Radiating out from the tree came soft grasses and flowers that spread over immeasurable ground. Hecate imparted in three voices what she saw. "Embrace and cherish these visions, Aidoneus. They belong to both of you."

Aidon opened his eyes. Hecate was again seated on the column base as though she hadn't moved at all. In all likelihood, she hadn't.

"You need to feel her again and know that she feels you— don't you, Aidoneus?" Her voice was once again singular.

"Yes," he whispered hoarsely. "Yes, I do."

"I will search for Persephone for you," she said, and closed her eyes. Silence filled the room, and Hades stood still, waiting. A moment later, Hecate spoke of her vision.

"Nysa," Hecate said, reaching into the earth goddess's mind from afar. "She's sheltering Persephone in Nysa."

"The fields of Nysa?" Aidon shook his head in partial relief. "If I can count on Demeter at all, it's to not think anything through when she's angry," he said under his breath.

"It's too early for dreams; don't bother waking Morpheus. You must go to her yourself, but Demeter must not see you, or sense your presence at all. She is ever alert to you and the Helm will not help you. I'll send you in the wind this time."

"How will I find Persephone?"

"You won't have to. She will come to you."

4.

DEMETER AND KORE EMERGED FROM THE BLADES OF barley into a rolling grassy meadow surrounded by groves of trees, each grove sacred to a deity. Nysa was the eternal field of the gods, and Kore's home as a child. She had played with her friends here. Kore remembered Ares swinging a wooden sword against the grasses under the watchful eye of Hera. Little Apollo once brought her a fistful of larkspur and recited awkward love poetry, to her mother's great consternation. Athena and Artemis ran with her in the field and played games of knucklebones by the creek. When Kore flowered into womanhood, her mother abruptly took her from their company and she hardly ever saw them again.

"Kore!"

She heard her cousin Artemis call to her from the edge of the valley. She jogged toward them with her long, sandal-strapped legs. Artemis wore a quiver of arrows on her back, its leather strap holding her short white hunting chiton against her body. The virgin huntress's honey colored hair was short and simple, coiffed into a messy chignon at the base of her neck. She waved a hand to them as she ran.

Kore waved back, then turned to Demeter. "How long do I have to stay here?"

"Until I know for certain that you're safe. I will tend the harvest alone this time." She held Kore close and kissed her on the cheek. "They will look after you, my child. Do not leave the meadow. Do not talk to anyone or anything while I'm gone."

Kore watched her mother vanish into a rush of barley, bound for Eleusis. Nysa was the perfect place to keep her while she attended her responsibilities to the mortals. The virgin goddesses were usually here during harvest time. The humans seldom waged war during harvest, which freed Athena, and seldom hunted, which relieved Artemis of some of her responsibilities. They tended to avoid Olympus during the harvest as their divine siblings were usually bored and making mischief. Both Artemis and Athena were younger than her, but looked older, having already fully taken on their divine roles. Although she felt a faint twinge of envy, Kore was thankful to see them. Artemis, athletic and sun flecked, bounded over to Kore and gave her a hug. "Finally we get to see you again!"

"Artemis!" she embraced her back. "I wish it were under better circumstances. I feel like I'm imposing."

"Nonsense." Fair-haired Athena stood up from the grasses next to them, and quickly rolled up a short scroll before stashing it in the folds of her peplos. She adjusted the plate armor that held her flowing gown in place and joined their conversation. "We will make them better," she said. "And don't worry. Arte and I scour the plain regularly this time of year in case any troublemaking satyrs come along. Brutish creatures… You're perfectly safe here."

Kore smiled thinly to hide her feelings from Artemis and Athena. That meant the man from her dream wasn't here and would most likely never find her. She absently picked the last remains of the asphodel out of her hair. Her mother had cowed her about the flowers throughout the journey to Nysa until she had relented and plucked most of them out. "What were you doing before I arrived? Can I join you?"

"Well," Artemis said, "as soon as we heard you were coming, we started making a garland for you, because we hadn't seen you in so long. But… you know me; I'm no good with flowers."

"We hope you like it," Athena added, shyly holding it out for Kore's examination. The garland was a tidy braid of laurel and olive sprigs laced with wild celery, whose tiny white blossoms provided the only break in the greenery.

"Oh, thank you!" Kore said, accepting the gift from her cousin's calloused hands. She sat down in the soft grass and let Artemis wind her hair into a coronet.

"Your dress is still so short," Artemis said. "Do you keep it that way for the hunt?"

"No, I don't hunt like you, Arte," she said, smiling and lowering her head to hide her embarrassment.

Athena spoke. "Well, have you ever thought about letting it down?"

Kore looked at her bare knees and blushed. "Mother doesn't approve."

Athena stepped in front of Kore and pointedly looked to the right, then the left. She smiled and leaned down. "I don't see her here to disapprove. Come on! You can change it back when she gets here. We won't tell."

Kore fidgeted for a moment. "I'm— I can't do that to her. I've already put her through enough for one day."

Athena gave her a pained smile. "I understand. Sorry; I didn't mean to upset you."

"There! And beautiful, I might add." Artemis finished winding and weaving Kore's hair and placed the garland on top.

Persephone...

She froze, hearing her name on the wind.

"Who's there?" She looked at her cousins, her eyes wide. "Did... did you hear that?"

Athena and Artemis stilled and exchanged a quick glance. Artemis swallowed. "H-hear what?"

"Nothing... it must have been my imagination," she said, walking into the field.

Athena and Artemis joined her, keeping back a ways as Kore explored her girlhood home. She had spent her childhood in the shadow of the sacred groves of the Olympians. As a young girl, Kore had laid a circle of river stones in the meadow and filled it with all her favorite flowers, hoping someday to have a sacred grove of her own.

"Do you remember the secret garden I planted?"

Athena smiled. "Of course I do! But it wasn't as big a secret as you thought it was. Father loved it! Said it was his favorite 'sacred grove'. I think your mother knew about it too."

"Oh," Kore blushed. "I'd wondered what happened to it. Want to visit it with me?"

"We'll finish gathering the leftover twigs from the garland. And I think I may take another pass around the meadow," Artemis said, "Can we join you later?"

"Of course!" Kore said cheerfully as she walked off into the grasses.

My queen... the wind whispered.

Her heart thrummed in her ears. She recognized that voice and turned in its direction, a narrow grove of cypress. Kore looked back at Artemis and Athena, still bent over in the grass picking up remnants of her floral crown. They must not have heard it. She walked slowly, one foot cautiously following the other toward the cypresses, her heart beating out of her chest.

Athena looked up to see her walk away. Demeter had enlisted their protection long ago in case anyone came for Kore. She shuddered, remembering dark Aidoneus stalking through the throne room toward her father yesterday, demanding his rights to Kore as Demeter cried out against it. Athena looked back to Artemis, who was biting her lip, her eyes welling up with tears. The huntress looked away to watch Kore walk toward the cypress trees, and moved to stand up and follow after her.

"Don't," Athena whispered, clasping her sister's trembling hand. "Father told us not to interfere. It will be alright, Artemis."

* * *

Demeter planted one foot after another in the sun-warmed soil. The Eleusinian priestess had plucked a single sheaf of barley and held it aloft, signaling the start of the harvest early this morning when Demeter had returned, sight unseen to oversee them. The priestess's acolytes had wandered through the fields all afternoon pouring offerings of *kykeon* and honey on the freshly threshed earth, singing praises to Demeter and Kore, carrying their effigies before them. The wheat waved across the fields, a sea of ripe sheaves that shone in the sun like swells on the ocean. Walled Eleusis stood on the other side of the hills, a beacon of rough-hewn white stones and whipping saffron banners. Wisps of white clouds moved across the azure sky, traveling on the breeze that wafted across the Eleusinian fields. Under an oak tree by the creek, a few elder women wrapped in dark linen himations, their backed bowed with age, hobbled after naked laughing children. They nattered after them to stay in the shallows and not splash too much water at the littlest ones. A toothless man with wisps of a white beard clinging to his face shared a cup of *kykeon* and laughed with his equally ancient wife.

The villagers dressed in bright reds and golds, the women with the hems of their *peploi* gathered up into their girdles, their hair wound back with strips of linen into tight chignons. They would stoop to gather large bundles of wheat, carrying them over to the ox drawn cart, giving the beasts a few sheaves here and there to keep them content. Most of the men dressed in nothing but loincloths, their skin glistening as they labored under the bright sun, sickles flashing. The rhythmic thresh of iron blades drummed a steady beat under their gossip and laughter.

Demeter was invisible in their midst, and could barely hear them. Hades was coming for her only child and she was preparing herself to meet him directly, to protect Kore from the Lord of the Underworld at all costs. She wiped a tear from her eye. Her daughter was safe for now in Nysa, but it was only a matter of time before he learned where she had fled.

She came upon the thistle her daughter had planted yesterday, its bright purple crown host to two of the little orange butterflies. They flitted around each other, one giving chase to the other before they settled, joined together on the flower. The small display of the earth's fertility and Kore's innocent wisdom should have given her joy, but she gritted her teeth, only able to see ghostly stalks of asphodel in her mind. The tall thistle withered, its flower drooping and blackening as she walked away.

Hades had profaned Kore's sacred house with his ugly bog flowers. He'd sown them around her daughter's sleeping body. Demeter angered, and the ripe silvery sheaves around her shriveled and turned brown. She walked away from the withered millet, barely aware of the dismayed voices of the villagers behind her.

There must be a way she could save her daughter from the Land of the Dead. She thought of the beautiful and virginal naiad queen Daphne, lustfully pursued by Apollo. To save herself from rape and destruction she had cried out to Gaia, the earth, who had answered her desperate prayers. Gaia had turned Daphne into a laurel tree, and she was saved and made sacred for all time.

For a moment she stopped breathing and stood where she was. The barley around her turned from living gold to dead gray. How could she even contemplate such a thing?

All she loved about Kore was wrapped up in her free spirit. Demeter thought about her light, her life, her every footprint filled with larkspur and roses, and the new ones— lilac, she remembered— flourishing wherever she went. She was pure and fresh and honest. Even in her defiance…

Demeter's eyes filled with tears. How could she let all these things about her daughter be wrested away to the land of the dead? For everything about her to turn cold and lifeless under the earth when she was made into Persephone? If she did nothing, Kore would be sacrificed on the marriage bed of the Lord of Souls.

Ice filled her heart. If she did this to their daughter, Zeus would never forgive her. She would be banished from Olympus, her high seat among the *Dodekatheon* removed, and she would be cursed to walk the earth as a minor goddess. But at least Kore would be safe. At least Demeter would know that her beloved daughter was saved forever from that fate. When Hades came to claim her, all he would find would be a new tree— a beautiful, flowering tree to honor her. Kore would be the loveliest tree in existence. Demeter wept. The waves of barley next to her rotted on the stalk and the grains filled with poisonous red dust.

Demeter would bring her back to Eleusis and Kore would be these people's sacred tree for all time. She sobbed, remembering her sweet girl toddling through the fields of Nysa as a young child. She knew that she would never see Kore running through the field, never hold her, never see her weave another garland or give life to another new flower, and her daughter would never forgive her for it. But if she did nothing, her warm and vibrant Kore would be trapped for eternity in the gray nothingness of the Other Side, prey to the will of cold and unfeeling Aidoneus.

* * *

The crisp smell of cypress met her as she stepped into the shade. Kore's eyes adjusted to the dappled light of the grove, and she saw soft wild celery covering the shaded soil with bursts of white asphodel growing in the patches of sunlight. Defiantly, she picked the flowers and wove them into the garland crown her cousins had given her.

The grove was silent except for her breath. In the meadow she had either heard his voice calling to her, or she was going mad. She picked a tiny asphodel bloom and twirled it in her hand. Her body warmed, feeling his presence. "Listen to me… I know you're here! And I know you came to me in my dreams last night."

Cypress boughs rustled thinly as a breeze swept through their upper branches. She looked up, searching for him. "Why did you bring me here? And why did you plant the asphodel in my shrine last night?"

The wind in the grove closed in around her, words forming in its wake. "Your crown…"

Kore touched the flowered wreath in her hair. "You don't like it?"

"On the contrary," the wind whispered to her, "Your bridal crown is beautiful…"

"Bridal crown," she echoed breathlessly, her voice faltering as she remembered his words from last night. She reached without thinking to the wreathed branches. Her heart jumped into her throat when she realized what she was wearing: laurel and olive were for weddings. Kore looked around her, wishing she could see him.

"When I take you as my queen, Persephone, your crown shall be every jewel in the earth. Every ounce of its wealth will be your adornment…"

She spun in a circle, wishing she could find a source for his voice. It made her dizzy, this phantom wind, and these thoughts of leaving here with him, of being a queen, showered in wealth and jewels. And strange too, how he kept saying the name her father gave her.

"Why do you keep calling me Persephone?"

"It is who you truly are," Aidoneus said on the wind. "It's who you were born to be."

He wanted to give her anything. Anything and everything. His heart and mind raced at merely seeing her, knowing that she was real, just as beautiful as she was in the moonlight and not some illusion of dreams conjured by the golden arrow to torment him. When she was with him last night, she was a woman. A sensuous woman with delicate curves and warm skin. But she looked like a girl in the daylight, her clothes too young, too loose fitting, disguising her hips, her breasts… Aidoneus shuddered. He wanted to see her as she was. Who she truly was…

A breeze whipped past and she felt warm hands on her shoulders and arms. She flinched involuntarily, then settled into their grasp. "And what do I call *you?*"

His mind raced, thinking of all the horrifying things Demeter must have said about him. And not just her mother. Hades was a curse word to the mortals— only the gravest of sworn oaths invoked his name. But he had to tell Persephone something. He willed himself to coalesce enough to touch her and with a sigh of the wind, brush past her lips. "Please call me Aidon."

"Aidon…" she repeated, her voice smoky from his light touch.

"Yes…" He felt himself quicken when she said his name for the first time. Relief washed over him as she relaxed, unafraid. He brushed past her breasts, feeling the nipples pull taut under the thin chiton.

Kore felt his breath, warm against the shell of her ear, and felt arms encircling her as though the breeze itself were embossed with his form. The fresh and woody smell of cypress filled her, and she let out a soft sigh.

Aidon could feel her, not just in the dream world, but real and present. He was the very air around her, engulfing her. She was no figment of his dreams. He could feel the pulse of every vein, every twitch of flesh, and every small bead of perspiration as her heart beat faster from his incorporeal touch. His senses were suddenly filled with the heady scent of flowers. He concentrated, solidifying, wanting to touch her skin with his own hands.

Kore closed her eyes. He surrounded and embraced every part of her, lifting her gently. She could feel her heels start to rise from the ground, and the loose fabric of her sleeve slipped down one arm.

"I will come for you tonight, sweet one." Aidon tugged down the fabric and blew a kiss on her neck, whispering into her ear. "I'll come for you at sunset and we'll journey to my kingdom together with you as my bride. I promise. But forgive me; I couldn't wait that long to see you again."

Kore felt the edge of her chiton roll over her nipple. Her areola pulled taut, exposed to the air and to him. "Aidon…"

She moaned his name. Aidon felt pleasure roll through him and blew on her exposed nipple, watching her shudder and arch closer to him with a gasp. Kore felt a warm rush of air wrap its way behind her knee and around her hip. She felt a solid arm, a hand and fingers pressing into her skin.

She gasped as he encircled her, her feet finally lifting off the ground, her body supported by invisible arms before being set down on the soft wild grass. The skirt of her chiton blew back, exposing her thighs.

"You're almost too beautiful..." he whispered, his voice sounding as though he were smiling, though she couldn't see him.

"This isn't fair," Kore pleaded. "I want to touch you, too... I want to hold you..."

This woman he'd patiently waited aeons to have... she desired him; she wanted him. Aidon's heart swelled at the idea. She wanted to do all the things with him that he needed to have from her. To hold him. To touch him. To lay down as husband and wife and— dare he even think it— to make love with him. "Soon, sweet one..." His hands trailed over her exposed breast and her stomach, dancing along her flesh. "...very soon."

Her body reached for his touch and he wanted to give her more. *Anything. Everything.* He was overwhelmed. Aidon would give anything in this moment to materialize in front of her, to be as they were in their dream. He knew too that he wouldn't be able to stop himself from having her completely, and doubted she would stop him either. Moving across her body, he caught the scent of wildflowers again and delved for its source.

A hot exhale of air teased the curls between her thighs. Kore arched and parted them, feeling a hand brush over her mound. Unlike last night, she didn't stop him. He was mesmerized by the sight of her most intimate places, her deeper mysteries unknown to him. He wanted to bring forth everything he'd felt rise through her last night to completion. Her flesh jumped as he stroked her, learning her. Her creamy thighs were open to him, her scent pouring out on the wind. A fine down of dark brown curls covered her nether lips. He traced their seam; watching as her hips moved from side to side and her breathing became shallow.

Every shiver of her flesh, every arch of her body made Aidon's heart beat faster, urging him onward in his discovery. The tips of his fingers were met with slick warmth, and a punctuated gasp from Kore that made him inhale sharply, feeling the unfulfilled pains of his own arousal. Shaking with anxious longing, his fingers glided down to her entrance and lingered there for a moment before traveling upward slowly through the folds.

When he neared the apex, she let out a sharp cry and sprang back from his touch. Aidon instantly rose up along the length of her body, alarmed, smoothing his hand over her shoulder. "Did I hurt you?"

She shook her head. "No. It… Can you please do that again?" she said meekly.

He smiled in relief and trailed his fingers downward through the valley between her breasts, over the tautness of her stomach, and gingerly steadied her mound with the palm of his hand. His finger met soft heat and sunk between her labia, tracing a path upward through the center until he felt her writhe anew. He stopped, memorizing the spot, feeling the tiny nub of flesh pulse under his finger. He waited for her to still and relax against him. When she rolled her hips forward and pressed the tight bud against his waiting finger, he started moving it in a slow circle.

The feel of his unseen hand stroking her filled her body with fire and familiarity, a longing she couldn't place for something she never knew she needed. Her hands and feet clenched and tingled, flames licking through her.

His winding finger moved faster. Every stroke of his hand against Kore's new-found epicenter shook her. Her lips, the tips of her breasts, her thighs twitched. Her voice wasn't hers anymore; it responded only to his caress. Every motion was a new thrill of pleasure. Something primal and inexorable began to wind within her, tightening every muscle of her body, searching, deepening, arching her closer.

Aidon felt her rising to him, her cries heating him and spurring him on. Her voice made his need a torture, unquenchable and unrelenting in his current form. He leaned over her and took the exposed nipple into his mouth and sucked it gently, driving her over an unseen edge.

Kore burst. Light danced behind her closed eyes and her head tilted back. She twisted and flailed, cried out his name and gasped, and the world fell away. Waves rolled through her as she felt his hand move away and travel up the length of her body to hold her. His lips teased along her cheek and she heard him breathing in time with her, steadying her body and supporting her until the tremors stopped and all she felt was his unseen hand grasping her arm.

"Persephone, I—" his voice shuddered.

Kore felt cool grass against her back, the soft earth beneath it supporting her, and then the caress of the wind was gone. He was gone. The grove was quiet once again, save for the sound of her heart beating in her eardrums.

* * *

Aidoneus materialized in his realm, and looked around in shock, drawn away from her against his will. He stumbled backward and slammed his palm hard on the edge of his ebony throne, regaining his balance. His knees were shaking. Desire for her had come with him. He looked down at his erect flesh straining against his loincloth and robes, and cradled it against his body, covering and protecting himself as he doubled over and gasped for air. His blood coursed through him like the molten river Phlegethon.

Aware of his presence, Hecate's eyes were closed, her brow knitted. "Aidoneus—"

"How dare you!" he bellowed, "Do you have any idea—"

"A very good idea, yes. But leaving you there with her would have been more dangerous than delicious, I'm afraid. There will be trouble…"

He watched her eyes tighten again as she concentrated, listening for a voice in the ether. He didn't have time for this. Hecate needed to take him back. Persephone needed him. He needed to see her. To hold her.

"I have to have her," he growled as he waited for Hecate to speak, willing his legs to carry him to where he could sit down. "I *must* have her. When the sun sets—"

Hecate flinched and cried out, startling him to silence. A voice piercing her mind— a wail of grief from the ether that was bending slowly into madness. "It will be too late!"

"What do you mean?"

"Demeter. She's coming for Persephone."

"She can't stand in my way; not now," he said, feeling his control slowly come back, his pulse steadying, his lust subsiding.

"She won't. Aidon, she will do worse. I understand now— I could feel her fear distilling into something sharp and desperate, but I was too focused on aiding your visit to Persephone. To keep you immaterial was not easy, with you in that state..." Hecate stood. "You are familiar with the tale of Daphne?"

A pregnant moment passed before his eyes grew wide. Realization and horror scalded him like acid and what little color he had drained from his face. "Gods above…"

He stood and strode across the room. Hecate followed him down the halls and corridors, running to keep pace. His himation shifted its form, winding around his body. The folds of fabric hardened, becoming the golden cuirass of his armor. Aidoneus had not worn it often, and never for its intended purpose since they cast Kronos into the Pit and ended the war. His long black cloak unfurled behind him as he stormed out to the courtyard. He reached through the ether as Hecate had taught him long ago and felt his helm materialize in his hand.

"Hades!" she said as he raised it over his head.

He spun on Hecate, his face contorted in rage. "I'll cast Demeter into the Pit if I have to!"

She started and drew back, then followed him again as Aidoneus continued his march. The corridor opened up into to the massive open stable yard of his palace, its floor made of concentric ringed cobblestones of black granite. He grabbed his iron standard from inside the gate and walked out to the center of the yard.

"This madness is not fixed by fate, Aidoneus! If Demeter reaches Persephone before you, be assured that the world will know her only for her slender branches and the gentle shade she gives. But such eternal changes have rules, and you can still prevent it. And you can save your bride in a more peaceful way than throwing the goddess of the fruitful harvest into the depths of Tartarus!"

He hammered the staff on the ground, the ringing echoing through the yard. Dark granite cracked beneath it, a glow of orange light radiating out from the point of impact. Aidoneus calmly strode back to Hecate's side as the stones fell away, lighting the room with reflected fire. She looked up at him, remembering aeons ago how Aidoneus had single-handedly convinced her and Nyx to support Zeus's cause during the war. That same taciturn warrior stood with her now, watching the rising smoke and listening to the approaching gallop of horses from the chasm.

"What way?" he said, finally.

Hecate looked into his eyes through the golden, black-crested helm that rendered him invisible to anyone he chose. She raised her voice as the ground beneath them started to shake. "Persephone can only be transformed that way if she is as Daphne was— intact."

Aidon's head snapped down to acknowledge the weight of what she said. A maelstrom of realization and trepidation ran through him, the helm barely hiding his emotions. "That's *not* how—"

With a shrill neigh, four dark coursers burst upward through the smoking gap, their manes and hooves sable black, their eyes glowing with fire. They pulled a great quadriga chariot behind them. It gleamed in the molten light from the chasm below, and then the ground started to close again with a grinding roar. The chariot had served Aidoneus well during the war, and would now serve him again. He returned the standard to the wall and stalked toward the cart. There was no time.

As Aidoneus grabbed the reins, a cloud of black smoke flowed out around the chariot, the chargers whinnying and stamping their feet. Hecate's voice rang out over the cacophony of the giant beasts. "If you love her, Aidoneus, if you want to save her, you will do what must be done!"

She watched from the gate as the chariot drove away. Aidoneus rode headlong for the living world and his Persephone.

5.

IT TOOK SEVERAL MINUTES FOR KORE TO RISE. HE HAD left her there, had disappeared in the midst of speaking, leaving her bewildered. Her chiton was wrenched out of place and her back was damp from the floor of the grove. She stood, confused by his disappearance, and scanned the empty grove. Had he truly gone? Was he still somewhere nearby? What would make him leave her so abruptly? She would ask him later. Kore knew Aidon would come back; that he would return tonight.

A heavy feeling settled in her chest. No matter how natural she felt with him, she had no idea who he was. She would be surrendering herself to him— a complete stranger. Her thoughts returned to the wedding party in Eleusis, how the man had taken the woman in the tent, pushing in and out of her, the pain on the woman's face when they first joined. Would she feel that same pain?

She remembered Aidon in her dream, the unseen part of him that had pressed against her thigh as hard as stone, pulsing and hot. She remembered him drawing his heat away, stopping himself from taking her. Her heart beat faster and a shuddering need flooded into her at the idea of Aidon lying astride her, entering her slowly. Her flesh still throbbed from his touch as she left the grove and returned to the sunlit meadow.

The sun was lower in the sky. In a few hours, it would sink below the horizon and he would come to claim her. His queen. *Queen of what?*

She could still hear her heart hammering in her chest as she gazed across the field of Nysa, its rolling hills blanketed in a host of flowers. There was no sign of Artemis or Athena. Down the hill from the cypresses, she saw the little stone circle she had created as a girl and walked toward it, readjusting her crown and tucking stray hairs back behind her ears. She felt around the garland's edges, making sure the leaves and flowers weren't crushed or lopsided from lying in the grove with Aidon.

Your bridal crown…

Kore shivered again, and stepped into the stone enclosure. Her little garden was almost exactly as she'd left it centuries ago. She knelt to pick a tall crocus, examining the wide scalloped petals in her hand. As she walked on, she was tormented by questions, trying to fit all the pieces together. Her lady mother must at least know of Aidon. His demonstration of his power— appearing in her dream, calling to her and caressing her on the wind— meant that he wasn't just any immortal, but a mighty god. Perhaps Demeter was mistaken when she saw the asphodel, thinking it meant something else. Maybe she would rejoice when she found out that her daughter was to become a queen.

She picked an iris and a larkspur, blushing the same pink color as the flower she had transformed last night. In the end, wouldn't Demeter simply want Kore to be happy? She imagined her mother coming to visit her in a beautiful palace once she was queen of…

What's this? she thought. The very center of the garden had been carefully manicured, and not by her. The grasses were cut low in a circle, and in the center stood the most beautiful bloom she'd ever seen. Kore peered at the flower. Its white blossom stood out against the velvety green carpet of short grass. She walked toward it, mesmerized, her gathered flowers falling from her open hand. White, rounded petals perfectly surrounded and radiated out from a short golden trumpet. She gently reached out and turned the blossom over in her hand, examining it. It smelled so sweet, its fragrance heady and foreign. She reached for the stalk with both hands and gave it a quick snap.

The earth trembled.

Kore fell to the ground as it split underneath her, a great crack in the earth yawning through the center of her little garden. She looked around in horror and crawled backwards along the shifting earth, then got up with one knee. A rush of dark smoke jetted from the center of the chasm, surrounding her and obscuring her vision, clouding the sky and turning the sun blood-red. Distantly, she heard horses galloping, their approach growing louder. She ran in the opposite direction, tripping once over the stone border.

A shriek from a horse split the air. She looked over her shoulder to see the silhouette of four horses against the darkened sky, drawing behind them a massive chariot. Their eyes glowed like fire and mist trailed from their nostrils. A cloaked shadow spurred them on.

Kore turned on her heels. "Athena! Artemis! Help me!"

The hooves drowned out her cries. They were gaining on her.

"Mother!! Mother, please! Where are you mother?!" Kore yelled.

The rumble of the wheels and the dark shadow they carried were almost upon her.

"Aidon! Save me! *Aidon!*"

Aidoneus leaned hard over the side of the chariot, balancing on the edge for support, and grabbed Persephone around the waist, holding her in the crook of one arm.

Kore's feet left the ground and she screamed long and loud, kicking and flailing against the shadow. Her feet met a shifting platform and a gauntleted arm pinned her fast to its owner. Persephone looked up to his face. It was covered with a dark gold helm, crested with long black horsehair. Only his bearded chin and mouth were visible beneath it. She screamed again, beating her hands against the hard plates of his golden cuirass until they were sore and bruised.

Her screams finally started to form words. "Let me go! Let me go!"

"*Hold on!*"

Her blood ran cold and she stopped moving. That voice… She looked up into his eyes through the helm and felt herself tilt backward, the entire chariot driving downward as she squeezed her eyes shut and screamed. The earth swallowed them whole. Persephone heard deafening cracks as chasms opened before them and shut behind them, each gallop bringing the heat of the earth closer to her.

The sound of grinding rocks was replaced with a roar of fire. She opened her eyes. They had broken through the earth into a great glowing chamber. The air wavered and scalded. Bits of rock hung from above, red and heated, melting like beeswax, drips trailing embers downward all about them. The chariot shook, falling, plunging through the air, the whinnying horses guided by their master. She looked behind her at the gaping maw of molten earth far below and grasped at his smooth armor, scrambling to find a handhold. Fathoms below, there was nothing but molten rocks and billows of vapor rising around them. She was going to fall. She needed to get away from him but without him, she would fall. What if that was what he wanted?! Persephone's eyes widened in terror pleading with the dark clad being who had stolen her. "Don't let me go! Please! Don't let me go!"

Persephone felt the heat grow more intense around her as they rode on. She smelled burning linen, and looked down to see flames licking up the side of her leg. The air itself had set the skirt of her chiton on fire, and embers started flying off the asphodel crowning her head. She shrieked and pulled it from her hair, using the laurels Artemis wove for her to fruitlessly slap at the burning fabric. Persephone felt her body wrench forward, the flimsy cloth tearing away from her, splitting along her back with a loud rip, her thin girdle jarring her waist when it snapped in half. The flaming garments and the garland from her hair burned away in his uplifted hand, their smoldering remnants turning to ash as they scattered behind the chariot. Left with little choice, she grabbed onto the straps of his cuirass just under his shoulders and looked up to see him pull off his helm and smooth back his hair.

Wide-eyed shock replaced her screams. *It couldn't be... it couldn't be...* She shuddered and froze as Aidon looked down at her.

"Persephone!" he yelled at her over the sound of the horses and the roar of twisting molten earth below. "Persephone, I need you to trust me!"

She scrambled and grasped at his neck, barely registering the fact that she was now naked. Her bare feet burned and she jumped, inching them up his greaves, then his legs, wrapping herself around him to escape the heat. The blistering vapors seared over her back until she felt his great black cloak wrap around her, pressing her against him, protecting her.

Persephone felt him pull the reins hard with one hand and bring her body further up along his with the other, his arm encircling her. She locked her legs around his waist and was face to face with Aidon, his skin glowing in the red heat. Their eyes met. He looked tenderly at her for a brief moment, almost disbelieving that she was actually in his arms, then turned away from her to concentrate and steer them onward. She pleaded with him in sounds that weren't quite words to turn back, to not burn them both alive.

The molten earth rushed toward them ever faster. She closed her eyes against the heat and buried her face into his neck with a sob, surrendering herself to her fate, waiting to feel the deep fires of the earth consume and devour them. Instead, the roaring heat stopped, and all grew quiet and cold around them.

For a moment she doubted how deathless she really was. Her eyes were awash in blackness and void. Her ears still rang from their passage through earth and fire. The horses pressed onward, quietly shaking the cart. Their cries grew silent, the only sound an occasional snort or nicker. Lifting her hand up in front of her face, she realized with a gasp that she couldn't even see its outline against the darkness. She ran her hand through the messy tangle of her hair, checking to see if it were still there and unburnt. Her face was still smooth, unharmed. Persephone cautiously turned her palm until it met the side of his face. He was still there, unburnt as she was. She traced the outline of an ear and high cheekbones, making sure that he was whole and unharmed.

As her hand passed over his nose and in front of his lips, he quickly kissed her palm.

Persephone drew her hand back, startled and relieved, and listened to the sound of their breathing, the only noise now as the horses charged silently forward into the abyss. Persephone felt the heat of his face, the shortening of his breath against her cheek. She angled her head as he turned toward her and captured her lips. Aidon's arm closed tighter around her and she melted into his embrace with a tiny moan, feeling his mouth hot against hers, sighing against her lips in relief. She kissed him back, shy at first, then eagerly when he responded to her.

Her fingers bunched in the dark curls of hair cascading across his cloak. His lips possessed hers gently, nipping and pulling, his kiss filled with relief, need and an anxious hesitancy that flowed into her from every place her skin came into contact with his. Persephone was suddenly very aware of her naked body wrapped around him. Her hands felt the pulse and cord of tendons in his neck and shoulder. Her ankle brushed against his thigh. His free hand pressed into her back and she leaned onto his breastplate, shaking nervously. Aidon broke away from her to kiss her cheek and neck, and then lightly pulled on her earlobe with his lips.

"Don't be afraid, sweet one," he said quietly, sending a shiver through her. "We're only passing through Erebus. The light will return."

"My dress…"

"And your crown. I apologize. Nothing mortal from your world can pass through the fire on the way to the Other Side."

"Wh-why… Aidon… Why did you take me like this?"

"You were in grave danger," Aidon said, relieved to hear his name on her lips. "I had no other choice."

He tightened the reins and leaned toward her, feeling her legs locked around his waist. Persephone pressed against the front of him, and need started to consume him. Heat flowed from between her legs, and the scent of her body enveloped him. She was still drenched from their time together in his sacred cypress grove. He felt the muscles of his stomach clench as instinct drew his entire body closer to the source of that heat.

Aidon kissed her, relishing the softness of her lips, the feel of her fingers weaving through his hair. Locking her arms and legs tightly, she copied him, kissing his cheek and earlobes. She pulled on one of them with her lips, tasting the edge with her tongue. Persephone listened to him take a long, ragged breath as he arched toward her, his hissed exhale grazing the shell of her ear and sending heat through her.

Persephone shivered, repeating his words in her head. *Erebus... the Other Side...*

"Who are you?" she whispered low into his ear.

"I am Aidoneus," he whispered back.

Ice ran down Persephone's spine.

Aidon...

Aidon...

Aidoneus...

Hades Aidoneus Chthonios, Polydegmon. The Unseen One. Receiver of Many. Ruler of the Other Side and Lord of the Dead...

Aidon crushed his lips against hers before she could respond. Persephone surrendered, opening to him and racing her tongue across his teeth, trembling. He moaned and smoothed his hand down her back to calm her. *He is... he is...* Her mind couldn't, wouldn't process it.

I am your lord husband. The lover from her dream, who possessed a tender fire, who had inflamed her, entranced her, awakened her, was none other than... She felt herself burning for him as her mind battled between the truth of the man encircled by her naked body and the feel of his tongue tasting and possessing her.

His hand rounded over one cheek of her rear and gripped her flesh as she returned his deeper kiss, savoring him. Persephone mewled a soft moan into his mouth, feeling his hand drift lower, fingers brushing lightly over her vulva.

He pulled back on her bottom lip with his teeth, before plunging his tongue into her mouth. As he canted his head, he curled one digit forward to caress the wetness of her crease, cupping her intimately, hearing her mewl at his touch. He sighed and broke off the kiss suddenly, leaving her gasping.

"I'm sorry." His hand left her for a moment, reaching below her sex as he lifted the front of his short tunic and moved his loincloth aside. Persephone felt him grasp her below the tailbone, his fingers burying into her flesh. "I wish there were more time and some other way."

She didn't understand what he meant until she felt herself sliding imperceptibly down his body, a hard heat butting up against her entrance. Every jump of the chariot slid her closer to him until that heat parted her folds, perched outside her gate. She remembered the wedding in Eleusis and the feel of him pressed against her in the dream. Her eyes shot open and she searched in the dark for his.

The faintest of light grew underneath them, finally showing Aidon's face. He looked at her with a gentle intensity; his eyes dilated dark with passion and determination. She eased against him and sunk lower as he pressed closer, lingering at her core, throbbing against her, then a slow stretch as he slipped a fraction deeper.

Aidon looked at her as she stared up at him. The growing light framed lips swollen from his kisses, a thin Grecian nose, and wild and wide pale blue eyes. He heard her heart beating, listened to her shallow breathing. He felt her open to him with a shiver and a gasp, and her flesh start to envelop and close around his, heat pouring out from her in this final moment.

Eyes locked to hers, Aidoneus quickly thrust upward.

. . . and now she was his Queen.

Persephone cried out in pain and squeezed her eyes shut, stars trailing behind her closed lids. The length of him sent fire through her as she struggled to stay still and not make the throbbing of her torn barrier worse. The fullness stretching her made her legs shake around his waist, offering no quarter against how completely he possessed her. Persephone realized that he had not moved within her at all as she adjusted to him. She slowly opened her eyes and looked up at him; his head was tilted back, his face strained, his eyes shut, his breathing shallow.

Aidon lowered his gaze to her, pleasure and remorse feuding within him. But above all else, he could feel the exquisite pressure of her— surrounding, enclosing, the heat within her seeping into him. He gripped the reins with his free hand and watched her face, not moving until her pain subsided. Aidon kissed away a tear from the corner of her eye, and muttered half-formed words against her skin that wavered between an apology and a prayer. Her breathing started to grow ragged as his lips trailed down her cheek, searching for hers.

Trembling, she kissed him back, her heart at war with itself. *Maiden no more.* The man from her dreams that she desired so, who had caressed her in Nysa, who had just consummated his union with her in the dark, suddenly, fully, completely joined with her was… *Hades.*

Her anxiety melted in searing heat as he withdrew ever so slowly and reclaimed her gently. The pain dulled. She felt him touching every nerve within her, pushing upward, unfamiliar pleasure shooting through her. Her arms tried to gain purchase on his shoulders, holding him closer to her. Persephone willed herself to look at him, to know him, to see the face that had burned itself into her dreams— the face of the man who burned inside of her. His gaze met hers with the same intensity.

She instinctively squeezed around him and saw his eyes roll back and close. A low growl emanated from deep in his throat. Persephone met his next thrusting response to her with a sharp gasp of pleasure. The pain dissipated into the background as he pressed into her again, forming a rhythm between them. It was too much— too raw to look and feel and know all at once. Persephone closed her eyes and kissed him again, feeling— choosing to feel. She moaned into his mouth, everything but their joined bodies disappearing and falling away as he held her to him and she held him within her.

Persephone raked her fingers through his thick black curls of hair and felt his beard graze and chafe her chin as their tongues mated in concert with their bodies. She broke away and he gasped for air. He rested his forehead on hers and she locked eyes with him again. Aidon pushed into her, their breathing becoming one, her fingers interlacing behind his neck to pull back and see him. The angle forced him deeper and she cried out, feeling his fullness within her, her insides coiling again, reaching.

His eyes darted across every inch of her body, watching her breasts rock back, the liquid flesh moving of its own accord. Aidoneus saw surrender cross her face and felt her tightening around him with every thrust. He brought her against his body, looking deep into her eyes. "Persephone…"

Shuddering against him, she tilted her head back and exposed the long line of her neck. He kissed it as she rocked forward, moaning wordlessly, rippling around him, her fingers clawing his neck, heat pulling and stroking his shaft as he made his final thrusts into her depths. Molten fire shot through him rising from where they were joined, arching his spine and erasing all conscious thought, the sharp pleasure of it shocking him. Aidon threw his head back and cried out loud enough to nearly spook the horses. His shuddering body matched hers as she clung to him.

They stilled. In the distance, the outlines of his kingdom came into view. They were nearly there, and his shattered thoughts started to piece themselves back together, considering the gravity of what had just been done. He focused on her. Persephone. *His wife.* Aidon wrapped the heavy cloak around them once again, cradling her, protecting her. Her eyes fluttered closed.

Very slowly, he slid out of her with a shudder, the cool air hitting his softening flesh. Her shaking legs disentangled from his waist and her body started to go limp, overwhelmed and exhausted. Aidoneus held her close. The arm she had wrapped around his neck draped outside the cloak, her head craned back against his shoulder. Her breasts rose and fell in shallow breaths.

The River Styx came into view, its calm light caught in the afterglow of the setting sun in the living world above. The horses started to slow, the ground looming into view. Aidon landed them in the great stable courtyard and brought the chariot to a halt, finally testing his shaking knees. Behind the cover of his cloak, he adjusted his loincloth and smoothed down the front of his tunic, both stained with their combined essence and her blood. Persephone breathed lightly into the crook of his arm.

Aidon unclasped his cloak and brought the other side around her, covering her slowly so he didn't wake her. He wrapped Persephone in its dark and heavy folds; her bare feet protruded from the edges. Kneeling down with one hand still supporting her shoulders, Aidoneus brought the other under the crook of her knees, lifting her into his tired arms.

Persephone turned toward him in her sleep as he crossed the length of the courtyard to the dark gates and corridors beyond.

6.

Waiting dormant for untold aeons, the seeds took hold of the gray earth. They burst upward, writhing through soil made alive and fertile only for them. Carefully, the sprouts broke the surface, stretching. One pale leaf appeared after the other as they took their first breath and came to life. Each gasp for air grew a new branch as fragile as the gray flowers above them. They quickened and strengthened; sprouting new life, green, thriving. . .

WARMTH.

The first sensation that Kore could feel was warmth. She lay with her eyes shut against the dappled flickering light. It had been a dream. The scent of warm olives hung about her. She had fallen asleep in the sunlight, under an olive tree in Nysa, and all this had been a dream. Mother would be there any minute.

But the ground under her was soft— too soft. It bunched in Kore's hands in waves of warm spun wool smoother than any chiton she had ever worn. Her feet lay under it. It was tucked around her breasts.

She opened her eyes. There was no sunlight. What greeted her instead was the light of small oil lamp flames, hundreds of them, each housed in a separate niche in the wall, stretching upward in a cascade of light and perfuming the room with olive. She shifted. As Kore moved she flinched in pain, feeling the heat of the path Hades had blazed inside her. She muffled a sob.

Kore. Maiden. Maiden no more.

Her hand flew over her mouth. All her life she had been Kore. But in the mortal tongue, Kore meant 'maiden', and as she felt the soreness overtake her center with every movement, she knew she was no longer a maiden. No longer Kore. Kore had burned away in the fires outside Erebus. She was Persephone. What was she now to this world when she had always been The Maiden? And *where* was she in it?

Surrounding her, walls of solid black marble with fine white veins reached upward to a domed ceiling above the bed, their smoothly hewn surface glowing in the flickering lamplight. The room was at least three times taller than Persephone. The vaulted ceiling above her was a translucent white onyx filtering soft light from outside.

At the base of the softly lit dome were intricately carved images of beautiful nymphs playing in the fields, carrying a garland of asphodel. Cascading down from the lower edges of the carved garland, six soft panels of white fabric draped down and pooled on the floor around the bed. The diaphanous panels caught and softened the lamplight, mimicking sunlight through leaves. She traced the panels down to the ripples of black sheets surrounding and enveloping her naked body, then looked back up to the thick base of one of the columns, its fluted edges framing one side of a great ebony door.

A woman sat against the column, her eyes shut.

Persephone gasped and shrank back, pulling the sheet up to her neck. The woman was barefoot, a cascade of selenite beads woven through her red hair. Wispy white curls framed her face, and crow's feet stretched from the corners of her closed eyes. She listened to Persephone, feeling confusion sweep over the young goddess.

"So many questions. You are full to overflowing, poor child. I have answers for you," she said, opening her eyes and lifting them to meet Persephone's. "You are in the Palace of Hades. I am Hecate. Aidoneus asked me to watch over you. Those answers come in a good order, I hope?" Hecate smiled gently. "I must leave you soon, though. Aidon wants to know as soon as you are awake, and I have that news to bring him now."

While the questions to those answers had crossed her mind, Persephone had not yet said a word. She wrinkled her brow at this woman.

"Ah yes— your last question has an answer too. No, I have never coupled with him."

"Stop that!" she snapped, realizing that the woman had been reading her thoughts.

Hecate inclined her head in a slight bow. "As you wish, my queen."

"What is this place?" Persephone said, looking around the room again.

"This room was created for you long ago," Hecate said, standing from her perch. Persephone gazed around the room. This was all hers? What did this woman mean by 'long ago'? Hadn't she just met Hades? She sat up again and winced. Hecate gave her a compassionate smile. "You will heal, and quicker than you fear. Stay here, child, and rest yourself well. The journey through the earthen depths is long and… tiring."

"How long was I asleep?"

"A handful of hours. It's the middle of the day," she said, opening the ebony door.

"But the sun was setting a few hours ago. How can it be daylight?"

"This is the Other Side," Hecate said as she left the room, "we pass our days when it is night above."

Persephone swallowed hard. She was in the Underworld. *Lord Hades rules the Land of the Dead...*

She puzzled how a place deep under the earth could have any kind of night or day. She covered her body again with the sheet and looked through the opening door as Hecate disappeared from the room. The bedroom opened into a large antechamber, with ceiling and walls of solid, smooth amethyst illuminated by the soft light entering through the columns outside.

Persephone turned to the delicately carved ebony chair and raised table next to the bed. She gathered the sheet around her and slowly walked over to the chair, seeing a length of fine black cloth with a gold braided belt folded over it. Beside the garment, a necklace and two fibulae were laid out for her. The golden jewelry was set with rubies, fire opals, and garnets, and it glowed even in the gentle light. The gems were arranged in the same shape as the fateful narcissus she had picked in Nysa before the earth cracked open beneath her.

Persephone wrapped the sheet around her and picked up the necklace with shaking hands. She raised it to her throat and jewels cascaded perfectly across her collarbone and the top of her breasts, as though the necklace were designed to fit only her. She looked up and saw her reflection in a long mirror of polished hematite. The sheet slipped from beneath her arms and fell to the floor, and she stood staring at her naked form draped with blood red jewels. She shuddered and unclasped the necklace, nearly dropping it on the table. Persephone picked up the sheet and pulled it around her, feeling more naked than she had ever felt in her life.

When I take you as my queen, Persephone, your crown shall be every jewel in the earth. Every ounce of its wealth will be your adornment...

She sat back down on the bed and shuddered. Was this how the Eleusinian woman had felt after her wedding? And was she even married to Hades, or had he merely enjoyed her in the dark of Erebus outside his bonds? There was no ceremony, no words that bound one to the other. Tears fell on the sheet she clutched at her breast. She lifted the black cloth in her hands, buried her face in it and silently wept.

Persephone felt a hand stroke her shoulder, and looked up to see Hecate. She sobbed aloud, leaning her head onto the strange woman's hip.

"You burn in many ways, many places, dear child, I know. It will be no worse, and then it will pass, and you will heal," Hecate said, stroking her hair.

"My mother—"

"—Ill prepared you for what to expect of this day, and fought the Fates too long trying to prevent it."

"Expect? None of this was supposed to happen! I— one minute I was— I was *with* him, and he tells me he will come for me tonight, then— then I picked a flower and— and—" Words disappeared as tears ran down her face and collected on the soft folds of Hecate's peplos. The woman stroked her hair silently, letting her cry. "My mother was coming back for me! He could have waited at least *that* long. I didn't even get the chance to tell her or say goodbye! She doesn't know where I am," Persephone said. "I don't even know where I am."

"You are with me." Persephone looked up to see Aidoneus standing in the doorway, his forehead etched with pain from listening to her sobs. A plain black tunic covered his chest, and a heavy dark gray himation was slung across it from his right hip over his left shoulder. His hair was bound back with a simple gold band. Three rings with enormous red stones glinted on his left hand as he motioned for Hecate to leave.

She narrowed her eyes at Aidon and looked down at Persephone, petting her hair. "I'll return if you need me," Hecate said, and bowed her head as she stepped away, "my queen."

Aidoneus watched Hecate leave; confused by the way she glared up at him when she passed by. He slowly walked over to Persephone and sat beside her on the bed. Her skin glowed in the lamplight. She wiped her tears away, trying not to look him in the eye. They sat in silence, Aidon searching for the spot on the floor Persephone seemed to be staring at so intently.

"I couldn't sleep either," he finally said. Sleep never came easily for Aidoneus under any circumstance. But restlessness and strange dreams had plagued him in his own room until he finally gave up on sleep and waited for Persephone to wake. He ran a hand down her shoulder, cautiously trying not to touch her too much. Aidon was mildly surprised that she didn't shrink away from his touch. Seeing her wrapped in the bed sheet, her back and bare shoulders exposed to him, started to inflame him. He had heard her cry out in pain in the dark of Erebus, and dared not be so intimate with her so soon. It was bad enough as it was, knowing that he'd hurt her. There would have been no blood at all if he had done as he should have— been gentle, been a good husband. But his guilt warred with the desire to hold her as close as he could as soon as he could. His body was drawn to hers like iron to a lodestone. He needed to get them out of this bedroom.

"Why didn't you tell me?" she whispered.

"Tell you what?"

"You said your name was Aidon. You are Hades," she said aloud, his true name heavy on her tongue. "Why did you lie to me?"

He found the will to put distance between them and stood, facing her. "I prefer to be called Aidoneus; Aidon for short. Hades means too many things. It was the name my father gave me. It is the name the mortals give my realm," he said, kneeling in front of her and lifting her chin to face him. "It's a name that would have lost you to me."

The sadness and fear in her pale eyes cut through him like a knife. "Don't you think I at least deserved to know?"

"I wanted you to know me: Aidon. The person I am; the man who is your husband. If you had known me only as Hades, Ruler of the Underworld, would you have let me hold you? Would you have kissed me in our dream last night?"

Persephone turned away and blushed, heat rushing into her as she remembered Aidon caressing her, his hands running along her skin, and his tongue parting her teeth as they tasted each other. The heat flashing through her started to lessen the pain at her core. She cursed her traitorous body. "That's not a good excuse. You lied to me."

"Hades is also the name your mother would have used to turn you against me; to lie to you about me."

"She only told me your name and your title once, and said that the mortals cannot call your true name above ground. She never said anything further about you," Persephone said, narrowing her eyes at him. "Maybe she should have. And do not speak ill of her: ever. You stole me from her."

His mood darkened as she unknowingly mentioned the woman who had shattered all his careful plans. Aidon had prepared everything— he would appear to her in the living world just before sunset, ferry her across the Styx at dawn when his kingdom was at the apex of its beauty, and gently guide both of them when they consummated their marriage that night. Demeter and her madness were the reason he had been forced to abduct Persephone and hastily couple with her in the first place. "She doesn't own you."

Persephone stood up in a flash of anger. "Oh, so you own me, then?"

Aidon came up from his crouch to rise in front of her, standing a head taller than Persephone. Calm dark eyes stared down at her. His hands moved gently to her shoulders, dancing over her hot skin. She shuddered, inadvertently dropping the clutched sheet and revealing herself to him. Aidon inhaled sharply before he averted his eyes, trying to look anywhere in the room that wasn't her inviting body.

He turned back to her and stared directly at her frightened face and nowhere else. "You may be my wife, but no one owns you, Persephone."

"Then let me go home."

"This *is* your home."

"You know what I mean!"

Aidon released her shoulders and turned his back to her. Once he'd offered her some privacy, he spoke again. "It isn't that easy. One cannot just cross the River here and go back to the corporeal world."

Persephone gathered the sheet around her again and sat down on the bed. "You flew me here; you can fly me back."

"If I do, then we might never see each other again," he pleaded with her. Aidon thought about all the other ways Demeter could separate them forever. He softened his voice. "Your mother would— she already did too much to prevent our union."

"Then why am I even here? Who says we're even married?"

Aidon turned and looked her in the eye. "Your father."

She creased her brow, thinking of Zeus—the distant and powerful god she hadn't seen since she was a young child. This was the way of the world. If Zeus had given her to

Hades, then that was the end of it. Her shoulders slumped in acceptance. "At least take me to my mother so I can tell her what happened."

"Persephone, I cannot—" he stopped and sat next to her again, moving her long hair over one shoulder to stroke her back. He fought to keep calm. "I can't surrender you to Demeter. You're my wife; I need you here."

"Then I am your prisoner."

He pursed his lips and stood up, walking to the door. "Please get dressed," he said with a backwards glance. "As long as we're both awake, I might as well show you some of your new home. Our home."

Her prison. But this was the way of the world. Her mother had told her so just yesterday. Women were passed from father to husband. It was inevitable.

Persephone watched him leave and looked back to the folded black fabric on the chair. She slowly wrapped it over her body, then fastened the cloth at her shoulders with the fibulae before winding the golden ribbon so it girded her waist and wound under her breasts. She pulled at the fabric, draping it around her slim curves into an elegant chiton. Persephone looked down, sumptuous layers of fine black cloth cascading from her hips to her feet. She decided against wearing the necklace.

* * *

Outside in the long hallway, Hecate stood next to the door, her arms folded and an eyebrow raised. Aidon glared back at her. "What?"

"I am not the Oracle at Delphi, Aidon, but next time, perhaps, you will trust that I don't need to be in order to give you a clear foretelling. She was not glad to awaken to me. You were in her heart, and you should have been beside her."

"I had my reasons."

"She is alone here—"

"She has *me*!" He spat at her.

"Now, or soon? By the time you arrived, certainly. But not this morning, when she needed you," Hecate said quietly.

"I couldn't stay with her. If I was tempted again so soon, I— I wouldn't have been able to…" Aidon was afraid of what he might have done to her, what little control he would have had if both of them awoke in the same bed. He had barely been able to rein himself in when the bed sheet fell and exposed her to him.

Hecate watched each unfamiliar emotion dance across his face. She gave him a pained smile and shook her head. "How little you know about women."

"I think you've made my lack of experience abundantly clear to me over the last two days," he said through his teeth.

"In that way the two of you are well matched. The river before you flows wide and wild. You can swim out alone, and be swept away by its currents," she said looking up at him, "or you can build a boat together."

* * *

Wherever she stepped, the plants withered and died. Hoary frost covered the fields of Nysa, each shocked blade of grass sparkling with ice under the waning full moon high overhead. Cloaked in indigo, her lustrous copper blonde hair newly streaked with brittle strands of white, Demeter carried a torch in her hand and cried out on the wind. Her voice was thin and hoarse, her words torn and scattered by the howling gales that whipped around her as she walked.

"Kore!" Demeter walked into the valley away from the sacred groves that stood on the hilltops. Rivulets of tears were dried on her face. "Kore! Where are you?"

She had to be somewhere. Demeter cursed Athena and Artemis, and then cursed herself for trusting Kore with Zeus's virgin daughters. When she had arrived in Nysa at sunset, both had told her they thought Kore was already with Demeter.

They were lying to her. She could feel their lies.

"Kore!!" Storm clouds moved across the surface of the moon and the only light Demeter had now was her torch. She looked frantically around her, hoping against hope that her daughter would come running out of the darkness and into her arms.

She tripped forward, falling over freshly uplifted earth. The clouds parted again and Demeter saw a great scar running through a small stone circle filled with trampled flowers. She could see the gaping outline of the earth where it had been pushed apart from below. Her eyes watered as she surveyed the ruined remains of the secret garden her daughter had planted as a young girl. "No…"

Demeter stumbled to the widest part of the crack in the center of Kore's garden and fell to her knees, her eyes brimming with fresh tears. "No! My Kore!"

She beat her fist on the cold ground, as the mortals did when they wanted answers from the dark god. "Hades! Hades Aidoneus, I know you can hear me!"

There was no answer.

"Hades!" she yelled, beating the ground with each word, "Cold-hearted ravager! Return her to me at once!" She opened her bruised fist, clenching the earth, fingers sinking into the upturned dirt. Tears fell down her face again and she shook, sobbing. "Aidon, please! You could have had anyone. She was all I had left…"

She looked skyward and wept, the wind churning around her as dark clouds rolled across the firmament and blotted out the moon. Lightning arced in a fan across the base of a cloud. "Is there nothing you cannot take from me? I've only ever asked you for one thing! And still—"

"We swore…" his voice answered her on a soft rumble of thunder.

Lightning illuminated the field and the trees, their leaves shriveling and falling to the wasted ground. Demeter pulled herself to her feet. "And you swore yourself to me, long ago! How can you answer for that?"

A loud boom split the air as a bolt crashed to the ground, its force nearly knocking Demeter off her feet. Zeus stood in its wake, his brilliant white himation wrapped around him as a cloak and hood against the icy wind.

"I couldn't take you as my queen, Demeter. The earth did not yield any help against the Titans, and you did not seek aid outside your province."

"You know I tried," Demeter cried to Zeus. "Gaia would not help me."

"No, indeed. Instead, she spit out Typhoeus, who nearly destroyed us all. The Titanomachy would have been lost if I had taken so weak a consort for my wife."

"It didn't mean you had to stop loving me!"

"We settled this aeons ago, Demeter!" he turned his gaze away from her and spoke under his breath. "You would not want me for a husband as I am now, anyway."

The truth stung her. "Yet you couldn't leave me one thing. Just one reminder of how much you once loved me!"

"Is that what our daughter is to you? A token of my affection, to be preserved forever in sentimental reflection? The toll on her was too great, Demeter. You sought to keep Persephone an ignorant child forever."

"Childlike innocence was her nature—"

"It was the only nature you gave her!" he yelled, the sky cracking with blinding light.

Demeter fell to her knees in fear, her head bowed. "Mighty Zeus—"

"Do not interrupt me, woman!" he bellowed, the thunder rolling and echoing through the hills. "You taught my eldest child *nothing!* I did not choose to keep Persephone ignorant to her divine destiny. But because of the love I once bore you, I allowed you more leeway with our child than I allowed the mothers of any of my other children. Including my own wife!"

She was weeping. He loved her once. Zeus placed a hand on Demeter's shoulder as she knelt, shaking in front of him. He knew her; anger was not the way to appeal to her. Her once golden hair was turned white with grief. The storm calmed.

"Demeter, Persephone is a queen now, and Aidoneus is not an unfitting husband. He rules over the richest part of what we divided at the end of the war."

Demeter raised her head to meet his gaze. Zeus's bold blue eyes softened.

"You must let her go," he said softly, the wind starting calm. "You are the mother of the fertile fields. The earth's people will be your children for all eternity."

Demeter stood up slowly before the king of the gods, her eyes narrowed, her voice iron. "I forsake them. Just as you abandoned your child, I forsake mine."

"You cannot," he growled, thunder rolling again across the sky.

"Stop me, then," Demeter replied, icily. The wind howled fiercely, turning cold, stripping more leaves from the trees, their dried edges cutting past them. "Return my daughter from the Pit, from the hands of that monster, and I will tend the earth. Until that time, your worshippers, and all the worshippers of the Olympians who betrayed me, will feel my wrath."

7.

THE PALACE WAS BEAUTIFUL AND COLD. EACH ROOM was different, displaying one rich color after another. Each step she took echoed empty and hollow, and she felt the profound silence closing in around her. Wide pillars and reliefs decorated each room, quartz giving way to marble, marble giving way to onyx, malachite, and granite. While the memory of Mount Olympus from her one childhood visit was hazy, she most clearly remembered stark white walls, absence of color, and an abundance of people. The Palace of Hades was its opposite.

One passage opened to an immense quartz-domed great hall with gold columns. Woven tapestries hung on each wall, their threads telling the story of the war long ago. She ran her hand along one such panel, tracing the outline of a golden chariot wheel, then stepped back to view the entire scene. Hecate stood to one side of her, Aidoneus to the other. He paid no attention to the tapestry, only to the wispy lock of hair on her neck that had escaped her chignon.

A warrior stood on the chariot, holding a raven-crested standard before a host of the Underworld. The threads told a tale of frightening creatures— a dark haired woman wrapped in black standing with towering Cyclopes, bronze armored men with black and silver wings hovering in front of dark, unknown creatures, their hulking forms hidden in the shadows. A small girl dressed in white with strawberry blonde hair and a silver half moon hanging on her forehead stood ahead of their ranks, her arms outstretched and holding up a massive golden helm.

"The Helm of Darkness; our gift to Aidoneus to render him unseen to whomever he chooses. That was me, long ago," Hecate said, pointing at the small girl, "But not *so* long ago..."

That surprised Persephone. Intuitively, she had guessed from the way Hecate carried herself and spoke that she was ancient. If she were just a child when the Titanomachy happened, it would make her not much older than Persephone. Her eyes followed the upheld helm and looked at the warrior's familiar face. She moved to the widest of the panels. The central scene was wreathed in laurel branches. It showed the gods' victory over Typhoeus, the deadliest of the Titan's allies, before her father buried him under Mount Aitne. In each corner was a depiction of the Olympian alliance. On a bottom corner stood three figures. A man and a woman dressed in white stood on one side of a river, and the helmeted warrior dressed in black stood on the other, his hand outstretched toward the woman's swollen womb. Persephone peered at the woman's face and her copper blonde hair.

She felt Aidon's hand come up to hold her at the small of her back. "Do you recognize them?"

"My mother... the man next to her is my father..."

"And you," he said pointing at young Demeter's belly. "And I."

She felt a chill crawl up her spine. If their betrothal was as old as the alliance of the Olympians, why didn't her mother ever tell her?

"This is where *we* started, Persephone. And one day," Aidoneus said, pointing at the vast empty wall opposite the entry, "Clotho, Lachesis and Atropos will finish weaving the tapestry that tells our story."

Clotho, Lachesis and Atropos, Persephone thought. *The Fates themselves. Mother knew of this; swore it on the Styx. Why didn't she tell me?* The last question repeated over and over again in her head. The walls felt suffocating and close, trapping her. A lump formed in her throat. She turned to Aidoneus, who was still smiling down at her. "Can we go outside? I… I want to see what it looks like beyond the walls."

"You've never lived indoors, have you?"

"No. Even the shrines and temples I rested in were open to the sky."

Aidoneus cursed himself for forgetting where she came from and what she had known all her life. At the very least he should endeavor to make his wife more comfortable with her new home. He smiled at her and pushed the stray lock of hair back behind her ear. "It would be my honor to show you the Fields."

Hecate followed them down the corridors through the portico to the gardens. Aidoneus opened the door before them and stepped out with Persephone while Hecate hung back. She watched him introduce the young queen to Askalaphos, the pudgy little gardener who knelt to one knee before Persephone touched him on the shoulder. Hecate smiled. Once they had moved on, Hecate walked to where the gardener was pulling at something near the enclosing walls.

"Stop," Hecate said firmly.

"My lady?" Askalaphos pointed at the tiny sapling. "It's just a weed, and it'll become a mighty big one if I don't pull it now."

"Let it become what it will, Askalaphos. If you see more like it, leave them untouched as well," she said. "Don't let *anyone* touch them."

"Lady Hecate, do you know what they are?"

She remembered the rush of imagery that had come to her yesterday as she had counseled Aidoneus. The flashes had been vivid, but understanding had escaped her. "I do not. But let them grow just the same."

Aidon took Persephone to the edge of the garden, replete with blossom after blossom of asphodel. White poplar trees shaded the boundaries of the garden, set inside the tall stone walls. Gray mist, unmoving, hung high overhead. Beyond the garden, a gray field stretched on to the horizon, cut in half by a thin black river snaking toward them.

Persephone looked out over the field, and thought of her mother kneeling down and ripping these same plants from her shrine. She had known this entire time. When Demeter saw the asphodel growing where her precious Kore had slept, her mother had known who was coming for her. *Why didn't she tell me?*

She reached out and brushed her hand across one of the asphodel buds, expecting it to open for her. The white petals remained closed and motionless. She chewed on her lip and tried again. Still nothing.

Persephone took a couple wide steps to catch up with Aidoneus, who was following the garden path to a large ebony gate. The gate to the garden creaked, and a man clad in black held it open for them. After they passed through, he closed it behind them and limped to the wall to retrieve a crooked herder's staff. A flat expanse of gray earth stretched before them. Here and there, clumps of the white flowers grew out of the rocky soil.

"Menoetes, my friend, how are you? How's the leg?" Aidon said with a smile.

"Well, milord; doing better today. But that ram they gave us did a real number on me," he said, smiling with missing teeth at Persephone. "And your ladyship must be..."

"Kor—Persephone," she said. The herdsman bowed to her, favoring his leg as he clung to his staff. She was struck by the fact that Aidon addressed everyone by name— even his gardener and bondsman— called them 'friend' when he spoke to them, and asked after each of them.

"My Queen," Menoetes replied before Aidoneus and Persephone walked on.

The plain itself was as bountiful with the dark stalks of asphodel as the garden. While the garden hosted rows of carefully pruned flowers, these grew wild and unruly, their roots thick and tangled. From the corner of her eye, Persephone saw a translucent white hand reach around a tall stalk, followed by short curls of brown hair, a stubbly beard, and finally a set of gray eyes peering out at her. She gasped and turned to look, but the ghostly face startled and vanished into a dark mist, disappearing as quickly as it had appeared.

...the Land of the Dead... Words from long ago teased her memory *...drink no wine, eat no bread...*

A young woman with pale skin, clad in a long black chiton, her hair bound up with black ribbon, stepped out from between two more stalks, absently twirling a white flower in her hand. Persephone could nearly see through her, and stopped for a moment to watch her. A serene smile lit the face of the shade as she pulled the anthers from the bloom. She glanced up at Persephone with a surprised gasp that melted into a soft smile. The woman cast her eyes downward and drew out the skirts of her chiton as she dipped into low curtsy. Rising again, she faded into a smoky mist that wafted back into the stalks of asphodel behind her, the flower falling from her hand to rest on the ground.

Lord Hades rules the Land of the Dead, where they drink no wine and eat no bread. . .

When Persephone was a child in Nysa, she and Artemis and all the Olympian children were taught simple rhymes to memorize the names and domains of the immortals. Before today, those long forgotten lines from her childhood were all she had ever known about her new husband, betrothed to her since she was in Demeter's womb. *Why didn't you tell me?*

Pale shades of mortals clad in black flitted between the plants, appearing one moment, and vanishing into mist the next. Two middle aged women looked at her and whispered, smiling. Both knelt to the ground as Persephone and Aidoneus walked past. An old man leaning against a staff clutched his hand to the front of his black himation and silently mouthed 'at last'. He bowed low before vanishing. Five young women, three carrying newborns and two with empty arms, traipsed across their path. The childless women silently fawned over the shade infants, then disappearing into the flowers as quickly as they appeared.

"Are those mothers who died on the birthing bed?" Persephone asked Aidon, remembering the Eleusinian woman and what her mother had said about the mortal's fate.

"There are too many," he said grimly. "Far too many if you ask me. You'd think the mortals would have solved that by now."

As they walked on through the fields, Persephone gathered a single white flower from each plant she passed and wove them into her hair. Aidon's mouth curved into an amused smile as she did it almost unconsciously, fashioning a beautiful crown from the flowers of his realm. They heard a desperate bleat behind them, and a black lamb bolted past them and away into the fields, becoming a blur of rustling asphodel. "You have sheep? How did they get here?"

"Mortals do not build temples to me, as they did for you, and they rarely pray to me." He placed his arm around her shoulder, trying to match pace with her smaller steps as they walked on. "But when they do, they send me their black sheep, and Menoetes takes care of them. It's why all of the cloth woven in this realm is black."

Persephone looked down at her own gown. "Aidon, would you mind if I changed mine?"

"Of course not," he said, smiling as he heard her say his name. He spread his arm to show her the color of his himation. "I keep mine gray, after all."

Aidon looked on as white framed in dark vermillion swirled across her gown to match the asphodel in her hair and throughout the open field.

"There we are!" Persephone smiled and smoothed down the edges of the chiton before looking up at Aidon, who stood transfixed, his eyes glinting as he shook his head in adoration.

"You're beautiful." Aidon pushed the same wayward lock of hair behind her ear, and brushed his fingers down her neck.

She stared up at him, the nervous smile on her face melting into desire as his fingers trailed slowly over her collarbone. Persephone felt his hand come up to her cheek again as her head tilted up, his face moving toward her.

A growl broke the silence, followed by loud baying. The ground started to shake. She turned chalk white in horror as a great monster came galloping toward them, its three dark heads baring sharp white teeth.

"Cerberus, *down!*" Aidon yelled out.

Persephone backed up and felt her feet start to carry her away. She picked up her long skirts and ran as hard as her legs could move, sharp gravel punishing her feet through her sandals. She didn't care.

One cannot just cross the River here...

The thin black river. It lay just up ahead. The field was hidden by mist, but now, caverns were visible beyond. Passageways to the upper world. She could run away back home. It was just a little further...

Aidon's back was still to her. He patted one of the heads of the enormous hound. Another head yawned. "There, you see? He's— Persephone?"

He saw her running headlong toward the river Lethe.

"Persephone! Stop! Don't touch the water!"

She looked behind her to see him running after her, yelling for her. The great beast sat in the field behind him, blood red tongues lolling out of its mouths. She ran harder. She was almost to the river. She was going to go home, and be free of this gray waste. Persephone would feel the sun and the wind, see the green fields and her mother again. She had so many questions for her...

It was such a shallow stream; the silted bottom was clearly visible even at the widest part. She could cross it easily. Persephone dipped one foot into the water, then the other and... it was warm. Why was she standing here? She heard someone in the distance saying a name. The water was warm. Why was she here? The water was warm...

Aidon leaned forward and grabbed her wrist, dragging her dead weight from the shallows of the Lethe and back to the shore as her heels scraped across the ground. He knelt with her in his arms. Her body was limp and her eyes stared off into nothing.

"No..." he whispered. "Fates, no... please... Persephone, wake up! Persephone..."

Kore looked out at the gray sky and the endless field. White flowers covered everything. Someone was holding her and shaking her. She heard her other name as though it were coming from the bottom of a well. Kore knew that voice. It was closer to her now. She turned toward him, "Aidon?"

"Persephone…" Relief washed over him. Aidon held her against him, her arms slowly starting to move. "Thank the Fates…"

"You… came for me? Oh, I knew you would come!" she said, clumsily throwing her arms around him, still disoriented. He looked down at her, shocked as she continued. "But it's not sunset yet."

He gently broke their embrace and looked into her eyes. "Persephone, what do you remember?"

"I wasn't expecting you so soon. I was just about to visit my garden but… this place isn't Nysa," she said, scanning the horizon. Kore saw a palace in the distance, set against a hillside, a waterfall cascading next to it. "Wait— I am with *you.* Is this where you live?"

Aidoneus relaxed and sat back. She wasn't lost to him; she had just forgotten the past day. He could still save her memories. Relieved, he stroked her hair. "Yes, sweet one. You are with me in my kingdom… Persephone, you—"

"Aidon!" She wrapped her arms around him and kissed his neck. "I thought you were only in my dreams, or I was going mad, but… you're here. You're real… Now I can finally see you in the light and— and you're beautiful and…" she said, smoothing a hand across his chest, then stopped. "No, beautiful isn't the word. It is, but, you're a man, after all. Handsome! Yes that's the word." Kore looked down the length of her as she lay in his arms. "Did you give me this dress?"

"Yes," he said quietly.

Kore brushed her hands over a glittering ruby and garnet narcissus fibula pinned at her shoulder and stared down at the diaphanous fabric clinging to her legs. "Why is it all wet?"

"We need to get away from here. You need to drink from the Mnemosyne pool."

"Where did you go?"

"What?"

"In the grove just now we— I had just…" she blushed and looked back up at him. "You were going to say something to me. At least it sounded like you were going to, but then you went away."

"I'm so sorry," he said, holding her. "Persephone, I wanted so badly to stay with you, but I was forced to come back here. I— there was something that I needed to do immediately."

"So you didn't leave because of me?"

"No, of course not," he kissed her forehead. "But, right now we need to stand up and—"

"Wait before we go, just… stay. Please hold me," Kore said as her hand slipped under the folds of his himation and stroked his collarbone, running her hand over his skin and tracing the edge of his tunic down to his chest. She could feel Aidon's heart beating faster, and ran a finger back up the vein throbbing in his neck. She heard his breath hitching.

He whispered to her. "Please… Persephone—"

She cradled his face in her hand then leaned up and whispered in his ear. "I love you."

A flash of hot, unwanted tears stung his eyes. Aidoneus tried to force them back, his voice choking. "Sweet one… we need to leave this place. Here— stand up with me."

He rose and took her with him. Kore staggered forward, losing her balance, and leaned against his chest as he held her. Aidon braced his feet to hold her up. She peppered any piece of his exposed skin she could find with small kisses, her lips dancing along his neck and collarbone. Each press of her lips stoked the fires raging beneath his skin. Her breath came out in a warm whisper against his neck. "You make me feel so alive. I know you feel the same..."

She pressed her thigh into his groin. Aidon cursed himself and the growing hardness she had deliberately sought out as she rubbed against him. Persephone still wobbled on her feet and he supported her and held her close. The heat of her body through their clothes became a delicious torture. Persephone pressed against him again and heard him hiss through his teeth. Her lips brushed past his.

"My husband..."

Aidon captured her lips in a fevered kiss, inhibition dissolved, and heard her moan into his mouth. Her hands traveled down his chest as she fitted herself closer to his body. He embraced her, all sound drowned out by the blood coursing through him.

The cautionary voice that would have stopped him from kissing her was extinguished when her tongue snaked out against his teeth. He opened his mouth and deepened their kiss, pulling her against him. Kore trailed her hands down his stomach, feeling him tense and jump at her touch.

How terrible could it be if she doesn't remember how you brought her here? Look at her. Feel her. She is yours and she wants you. You could have her here and now...

Her hand reached lower, making him gasp. She whispered against his lips. "Lie with me. Make me yours."

Aidoneus broke off the kiss and stepped away from her, gently prying her off him. "I can't. I— Persephone, I can't..."

"You don't want me?" Kore said, her face falling.

"Sweet one, I do want you. Powerfully. But not here; not like this." He held out his hand to her. "Come with me."

Kore walked after him, her hand in his as they traveled through the silent field, passing one bunch of white flowers after another. They were nearly out of breath when they came to a pool reflecting the gray mist above, its shores ringed in white poplars.

"This may be easier if you're lying down," Aidon said. She blushed and the corner of her mouth twisted up before he realized what he had just said. "No, no… you need to drink the water, and the effects will be very strong and very sudden."

"Why do I need to?"

"Please trust me," Aidoneus said as he dipped the edge of his himation in the cold waters of the Mnemosyne pool. He watched her comply, lying on the flat stone embankment. A soft, expectant smile lit up her face and she closed her eyes. He shook his head at himself. Even now, she thought he was trying to coyly seduce her.

Cradling the wet fabric, he sat behind her. Aidon propped her up in his lap with her head leaned back against his chest and stroked a hand over her forehead to relax her. "Here; just a few drops. I'll be right here with you."

She opened her mouth and felt the cool water hit the back of her throat, then gasped and coughed. Stars trailed in her vision, then rushed through her in blinding white light. She shook violently, and Aidon wrapped his arms tightly around her. Everything around her disappeared and fell away. She could hear his calm voice echoing, as though it were emanating from the center of her. "I've got you… I've got you. It will be all right. Shhh…"

Her mind wound back to her first memories of her mother. The taste of ambrosia. Olympus. Meeting her father. The fields. The flowers. The harvests. The wedding she witnessed. The man who held her close that night. *Let me look at you.* The field of Nysa. Aidon. The cypress grove. *Your bridal crown.* The flower in her garden that split the earth. The chariot. The searing heat. The dark of Erebus. Her legs wrapped around his waist. Hades. Caressing her. Kissing her. *I wish there were more time.* The pain. Pleasure. Kore no more. Running into the Lethe. Memories escaping. Holding herself against Aidoneus. *I love you...*

Persephone's entire body screamed as she turned to the side, curling her knees to her chest and crumpling against Aidon. He embraced her, his hand smoothing over her arms to comfort her through wrenching sobs. She went limp and shuddered against him at the onslaught of memories. He rocked her from side to side in his embrace, his head leaned down against hers, until she had no tears left.

After she had been silent for a moment, he stood her up carefully and looked into her eyes. "Let's go home."

8.

Aidon held Persephone about the waist during their walk back to the palace, in case she faltered, and looked down at her tear-stained face. She looked ahead silently, leaning on him periodically to regain her balance. The rush of the falls grew louder, and the gray mist above them began to dim as they approached the gates.

"What happened to me?" she finally asked.

"You walked into the river Lethe. Its waters are drunk by the shades to erase the memories of their lives and the pain of their death when they first arrive. They cross over it and drink it once more when they are reborn to the world of the living."

"And that pond?"

"The Mnemosyne— where all lost memories go."

Persephone puzzled over this for a moment, then gasped and shrank back against Aidoneus as the great black beast from the field loomed into view. He was lying down next to the outer door, a low whine emanating from each of his three heads when he saw her.

"Persephone, it's all right," Aidon said, holding her. "Don't be scared. It's just my dog."

"Your… that's a dog?!"

"Mostly." He lifted his thumb and index finger to his lips and whistled twice. The three heads lifted up. "Cerberus! Cerberus, this is Persephone. Say hello."

Cerberus jumped up and trotted over to them before crouching down. He lowered two heads and raised one, lolling out a panting tongue. The beast's shoulder was as tall as Persephone when he was lying down.

"He won't hurt you," Aidon said, reaching a hand out to pet him. Persephone inched closer and gingerly reached out her hand. It met short wiry fur. She ran her hands through it, then stepped back with a start as the creature rolled over on its back, snorting.

Persephone stepped forward again and reached up to scratch his stomach, watching all three tongues hanging out of his three mouths. His serpentine tail smacked and shook the earth, his hind legs kicking in the air. She looked back to see Aidon crack a wide smile, showing his teeth. The expression looked foreign on him, and she guessed he didn't smile like that very often— if ever.

"I think he likes you," Aidon said. "He won't even do that for me."

Cerberus pricked up his ears. Persephone stepped back as he rolled away from them, then bounded across the garden, clearing the wall as if it weren't even there. Persephone heard him baying and barking. "What is he doing?"

"Cerberus helps me keep the world of the living separate from the world of the dead. He guards all of us."

"Would he… is he guarding me?"

"Yes, but he would let *you* pass him. Mortals, living and dead, cannot," he said as they made their way inside. He watched relief wash over her face.

Persephone followed him as they made their way back to her chambers, slowly learning the layout of the palace. The memory of him embracing her at the Lethe played out again in her mind. "Why did you stop?"

"Stop what?"

She sighed and looked down. "You could have… had me… on the banks of the Lethe when I lost my memory. I was willing. Why did you stop?"

Aidoneus opened the door to the amethyst room and took off his sandals before entering her antechamber. "I thought that would be obvious."

"How so?"

"When I am with you, I want it to be with you as you are, and I want you to want me as well. I'll not have you by way of deception. The girl who kissed and embraced me at the Lethe wasn't you, Persephone. Or, rather, it was you before…"

"Before you abducted me," she said, sitting down carefully on a chaise and removing her sandals. "Which begets my next question: why did you abduct me in the first place? You knew that I wanted you, that I was going to wait for you."

"You were in danger. I had to act."

"In danger of what?"

Aidon knew this would come. No matter how irrational Demeter had been, her daughter still loved her deeply. If he told Persephone what her mother was about to do, she would never believe him. "I can't tell you."

"Oh? Then I suppose you also can't tell me why you said you wished there were more time, before we—"

"To save you I had to…" he stopped and took a long breath. "The threat to you would be ended only after we consummated our marriage."

Persephone looked up at him skeptically, her brow wrinkled. "Aidon, at every turn you've asked me to trust you. How am I supposed to do that, exactly? You didn't tell me your true name or reveal anything about yourself, when you very clearly knew all there was to know about me."

"Persephone—"

"You took me from the world above, the only home I've ever known, and you can't even tell me why."

"Persephone, I promise you, all will be revealed in time."

"Revealed in time…" she scoffed. "You wonder why I cannot trust you? This is why I had to ask you why you didn't just take me at the banks of the Lethe when—"

"Because I love you!"

Persephone stared up at him in shock, his face echoing hers. He turned away, wide-eyed, trying to process the words he'd just said. She sat there, her skin prickling as she brought her arms around her body, feeling raw and exposed, remembering when she said those very words to him not an hour ago.

"Because I couldn't do that to you," he continued. "There was a reason and a purpose for everything that happened when I brought you here, and I know that it destroyed your trust in me. Believe me when I say that to save you, that was a price I was willing to pay. I— I don't expect you to love me right away, Persephone. All I ask from you is for a chance to rebuild that trust."

"You're asking for a lot, Aidon," she muttered under her breath.

"I know."

"And even if I do come to trust you… or love you… it doesn't change who we are. Who is to say that I'd want to live in this place… forever? Mortals pray to my mother and I for fertile fields. For life— not death. I don't belong here."

"Believe it or not, I felt the same way when I first arrived here." Aidon stretched his hand out to her. "Come; I want to show you something."

She curled her fingers around his and he helped her to her feet. They walked through the sweeping portico columns onto the terrace. Aidon stood behind her, his hand resting on her arm and a thumb rolling along the skin of her shoulder. She leaned toward him, almost dizzy as she took in the sweeping landscape. The palace sat on a rocky cliffside far above the gray plain. From her left, a vast river wound its way before the palace and continued outward, meeting an endless black sea. Thin mist hung over the still waters.

From her view on the terrace, the palace was far more massive than she could have guessed from the few rooms Aidoneus and Hecate had shown her. The polished black marble of the palace's outer walls belied the wealth of colorful stone she had already seen inside. Its hundreds of rooms and terraces were connected by winding hallways and staircases between the levels. Several rooms and passageways were embedded in the cliff side, framed by columns carved out of the stone itself. The gardens and the flat plains surrounding the Lethe and Mnemosyne lay behind the palace, high above the river lands. Far below the terrace, a towering poplar tree grew, its shining golden boughs overhanging the entryway to the palace atrium.

"Did you build all this?" she said quietly.

"Yes, bit by bit. I had aeons to do so."

The calm waters of the river shone a blue darker and richer than the sky in the world above. Suddenly, its color changed to a brilliant purple, fading to orange, lighting the land and the mists above in a soft glow. The river shone like a brilliant sunset, its light illuminating the crystal room behind them. Persephone's eyes danced. She had never seen a sunset this beautiful in all her existence. Overwhelmed, she looked up at Aidon, who smiled back at her.

"That was my reaction the first time I saw the river change from day to night," he said, running his hands along her shoulders and down her back.

"What makes it change color?"

"The River Styx has no bottom. Beyond that, we don't know. The river is far older than you or I— older than Hecate, or Nyx, even. Hecate says it's been here since Chaos gave the cosmos form from the void. It is the mother of all waters above and below the earth."

Persephone stood mesmerized as the river shifted from orange to bright fuchsia. She felt Aidon's hand stroking her back and leaned closer to him. "You didn't feel like you belonged here… A strange thing to say since you rule over everything we're looking at right now."

"I didn't choose to rule here. But I've come to believe that this place chose me. We drew lots. Your father received the skies and rulership over all, Poseidon the seas, and I received the Underworld."

"But you were the eldest…"

"Yes. The lot I received embittered me for aeons, but I eventually grew to love this place. In retrospect, I don't think Zeus's position would have suited me. I was callous and short tempered in earlier days. And I'm afraid of what that would have turned into if I were ruling in his place."

She turned to face him as the light faded from the river, turning it violet as night fell in the Underworld. "This is all very beautiful… but it's not the same as the sky and fields of the living world. I worry that it will take aeons for me to fall in love with the Underworld, just as it did for you."

"I'm fairly certain loneliness prolonged it for me," he said, taking her hands in his. "I'd like to think I could help relieve that for you."

She looked up into his eyes. "You couldn't have been completely alone this whole time. I mean, the men of Olympus all have… companions…"

"I'm not an Olympian. And I knew I would have you beside me one day," he said.

"What about during the war?" she said quietly, moving closer to him.

Aidon brought his hands up to her shoulders and a vulnerable smile lit up his eyes. He shook his head slowly.

Persephone's lips parted and she blinked in startled revelation, her body shuddering, pushing her closer to his. "So that means… when you and I were in Erebus…"

"Yes," he whispered softly.

She returned to that moment and the look of shocked pleasure on his face as he trembled and struggled to remain still, trying to soothe and comfort her after their bodies joined. Persephone remembered his arm locked around her, supporting her. Her body drew instinctively closer to his and she lightly traced her finger around the edges of his face, brushing across the trimmed beard framing his jaw line.

Aidon kissed the edge of her hand just as he'd done in the dark of Erebus when she'd reached out for him. He cupped her face, and leaned down to meet her waiting lips. She deepened their kiss, first tasting his lips then mating their tongues. Her body melted against his, feeling him arch toward her. Persephone's fingers raked down his back as he encircled her within his arms, pulling her ever closer. He felt his flesh awaken yet again, and sighed against her soft lips.

"Erebus was unforgettable for me," he said hoarsely. "But that wasn't what I wanted for our first time. I owed you so much more. So much more tenderness, so much more consideration…"

Persephone renewed their kiss as heat filled her body, her breath shuddering through her as he held her. Her knees shook and she felt her heels lift up to stand on tiptoe, getting closer to the heat from him that pulsed between them.

"Show me."

"Show you…?" He drew away breathlessly to look at her face, her lips red from their kiss. "Are you sure?"

"Yes," she said timidly. "I'm sure."

"I don't want to hurt you."

She leaned up to his ear, nervously. "I believe you, Aidon— I want to trust you. I want to try…"

"If you want me to stop at any time—" She put two fingers to his lips. He kissed them, then turned to capture her lips again in a kiss. He cradled her shoulders and held her up to him as her knees shook in nervousness and delight.

Aidon dropped down and scooped up the back of her knees with his other arm as Persephone folded her body against his chest. He quietly carried her from the balcony portico to the faintly lit amethyst antechamber, following the pathway of lamplight to her room. His eyes locked to hers in a smile as he walked through the ebony doors.

He thought back to just before dawn, when he had carried her sleeping body in this same way to this very room and laid her down on the bed. Aidoneus had spent several minutes carefully untangling the ruined braid that had held her hair through the journey, before unwrapping her from his cloak. Wiping her blood and his seed from her thighs with the edge of his cloak, he had cursed himself for hurting her. But despite his guilt, and exhausted by the journey from the living world, he had still felt himself harden painfully under his armor and tunic, her beautiful naked body spread out before him. Aidon had quickly covered her with the bedclothes and left the room, fighting his desire for her the entire way.

Persephone felt her foot pass gently by one of the gauzy panels draping from the ceiling to the bed— her bed— as

Aidon raised a knee for leverage on the soft down mattress and placed Persephone in the center. She felt her body sink into the cool sheets.

Aidon closed the great ebony doors with an echoing thud and looked back at her, the room now theirs alone. He walked toward the center of the chamber and raised his hand above his head, looking at the surrounding lamplight. Slowly closing one finger after another, the lamps dimmed to flickers of orange dancing on the edges of low blue flames. Only a scattered handful of the small lamps held full light. Persephone shuddered at this subtle demonstration of his power, her eyes transfixed as he walked to the side of the bed and sat down.

Persephone stretched out her hand to him and he pressed her fingers to his lips. He kissed down the length of her bare arm and up to one of the fibulae holding the chiton onto her body. Aidon lay alongside her, propped up on one elbow as he moved his hand to the brooch and slid out its pin. He looked up into her eyes for approval and was met with lids half closed in passion and her parted lips. Unable to resist he kissed them again, pulling the jeweled pin away. Her hand danced over his shoulder and neck to the golden band containing his hair.

Tugging on it, she felt his hand come up to help her, pulling the thin torc away from his locks and letting it fall. Long curls of black hair fell freely down his back. Aidon took the three large rings off his left hand and carefully set them aside with the rest. Supporting her neck, he pulled at the ribbon holding her chignon and unwound her hair, spreading the dark russet waves on the pillow behind her.

Persephone watched his eyes dart down to her breast, now exposed by the missing fibula. His hungry gaze caused her to inhale sharply, and the nipple tightened to a point as he unconsciously licked his lips. His hand traced and molded her breast, a thumb circling inward. Aidon's tongue darted out to taste the very tip, then sucked the puckered flesh into his mouth as Persephone moaned from deep in her throat and thrashed on the bed.

"Should I keep going?" he whispered against her breast.

She didn't answer him aloud; she only nodded with her eyes shut. He smoothed a hand over her hot skin and the soft fabric until he reached the ribbon girdle that bound her chiton. The tie was easy to undo, but unwrapping it from around her was a little harder. She smiled at him as he fumbled with it, holding her at her lower back. He unwound it in each direction, then pulled it from under her and cast it over the edge of the bed.

His face scanned her body before he looked back at her and moved partially over her, that familiar heat pressing against her hip. His lips met hers in a long kiss as she moved her leg against him, causing him to groan into her mouth. Aidon pulled away the second fibula and set it aside. The chiton was now a long piece of unbound fabric, its shape held aloft by the curves of her body underneath. He sat up and unwound the shoulder of his himation, propping himself up to pull it from underneath where he lay, letting the heavy fabric fall softly to the floor.

Persephone stared down at sculpted calves that had spent aeons walking across stone floors, following their lines up to his thighs, and an unmistakable outline, hard and upright, concealed beneath his tunic and loincloth. Persephone's breath hitched and she blushed and shuddered in anxious heat. Admiration and restlessness played across her face before moving closer to him. He took off his belt and removed the golden fibula pins that held the fabric in place at his shoulders. Aidon cast it to the floor, his loincloth all that remained.

She squirmed in pleasure at the sight of him and reached carefully toward his body. Aidon forced himself to stay still as her fingers landed lightly on his chest. She traced each rise and fall then curiously ran her ring finger around a flat nipple. Aidon inhaled sharply through his teeth. She shifted course, trailing her fingers down his stomach, mesmerized. A deep line arched from his waist to his groin over one hip and into the dark curls of hair that started in a thin line at his navel and thickened as they moved lower. The pronounced hip line met its match from the other side just below the straining cloth, all paths leading to…

"Not yet," he said, picking up her wrist before her fingers drifted any lower. All his energy was focused on fighting the urge to throw the remainders of their clothes to the floor, wrap Persephone's legs around his waist, and plunge into her. If she explored any further, it would end him.

Instead, he set her arm gently down at her side again and pulled slowly at the fabric still covering her. His lips touched her neck and she moved her hand up to his shoulder, gripping at his skin.

Aidon stopped. "Is this still what you want?"

"Yes…" She looked into his eyes.

Persephone helped him, raising her hips off the bed as he moved the fabric out from under her. She felt it scrape over her breast as more of her flesh was revealed to him. The newly exposed nipple puckered from the cool of the room and the heat of his touch. Aidon sat up and pushed the remains of Persephone's chiton over the side of the bed before turning back to her.

He paused there, taking in the swell of her breasts from the underside, the curve of her stomach, the mound of gently curling dark pubic hair, her legs, her ankles, each individual toe. He reached behind him and untied his loincloth, then cast it away with the rest of their clothes. Aidon sighed in relief and heard her shift and hold her breath.

Persephone took in the full sight of him for the first time. In their dream, her view of his most intimate parts had been obscured by their bodies, and in Erebus, the darkness had covered him completely. When he took her, he had sheathed himself fully within her. She had only felt, not seen, him until now. His manhood jutted from his body as he sat up. She watched it fall against his stomach as he lay back down beside her, the weight of his engorged flesh tipping it toward the sheets. She felt her skin flush hot, and her breath grew short. It was no wonder the pain had been so great. She wondered how he could fully enter her again without it hurting.

"Are you alright?" Aidon startled her. He ran a hand down her shoulder, feeling her shake.

"It's just—" She licked her dry lips. "I'm afraid it will hurt again."

He cupped her face and kissed her forehead. "We can stop anytime you want. Say the word and I'll stop right now."

Persephone looked into his eyes, burning yet sincere as he stroked her cheek and sighed. He meant every word of what he said. "I don't want to stop— not now. Not yet. But if I do... do you promise?"

"I promise."

She leaned into Aidon and felt him press against her. He shuddered at the contact. His lips found hers again as they held each other skin on skin, their hands moving and exploring, running across each angle and curve.

Persephone's arm slid under his waist and held Aidon against her. He leaned down and kissed one breast, then the other, moving back and forth between them. Persephone moaned as he pulled each hardened tip into his mouth before kissing her along her collarbone and up her neck. Carefully, he brought his hand up her thigh and moved inward. Her legs wriggled open at his touch, her body seeking him of its own volition. His hand trailed along white-hot skin, her knees shaking as he drew closer.

When Aidon's hand met the apex of her thighs he looked back up at Persephone, watching as desire played across her face. Fingers stroked across the soft hair covering her vulva as his palm came to rest on her mound. She felt that familiar coil tightening in her stomach. Aidon slipped a finger between the folds, sinking into the slick heat pouring out of her. He groaned. She arched against the finger moving down her seam, the flesh pulsing around him. He found her entrance and circled back up, her body shuddering a halted moan as he brushed over the hooded bud at the top.

Persephone pulled him in for a kiss as his finger circled that spot. Fire shot through her as she turned her entire body toward him, aching for him, needing to feel him closer. She brought a leg over his hips, opening herself to his touch, his finger massaging and stroking the nub.

Aidon shifted her back down to the bed underneath him and lay astride of her. He balanced himself above her on his elbows and knees, his lips locked with hers as his hand returned to the heat of her crease, gently rolling his fingers through the folds. Her feet rested on the backs of his knees, opening herself to Aidon's careful caress. He rose above her and Persephone looked up into his eyes, feeling the weight and heat of his arousal fall against her stomach. He watched her gaze trail down between their bodies. She saw the tip pointed straight at her, a tiny pearl of fluid glistening on the crown, and trembled.

"If you're afraid—"

"I'm not." She looked up at him, his hand smoothing hair back from her forehead. "I'm not," she whispered again.

She ached indescribably, needing him closer to her. She sighed under her breath. "I want you, Aidon."

Relief washed over him as he moved his body back, and felt her raise her legs to the side of his hips. He kissed her neck and came up to her ear, returning her gentle susurrations. "I'll go slowly. This isn't supposed to hurt. I didn't..." He fought to find words, to ensure her that he would be careful, tender with her. "It was never supposed to hurt. But if you feel any pain, Persephone, any at all, I'll stop. I promise."

She ran her fingers through the curls at the nape of his neck and felt the tip part her folds at her entrance. Tensing, she breathed shallowly through her nose as Aidon moved his hand between them. Persephone bit her lip, her heart beating out of her chest, waiting. He drew back for a moment. Instead of entering her, he traced the tip up and down her crease, rolling it through her wetness as she relaxed and gasped. The feel of him hot, needy, and barely restrained while he touched the folds of her labia from top to bottom was exquisite. Persephone could feel every twitch of his flesh, the blood pooled at his groin reflecting his heartbeat.

For Aidon this was slowly becoming torture. When he moved the tip up to brush against the center of her desire, she moaned and pressed her fingers harder into his shoulder blades. When he pushed it down to her entrance, he shuddered at the heat pouring out of her, beckoning him forward. He fitted himself over her body. Coated in her wetness, shaking with the primal need to bury himself within her, he kissed her jaw line. "Persephone..."

"Aidon, please..." she brought her legs up higher and locked them around his waist, opening to him. She watched him rise above her on one arm. He guided himself toward her entrance and Persephone felt him pitch forward as the width of the head opened her.

He moved slowly, finally taking his hand away when he knew his own motions could carry him forward. He looked into her eyes, searching for what she felt as he entered her.

Aidon watched her wince as he slowly pushed past where her barrier had once been. When she cried out sharply in discomfort, he stopped and ran a trembling hand along her cheek. "Did I hurt you?"

"Only for a moment," she whispered back to him, smiling up at his worried face.

"Do you want me to stop?" he said, drawing back.

"No! No. Please…" She closed her legs around his waist, pushing her hips forward to reclaim the fraction of space he'd withdrawn. "I need you."

He closed his eyes as they rolled back in pleasure at her words and movements, feeling her inch herself forward, enveloping him. It was too much. Aidon grasped her thigh to steady her and moved forward again, hearing her gasp as he slowly filled her.

Her world started tipping back and falling inward, heat sinking into her. The center of their universe became where he was carefully joined her, and Persephone felt her head spinning in pleasure. The only sound she could hear was her heart beating out of her chest and his ragged breathing. Persephone let out a short cry and felt Aidon stop again before he realized that it was from pleasure, not pain. He kissed her open mouth on each of her lips before capturing them fully and tasting her. They moaned in unison as he sunk in the rest of the way and held there.

Velvet heat closed in and rippled around him as he waited for Persephone to open her eyes. When she trailed a foot along the curve of his spine, when she dragged her fingernails across his shoulders, when she simply breathed, she felt him within her body. When she opened her eyes to him, Persephone felt Aidon within her soul.

She gazed up at him, her eyes dilated with need, and the instinct to move overwhelmed him. He withdrew slowly as she whimpered, his absence aching within her. When he pushed forward again, she tightened her grip on his body, welcoming him back into her with a cry of pleasure. He pulled away again, this time nearly every inch and looked down the delicately curved length of her shuddering body to where they were joined.

He cradled her head forward, his hand tangling in her hair, wanting her to see their flesh together as one.

Persephone's eyes dizzily trailed down the clenched muscles of his stomach to the nest of curls between his legs and the thick shaft penetrating her, slick with her essence. They watched and felt as he pushed slightly forward and drew back, each short thrust drawing a moan from both of them. She looked up at his straining face as he slowly drove back into her, the space between their bodies disappearing as his hips met her soft thighs.

Aidon shook and smiled down as she stared back up, pleasure written across her face, the pain now only a memory. He smoothed his hand over her forehead and carefully withdrew and thrust into her again.

She looked up to see his eyes darkened with pleasure, the curls of his long black hair falling to one side. He moved up on his elbows once again and held her back and neck, embracing her as they moved in a slow rhythm. She gasped at how incredible he felt within her. His lips covered hers in a kiss.

Arching underneath him, she felt him rock her back with each thrust. Her stomach and thighs, the palms of her hands, the tips of her breasts and the soles of her feet began to spasm, edging her ever closer to that glorious crest. She reached down to his waist and pressed her hands into the hard curves of his hips, angling him deeper with each push.

The waves that rolled through her started to echo within him. Aidon could feel every nerve of her channel starting to pulse around him as he quickened his thrusts. Her arms and legs shook as she brought her hands up to his shoulders again, the pressure of her sheath tightening around him. He wanted to arrive there with her. "Persephone," he whispered into her ear. "My sweet wife… just let go… Let go…"

She rested her forehead on his shoulder, her body curling forward to his as the paroxysms started, their waves as uncontrollable as her voice. She cried out, hearing her voice only distantly shouting his name and wordlessly pleading with him for more as he started to quake. Her back arched and her eyes squeezed shut, Persephone held fast to him as he rose above her and made one final deep thrust. Aidon answered her cries with a shout that echoed off the marble walls.

The swell rising through his body held him arched there as he came forcefully inside her before collapsing into her arms. Their breathing was erratic, their limbs tangled and their bodies covered in a sheen of sweat. Persephone felt him breathing hot on her neck as a last moan shuddered through him.

Her chest rose toward his, their breathing paced and slowing in unison. Their bodies remained otherwise motionless. Any movement was too much. Persephone opened her eyes. Her fingers were still twined and tangled in the curls of his hair as he lay still inside her.

She felt him shift and met his gaze. Aidon. Her husband. Her lover. His eyes scanned her face as he brushed a lock of her hair from her neck that had been trapped there by friction and the heat of their bodies. Hades. God of the Underworld and Lord of the Dead, who she had just given herself to willingly, who had just filled her with his seed. Her abductor, who would keep her here forever from the sunlit world, from ever seeing her mother again. Persephone had just proven herself his willing captive.

He watched her face fade from bliss and tenderness to fear and shame as she turned away from him, her eyes watering. Aidon pulled away from Persephone with a shiver. He watched her roll onto her side, away from him, her legs curling into fetal position. She shook, tears streaming under her eyes and over the bridge of her nose to land on the pillow. He turned away and sat on the opposite side of the bed staring despondently at the small heaps of their scattered clothes.

She is not to marry. And certainly not to someone as hard hearted as you.

Demeter's words from long ago rang through him. Why else would she shrink away from him in revulsion? He looked back at her shaking body and pulled the bedclothes over her, feeling her tremble as his hand smoothed the covers down over her shoulder.

Persephone listened to the swish of fabric as he wound his himation around his waist and over his left arm. Aidon gathered his tunic and scattered effects. *Please stay.* The words caught in her throat and she choked back tears. Hades had taken her. Kore, the maiden of the flowers. Persephone, maiden no more. Cypress, his clean and spicy scent, still clung to her and she could feel their warmth radiating from the sheets. This was how he had wanted to make love to her before circumstances forced him in Erebus. Aidon had held her, making every moment careful and intimate, focusing on her pleasure as he relished in her and guided her. *My sweet wife...*

"Aidon?"

He stopped at the door. "Yes?"

"I'm sorry," her voice cracked.

"You don't need to apologize, Persephone."

"It's just— I know what you said you felt for me, and I—" The lump grew impossibly large in her throat.

"I didn't expect to win you over in one night, sweet one." But Aidon had, hope against hope. He had seen the look in her eyes as they stood on the balcony, had felt her absolute trust in him as he slowly revealed her to his gaze, had felt her body keening for him, her voice crying out for him when he was within her.

"I— I need time, Aidon."

"I know." Faint hope flickered in his eyes. "But tonight, just rest. I've put you through enough as it is."

The door creaked again. "Aidon?"

He turned back to her.

"Can you hold me?"

His eyes widened in shock at her request. He gently shut the door. Moving cautiously toward the bed, he unwound the fabric from around his shoulders and let it pool at his feet, naked before her once again. Aidon gestured to the walls with a flex of his fingers, the last light of the oil lamps around them extinguishing. Persephone moved over in bed as she felt his weight press into the mattress in the dark. He lifted the sheets and slid back under them with her, the bed already warm.

Her skin was soft against him, and her thighs shifted as he settled in behind her. Aidoneus curved around her body and stretched an arm out underneath her pillow to support her head. He ran his hand down her outstretched arm then twined his fingers over hers. With that, Hades and Persephone fell into fitful sleep.

The shoots hardened to the air. Their new skin would protect them—strengthen them. Hard branches drooped under the weight of larger leaves, testing and hurting them as they rose free of the cold earth. Rising at last over the gray flowers, they could now see each other for what they were.

9.

"YOU'RE WRONG!" THE FLAXEN-HAIRED GIRL SAID. "I know all about the act of love."

She was met with a sardonic laugh, tenor and melodic, coming from behind her as a hand brushed over her exposed breast. Its owner circled her and spun around, a chlamys draped across one shoulder, his only garment. "Oh, Elektra…"

"Voleta," she pouted.

"Voleta. My apologies," he said, pulling the fibula pin from a brooch with a stylized *theta* etched on its surface. It clanged on the floor like a bell. The black fabric followed it, slinking off his shoulders to revealing his pale, smooth frame. His black hair was cropped short on his head and between his legs. Piercing silver eyes stared out of a flawless, angelic face. "You know nothing about the act, other than which parts fit together. It's why you came to me so readily. You're curious."

"But, the Great Lady—"

"Yes, yes… Hecate sent you to some village or another for the great rite of *hieros gamos*," he finished for her. "And then some noble youth climbed up your body and squirted inside you to bless the planting of the fields, or founding of a city, or what have you…"

Voleta gaped up at him, shocked at his flippancy. He ignored her and continued.

"And because of this, you think you know anything about the act of love," his smiling face came within inches of hers. He slid a finger under her chin and pushed up. "The first thing I'm going to teach you is to never open your mouth like that unless you intend to use it."

"I came to you because I saw you and wanted you," she said indignantly. "Our Lady said that after the rites we could have as many men as we like as long as we are mutually fulfilled."

He laughed again. "And do you have the faintest idea what she was talking about?"

Voleta bit her lip.

"Well despite your ignorance, your Lady is at least right about that," he said, pushing Voleta back against the sheets with a finger, "and I intend to make good on it. Allow me to educate you."

"And what is it about *you* that makes you such an expert on something meant to create life, anyway? You're—"

Voleta's breath hitched as the beat of large, black-plumed wings guttered the flames of the oil lamps and fanned her hot skin. She saw them in full for the first time as he stretched them, their span spreading into the darkness of his room, eclipsing the lamps. Voleta suddenly felt very small.

She wavered again. "Y-you're…"

"Death," Thanatos finished for her. "Very clever. But consider this…"

He folded his wings back and knelt in front of her. Thanatos kissed her on her right foot, then her left.

"There isn't anyone I cannot have, the old, the young, maiden or youth…"

He placed a kiss on her right knee, then her left.

"…because in the end, I take them all."

He planted a kiss on her womb and slowly, deliberately slipped a finger inside her, curling it upward, beckoning her in pleasure. Voleta wriggled on the bed, her breath catching.

"The occasional young man is quite fine, but I prefer the maiden when I come for her."

He placed a kiss on her right breast and on the slow withdrawal of his lips, teased the nipple to a point. Thanatos added another finger inside her and curled them in a fast cycle, brushing a spot she didn't even know she had. Voleta gasped as he smiled up at her.

"Sometimes, she pleads to go. Other times, she pleads to stay. But out of the scores I send every day to the shores of the River …"

He kissed Voleta's left breast, sucking the nipple upward with a nip of his teeth as his mouth came away. He stroked his fingers inside of her, then added his thumb over her nub to rock back and forth across its swollen surface. He watched intently until her breath became ragged and her eyes glazed over.

"…there is at least one…"

He pecked a kiss on her lips.

"…who pleads for *me*."

Thanatos pushed the pads of his fingers up into the secret spot and Voleta screamed out loud, her back arching and falling as she came, fingers gripping the sheets. Liquid coated his hand. The smirk never left his face.

When her shuddering had ceased and her breathing had settled, Thanatos slowly withdrew his fingers. Voleta opened her violet eyes wide and stared up at him. "What was… How did you—"

"Make you come? That's my trade secret. Tell me— that sniveling mortal boy who took you maidenhead— did he do that for you?"

"No," she panted. "Wait— was that the Sacred Kiss?!"

He smiled at her, showing all his teeth. "You are a clever girl. And yes, it was. I figured I'd start with something you were familiar with before moving on."

"You profaned it!"

"I enhanced it," he shrugged. "Which brings us to our next exercise…"

Thanatos knelt down between her legs and ran his tongue through the wet lips of her vulva. He firmly pinned her thighs to the bed beneath his sinewy arms, and pressed down on her mound with both hands.

"Thanatos… what are you— oh!"

With his hand gripping her mons, Voleta couldn't squirm out of reach of his mouth. The universe tilted over again for her. Words disappeared, lost in her cries as he extended her pleasure, chasing her long climax from peak to peak. Thanatos kept drilling the sensitive bud with the tip of his tongue. Voleta spasmed and cried out as every touch became a little death. He paused for a moment, giving her a small reprieve from his torment, then dove in once more, drinking her, and sucked the hooded nub hard into his mouth. He quickly pushed three fingers into her and curled them around to just the right place. She bolted upright and screamed, eyes rolling back in her head, finally forcing Thanatos to lose his grip on her.

He rolled back onto his haunches to admire his handiwork as Voleta fell limp against the bed, gasping for air. Standing up, he picked her discarded chiton off the floor and wiped her juices from around his mouth. "I couldn't let you get up without at least having a taste. I take it he never did that to you either."

She shook her head and reached out to him with one hand, eyeing his fully erect cock hungrily. Her tongue was thick in her mouth. Slowly, words started to form again. "Do I get to taste you?"

He thought about it for a moment, cocking his head to the side. "No. I don't think so."

"Why not?"

Thanatos sat next to Voleta and traced a finger along her trembling lips. "Because— and this is impatient of me, I'll admit it— you don't have enough experience to pleasure me with those lips."

Her face fell. He ran a fingernail between her breasts and across her stomach before clamping his fingers on her mound, his palm squeezing and massaging her wet flesh. "But these lips on the other hand..."

She stared up at him, wordless and wide-eyed as he rose above her and moved between her legs, spreading her knees apart. Thanatos craned her ankles up over his shoulders.

"And since there's no hymen to worry about anymore, thanks to the goddess you serve and that idiot who had you..."

Thanatos spread his black wings with a shake, startling her, and held Voleta at an angle so she could watch him enter her. Voleta winced once, expecting pain, until he moved his hips around in a circle, stirring her insides with his cock, working his way into her depths. Her soaked and quivering channel offered no resistance. Voleta's face and shallow staccato breath told him all he needed to know— he was filling her far deeper than what she had experienced in the rite. She was expecting him to stop, to be at the hilt much sooner, and opened her eyes wide to him as he continued to drive into her in slow methodical circles. He finally settled into her as both looked down to see short black hair touching short blonde where they were joined, his length sunk all the way inside her.

"…With that wretched barrier gone, I don't have to worry about preventing pain. Only giving pleasure," he said, withdrawing all but the crown. Voleta whimpered at his absence before he thrust in again and she rocked her head back. Thanatos pushed in deeper and stayed there.

"Please…" Voleta whispered.

He cupped his free hand to his ear and leaned in close to her face. "What was that?"

"Please…" she said louder, trying to breathe around the word.

"Please what?" Thanatos pouted his lips with a sarcastic smirk. "'Please stop'?" he said as he slowly withdrew.

"No!" she cried.

Thanatos returned her ankles to his shoulders and held only the tip of his cock steady inside her. He came down an inch from her face and smiled, wings outstretched behind him, blocking out the lamplight. "You want me to fuck you, don't you?"

"Yes!"

"Before I do," Thanatos said against her whimpering protest as he came back up, "I'll ask you again. What is it you know about the act of love?"

"N-nothing!"

* * *

As soon as he rounded the corner outside Thanatos's apartment, Aidoneus knew that Death was entertaining a guest. Shouts of female pleasure, half-hearted protestations, and full-throated exclamations were barely muffled by the heavy ebony door. Every so often, soft cajoling and hard, lascivious words from the Minister of Death interrupted the loud moaning. Aidoneus slowed his pace.

He had passed by this room under these circumstances many times over the aeons and had quickened his pace, bitten his tongue, and rarely voiced his opinion of his friend's private life. As long as Thanatos did his job, and didn't flagrantly disregard the rules or create discord, Aidon figured that he could be left to his own vices.

But today the sounds echoing from his Minister's chambers made his blood burn. He had known those pleasures, or at least had a taste of them. He thought about his wife, the very subject he'd come to discuss, and wavered, wondering if he should reconsider. The crescendo of voices from inside only heightened his frustrations. *Enough of this,* he thought. He gave a slight knock against the frame.

Nothing.

Impatient, Aidoneus clenched his jaw and rapped loudly on the door.

"Just a minute!" Thanatos yelled from inside.

Arms folded and eyes trained down the hall instead of on the interplay of shadows flickering from under the door, Aidon tried to ignore the sounds of them in extremis. Near silence followed. Still, the door remained shut.

* * *

Thanatos drew himself away from Voleta with a long, hard exhale and staggered a few steps backward, stopping with his hand on his knees, the muscles of his stomach clenching as his wings curved over his shoulders while he recovered.

"Thanat—"

He hushed Voleta with a glare, holding a finger outstretched toward her. Thanatos gasped for breath and turned his head toward the door. "Who is it?"

"Open the door."

Thanatos spun back toward Voleta and smacked her lightly on the rump. "Get up."

"But—"

"Do you have any idea who I'm making wait outside that door right now?" he whispered to her. "Lord Hades Aidoneus Chthonios."

Her eyes grew as wide as the full moon as she scrambled off the bed, picking up her soiled chiton and wrapping it around her. Thanatos slung his chlamys over his shoulder again, pinning it in place.

The door finally opened. Aidoneus watched a blonde woman dart past, barely nodding her head to him, a quick 'milord' escaping her lips as she ran. He heard her bare feet pad down the stone hallway as he entered his minister's chamber. Aidoneus closed the door behind him, wrinkling his nose at the heavy smell of sex hanging in the air.

"My lord," Thanatos said with a slight bow, adjusting the draped fabric under the base of his wings. "I would apologize—"

"I don't expect you to," he said. Thanatos lit a censer next to his bed and sat down to catch his breath. The smell of pennyroyal and wormwood started to cover the scent of the Minister of Death's latest conquest. "Who was she?"

Thanatos looked at the ceiling, mouthing names as he thought back. *Phaedra, Elektra, Voleta...* "Voleta," he finally said.

"One of Hecate's Lampades nymphs?"

"I think so," he said with a shrug.

"Thanatos, please tell me she wasn't a new initiate. That you know a little more about her than barely remembering her first name," Aidoneus said as he looked for a place to sit. He squinted at the surface of a chair near the bed, making sure it was clean before he leaned back into it.

"I'm not an idiot," he laughed. "The only ones I take to my bed have already undergone the *hieros gamos.* The white witch would make my cock disappear if I touched any of her virgin initiates."

"Hecate's none too happy with you having them once they return, either."

"They come to me willingly, and she's none too happy with me in the first place, whether I fuck them or not." He leaned back with a smile and a sigh. "I swear by the Fates, Aidon, I found this one already standing in my chambers when I got back. It was almost adorable how she tried to seduce me. She just looked at me and pulled the pins on her chiton before I even shut the door," he guffawed, then grew quiet, watching Aidon blush. Thanatos leaned in closer to him. "Now that's new!"

"What is?"

"In all the aeons I have known you, the only reaction you ever had to hearing about the women I've fucked has been disapproval."

"It still is," he said, cocking an eyebrow at his minister's vulgarity.

"Yes, but there's more now! Your chief concern was always about how my behavior might cause problems with Hecate. I couldn't even get you to blink when I talked about sex. But now," he said with a smile, "our new little queen has changed you."

Aidon's lips thinned and he looked at the ground. "I suppose."

"And that's not a bad thing." Thanatos grew serious, the constant smile finally leaving his face. "I take it you didn't come here to talk about Voleta or Hecate?"

Aidoneus shut his eyes. Every day at dusk he had come to Persephone as she looked out over the shifting colors of the river. Each time, he would take her to bed, reenacting their night three weeks ago. When he made love to her, he would extinguish the lights and just feel the press of hot skin, listen to her ragged breathing and sharp cries of pleasure as she held him ever closer. Tangled together in the dark of her room, he could feel passion and joy. But as soon as their embrace ended, her fear and sadness would return with a shiver. When it was over it wasn't love she felt for him— just a potent mix of desire and fear. With the lamps doused, at least he couldn't look into her eyes and know it.

"Aidon?" Thanatos said, watching sadness wash across his friend's face.

"It's becoming unbearable," he started slowly. "I love her."

Thanatos snorted and shook his head. "If you're coming to me for advice on love, I'm the wrong person to give it."

"My experience with women begins and ends with her. Yours, however— Honestly, Thanatos, how many have you had?"

"Gods, I don't know. How many days has it been since Prometheus handed fire to those fools?"

"You mean to tell me that you've been with one woman each day since…"

"At least, if I can help it; and you can't blame me for trying! My job isn't exactly pleasant, you know. I need diversions, and you don't allow wine down here. Or ergot *kykeon*— a barley mead hallucination would do me good, just once in awhile." Thanatos cleared his throat. "So when someone sees through that hideous shell I become in the mortal world, and wants me all the same, I give them what they want. It's only fair if it's someone's last request. Wouldn't you agree?"

Aidon narrowed his eyes. "No, I wouldn't. These women throw themselves at you thinking that you'll find it in your heart to save them from… you."

"Entirely untrue. I tell each of them plainly what is about to happen to them and why I'm there. They know there's no going back; I only show them how sweet death can be," he smiled.

"All the same, I don't understand the appeal. I thought you would have gotten bored with it and settled down by now."

Thanatos laughed. "You're talking to me, remember? It's hard to settle down when you make a habit of never fucking a girl twice. Believe me, I only had to make that mistake with the one."

"Dare I ask who?"

"Eris," he muttered.

Aidon curled his lip. "Eris?!"

"Multiple times. Sometimes I still— I can't help myself. She's just…" he looked off into the distance and whistled low, running his hand through his hair. "Look— crazy women make for an amazing lay."

"I wouldn't know."

"My dalliances aren't what you came to talk about, in any event," Thanatos said, "This is supposed to be about you. Now, my king, what advice could you want from your humble minister on matters of love, knowing full well that I'm only interested in love's counterpart?"

He was silent for a moment, deciding whether or not this was even a good idea. Thanatos waited.

"Sex itself is hardly a problem for us," he said quietly.

"Really!" Thanatos smiled and leaned forward, his wings relaxing and spreading out behind him. With a glare from Hades they snapped back. "I mean no disrespect to our queen, of course. I'm just glad for you."

"This isn't easy for me to speak about," he said, looking away.

"The door is shut, and nothing will travel beyond it. You can speak plainly to me, Aidon," he said seriously, the smile gone from his face.

Aidoneus squeezed his temples with his fingers and began again. "That part of our lives is… it's wonderful. Incredible, really. But it's all we have right now."

"Then keep it as it is," he said with a shrug. "So many men would dream to have even that."

"But that's not what I want. I can't keep doing this in perpetuity."

"So what is it that you want from her?"

"I want her to want me to be more than just her lover." Aidoneus paused, frowning. "I want to be her husband. I want her to be my wife; my queen."

"Well, sorry to say, you can't will her to love you, or make her love you with what both of you are doing right now."

Hades looked down and ran his hand back through his hair again.

"Aidon, it's not as dire as you seem to think."

"No?" he snapped. "I know I can't make her love me, or trust me, but Persephone can't bring herself to do either." He stood up and turned toward the door, muttering to himself. "This is foolish. I should just take your advice, and enjoy the way things are now. She is my consort; she's ready and willing for me when I go to her, and I should just be content with that."

"Wait," Thanatos said. "Stay. You just said 'trust'. How much trust do you put in her, exactly?"

"I don't understand."

"Well, from what I hear, our little queen has been wandering in circles around familiar parts of the palace for the last few weeks, either with Hecate, or to the garden with Askalaphos and Cerberus. Where were you?"

"This realm doesn't run itself—"

"Except for at night when you're with her, you mean."

"What is your point, Thanatos?" he bristled.

"That it's hardly a question of her trusting you. How much do you trust her? How much of our world has she seen?"

Aidon sat down again. "The last time I took her anywhere, she ran away from me and straight into the Lethe. I almost lost her."

"She'd only been here for a matter of hours, and from what I heard from Menoetes, your big black three-headed puppy gave her quite a scare."

"I keep her in the palace to protect her."

"Like Demeter did?"

Aidoneus glared at him.

Thanatos stood firm. "Put some trust in her, Aidon."

"How?"

"I don't know. I'm sure the situation will arise if you actually spend time with her outside her bedroom."

Aidon sat there, absorbing his friend's advice. For all Persephone knew, traveling beyond the palace would bring the same pain she had experienced at the Lethe.

I just worry that it will take the same aeons for me to fall in love with it as it did for you…

If she was ever going to love him, she would also have to love the land he ruled— the place that bore his very name in the world above. "I'll speak with Charon. The best view of our realm is from the Styx."

"There's a start. Now, as to the *real* reason you came here…"

"What do you mean?"

"Oh, please, Aidoneus, if you wanted to talk about women and love you could have gone to Mother Nyx or even Hermes when he comes down here."

Color started to rise into his cheeks. "My biggest concern was discussed. Anything else is… incidental."

"Hardly; you said so yourself. 'How many women have I had?' The reason you came to me was to talk about how you can better please your queen."

Aidon felt heat rush to his face and saw a smile curl his friend's lips again. "Well—"

"I thought so," Thanatos said, leaning back and clearing his throat. "Lesson the first: in every way imaginable, know every inch of each other…"

* * *

She felt different. Persephone stood in front of the polished hematite mirror, turning this way and that, examining her figure under the long peplos in the glow of the oil lamps. Her hair was darker and thicker. She could dismiss that change— it may have been the darkness of the reflection itself. Her hips flared out more than before, and effortlessly held up a jeweled girdle, another gift from her husband.

She cupped and shaped her hands under her breasts. That definitely wasn't from the reflection. Her cheekbones were more pronounced. Persephone sucked in her cheeks, rounded and girlish three weeks ago, and saw the face of a woman staring back at her.

The changes grew more noticeable every passing day. After wandering into the Lethe, she had slept on and off for almost three days, according to Aidoneus and Hecate. It took a great deal of time to adjust to the opposite schedule of this world. Day was night, and night was day.

Persephone would stand at the balcony when the River Styx started to change color at dusk, her knees shaking, knowing that Aidon would come to her. As the river darkened, she could feel his presence beside her. His arms would wrap around her waist as they stood silently, watching the last light of the daytime dance across the water. His hands would caress her skin, running across her arms and her hips, curving over her breasts and thighs until her body ached with need and she turned to kiss him. Each night he would carry her into her room as he had after they first watched the sun set three weeks ago.

Before he extinguished all light in her room, she would watch his face as long as the flicker of the lamps allowed, his eyes filled with a longing that went beyond desire and pleasure. Persephone would surrender to him in a tangle of embracing limbs, alive, afraid, reaching, and fulfilled, then listen to his breathing as he held her to his chest until she fell asleep.

I love you… She had said it first. She had lost hold of her memories for the moment, but she had said it just the same. She couldn't bring herself to say it again.

Last night, strange dreams of winding branches, growing leaves, and buds preparing to blossom alternated with visions of her home in Eleusis and nightmares of a widening maw of dark fire. She had cried out in her sleep and jolted awake to feel him rocking her back and forth, stroking her forehead. He whispered to her, tender words in the dark to soothe her back to sleep. It was only once she closed her eyes again and started drifting off that he whispered to her that he loved her. But when first light woke her that morning, he was already gone. She wanted him to stay, but how could she ask? The next time she saw him it would be for the nearly silent ritual they played out every night in her bed.

Hecate accompanied her each day. She toured the palace and gardens with Persephone, explaining the myriad complex rules of the Underworld by way of hints and riddles. During those first few days walking with Hecate, Persephone thought her mind was playing tricks with her, echoing the cryptic words of the selenite-crowned goddess.

But Hecate had in fact aged rapidly before her very eyes, her brilliant red hair streaking with more and more silver every day. Her pale skin grew wrinkled and fragile. Their walks grew shorter and slower. Three days ago, she had stopped visiting Persephone entirely.

When she asked Askalaphos the gardener what had happened, he simply shrugged. "She just does that," he said, then returned to carefully pruning the poplar trees. For weeks Persephone had tried with all her might to make a flower— *any* flower— grow here. Even the flowers already rooted in the ground wouldn't respond to her. She'd spent several days in a row trying to open just one asphodel before eventually giving up, deciding that these flowers were as dead as everything else here, and that the life-giving powers she had spent aeons perfecting in the world above had no effect on them. Askalaphos wasn't any help there either, shrugging once more and telling Persephone that making the flowers grow down here was his job.

When he wasn't busy harassing the sheep and chasing down wandering souls, Cerberus had taken to trotting up to Persephone as soon as she reached the portico. Persephone had nearly trained him out of bothering Menoetes's herd by asking Askalaphos to fashion her a large stick out of one of the smaller poplar branches. Cerberus had gone tearing after it each time, tongues lolling out of his three mouths and after he dutifully brought it back to her. His long tail would wag and inevitably crush the asphodel in the garden, to Askalaphos's chagrin, until she threw it again. The herd of black sheep grew every day. Menoetes himself said that he'd never seen so many offerings from the world above as he'd seen in the last two weeks.

A rustle of cloth interrupted her thoughts.

"My queen?" a small voice said from the doorway.

Persephone startled and turned around to see a young girl with strawberry blonde hair staring back at her. Her hair was crowned in selenite beads and her white peplos draped and gathered over her hips and hung to the floor, worn as if she were an adult. A half moon hung on her forehead.

"H-Hecate? Is that you?"

"Yes, I'm me! It's very nice to see you again, Persephone," she said in a mature but tiny voice as she curtsied.

"What happened to you?!"

"Didn't Aidon tell you?"

"Tell me what?"

Hecate rolled her eyes and let out a small sigh before shaking her head and grumbling to herself. "Aeons and aeons… I should know better by now."

She walked over to where Persephone stood and cocked her head to the side. The young queen's eyes were wide with wonder, her mouth dry.

"Ooh, look at you! You're like a tree showing its first full leaves! And your hair got darker. It's very pretty on you!"

"Thank you. I'm still not sure what that means for me exactly…" Persephone said trailed off. She was still trying to absorb that this little girl and the ancient wise woman who had guided her through the Palace of Hades were the same person.

"Oh! Yes, I'm younger now…" Hecate said, remembering where she left off. "See, your parents are Olympians, so they won't ever die, as long as there are mortals who worship them." She paused and examined Persephone, wrinkling her brow. "Well, it's like that up above, but it's different for you down here. This world is changing you into the goddess you were born to be. Since you're the queen here, you won't need the mortals to worship you as much any more."

"That I was born to be…" she thought about her younger cousins, Artemis and Athena, Hermes and Ares, who all looked older than her though they were born later. The woman who stared back at her in the mirror was who she was meant to become. But what was that, exactly?

"I don't need worshippers to live forever either: I'm connected to the moon. That's because I'm even older than the mortals," Hecate continued with a giggle. "Up in the world above, the moon is small, but it's getting bigger. And when it is, so am I! I'm a woman when it's full, and then a wrinkly old crone when it's disappearing again. And oh, you should see this place when it's full! Its silver light shines through the Styx..."

"You're older than the mortals... are you not an Olympian?"

"Oh, no; I'm much older than that. I'm a Titan."

Persephone recoiled briefly and composed herself. Titans were the monsters her mother told her stories about as a little girl.

"It's okay," Hecate said with a laugh, reading her thoughts, "My mother told me all kinds of stories about the Protogenoi just like that. Oops! Sorry. I forgot I'm not supposed to read your mind anymore."

"Don't worry, Hecate, it's— Who are the Protogenoi?"

The girl rolled her eyes again. "Ugh, Aidoneus tells you even less than Demeter," she whined. "Chaos, Hemera, Gaia, Ouranos— my mother had the worst stories *imaginable* about him— You won't meet them. But Nyx and her sons live here. She's the goddess of the night. And Charon is the boatman, and Morpheus is the king of dreams, and there's Hypnos, who rules over sleep." Hecate paused to frown pointedly. "And Thanatos looks like a skeleton and makes people dead."

"What's the matter with him?" Persephone asked.

Hecate wrinkled her nose. "Nothing. We... don't get along."

She could feel Aidoneus approaching her room. Warmth washed over Persephone and her skin prickled. Her entire body pulled in the direction of the hallway beyond as he came ever closer.

"Persephone?" his voice echoed through the amethyst antechamber outside her room.

She twirled a lock of hair and fussed with the crown of asphodel she had made that morning before turning around to see him slowly approaching the door.

"May I come in?"

"Of course," she said. She thought it strange that he should ask since only last night they were tangled together in the sheets of her bed. Persephone glanced at the rumpled sheets and felt heat rush to her face.

Hecate failed to suppress a smile as she slid off the edge of the bed and walked toward the door. "Well… I have to go now. If you need me, my queen…"

"Thank you," Persephone said, nodding back at Hecate.

The small girl strode regally out of the room, leaving her alone with Aidon. He watched her eye the bed nervously once more and push a loose lock of hair behind her ear, her arms folded across her chest. Aidoneus shook his head. This was the only reason she thought he would ever visit her. Then again, it was the only reason he'd ever given her.

He cleared his throat. "I was wondering if you would like to come with me today."

A smile peaked the corners of her mouth. "Where are we going?"

10.

ONLY ONE POPLAR IN THE GROVE RETAINED ITS leaves and the sharp wind whispered through the topmost branches. The naiad laid her cheek against the leeward side, leaning against the tree just as she had leaned against her mother's hip so long ago. Minthe kissed her palm and planted it on the cold bark, then lingered until the icy wind became too much to bear. She wrapped her shawl around her and headed south toward Thesprotia.

Minthe knelt at the side of the road to tie her buskin boots and leather leggings above her knees. She disliked the heavy footwear, but it kept her warm. The ash and poplar trees surrounding her were covered with frost, their branches sparkling. The frozen landscape would look beautiful were it not deadly. Minthe tried to ignore her growling stomach. She wasn't a deathless god, and being ageless didn't exempt her from hunger.

Or death.

She shivered and turned off the wind-battered road, following well worn deer tracks. Her memory of the path was distant and feeble. She'd been here only once, as a child, gripping her mother's hand. Gray leaves crunched under her feet. She caught the faint smell of food as she came upon a stagnant creek, its banks shallow, its surface frozen solid. The falls that fed it were a cascade of icicles, but light shone from behind them.

This was the place she sought— the home of her father, Kokytos.

Go to him, Demeter had instructed. *Helios made it clear that he will not defy Zeus. Selene sides with Hecate in all things. The gods of the sky have abandoned us. But the gods of the waters might come to our aid. Go to your father. Do not fail my stolen Kore.* With that, the earth goddess had set off for Poseidon's court, hoping to sway her tempestuous brother. Minthe was glad to stay away from there. Her nymph cousins had too many stories about the Lord of the Seas.

She stepped around the pillars of clear ice, their surfaces faintly glowing in the light of a distant fire. Piles of wet leaves smelled sweet and rotten. Faint drums and pipes from within the cave mingled with raucous laughter. The warmth radiating from inside should have invited her, but she stayed on guard, not knowing what lay beyond.

She turned a corner and screeched, flailing back, falling hard on the ice. Her voice echoed loudly and the music in the cavern stopped. Minthe looked up again, her heart racing. It was only a drowned stag, partly submerged and mirrored on the ice, his tongue swollen, eyes open and frozen opalescent blue. His antlers dangled with icicles. Minthe swallowed and stood up.

"And who is this?" said a nasal voice behind her. She whipped around to face a creature with short horns, a toothy smile, and a hairy chest. A fleece was pinned over his shoulders with a silver fibula. His legs were like that of a deer, and emphasized by the deerskins wrapped around his hooves to keep out the cold. They had also silenced his footfalls, allowing him to creep up behind her. She gulped and averted her eyes from his exposed phallus. The satyr laughed like a goat. "Like what you see?"

"I…" Minthe stuttered as the woodland daimon twined his finger around a windblown strand of her hair.

"You are such a pretty thing." His organ twitched and thickened. Minthe could not take her wide eyes off it. "But familiar, I think. Have I not seen you before?"

She straightened her back and lifted her chin indignantly. "I am a lady's maid of the great Harvest Goddess and the daughter of Kokytos. I am here seeking his counsel."

He guffawed, ignoring her protestations, his golden eyes sparkling. "That doesn't make you very remarkable, girl. The river king has many sons and daughters."

"Phorbas!" A voice from within bellowed. "Who goes there?"

"No one, milord," he called back, cupping Minthe's chin and forcing her bright green eyes to stare up into his golden ones. "A wandering naiad… claims she's your daughter."

"Bring her here."

The drummer and piper picked up again and murmured conversation filled the air, the court within satisfied that Minthe's scream hadn't signaled danger.

Phorbas nodded and offered her his arm, escorting her into the hall. Minthe pulled back from the satyr with a scowl and walked ahead of him stiff as a plank, arms folded, her insides shaking. She could have been ravished. But if Kokytos had saved her from a man of his own court, perhaps he would be willing to hear her…

Once she passed the threshold, the smell of food and drink was overwhelming. Roasted hind and broiled rabbits lay on a long table, surrounded by amphorae of dark wine. Pomegranates with ripe red seeds and split figs with tender sweet flesh beckoned to her. Spiced olives glistened with oil and brine. Her stomach rumbled painfully.

The music died down upon her entry, and loud laughter and voices echoed from every corner of the hall as nymphs and mortals and woodland daimones of every sort drank and feasted in various states of dress. She shrank away from one pair copulating in a niche and faced the throne. Kokytos regarded her, his mouth hidden by folded hands. Silver hair cascaded over brown fur robes and a circlet of interlocked antler bone embedded with blue topaz hung above his sharp, beardless face. Dark eyes glowered at her. The music stopped again, all eyes turning to the fresh arrival, many with lascivious intent.

"Speak," he commanded, startling her. Minthe knelt at her father's feet, her eyes cast to the floor, and placed a hand on his right foot in submission and supplication.

"Milord, I am Minthe, y-your daughter b-by—"

"I know who birthed you. Her tree stands in a copse of poplars to the north."

"M-milord," she began again, "A-as you know by the desolation outside your halls, the Corn Mother has w-withdrawn her favor from the earth. She mourns her lost daughter."

A wizened satyr whispered something into the king's ear. "Everyone knows that. Why did you come all the way from Eleusis to find me?"

Minthe stood and opened her mouth.

"Let me guess," Kokytos said with a wry grin. "Your great mistress wants my help, to bring back her dear, unfortunate Kore from the halls of the Unseen One."

"Yes, milord."

"And if I do, will the mighty Demeter grant me her protection and promise to deliver bountiful harvests to me and my beloved subjects?"

"Of course."

He smiled. "And would she raise me above my lowly station as a rustic god?"

"She gladly would, milord!" Minthe said brightly. "That and more. We greatly value your assistance. How soon can you help us?"

Kokytos raised his eyebrows and Minthe heard snickering behind her. It grew until the whole court peeled into open laughter. Her cheeks burned red and tears stung her eyes.

The musicians took up a fast tune and the court returned to their feast. Her stomach twisted; it wasn't safe here. Minthe was ready to bolt from the room when Kokytos descended the dais. "You ask me to challenge the Receiver of Many, do you? Because your mistress cannot abide her daughter being *rightfully* delivered to her promised husband?"

"But the Notorious One didn't— H-he *stole* her, my lord. She was screaming when he took her. Helios saw it happen in Nysa."

"I expect she did scream." Kokytos laughed. "I think I might scream too, if the Lord of the Dead was hauling me off to his bed in the lands below. Did you think he'd woo Demeter's sheltered girl with a poem and a bouquet of roses?" His voice turned grim. "You mistress takes me for a fool. And you too, sending you on this errand. She asks me to draw up arms against the hosts of Hades? Look around you." Minthe turned, seeing faces frozen in contempt. "They have nothing now. They bartered what they had for my shelter and my protection. How many do you wager would be willing to march through Demeter's desolation and storm the Underworld to take away its new queen?"

She gulped and her eyes welled with hot tears. "Father Kokytos, please, I beg you as your daughter—"

"Daughter?!" His advisors mimicked his laugh as Kokytos sat back on his throne. "I've sown my seed a hundredfold across this land, girl. There's a long line of begging bastards ahead of you, and most of them would be content with bread and a roof."

A tear rolled down her cheek. "But… I… you and my mother, she—"

"Your mother cried out another's name when I lay with her, the very night you were made!" He guffawed. "She spent her days in the world below tending the poplars and doing who knows what. I don't even know that you're mine, but let's suppose you are. If you were to come to me on behalf of *Zeus himself* begging favors, I *still* wouldn't be so stupid as to cross the Lord of the Dead!"

"I *cannot* return to Demeter empty handed," she sobbed.

"Then don't," he said. Minthe wiped her eyes and stared up at Kokytos. "Stay here, if you must. But…" He motioned to a group of men in the corner eyeing her hungrily. "If you do there will be… expectations. Are you still a maiden?"

"Y-yes," she lied. They would regard her more carefully if they thought she was a maid. Her kind was prey to immortal men, otherwise. They would believe her. Men arrogantly thought they could tell. Most could not.

"A maiden *nymphae*? What luck for you! That will serve you well here. At least tonight."

Minthe burst into tears and backed away from him. "How can you suggest— you're my father! How could you even say—"

"You won't survive in the cold, girl. You know it. You were right— you cannot go back. The Olympians do not abide failure. Demeter will cast you out… at best."

"I'll leave, then! I'll go—"

"Where? There is *nothing left*. Dryads and naiads are frozen everywhere in Hellas. They're not deathless, little one. I give the lost ones a home, where they can huddle and hope that Demeter comes to her senses."

"And mortals too, I see," she said, raising her chin.

He shrugged. "If they bring enough wealth with them."

"But mortals are gluttons, especially the wealthy ones! They eat more than our kind ever could. Why are your wasting your stores on them?"

Kokytos gave a furtive glance around the room, then focused his hard eyes on his daughter, speaking low. "If your mistress doesn't relent… if this famine stretches on, then it behooves me and mine to make sure we have other sources of sustenance. I provide for those mortals who can afford our company. And I put meat on their bones… as a surety."

Minthe looked around the room in horror, watching mortals feast alongside nymphs and daimones, satyrs and woodland creatures, fattening themselves, marinating their brains and blood in strong wine.

It was the price to be paid. She straddled the yawning abyss between survival and damnation. Minthe sobbed in disbelief, her eyes red and raw. *The lost ones…* she was one of them now that she'd failed the Mother. Failed *her* mother.

"Without my protection you'll be lost. Now, stop this crying. You're valuable. Tears don't become you."

She wiped her eyes. Lost… lost… Minthe's shoulders sank. She gave him a nod, and nothing more.

"It's settled, then!" He raised his hand and the music ceased. Kokytos smiled and descended the last step, gripping Minthe's shoulder, presenting her to the court. He bellowed. "Who will offer for this maiden daughter of mine?"

Minthe stared out at them in a daze, her vision blurred, listening to the menfolk barter for her company for the night. Phorbas and a wealthy mortal herdsman bid back and forth using their sheltered flocks of sheep as tender. The satyr surprised his opponent, pulling out a small leather bag and throwing it at Kokytos's feet. The room gasped when a *minae* of silver coins spilled out. Kokytos picked up up the heavy purse. And with that Minthe was sold for six skinny ewes and a handful of silver.

Phorbas took her by the wrist and led her away with a triumphant smile. He stopped next to the food-laden table and handed Minthe a large *kantharos* cup of unwatered wine. She sipped it and gagged, then took a draught to numb herself. The drink made her head spin. The mortals and immortals forgot the chill and desolation beyond, drowning in a sea of feast and flesh. They danced and swaggered all around her, their bellies filled with the same drink. Minthe saw a man sit a woman in her lap, nibble her earlobe and kiss down her neck before pulling the fibula from her one-shouldered *exomie* with his teeth. Her bared breasts were quickly covered with a pair of hands and her mouth claimed by the lips of another.

A plate of seasoned deer meat was thrust in front of Minthe and she nearly vomited, her stomach rebelling, her mind screaming for her to run as far and as fast as she could.

Women and men shed their clothes, and out of the corner of her eye she saw Kokytos beckon a nimble dryad to his throne. A nymph against the wall moaned, gripping a satyr's curved horns as he burrowed his face between her thighs. Next to them she saw a youthful man's hand, then lips wrap around a satyr's member, his mouth forced further down as the same herdsman who lost the bid for Minthe sharply thrust into him from behind. She turned quickly back to the plate of meat, then bit down, juices flooding into her mouth.

"Hungry, were you?" Phorbas fed her a few olives. His thumb lingered on her lips.

Minthe nodded quietly and he gave her a bright smile. This satyr seemed pleasant enough. She was lucky, she supposed. He seemed kind. To stay here and eat and survive, the men had given away their fortunes, the women their bodies. But there were far fewer women here, she realized. Most would be pleasuring more than one man.

Minthe froze, and what she had foolishly agreed to undertake dawned on her. She panicked. Perhaps she could get Phorbas intoxicated and escape. The whole court would collapse into a drunken stupor soon enough and she could flee with a full belly… perhaps take some fruit with her. Pomegranates and olives would keep in the cold. She would have a chance. She could board a ship in Ephyra and sail south, beyond the cold, beyond talk of Kore and Demeter and daughters traded like chattel.

The plate before her was removed and Phorbas held up the strong wine, raising the glass to her lips and tipping it back. She let it fill her stomach. The cup pulled away, and the hard rim was replaced with the softness of his lips. She swallowed. Her limbs grew heavy. She floated. She felt him crush her against his body, his hard shaft rising against her pelvis. Her chiton was missing, she realized lethargically. He rubbed his cock between her closed thighs, hissing his restrained pleasure. Phorbas kissed Minthe again, his tongue pushing past her teeth to caress hers, suffocating her.

"It's better this way," he muttered against her neck. "Now that you're relaxed."

"Now that…" she slurred, then cried out as he took her where she stood, pulling her closer to him. Her legs stopped working, her head swam. She flailed her arms and tried to push at his chest but he held her tightly, inescapably. Phorbas pulled out half way, then pushed in with greater force. *Lost,* she thought, her body slackening. *Lost.* She surrendered and grew quiet.

He dragged her under the table where they would be uninterrupted. Phorbas laid her back, supporting her head in one hand and pulled her thighs up to his waist with the other. He mounted her. Minthe turned away from him and stared at the wall. He grunted into her ear and her back rhythmically scraped against the cold floor. He kissed her tenderly and moaned soft praises that contrasted sharply with each painful thrust. A last tear fell into the tangle of her hair and she closed her eyes, nearly unconscious, the wine mercifully pulling her away from her aching body.

Lost... lost... lost...

* * *

Aidoneus and Persephone took the winding staircases down to the atrium entrance of the palace. Persephone lingered for a moment to look up at the dizzying heights of the great golden poplar tree that overhung the entryway before they made their way down the path to the river's edge. Outside, shades flitted about, appearing from and dissipating back into the asphodel. Persephone walked at Aidon's side. He looked to their left and held her back for a moment by the shoulder. A young girl in a tiny black chiton ran out and toddled across their path with a flower in her hand, giggling to herself without making a sound before vanishing into mist within the asphodel. Persephone smiled in the direction of the little shade, and realized that Aidoneus could hear her coming before she ran across their pathway.

The River Styx looked far vaster once Persephone was standing next to it. Stalks of asphodel grew even higher here; a few were taller than she. The still water seemed to stretch on endlessly, the far shore lost in mist. The pathway from the palace atrium to the river itself was lined with carefully clipped cypress trees— no doubt the work of Askalaphos. They were a far cry from the unruly, gnarled trees in the grove at Nysa.

"Charon was the first person I met when I arrived here. When I came to the shores of the Styx as the new king of this realm, he asked me to give him one of these," Aidon said, fishing out two gold *obolos*. He picked up Persephone's hand and folded her fingers around one of the obols. "And aeons later, I can't for the life of me figure out what he does with all those coins."

She met his smiling gaze as he closed her palm and brushed his fingertips over her knuckles. Waves lapped against the shore, breaking the comfortable silence and drawing their attention. Persephone looked out to see a long gray boat bobbing on the water, its bowsprit peaked upward into three metal hounds' heads, the center head holding a lamp in its teeth high above the water. On the stern, a dark figure sunk a long oar into the river and pushed toward them. The prow raked across the gravel of the shore as the hooded man walked the bracings to where they stood. He knelt low at the bow, his oar still in hand, and looked up at them from under the hood with a half smile. "Did you intentionally keep her from us for so long?"

"Persephone, may I present Charon, son of Nyx, the ferryman of souls. And no, my friend, that was not my intention," he said holding out his coin. Charon pocketed the obol and looked to Persephone's extended hand holding out her own coin.

"You..." he said with a voice like gravel as he waved her hand away, "You ride for free, my queen."

Aidoneus gaped at him before composing himself. "In all the years I've— Why?"

Charon removed his hood, revealing a smoothly bald and very pale head with ashen gray lips and sunken cheeks under high cheekbones. He looked up at both of them with eyes that swirled with the deep grays and blues of the river, "Why ask questions to which you already know the answer?" He extended his hand to Persephone with a smile. "Come, my queen."

Persephone looked to Aidon first. When he nodded, she accepted Charon's hand, picking her skirts up above the water's surface as she stepped in. Aidon followed, settling beside her in the stern. Charon pushed the boat away from the shoreline and back into the calm waters of the Styx.

As he steered the craft into the wide part of the river, Charon began humming a gentle song to himself. Persephone's eyes opened wide and her lips parted. Her mother had sung that lullaby to her when she was a small child. He looked at her, and smiled when he saw that she recognized it.

She squinted when a wisp of cloud passed under the water, echoing the sky in the world above. The wispy streak reflected in Charon's changing irises. "If you don't mind my asking, why do your eyes reflect the River?"

Aidon snorted, then cleared his throat to cover his amusement, knowing how the boatman might respond. Charon didn't disappoint. "Is the Styx not my home? Do your eyes not reflect the blue sky of the world above and the gray fields of the world below?"

Persephone paused for a moment, looking away as she pondered his words. Hecate had spoken earlier about her coming in to her powers now that she was Queen of the Underworld— her new home. She knitted her brows together at the boatman. "Do you always answer questions with questions?"

He smiled. "Why should I give clear and solid answers to questions that flow as dark and mutable as the Mother River?"

Aidon smiled as Persephone wrinkled her nose. "Forgive him, sweet one. He spends his days being interrogated by the shades."

Charon smiled apologetically. "Your husband speaks the truth. The sad thing is that it's always the same question I'm asked, and I can only give them one answer: 'Because you are dead'. So please forgive me, my lady, for my puzzles and riddles. My job demands them so I might comfort those who make the journey across the river— and also to keep myself entertained." He dipped his oar into the Styx once more, then turned his head back toward Persephone. "Speaking of, my lady, I take it you recognized the song?"

The lullaby. He knew. Persephone smiled in answer, saying nothing. Charon nodded his head to her and guided the boat onward. They floated slowly downstream toward marshes so wide that both shorelines were obscured by mist. Drowned cypress trees reflected deep into the mirror of the water, broken up by tall clumps of feathery gray rushes. A handful of shades of every age and station stood together on the far side of the river.

"I'll come back and get them later," Charon said.

"Who are we receiving now?" Aidon said absently, leaning his foot against the center bracing of the boat.

"Well, the deluge of the very young and very old has ceased for the most part. But even now there's more standing at the shore than I'd like. Can we safely assume the bad harvest is winding down?" Charon asked.

Aidon held his breath and looked at Persephone, wondering whether or not he should have told her, and if she would be angry at him for not saying anything. She simply sighed and looked at the thin shades. "My mother…"

Demeter throws a tantrum, Aidoneus thought, *and the mortals suffer.* He thinned his lips, remembering when Hermes first delivered the news. He looked down. "I should have told you."

Persephone hated to think that the mortals were suffering on her account. It was likely temporary. Her mother was none too happy about her coming here, but she had been part of arranging her betrothal to Aidon all those years ago. Persephone thought back to the tapestries hanging in the palace's great hall, showing her mother, father and her husband during the war with the Titans. Their promise had sealed the Olympians' pact.

"I *will* see her again," she said, as Aidon's breath hitched. "Won't I? She can visit me here, can't she?"

Aidoneus smiled in front of clenched teeth before he could speak without betraying his anger. "Of course she can."

He squeezed her hand protectively. What could Demeter possibly do to Persephone in a kingdom where he held absolute power?

She saw four women, two standing and picking asphodel, two more weaving them into garlands. Another held a long stalk of the wispy grass, plucking a frond and tucking it into her hair. Their forms were as solid as her own. They were beautiful and dark haired, stood as Charon's boat passed. Wings, as delicate and transparent a butterfly's own, unfolded behind them. The bowed their heads when they saw Persephone.

"Who are they?"

"Stygian nymphs. They lived here long before I arrived," Aidon said, leaning back.

She remembered what she knew of Olympus and the station of nymphs there. "Are they your servants?"

"No. I leave them to their own devices." His mouth perked up. "I pride myself on having no need of slaves here. That is a… decadence of the world above."

Charon piped up. "Would you like to see the marshes and river lands of Acheron up close, my lady? The Styx flows into and out of it to the black sea beyond— Oceanus. From there we receive the souls lost at sea in the world above. Usually I land here." Charon pointed to the smooth limestone docks leading from the marshes to the fields beyond the near shore, "and the shades go up that wide path to be judged at the Trivium," he said, motioning up the cobblestone path. At the distant end of the path loomed an enormous frieze of black granite supported by four rows of columns.

"Where do they all go?"

"To Asphodel, mostly," Aidoneus replied. "It's very rare that we send someone to Tartarus."

"We?"

"Aeacus, Rhadamanthys, and his brother Minos. They were kings of men and mortal sons of Zeus when they were alive. They sit in judgment over most of the shades and decide by vote," he said. "There was a time when I presided over all the judgments, but the mortals' numbers grew too great. Now, I only personally preside over the trials of kings and other rulers, so that my judges will not be prejudiced either for or against them. I don't want rivalries from their temporary lives affecting the eternal fate of those sent here. I also need to remind the wealthy and powerful that their status in life means nothing once they get here."

Persephone's mouth grew dry. "A-are we going to visit Tartarus?"

Aidon ran his thumb along her clenched knuckles. "No, sweet one. Rest assured I will never take you there."

"But it *is* part of your— our kingdom."

"There are things down there that no one has seen since the war. And certainly not anything I should expose you to."

The reeds of the marsh parted and Charon rowed the boat toward the delta of the rivers. More caves emptied onto the shoreline and she knew that they led to the world above. Lone figures, pale and dressed in funerary garb, walked listlessly from the caverns to stand and wait.

"The other shore… is this river the boundary of the Underworld?"

"The physical boundary, yes."

"Physical boundary… what do you mean?"

"Well, surely we require more… *hindrances* to keep the living from the dead. The Styx is one such boundary. But there are more. Many more."

"Fates," Charon interrupted. "Can you imagine living souls standing at the shore trying find their dead kin?"

"Precisely," Aidon said, remembering the last time a mortal had trespassed. "That's why there must be more boundaries between worlds than just the physical."

A tributary, red as blood, flowed away from the Styx and into the distance. Its banks were lined with black hooded shades staring vacantly into the waters.

"The Cocytus," Aidoneus said. "The judges will send some there for a time, to reflect on their actions in life. They stare into the river to see the pain they have caused. Some must stare for… a long time."

The tributary disappeared behind a hill, the land and gray clouds flickering and glowing orange and red in the distance. Persephone swallowed and pointed at the smoldering horizon. "Is that light from Tartarus?"

"How does something shine when it destroys the light?" Charon mused, turning to look back at her.

Aidoneus shot the boatman a warning glance. "The glow comes from the fires of the molten river Phlegethon. It surrounds the Pit of Tartarus and keeps us safe," he said, wrapping an arm around her waist.

"Safe from what?"

Charon and Aidoneus exchanged a glance, then stared at her.

Persephone shivered before answering her own question. "The Titans."

"Yes," Aidon said solemnly. "You'll never need to worry about them, sweet one. Tartarus is as far below us as Chthonia is below the living world."

"Chthonia? I don't—" Persephone looked away, embarrassed. She should have learned all these things long ago. *Lord Hades rules the land of the dead…* She knew no more than that. Persephone looked down at her lap and plaited her hands together. Aidon brought his arm up her back, massaging her shoulder.

"In the old tongue, Chthonia means 'beneath the earth'. The mortals call this place 'Hades', but it's been here far longer than I have ruled it," he said quietly. Her face fell. "Persephone, it's all right. I imagine this is a bit overwhelming. Honestly, I think I had far more questions than you when I first arrived…"

"Oh, you were terrible, Aidon!" Charon interrupted, making Persephone smile. The ferryman stood upright, stiffened his shoulders so he looked taller, and lowered his voice doing an impression of her husband in his younger days. "'What's this? Who's that? How does this work? I want to change the way we do that! Why can't I change it?' You were an utter terror your first century here!"

Charon rowed on one side, turning the boat around. Aidon would have reprimanded the boatman, but he was too busy melting. It was the first time his wife had laughed in his presence— by far the most beautiful sound he'd ever heard. Persephone covered her mouth and stopped, thinking she had offended Aidoneus. She looked up at him smiling broadly at her and relaxed as he held her by her arms again, leaning her back onto his chest. She giggled once more. He planted a slow kiss on the top of her head and breathed in the scent of her hair, sending a shiver down her spine.

They docked on the far side of the river, the waiting shades kneeling as Aidoneus climbed out of the boat and landed shin deep in the water. He lifted Persephone into his arms and walked up the embankment, setting her down once they reached the shore. With a quick brush of his hand, his sandals and the soaked edges of his himation instantly dried.

She waved goodbye to Charon as the assembled souls stood and climbed cautiously into his boat, a coin in each of their hands. Charon's soul-laden boat pushed off from the shore, and Persephone felt Aidon wrap an arm around her. The boatman raised his long oar to salute them.

She turned to her husband. "All these shades… If most go to Asphodel and the especially evil go to Tartarus, where do the good ones go?"

"What do you mean?" he said.

"The good mortals— the ones who were especially brave or kind. There's no place for them?"

"Mortals are mortals and Asphodel is there for them. There's little difference between them individually. All people are a sum of their parts, good and bad," he shrugged. "The better they are in life, the easier a time they have here; the better chance of being reborn to the living world."

"And that's their only reward?"

"Unless they defied the gods or committed despicable acts in their lifetime, yes."

Persephone knitted her brow again and silently looked across the marsh to the Plain of Judgment.

"Are you ready to go home?"

"Yes, but it will take Charon a while to come back here."

"There's no need to bother him. We'll just travel to the palace through the ether."

Persephone lowered her eyes once more, as she had on the boat. He looked at her in confusion. "You don't know how?"

She turned away from him and balled her fists, saying nothing. Her shoulders tensed forward.

Aidon cautiously put his hands on them. "Persephone, I didn't mean it that way."

"I don't understand why you have any interest in me at all," she said under her breath. "I know nothing about your kingdom—"

"Most don't."

"—I don't even know how to travel the way gods are supposed to," she said, tears stinging her eyes. "You are the eldest of the three most powerful immortals in existence and I'm just— I know nothing."

"Look at me," he said, leaning over her and turning her toward him. "There is nothing wrong with you. I don't understand why Demeter didn't—" he stopped and closed his eyes before saying something he would regret. "She was only trying to protect you."

"I'm just a flower goddess, Aidon; I'm an afterthought compared to my mother. I have no idea what I'm even doing here…" A tear traitorously spilled down her cheek. Aidon caressed her face, catching the droplet as it fell. He lifted her chin so her downcast eyes met his.

"Persephone, you're my wife; everything I rule I lay at your feet. You are Queen of the richest part of what we divided after the war, and the Fates decided you were destined to rule before you were even born."

"What kind of a queen am I? I've hardly left my room since I got here—"

"That's more my fault than anything—"

"—and I didn't even know the true name of where I've *lived for over three weeks*. There is so much I *need* to know."

Aidon startled and looked away from her for a moment, remembering what Thanatos had said to him that morning. This was the perfect opportunity.

Persephone saw light dance in his eyes. "What is it?"

"I could teach you."

"H-how to travel through the ether?"

"It's not as difficult as you think."

"Are you sure?"

"Yes. It would be my pleasure to show you how," he said. "All you have to do is hold on."

"We should wait?"

"No," he said with the faintest hint of a smile. "I meant hold on to *me*."

"Oh," she murmured, feeling heat rush to her face. Persephone carefully put her hands around his waist, feeling the heat from his body through the heavy wool himation.

"You'll have to hold on tighter than that," he said quietly. She brought her arms up around his neck and stood on the tips of her toes, her lips tingling as she came face to face with him. His arm braced her against him, his palm spreading across the center of her back between her shoulder blades, crushing her chest to his. Aidon reached toward the shore with his left hand, his rings glinting against the backdrop of the palace.

"First of all, everyone does this differently. The gods all have their own strength; their own sigil, theirs by birth or deed. I live in an unseen realm, shrouded in darkness, and draw my strength from that. You however, are from the world above, and your own pathway will likely reflect that. You will see it," he whispered into her ear. "And once you make it *yours* everyone will see it."

His closeness made her shiver. Her breath hitched as black smoke started to swirl around their feet, moving outward, upward, surrounding them. Persephone held her cheek against his, her shallow breathing so different from his focused, measured breath.

Aidoneus leaned closer and whispered in her ear, "You have to concentrate on where you want to go. Picture that you are already there, that you were there the entire time."

She wrapped her arms tighter around his neck, her entire body shaking as the smoke closed in around them, blotting out everything. She remembered the sun turning red from the smoke in Nysa when he pulled her into his chariot. She remembered how she wrapped her body around his in the darkness of Erebus and shuddered.

"All you have to do is let go—" he whispered. She felt the rush of the ether take them in a blink of silver and crimson light. She didn't even have time to breathe before they were standing under the golden poplar tree overhanging the entrance to the palace. "—and there you are."

She gasped, and looked around. Persephone felt his arms tighten around her shoulders as he bent slightly, gently returning her feet to the solid ground. She looked up at him, suddenly cold as the heat from his body vanished from her skin. Her arms and thighs prickled. Aidon's gaze scanned over her body, his eyes stopping just below the neckline of her chiton. With a sharp inhale, she realized that the tips of her breasts were chafing the fabric and very visible to him. His nostrils flared before he took a long breath and averted his eyes.

"My mother didn't take me with her through the ether very often. We only ever visited Olympus twice; both times were when I was a very young girl. When I started… becoming a woman, we left Nysa through the ether to live in Eleusis. Then once when the mortals were waging war on each other in Attica. And the last time I went with her was to Nysa so she could hide me from… from you."

His face was solemn as she spoke, but she saw a hint of sadness in his eyes. Aidon masked it with a pained smile and let her continue.

"So, I didn't have much experience with it," she said, her mouth mischievously twisting up at the corners. "But I know for certain that I didn't have to hold on to my mother like… that… when she began the journey."

Aidon narrowed his eyes and leaned toward her. "In case you think that I was using it as an excuse to press your beautiful body against mine," he flirted, making her shiver as his gaze slowly moved over her once more, "I assure you it was necessary. We were traveling through the ether between points in the Underworld. You will need to practice first. Even an experienced god has far less control over it here than they do in the world above; including me."

She shook her head incredulously and muttered, "Everything about this place…"

"You don't like it here…" Aidon's face fell and his eyes looking away.

"No!" she said wide-eyed. "No, that's not what I meant. Chthonia is just so very… different. Beautiful and different. I— I like that I had to hold on to you," she blushed.

Aidon straightened, taken aback, before he took a step closer to her and cupped her face in his hand, running his thumb across her cheek. He carefully leaned over and rested his forehead against hers, letting her make the first move to kiss him. Persephone stared up at his dark eyes and saw a soft smile on his face. She stepped into the kiss, feeling his arms close around her. She crushed her lips against his. Her hands came up to his collarbone, her index finger slowly winding through her favorite lock of hair at the nape of his neck; the one that was always too short to be caught in the band he wore to pull back his unruly hair.

He wanted so badly to deepen the kiss. Aidon could feel himself pulling toward her, entranced by her as his fingers spread out along her waist and shoulder blades. Instead, he pulled away from her lips, listening to her shudder. "We should practice."

She could feel his voice, just a little above a whisper in the center of her chest. Her lips moved forward again, but he tilted his forehead to hers to avoid the kiss. Aidon looked into her eyes, smiling as Persephone echoed him. "Practice?"

"I said I would teach you. But not here." He took a step back and held up his left hand to show her his three rings. "Do you know what these are?"

She shook her head, watching light glint off and reflect within each deep red cabochon.

"They are called the Key of Hades."

She bit the corner of her lip and tilted her head.

"Trust me; I didn't name it," he said with a smirk. "But to protect the world above, the Key was given only to me. If the unthinkable happened and something escaped Tartarus, I alone would be able to seal off Chthonia. This represents the only pathway between the worlds through the ether."

"But others come and go from here, don't they? What about Thanatos, or Hecate? Or Hermes?"

"You've met Thanatos?"

"No," she said, "but everyone knows who Death is and where he's from. He's a skeleton cloaked in black."

"Most of the time in the world above, yes, he is. Down here, though, he looks very different. Thanatos and his brothers cannot truly cross over through the ether. They only appear as shadows of themselves in the world above." He held his fingers out to Persephone and watched as she took his hand and gingerly touched the cold stones, closing her warm hands around his. "Hermes doesn't use the ether to travel; he's too fast to need it, and only comes down through the passageways guiding lost souls back here. And… well, Hecate is never really *here.*"

"I've seen her almost every day, though."

"What I mean to say is Hecate never really leaves the ether. She is its goddess— as much a ruler of all the spaces and pathways between the worlds as I am ruler of the Underworld, or your father ruler of the sky. While she prefers to appear most often in Chthonia, she's not ever truly, bodily here."

"What will happen to me if I cross over? Will I become a shadow?"

"No," he said, "Nothing will happen to you. You're from the living world; which is why it will be easier for us to practice there."

She stared up at him, wide-eyed, almost disbelieving what he'd just said. Was he going to actually take her above? She would be able to see the green fields again, to see the sky once more. "I won't run away," she blurted out.

"What?"

"I won't run away," she repeated quietly.

He couldn't let her go now, not when he was so very close… Her lips were parted and he dove back into their kiss, unable to stop himself from tasting her. Her arms crept up his shoulders to his neck. The tips of her fingers danced across his skin as she held onto him.

Persephone broke away from the kiss. "Teach me."

11.

DELPHINIA WINCED.

She didn't expect him to be gentle. Few men were taught how to be gentle, whether it was with their wife or a *hetaerae.* Delphinia was neither, and softness was not needed for this act. She silently forgave him and tried to refocus on the rite itself. *The earth. The earth. The gods must be appeased. The earth must heal. For the sake of all humankind, every man, every woman, every child...*

He pinned her to the floor, and her attention snapped to her bruised shoulders and her lower back roughly scraping the wood planks. She whimpered and wanted to tell him to stop, to have a care for her, but she remained silent. This man was a powerful king— practically a god among his own people. She didn't dare anger him. His guards stood outside her home in the cold.

Delphinia had heard things— that the king's guests often disappeared only to be found later, floating in the canal. She heard that the king had once defied Zeus himself. Delphinia knew better than to trust country gossip. Peasant folk would always whisper about those with power. Especially when that power was not of this world. She knew that from her own experience.

Despite all she'd heard, she *needed* to trust him. He was reported to be ageless— if not immortal, by his own will. His countenance seemed such. He looked younger than he ought to be. He also knew the rite of *hieros gamos* when few did. He knew the sacred words of the rites in Theoi— the language of the gods, and though lesser in stature than she thought he'd be, the king had a bearing about him that spoke of great charisma and power. He wasn't one to be trifled with.

She closed her eyes and strived to refocus her energy on the act itself, on taking up the part of Gaia to his Ouranos. She was the earth. He was the sky. And the fervent prayers offered up with the rhythm of their bodies might be enough to render the earth fertile once again. The very thought sent a wave a pleasure charging through her. His path within her was eased and she heard him hiss at the slickness that freshly enveloped him. Delphinia could control this— control *him.*

The *hieros gamos* was her sacred rite— this was what she had trained to do since girlhood. She had taken unskilled youth and wise hierophants through the ritual. She could do so again. Delphinia pushed against his flanks with her heels and arched under him, shifting so his thrusts would push against the places within that would vault her to ecstasy.

Delphinia's whole body tightened, and she could feel his heart beat faster against her breast. She could sense the blood pumping through his veins and his phallus thickening within her. She angled down so he could ride high and stroke against the bundle of nerves atop her entrance, then canted her legs up so he could thrust deep. *The earth must heal... the earth must heal... Gaia... sweet Gaia...*

Her toes curled and her thighs went taut, a wave of exaltation taking her. She let it grasp at her soul, and she channeled it through them both, then beneath their connected bodies and into the earth itself. The causeway was opened. She was open to him and he to her. He gasped, his breath hot against her neck, his voice strained as he shook and gave her the gift of seed. They lay still, with her beneath him, their bodies glistening with oil, anointed with frankincense. The blood rushing through her ears abated and she could hear the crackle of the hearth fire— feel its heat. She sighed and relaxed as he withdrew.

"Well." He stood. A smirk lit his face as he washed his face and genitals, then donned his ceremonial golden robes. He smiled politely at her. "I appreciate you… accommodating me on such short notice."

"My lord, there is no such thing as short notice when the survival of all is at stake," Delphinia said. "And I needed… one who had been anointed by the gods for it to have meaning. So I thank you."

"This wasn't for *all*, priestess."

She amended her words. "Of course, my lord. It was for the gods. For the earth."

"Again, no. I care not for the gods."

Delphinia propped herself up on her elbows. *Run,* a voice told her, *run now.* She shook it away. She'd misheard him. "Surely you don't mean…"

"I do. And in your heart of hearts, I doubt you meant this for them either." He fastened the long *chitoniskos* at the shoulders, and draped his finely-embroidered himation about himself. "Ask yourself: what have the gods done for you?"

"They've… they've nurtured and protected me… they've…" Delphinia covered her bare breasts. She had served them all her life. First as a virgin oracle, then as a priestess, indoctrinated into the rites with the priest of Delphi. She had become a servant of Hecate, of Demeter and

Kore… How could he cheapen this act with his talk? "Why did you come? Did you lay with me for your own amusement?"

"Oh, certainly not. I admit, you're more skilled than most *hetaerae,* but you'd have to be, since you are willing to lay under any man who fancies himself Ouranos for one night."

"You speak blasphemy, my lord."

"But only blasphemy toward those that punish us with plagues and famine. With death."

"Death is—"

"Merely a facet of life?" He chuckled, placing his golden crown on his head. "Spare me. That's peasant talk. Is that what you really think?"

"What else could there be? The proof is all around you. The plants must be plucked from the earth to feed the animals and they must be slaughtered to feed us." She wrapped her cloak loosely around herself. "And when we die, we nurture the worms. And our immortal souls—"

His low laughter interrupted her. He donned his shoes, lacing the leather buskin with his sandals. "Do not speak to me of souls, woman… So many of your kind have nothing but laws and rules for where a soul is to go when *they* know even less than I do. You are but dust— the very *earth* you try so fervently to bring back to life. I am not. I am beyond the constraints of this world and the next. It's why you took me in."

Tears stung her eyes, but she bit her cheek, willing them away. "Why join me in the *hieros gamos* if you harbor such animosity in your heart?"

"Because our goals are the same. We wish to create a better world."

"I do this to bring fertility back to the earth whether or not Kore is returned."

"Then you defy them," he said, eyes wide.

"No, I—"

"Is it not their wish that you mortals should die like flies?"

"No… they wouldn't—"

"Are you not defying the Fates themselves, Demeter's will?"

"I," she choked, and his golden clad visage blurred in her vision. "I only wish to restore the earth. I want to stop the suffering.

"Restore? There is no going back. Kore is the concubine of the Lord of the Dead now. He doesn't let anyone leave his kingdom and I'm sure that goes twice over for her. She will not be returned," he said calmly, his back turned to her. "And neither will life to the earth."

A tightness strangled her throat. She bared her teeth as she spoke, her voice shaking. "You forget that it does not matter what you *think* or what resentment you hold." Her face resolved into a smirk. "Our essence will nourish the earth by this act whether you will it or not!"

"Perhaps."

"It was your willing sacrifice!"

"Yes. You see? We are of like minds. A better world does requires sacrifice." He turned around to her, a flash of metal, gleaming in the firelight, held tightly in his right hand.

She went cold. Her lungs refused to work. Her limbs went slack.

"You said so yourself." He advanced on her. "We all return to the earth. And through you its essence will flow into me. After all, the channel into the earth that our act has opened—"

She didn't let him finish his sentence. She couldn't cry out. It would alert the guards. Delphinia ran, bolting for the door. The air took her breath away, freezing her lungs. The frost on the ground tore at the skin on her bare feet. She tripped over the oak branch that marked the entryway to her home. She scrambled, flailing into a crouched run, like a hind bolting its hunter.

Colder... even colder now... why so cold? Delphinia's brain muddled, fighting to stay alert, to glean and understand... Gaia forgive her, she'd been a fool... Her thoughts were a haze and she was dizzy, the world spinning around her.

Wind bit at her skin, digging deep into her blood. Her footsteps were marked by drops of blood. *So cold...* He'd cast aside her linen wrap. He'd captured it as she'd fled out the door. *Hadn't he?* She swore it was tight around her shoulders a moment ago. The golden knife— no, it was a short, bejeweled sword— tensed in his hand. The guards stood motionless. "Help me! Please!"

One of them looked away from her.

"*Please*! I'm a priestess of your gods! Have mercy... mercy!"

She wrapped her arms around her. *A mile.* Delphinia limped. *I can run to the next house. Please...* she willed her legs to move, but they wouldn't. She wobbled as the man closed on her. The air grew colder still and she fell into warm arms. Despite all, she cried for help until the words lost meaning, and struggled until the cold sapped her strength.

"Your gods..." He rasped against her ear. "Where are they now, priestess? Do they deserve the power you surrender to them?"

"Holy Cerulean Queen hear my cry," she prayed, her words slurred. "Daughter of Rhea deliver me from—"

"Quiet now. She cannot hear you. And if she did, Demeter would not care. The gods *hate* us. But you, my lady... you will help me rebuild what they destroyed... set right what they ruin time and time again... and free mankind from the gods themselves. A better world..."

"You will burn in Tartarus! Your body will be ash... your screams will fill the Land of the Dead!"

He smiled. "I'm not going there except by my own free will. I assure you." He stroked her cheek. "Now fear not, priestess. Your beloved earth calls for you."

A sting of cold bit at her neck and warmth trickled over her freezing skin. Delphinia's fingers grew numb. Her legs went limp under her but he held her steadfast. The night grew brighter. Frost glimmered, each point of light blurring with the light of a thousand haloed stars. She felt the sensation of him letting go, of her falling. The earth cradled her and the light blindness and cold ceased.

He stood over her body. Her warmth and the tendrils of her connection to the earth flowed through him. It filled his veins and bones and loins. He hardly felt the wind. His hand pressed against the oak tree that shaded her home. The full strength of the earth rushed through him, filling and renewing him. His men put the priestess's home to the torch.

The oak's leaves shook and gave up their hold on the branches all at once, drifting across the barren meadow. Mingling with their dark edges were flurries of white flakes, frozen and beautiful, biting at his skin as they drifted on the wind. He felt all the woman's essence, her connection rise into him, becoming part of him. Then the wind stopped, and white flakes and clumps fell from the sky and covered the ground.

Sisyphus smiled.

* * *

Teach me...

Persephone's whispered words scalded Aidoneus. All he could think about was her body pressed to his, the thin layers of cloth the only barrier between them. He brought her harder against him with one arm and locked his lips to hers.

With his left hand, he reached out, enveloping them in black smoke, ready to transport them through the ether to the world above. Her eyes closed and her tongue danced with his as the Underworld vanished around them.

Nysa, he thought.

She felt them being pulled through, the silver and crimson light of the ether whipping about them as they traveled together. Persephone broke away from their kiss. The black smoke that had lifted them out of the Underworld condensed under their feet to hold them aloft, solid against the infinite expanse of the Void. All was quiet. Vertigo gripped her as it had the few times she transported with her mother. Persephone didn't know if the silver light and clouds were twisting about them, or if they were falling headlong through them. The journey took much longer this time. She looked down to see the rings on Aidon's hand glowing fiery red. She gripped his shoulders tighter, and he responded by pulling her closer to his chest. She felt safe and secure against him as she tried to blot out the very real fear of falling through the ether forever, lost in the spaces between worlds.

"We're almost through," Aidoneus said, then braced himself, his legs apart, supporting her. She watched as the light gave way, threads of silver pulling back from them to be replaced with darkness. Stars appeared, the brighter ones with peculiar haloes around them. Silhouettes of wild cypress blocked out the midnight blue of the sky and the stars above. She knew this place…

The ethereal threads disappeared entirely and he almost reluctantly released his grip on her, watching as she slid down and away to stand on her own two feet and look around. Aidoneus could see his breath before he felt the cold. It was curious; foreign. He looked down and saw Persephone shivering, her arms held around her sleeveless shoulders. He quickly unwrapped his himation and draped her within its folds, gritting his teeth against the bite of the cold air.

She felt the warmth of his body radiating from the soft wool, his fresh, masculine scent caught in the heavy folds of cloth. Persephone startled, realizing where they were. It was the grove; this was Hades's sacred grove at Nysa. She closed her eyes, remembering when she lay here in the dappled sunlight, his unseen fingers teasing and caressing her naked skin as she reached ecstasy for the first time, her back arching in the soft celery grasses of the clearing.

It seemed like a lifetime ago. She reached down to the ground. The wild celery had dried brown, their dead husks turning to dust in her hands. The asphodel showed no flowers, and their black stems stuck up out of the ground. She saw her breath in front of her face and looked at Aidon. His teeth were chattering. "Aidon, you're freezing..."

"Don't worry about me," he said. She ignored him and pressed her warm body against his, wrapping the heavy fabric around both of them.

"Why is it so cold?"

"I don't know." They looked up, the frost-haloed stars disappeared behind dark clouds. An infinitely tiny speck floated out of the sky and drifted between them, vanishing as quickly as it had appeared. Another followed, then another, then the air around them was full of gently falling cold flakes. They clumped together as they spun through the air cascading into one another. One tiny clump landed on Persephone's nose, melting instantly.

Persephone wiped the droplet and examined it on her hand. "This isn't possible. It only snows on the very highest mountaintops. Higher than Parnassus, even..."

Snow fell about them in the field. It melted when it hit the ground, but the dead plants and tree branches held it aloft, their topsides slowly turning white. *Demeter wouldn't do this; she couldn't,* Aidoneus thought. "We should go back."

"No. Please Aidon. I want to try."

"Are you sure?"

"Well, I'm warm enough. Are you sure you're all right?"

He thought back to when Zeus, Poseidon, and he carefully scaled the wind-whipped face of Mount Othrys all those aeons ago. "I've felt cold worse than this. At least there's no wind. Something here is off balance, though. If you don't mind, I'm going to skip ahead a bit in our lessons and have *you* send us back to the Other Side."

"Aidon, I'm not powerful enough to—"

"Yes you are." He stepped away from her warmth and lifted her chin to look into her eyes. He closed his hand around hers, her fingers lacing through his alongside the rings. "I wouldn't have asked you to do this unless I knew you could."

"H-how do I even start?"

"Close your eyes," he said as she did so without hesitation. "Breathe with me, now. In and out."

Persephone inhaled through her nose and exhaled slowly, following as he breathed with her. She could only feel his hand gripping hers and the ground beneath her feet.

"Whatever you may be thinking about, Persephone— any limitations, any feelings, anything at all— let them go. There is only you, the immortal goddess, and there is only the place you want to be. Concentrate."

Grow, she thought. Persephone felt her other hand raise almost on its own, her fingers bending toward the earth, her wrist curling upward. Aidoneus watched as a dark stalk sprouted out of the freezing earth, turning green and almost glowing as it lifted. One six-petal asphodel blossom opened along its length, then another. She could see it in her mind as the petals peeled back, their anthers unfurling, their stamen standing on end. She frowned, "I only made a flower, Aidon. I'm not—"

"Concentrate!" he said sharply. Aidoneus felt an echo of energy surge all the way through him from the earth itself and flow out to her through their joined hands. His rings smoldered like coals.

Upward through her feet, outward through her hands, and pulsing like the touch of her husband through her core, she felt the raw earth and all that lay beneath it surge into her. With a turn of her wrist, she channeled it through her outstretched fingertips. The asphodel stalk grew faster, the top bursting with an impossible mass of buds.

In her mind she saw fire— Aidon's chariot in the bowels of the earth outside Erebus, just before he claimed her. She saw the wreath from her hair, in her betrothed husband's uplifted hand, the ashes flying away as the heat set it aflame. She remembered picking the asphodel to make that wreath from this very ground, how the red-orange anthers had ignited as they traveled through the fires of the earth.

As the buds opened in front of her outstretched hand, one ember emerged, then another, swirling, the flames increasing as more buds opened in orange flames. The fire itself became a blazing ring that stretched in front of them, flaring with heat, melting the snow that clung to the plants around them.

Through the ring of fire, Aidoneus saw the silver threads of the ether and smiled triumphantly. They pulled and tugged at the flames and latched themselves to a speck in the distance that grew wider, coming into focus and pulling their destination toward them. He could make out the garden of the palace, the stone walls, and the fields beyond. His mouth dropped open as a shiver crept up his spine in a mixture of arousal and astonishment. This was impossible— no one could bridge the ethereal reach this way. Except for his wife.

Aidoneus had been wrong— intriguingly wrong about her— Persephone was a goddess beyond his reckoning.

She opened her eyes and shuddered out a long breath, staring into the fire, her arm outstretched toward its center. She felt her husband's wonder and admiration; she felt the earth's energy and the pull of the fire. "The Phlegethon," she breathed.

It was only when she whispered it that Aidoneus recognized the circle of flame. He opened his eyes wide and a very old emotion he hadn't allowed himself to feel in aeons came rushing through him. Fear. She was drawing the fires from Tartarus itself. He swallowed hard. "Persephone…"

Help me.

The voice was small— too small for him to notice. "I hear someone—"

"Persephone, don't listen to him! Close the gateway now! *Close it!*" he shouted at her.

"No," she replied calmly. Persephone felt his fear pulse into her hand and looked back to comfort him. "It's all right, husband."

Aidoneus flinched and leaned back as she turned to him. Her pupils were rimmed in fire, glowing an orange that matched the circle before them. She calmly turned back to the pathway. For a moment he considered letting go of her hand, breaking the Key's connection to the ether and their home beyond, but feared that she would be pulled in and lost to either the Pit or the Void. He had to try to reason with her. "Persephone; wife, *do not* listen to him! No matter what he—"

"She. It's a woman," she paused, listening, "Her name is Merope."

"Merope?" He had never sent anyone to Tartarus by that name. His brow knitted in confusion, and fear was slowly replaced by curiosity. He closed his eyes and connected with

Tartarus all the way through her body toward her outstretched fingertips, focusing on the gateway she created. He listened for the voice.

Please help me, it said. *I don't belong here.*

"They all say that," he scoffed, withdrawing from it.

"Sisyphus..."

Aidoneus stopped. Now that *was* a name he recognized.

"Sorcerer king of Ephyra," Persephone continued. "Merope was his wife. He tricked them."

"Tricked who?"

"The brothers. Your judges, Minos and Rhadamanthys, with a glamour. They thought she was Sisyphus. They presented her as Sisyphus to you and you sent her to Tartarus."

"Impossible. No mortal could ever summon sorcery strong enough to fool—"

"Gods above..." Persephone cursed under her breath shaking her head in shock, "...the things he did to her. Listen, Aidon."

He closed his eyes and focused again on the crying voice.

...us both on the funeral pyre... imprinted his essence on me as I burned... calls himself a deathless god king in Ephyra, now... a kinslayer... blasphemer... sent me in his place. Please Lord Hades, Polydegmon, you are a just god...

"Aidon, please, we must help her," she echoed, looking back at him, her eyes rimmed in fire, her face pleading with him.

A pyre, he thought. Ephyra's people were Thessalonian. *The people of Thessaly don't build pyres; they bury their dead. Unless...* He nodded to Persephone. "All right. I'll speak to the Hundred Handed Ones."

"They hear us," she said. The fire told her everything. They were the guardians of the Titans and the wicked. The jailers of the Pit of Tartarus. The vision of their home faded from the center of the circle, replaced with the gaping maw of black flames from her nightmares last night. She shuddered.

Praxidike...?

This time, Persephone recoiled. A sound so deep and resonant it almost made her nauseous welled up in fifty voices speaking as one from the dark fires. Aidon could hear it too. He protectively tightened his grip on her hand. "I've got you," he whispered.

"Wh-who are you?" she said.

More importantly, the many-voiced one asked, *who are you?*

"Kottos," Aidoneus said to the Hundred Handed One, "you are addressing my wife."

Ahh, Kottos said, *my brothers and I have waited aeons for you, my queen. Persephone Praxidike Chthonios. She Who Destroys the Light. Carrier of Curses. The Iron Queen of the Underworld.*

"What am I?" she whispered to herself, trembling.

Aidon could feel her faltering. "Sweet one, it's all right."

We are yours to command, Praxidike.

She straightened, then looked back at Aidon who nodded to her. She spoke to the fire, "A woman is being wrongfully held in Tartarus. A glamour was cast over her. Her name is Merope, and she was sent there in place of Sisyphus of Ephyra. I command that you release her at once from the Pit."

And what should we do with her?

"See that she is brought to the Palace of Hades. We must learn all we can from her," she turned back to Aidoneus, her eyes flaring in anger. "The sorcerer king must be brought to judgment for what he did to her."

As you wish, Praxidike.

The fire flared once and the maw of black flames vanished back into the ring. The fires calmed and grew friendly. Their home once again stood on the other side. Persephone looked at Aidon, her eyes returned to normal and her hand shook in his grip. The sun started to dawn in the east, nearly obscured by storm clouds whipping flurries of snow around them. "Can we go home now?"

"Yes," he said quietly with a nod. She gripped his hand. He took a step forward and held her at the small of her back. Aidon just watched her, his heart racing. This was not the screaming girl he'd dragged into his chariot from the field of Nysa. His wife was a darkly magnificent creature, stepping through the ring of fire she created with him at her side. Persephone— his Queen.

* * *

The journey home was quick; mere steps. When the threads of the ether closed the ring of fire behind them, they found themselves standing in the palace gardens. The blanket of misty clouds above was awash in the brilliant colors of dusk, reflecting the light from the Styx. It was so much warmer here, and she realized that she still had her husband's robes wound around her shoulders. The cold from mere moments before still clung to him. Persephone took off Aidon's himation and draped the dark fabric around his shoulder once more. He closed his eyes and inhaled as she sweetly attended to him; it smelled like her now— lilies, ocean mist, and warm earth. She draped and wrapped it loosely about him, pushing the last heavy length over his left shoulder.

"Persephone…"

Aidoneus wrapped his arms around her, and she leaned into his chest. He pulled her closer, his hands gripping at her skin. They breathed shakily, both trying to understand what had happened, what it meant, what they saw, what she was able to do. The tension left his fingers and he flattened his hands against her back, soothing and holding her. She sighed and closed her eyes, listening to each slowing breath. Her ear pressed over his heart, she slowly opened her eyes.

Persephone blinked at what she saw. "Aidon, this is the garden, isn't it? I didn't accidentally take us somewhere else, did I?"

"No, sweet one. You brought us home."

"What is *that*, then?"

He followed her gaze and saw rough bark on a slender tree trunk. When he looked up through the canopy of branches, he saw vibrant green leaves unlike any he'd ever seen, the boughs winding through the branches of another similar tree. Aidoneus and Persephone turned in a circle to see that they were surrounded by six such trees that stood twice their height, each one spread out to touch the one next to it.

"My dreams," they whispered in near unison and looked at each other in shock.

"You've seen these too?!" Persephone said.

"I hardly sleep as it is, and I see them every time I shut my eyes," he said, stunned. "They started when I brought you here. What about you?"

"Same," she broke away from him and walked over to the tree, smoothing her hand over the rough bark. "Every night. Last night, when I woke up and you held me… I saw these trees; then fire."

He walked over to a different tree and reached up to run his hand along one of the waxy leaves. "This is impossible…" he said under his breath. "Persephone! Touch the leaves; they're warm. Like the sun has been shining on them all day. Do you have any idea what they are? I've never seen anything like them in my realm."

"Pomegranate, I think? …Hard to tell when they're so young." She walked around one tree and stared up through its branches at the mists above. "It's getting dark; I'll be able to see them better tomorrow."

They circled the small grove, touching the leaves and branches as they went, and met on the opposite side under one of the trees. Distracted by the winding branches, Persephone almost ran into the wall of his chest. The same astonishment she felt was written across his features. Aidon drew her close again and cupped her face in his hands. "In all the aeons I waited for you, I never dreamed—"

She cut him off with a kiss, interrupting him before he said something she wasn't ready to hear. Persephone kissed him hard on the lips, and felt Aidon surge against her. A familiar coil tightened in her stomach. His hands wandered down her waist and over her hips as her tongue played against his. She brought her hands around him, her fingernails raking over his clothed back. They broke away and watched the fading light of dusk frame the silhouette of the trees.

"Aidon, we have to tell Hecate."

"Yes," he said, "Though I have a feeling she already knows. If these are tied to our dreams I should also speak with Morpheus…"

She looked up at him for a long moment and swallowed. "In Nysa, when I created the ring of fire, I… I never thought I could do anything like that. Not ever. Thank you for showing me," she said, running a hand along his cheek. He turned his head and kissed her palm.

"You were magnificent."

"Then, you're not… upset that I can create a gateway like that? That I have more control over the ether than I thought I did— than you thought I did, and possibly more than you, even?"

"What?" he said in amused bewilderment.

"I'm just worried," she said looking at the ground and fidgeting, "that you don't want me, as your consort, to be able to just *create* something like that my first time out. That what I did would somehow make you feel… emasculated… and that you wouldn't want me afterward."

His lips curled into a half smile as he tilted her chin up to look into her eyes again. He grabbed her wrist and stepped toward her, pressing her hand over the hardness quickening under his clothes. He smirked when her eyes grew wide, then circled his arm around her waist and pulled her even closer. His heat arched into her hand, and he sucked in air through his teeth as her fingers closed around him through the fabric. Her lips parted and she shuddered, warmth flooding into her and echoing his arousal.

"Tell me again, Persephone, how you think I could feel emasculated by you," he crooned in the deepest register of his voice.

Her voice cracked, "I—"

He stole a kiss from her then, drawing her figure into his arms and tipping her back as she clung to him. Aidon mated his tongue with hers, the depth of their kiss a portent for all he wanted to do to her that night. His voice was low and dangerous, his words whispered against her neck when he broke away from her lips. "On the contrary, sweet one, I've never desired you the way I desire you now."

She kissed him just in front of his ear, feeling light headed, her stomach fluttering at his words and the sway he held over her body. "Aidon…"

"Please Persephone," he said grinding into her once more, "do not deny me anything tonight. I need you…"

He felt her tense.

He let out a long breath before continuing. "I would never dream of taking you unwillingly," he said, "but if this is what you want—"

Persephone kissed him hard, her body quaking. She felt her thighs twitch and moaned into his mouth as his hand came up to her breast, roughly cupping and molding her clothed flesh in his palm. She pulled back and whispered hoarsely to him, "Take me inside."

That was all he needed to hear. Aidon grabbed her hand and marched them out of the garden. He took them through the portico toward the entrance to the palace, pushing her against one of the heavy doors and kissing her hard as he wrenched the other open. She darted out of his grasp with a nervous titter as the door swung wide and ran along the hallways ahead of him, bidding him to chase her, stopping suddenly at the column base of the stairs and biting her lower lip. He stalked toward her and crushed her body between the stone column and his own, his lips moving over her neck, earlobe and jaw line before capturing hers.

She took his hand as they walked up the steps, pausing for a long kiss at each landing. When they neared her room she laughed and ran down the hall ahead of him, looking back to see him give chase once more as she disappeared into the amethyst room. He found Persephone again near her door and pulled her against him. He moved her backward, clasping her hands within his at their sides as they walked through the ebony doors of her bedroom.

Persephone broke away and sat on the bed, scooting back toward the pillows. Aidon slammed the doors shut while she untied and kicked off her sandals. She looked up at the lights in the room and back at him, expecting them to be extinguished. They were not. Her breath hitched as he strode toward the bed.

"Not tonight," he said, following her gaze to the lamps above. "I'm through hiding in the dark from you." Her eyes lit up hearing him say it, he sat next to her, quickly removing his sandals.

"Then don't leave before the light comes," she said.

He stroked her face. "I won't."

She kissed him, feeling him tug at the edges of her clothes, exposing her collarbone. He kissed her jaw line and across the hollow of her neck before sliding the fabric over one shoulder. "Why do you always go?"

He looked up at her, then back to the pins holding the fabric to her. "Rulership over this realm comes with many responsibilities," he said, avoiding her question. *I leave so that I don't have to look into your eyes and see that you do not yet love me,* he thought. He swallowed and continued. "Besides, I only ever sleep a few hours at a time. Holding the Key means constantly hearing the voices and prayers of everyone in this kingdom. It's why I remove my rings when I'm with you."

"Aren't you worried someone will take them?" she said as he pulled them off his fingers, their gold bands clicking together as he set them on the stand.

"If someone tried, they'd just return to my hand. They're bound to me alone."

The chiton clung to the curve of her breasts as he expertly pulled at the ribbon girdle, quickly unwrapping its length from her waist. He'd had enough practice removing it in the dark. Persephone grabbed for the pin holding up his himation and pulled it free of its housing, watching the heavy fabric fall around him. He pushed it away behind him, casting it to the floor, and lay back on the bed to watch her rise to her knees above him and remove one of the pins in her chiton.

The fabric fell away from one breast and exposed her all the way to her navel. Aidon shuddered, transfixed as she pulled away the long ribbon that bound her hair into a careful chignon. Persephone leaned her head back and shook free the long waves of her hair, emphasizing each motion for his enjoyment. She smiled and bit the corner of her lip as he eyed her hungrily. She took her time, moving her hand slowly up the length of what fabric still clung to her, watching him shift on the bed. He bit down on his cheek and clenched his fists until his knuckles turned white, willing himself not to tear the rest of her clothes off her body.

Persephone pulled apart the last clasp of her chiton and heard Aidon groan in appreciation as the fabric fell from her naked body and pooled around her knees. She brushed it over the side of the bed and tousled her dark hair once more, the curled ends falling over her breasts.

Aidon leaned forward and pulled her body to him, his mouth latching onto her areola. Persephone thrilled and gasped as his tongue laved the tender flesh, the tip twining around her hardened nipple. He gripped her waist and swung her smoothly to his side, pressing her back into the rumpled sheets and kneeling over her. Persephone pushed firmly against his chest until he was upright again and propped herself up with an elbow. She reached to his shoulders and pulled the pins from his tunic, the fabric falling to his waist. He breathed heavily through his nose and focused on her movements while she tugged at his knotted leather belt. She paused, distracted by that irresistible line that traveled from his hip straight into his groin and lightly traced its indent on his skin, watching his stomach jump.

"Persephone…" he ground out through clenched teeth, the scent of her arousal driving him mad.

"Hmm?" she said innocently. She fumbled with the belt once more, her wrists grazing his hardness as she struggled to free him.

"If you keep doing that, I don't know if I'll be able to stop myself…"

Persephone looked up into his eyes as the knot came loose. The released fabric fell and caught on his flesh before she tossed it aside. She met his eyes with a smirk and threw his belt to the floor, then quickly untied his strained loincloth, not breaking eye contact with Aidoneus. She leaned away from him. "What makes you think I want you to hold back?"

He inhaled sharply and pushed at her shoulders, lunging forward between her legs and pinning her underneath him. With all his might, Aidoneus thrust into her to the hilt.

They shuddered together and cried out in pleasure as he cleaved to her. He paused only to let Persephone wrap her splayed limbs around him, anchoring him inside her body, before thrusting in again. Her fingernails scratched rows of pink lines down his back.

Aidon gripped the sheets and laid his head beside hers as he formed their rhythm, his breath coming out in hard pants against her neck with each sharp thrust. She answered with punctuated cries, which changed to a long low moan as he took her faster, gliding through her.

Shifting his weight to one elbow, Aidon reached between her legs with his free hand and searched the top of her mound with the tips of his fingers. He smiled, feeling her keening against him when they found the source of her pleasure. Aidon coaxed the tender bud from under its hood and stroked it in time with each thrust, her body writhing under his. When her body started to tremble, he lightly pinched and rolled it between two fingers.

"*Aidoneus!*" She screamed, clinging to him.

She used his true name— the name she once feared, the name that declared him the Lord of the Underworld and master of all the souls within it. He startled, the realization jarring him. Then her sheath squeezed around him in waves and erased all thought in a blinding flash of pleasure. He cried out and strained forward, emptying himself inside of her.

12.

Aidoneus collapsed and Persephone held him close, listening to his ragged breathing. He slid out of her with a sigh, but stayed locked between her legs. She finally opened her eyes to the marble reliefs above them. The images seemed animated by the soft play of shadows from the flickering light of the hundreds of tiny oil lamps. Persephone tilted her head forward and ran her hand along the smooth muscles of Aidon's shoulder and back.

When her hand moved over a ridge on his skin, she felt Aidon tense and hold his breath. The line of a raised white scar stretched underneath her fingers. It thickened and pitted slightly, cutting a widened swath down his shoulder blade and traveling in a jagged line across the center of his back before disappearing under his right arm.

He stayed still, vulnerable, as she examined it. Persephone moved to sit up and Aidoneus slowly rose with her, his legs folded under him. She crawled behind him on her knees to view the scar in full. Closing his eyes, he willed himself to let her look. Just when he thought she would be repulsed and recoil from him, her palm gingerly touched his skin again and caressed his shoulders.

"What made this?"

"Kronos," he said quietly.

Persephone cringed. She knew the story well— how Father Kronos had devoured his children one by one as they were born to stop an ancient prophecy. How Zeus, her father, had escaped that fate and later freed the other five Olympians, her mother among them.

"I was the first. He saw himself, his likeness in me when I lay in Rhea's arms. He'd never done it, or thought to do it, before he saw me, and I was not devoured... cleanly."

He tried to stop himself from shivering as buried memories of twisting pain and half his life spent in claustrophobic darkness rushed back to him. He remembered screaming and crying as a child, wondering what he had done wrong. More children arrived, and he swallowed all emotion to stay strong for the others. Hestia came soon after him, and later Hera. Then Poseidon, and lastly, squalling and terrified, the infant Demeter. As they grew up in oblivion, they feared him— when they saw him in the dark, they saw their father's face. He'd earned his epithet, Receiver of Many, far before drawing the lot to rule the Underworld.

She felt his body shudder. His chin tipped forward to hide his face behind the curls of black hair that had come loose in the throes of passion. Persephone wrapped her arms around him, pressing her breasts against his back, and against the scar. She stroked her finger along what was still visible on his shoulder and gently kissed the top of his head.

"You shouldn't look at it so closely, Persephone," Aidoneus murmured, trying to pull away. "It's not a sight for someone like you."

"No," she said softly, her fingers tracing the scar once more as his shoulders tensed underneath it. "It's part of you, Aidoneus. It's part of what made you who you are now."

He sat stiffly and felt her body draw back from his. Just as he was about to turn, he felt her lips meet his shoulder and press a kiss to the scarred flesh. Aidon's breath caught in his throat and he stayed perfectly still while she slowly planted a trail of kisses down its length to the side of his arm.

She moved to face him. His lips were parted in shock, his eyes watering and staring deep into hers. Aidon rose up on his knees to meet her, and ran his fingers up her spine to tangle in her hair as he kissed her. "My love…" he whispered against her lips.

The words Persephone wanted to say to him burned in the back of her throat. In this moment, she wanted so badly to give in completely; to surrender to him and be his wife, to tell him how much she loved him. Instead, she kissed him again, feeling his arms come up her back, his hands caressing her neck. Persephone realized that after tonight this man, this king, this god, would never let her go— and she was certain now that she didn't want him to. But if Aidoneus knew that he'd won her…

She shuddered and drew back, looking at his face. Her gaze trailed across his body, taking in his wide shoulders and strong legs built with lean muscle. She reached out and smoothed her hands across his skin, learning him. Aidon sat still and let his wife's eyes, then her soft hands explore him. She moved in a circle around him, her knees pressing into the mattress. Persephone took one of his hands, drawing his long fingers out and tracing each knuckle, then his wrist.

"Did this place change you as well?"

"What do you mean?"

"Today I spoke with Hecate, and she told me that this place is changing me into the goddess I was born to be," she said, thinking about Kottos's words, and trying to picture her husband after he'd been freed from Kronos.

"This place calmed me considerably," Aidon said. "I was young and fresh from the war when I arrived; this lot was not what I'd fought for, and at first, I seethed. The Underworld tempered that anger, and turned me from a warrior into a king." He looked at the rounded curves of her breasts and hips, her darker hair, and understood what she really meant. Persephone was trying to picture him in earlier days. "Physically, I haven't changed much."

"What did change?"

"Well, I didn't trim my beard as often back then. And I got more sunlight on my skin. I kept my hair a bit shorter, but still wore it pulled back from my face for battle."

"The few gods I've seen keep their hair shorter than *that,* even…"

"I suppose that's the style, now. What— you want me to cut my hair?" he said with a coy grin.

"Oh no! I like it long," she said. "It suits you. And if you cut it short, what would I hold on to when—"

He watched her eyes widen and her lips part in shock at what she had just implied. Her face and breasts flushed a deep red as she looked away. Aidon grinned at her, and tipped her chin back up to look Persephone in the eye. "If that's how you really feel, wife," he said, planting a chaste kiss on her lips, "I'll *never* cut it."

Persephone gave him another shy smile and undid the gold clasp that bound his curls back. She ran her fingertips in circles over his scalp, massaging them through his hair as he sighed and relaxed. Her hands moved over his shoulder and along the length of his other arm until she saw a razor thin white scar cutting upward along the side of his bicep. "Did Kronos do that too?"

Aidon glanced down to where she was tracing her finger and wrinkled his forehead in thought, almost forgetting where he got it. "No; that was from the war."

"I've never seen scars on an immortal before..."

"I was young and we were all very weak once we were freed; the Titans could injure us as easily as mortals wound each other. And I didn't have bolts of lightning or a trident to help keep my distance. I needed to get up close when I fought them."

"What happened here then?" she said, tracing its ridge once more.

"I think that one was from Koios, when we crossed swords at the base of Mount Othrys."

She imagined Aidoneus in his youth, the formidable warrior god, mightier than Ares. She pictured the hard muscles and sinews of his long legs protected by metal greaves and leather, his dark crested helm and golden armor flashing in the sunlit melee of battle. The sound of bronze against bronze, wood, and even flesh echoed in her imagination. Persephone quivered at the idea of Hades cutting down his foes like blades of grass, fighting his way through to duel with the ancient and deadly god of the oracles and intellect. Her eyes lit up and a smile teased the corners of her mouth. "Tell me more..."

"Well, sweet one, there's not much to tell about that battle... The Helm of Darkness had been very recently given to me for freeing the hosts of the Underworld. I hadn't had it for long and foolishly thought that because Koios couldn't see me, he couldn't hear me either. He turned and slashed in my direction, and I ducked out of the way, just barely." He looked down at the scar. "Or not enough, truthfully."

"How did you beat him?"

He tilted his head forward. "Are you sure you want to hear this?"

She nodded enthusiastically. He gave her a half smile, noting how adorable she looked sitting there with her hands clasped in her lap, unaware that her arms were drawing her breasts together into a deep and delicious cleavage.

"All right, then… When Koios's blade glanced off my arm, and because he couldn't see me, it gave me enough of an opening to… ahhh… put my sword through his neck," Aidon said, mumbling the last words.

Her eyes and mouth flew open and she shuddered as the fight played out in her head in all its bloody detail.

"Persephone, I told you… these stories might not be for you." Between a horrific childhood and his exploits during the war, she was going to think he was a monster. He watched her face carefully. *Maybe I am,* he thought. *Maybe I should have just left well enough alone…*

"No!" she pleaded. She took a deep breath and composed herself. "Please don't stop! I can handle it," she continued calmly.

His mind played with the innocent double meaning of her words and the palpable heat of her flushed skin. Aidon's fought back a surprised smile as he caught the scent of lilacs in the air between them. His story was arousing her. He narrowed his eyes and smirked, indulging her. "With the Titans, we discovered that the only way to subdue them was to be quick about it. They were gods of time; a long fight was to their advantage. I ran Koios through and pinned him to the rocks with my sword still in his throat, then opened a gateway underneath him to Tartarus."

"You could do that?"

"All of us could do it, for a time. The cosmos was in chaos. The rules were not as they are now."

She nodded. "Go on…"

"When I slid the blade out, he fell into the Pit. His hosts saw that their lord god was gone and fled into the fields of Thessaly, where your father's Cyclopean army crushed them."

Her breath hitched and she leaned toward him again, her finger dancing across the scar once more. "Did it hurt?"

"It certainly stung, but it was just a flesh wound. Now this one," he said, turning to lay on his side and showing her a short scar on the outside of his right knee, "this one *hurt.*"

She leaned over him as he sat back against the pillows and ran her hand over the jagged white scar. "How did you get it?"

"I was… protecting someone," he said, freezing. *I've gone too far; I shouldn't be telling this story,* he thought.

"From who?"

"Iapetos."

Persephone paled. Her mother had told her stories about Kronos's right hand, Iapetos the Piercer— the cruel god of finite mortality itself, and the former ruler of the Underworld. "Wh-who were you protecting?"

"You."

She looked up at him in shock. "But my mother said he went to Tartarus before I was born."

"He did," Aidoneus said. "I sent him there."

Persephone leaned against his chest as he lay back and felt him take a long breath. He ran his hand through the long strands of her hair that had spilled across his shoulder.

"Right after Zeus freed us, and before we convened on Olympus, the six of us scattered across Hellas so Kronos couldn't find us. All of us were very weak, and it was only with the intervention of a few of the Titans and Protogenoi that we survived at all. Zeus retreated back to Crete with Rhea, Tethys took Poseidon and Hera to Samos, Themis hid Hestia on Cythera, and Hecate took Demeter and me into the ether so she could hide us everywhere and nowhere all at once."

"My mother never said *anything* about— Hecate took *both* of you?" Persephone ran her hand along his chest. No one had ever told her this. She leaned into him, eager to hear about a history that had been kept from her, secrets that her mother had shied away from when she asked too many questions as a young girl.

"She was our teacher; our priestess. Hecate is still my greatest mentor— more of a mother to me than Rhea ever was." *I shouldn't be telling this story.* He stroked Persephone's arm and wondered if he should continue. She needed to hear about his past and if he didn't tell her now, he would have to answer these same questions later, *after* she'd spoken with Hecate. He had trusted her with it this far. "Your parents were deeply in love with each other from the moment Demeter was rescued by Zeus. Nine years of bloody fighting passed before it was safe enough for the six of us to meet in one place on Olympus. We gathered to draw up plans for how we should end the war and what would become of us once it was over. We didn't come to any kind of an agreement. As far as I'm concerned only one good thing ever came out of that first meeting— you were conceived that night."

Persephone looked down. She had been told that part, at least. It was the part Demeter would talk about most— how the young rebel god had caught her as she fell from Kronos; how he had fallen in love with her the moment she landed in his arms, shaking and blinded by the daylight; how his was the first face she had seen since the darkness, his youthful mop of golden hair shining in the sun. Demeter told her how Zeus fell in love with her first out of all beings— that they waited for each other after he freed her. "She told me that part at least; she always told that story. But never any of the other… details. Mostly because she said I was too young to hear about romantic love."

"That's a pity," Aidon turned toward her, "because then you would know about how your mother crept up on the sleeping Iapetos and tried to steal his spear."

"What?!"

"Oh, she was very brave," he said. *Brave and foolish,* he thought.

"Why did she do it?"

"Because Zeus started… turning his affections elsewhere." He caught her stilled hand in his and looked down at her. "I'm sorry."

"Why? I mean, it's sweet of you to consider my feelings, but I'm all too familiar with those stories. You don't need to protect me from them," she scoffed. She masked her pain well, and must have masked it for centuries, but Aidon could hear the hurt in her voice. "His infidelities are nothing new."

Is this why you cannot fully open your heart to me, Aidon thought, *because you think I'll be like him?* He massaged her palm and wrist in his hand. "She was trying to win him back with an act of bravery. Demeter was already carrying you, loved you— grabbed my hand once and pressed it to her womb so I could feel you kicking at her. We hadn't become the Olympians yet, and all six of us were more or less fighting individually for our own survival. She 'borrowed' my helm in the dead of night and went to the heart of Mount Othrys itself, not knowing that its invisibility is tied to me, and only works for others if I explicitly allow them to use it. She took the spear, but Iapetos woke and saw Demeter run away into the ether with his favorite weapon. She led him straight to me."

"What did you do?"

"What could I have done? I woke up to Demeter flying at me through the ether with the deadliest Titan on her heels. 'Aidon, forgive me! Save my daughter!' she screamed. I pulled the three of us from the ether into Chthonia, where I had allies. Hecate and Nyx gathered up Demeter, and I met Iapetos at the river Phlegethon.

"I *had* him; I was about to push him into the Pit, but I forgot to keep an eye on his other hand. He plunged his knife into my leg here," he said indicating the raised, jagged scar above his knee, "and I lost my footing. Hecate took my helm from Demeter and pushed it to me through the ether. I put it on just as his sword was about to come down on me and disappeared, rolling out of his reach. But if I moved again, he would be able to hear me."

"How did you escape?"

"I didn't. Your father came charging in on his chariot, bellowing in rage, eager to defend your mother with the lightning he had just been given. The cacophony distracted Iapetos enough that I could rise to my feet. But with my helm on, Zeus couldn't see me standing in front of the Titan. If he used the lightning, he would have struck *me* down instead of Iapetos, and despite being in tremendous pain, I had to act quickly."

Aidon paused and looked down at Persephone, enraptured by his story, and didn't know how to continue. He had never told these things to anyone before. Everyone he knew was in the war fighting alongside him.

"Don't hold back," she whispered. "Tell me."

"I took off his head."

She shuddered against him, her eyes wide. He felt her hand trail along his chest and her thigh squirm over his.

"One clean stroke. We threw him into Tartarus. When it was done, Hecate had your father, your mother and me take an oath and drink from the river Styx. We began the alliance of the Olympians that very moment by sealing yours and my betrothal."

"Did Iapetos die?"

"He can't; Iapetos is deathless. He's chained down there with the others, but only speaks in whispers now. Your father and I went to Tartarus to make sure Iapetos stayed there, and won the alliance of the Hundred Handed Ones. Given their... history... with Kronos, they agreed with pleasure to become the Titans' jailers."

Persephone looked at him. "I want you to take me there to meet them."

"No."

"But—"

"Persephone, speaking to the Hundred Handed Ones and seeing them are two different things. These are beings that can *subdue gods.* And there are other ancient horrors in Tartarus that you shouldn't see— that no one should ever see."

She had drawn the power to reach into, the ether from Tartarus itself— had watched terror sweep across Aidon's face as she opened the gateway and looked back at him. *Ancient horrors.* Was that what she was becoming? "Aidon, I need to know why they called to me; why they knew me. What am I? Am I... a *thing* from the Pit?"

"No, my love, of course not," he said drawing her into his arms. "Why would you ever think that?"

"They called me 'She Who Destroys the Light'."

"But, sweet one, that's what 'Persephone' means in the old tongue."

She froze in fear. Was she cursed? She had been carrying that name all her life, though few ever called her that. The only one who had ever done so with any regularity was holding her right now. An invisible weight bore down on her chest. "Is that why my mother called me Kore, hid me, and kept me ignorant of you? ...of all of this? Because she knew that if I came here I would become..."

She didn't finish, her voice cracking. Aidon hushed her and held her as she shook. He kissed her forehead, and stroked her back. The world above was cold and dark without her in it. He wasn't about to tell her that. Besides, Demeter was to blame for that, not Persephone. Her mother would stop this nonsense soon enough. If not, Zeus would stop it for her.

"They called me Praxidike."

"It means 'justice'."

"It means 'vengeance'," she countered.

"It's the same thing."

"No, it's not!"

"Sweet one," he said, turning to kiss her on the cheek as they lay side by side. Aidon laid his head on the pillow beside hers and looked into her eyes, watched her tears spill out and spread on the pillow. "There is nothing— *nothing* evil about you. You shine like a light down here. The reason I won't let you go to Tartarus isn't because I think you'll become one with the Pit. It's because you're my consort and queen. You are my wife. I'm sworn to protect you and would never forgive myself if he— if anything happened to you down there."

She looked up at him as he took her cheek in his hand and brushed her tears away.

"I love you, Persephone."

She looked away, fresh tears brimming in her eyes, unsure of how to respond to him.

He closed his eyes and pulled her closer, whispering in her ear. "You don't have to say anything right now, sweet one."

She shivered against him as his breath tickled her ear and neck. Hiding her growing feelings for him would soon be impossible. Persephone could feel the same energy she called up from the earth flowing freely between them right now.

She knew he could feel it too. The reverberations of it raced through each other as though their very souls were merging. "What if there *is* something wrong with me? What if I'm actually an evil thing?"

He pulled back from her with a smile, his gaze traveling the length of her body. He ran his hand over her waist and slowly down her thigh. "If there were any evil part of you, I surely would have discovered it by now, no?"

Persephone blushed hot and tilted her face toward his. She kissed him, his hands running across her body, his flesh quickening between them.

"Of course," he said with playful eyes and half a smile, "I could look again."

She giggled and felt him draw away from her, crouching at her feet. He lifted one foot and then the other, running his hands from her toes to her calves and peppering her feet and ankles with kisses.

"No evil here," he said, smiling up at her. He ran his hands up her legs, and across her thighs, kissing the back of her knees.

Persephone squealed, surprised she was sensitive there. She felt the heat of his kiss shoot up her spine and bucked as he held her steady. Amusement crept over his face at her reaction.

Aidon turned his attention to her hands, massaging her palms while Persephone sighed and sank deeper into the pillows. He planted a kiss on each knuckle and then sucked one finger after the other into his mouth. Her breathing grew ragged. "None here," he whispered.

His hands, then his mouth moved up her arm to her shoulder. She shuddered when he reached her neck and gasped when he arrived at her breasts. He gathered the liquid flesh in his palms, carefully kneading them and teasing her nipples to points before sucking one into his mouth. She moaned as his fingers and tongue alternated back and forth between each peak.

"None here," he rasped between them with a last kiss placed over her heart. Aidon knelt between her legs and kissed down her stomach. She felt him grip her lower back, then her thighs, lifting and tilting her backward and drawing the back of her knees over his shoulders until at last he was facing his destination.

He looked into her heavily lidded eyes, then kissed below her navel and above the line of her dark curls, running a finger between her labia. "And certainly none here."

"Aidon…" she whispered.

She gasped and watched his mouth move lower, kissing along her hip bone and the inside of her thigh. "Wait, Aidon, I don't know if you should—" Her words were lost and her shy resistance to where he kissed her next wore off very quickly.

Aidon's eyes rolled back and closed, his senses filling with her heady taste and scent as he ran the flat of his tongue through her wet folds, then speared it to gently probe her entrance. She bucked forward and he wrapped an arm around her waist to steady her body so he could explore her with his mouth. Every kiss, every time he snaked his tongue into her, every nibble and every hum of adoration that vibrated into her wet flesh made her body twist and her voice cry out for him. Gods, why hadn't he thought to do this sooner?

Her thighs shook, splaying out one minute so he could hear her then trapping his ears the next, muffling her sharp cries. When he reached the top of her labia and flattened his tongue against her bud, Aidon opened his eyes to savor the sight of his wife lost in pure pleasure. He marveled at how profoundly each small movement affected her and watched her hands land hard on the sheets and pull the fabric into her clenching fists. Her half closed eyelids fluttered.

Persephone couldn't think, couldn't breathe. Every ripple of his tongue through her nether lips drove a new wave of pleasure through her, arching her back, rushing through her breasts and up her spine as he hungrily kissed and drank her essence. She felt him shift her body as he bent forward over her and pushed two fingers into her channel. Persephone wanted to cry out his name, but had lost her ability to form words. Now she hovered at the precipice, singularly aware that this time felt different. The room started to tilt back and fall away.

Aidon felt heat dripping around his fingers as he thrust them back in, curling them forward. His fingertips searched her channel carefully for the spongy ridges of flesh he'd been told to find, and when they reach their goal, he felt her hips rock and heard her voice cry out even through the wall of her thighs squeezing around his head. He sucked the hood of her clitoris into his mouth again, and the pull of his lips and the pressure of his curled fingers became an axis of pleasure piercing through her. She came with a scream, her channel pulsing wildly around his fingers. He stroked them through her as she climaxed, mimicking the motions of their lovemaking and prolonging her pleasure.

Her essence coated his lips and his chin. Aidon flexed his arm around her to steady her as she undulated, her head thrown back against the sheets. Her fingers threaded through his hair. Another wave rolled through her and she tugged at his scalp, not knowing whether to pull him closer or push him away, unable to withstand anymore. He opened his eyes to watch the peaks of her breasts rise and fall as she gasped in release. Aidon slowly pulled away from her and delivered one last light kiss below her navel, bringing her back and legs to rest on the bed once more. He shifted to lie next to her.

Persephone opened her eyes to see Aidon run his hand hard over his mouth and the point of his beard. He brought it up and carefully licked each of his fingers, humming in pleasure as if he were drinking the last ambrosia in existence. She stared up at him wordlessly as he fitted his body next to hers, the tip of his member slick and weeping against her thigh.

"And now I'm convinced," he said breathlessly and licked his lips with a smile, "that every last bit of you is good and beautiful."

She breathed through a grin and closed her eyes once more, unable to move. "That was… How did you…"

Aidon smiled silently as his hand glided along the light sheen of sweat covering her neck and breasts. She glowed in the lamplight. Persephone saw him position his arm at the side of her head, ready to move over her and fill her once more.

"Wait."

He stopped.

"My turn."

His eyes glazed over at her meaning and he exhaled long and low as she turned toward him. Aidon lay on his back, silently swearing to himself that he wouldn't stop her. Every inch of him wanted to take her under him this very moment and join their flesh as deeply and thoroughly as he possibly could. Instead, he watched Persephone kiss his chest, moving her hands over his shoulders and tensed arms.

She stared at one of his flat nipples then darted her tongue out, listening to him hiss through his teeth as his entire body quaked. That was unexpected for both of them. Veins pulsed under the skin of his forearms and his knuckles turned white from clenching his fists. Persephone knew then that he was using every bit of will not to take her then and there. She would have to revisit them later. Greater temptations awaited her and she knew her time to explore him was dangerously pitted against his desire to drive mercilessly into her. She kissed over Aidon's stomach and heard him sigh, allowing himself to relax against her careful exploration. She ran her hands carefully down the path of coarse hair that started at his navel, not touching his most sensitive flesh just yet. He drew his legs slightly apart so she could kneel between them.

Persephone stroked her hands up his inner thighs. She cradled the soft globes of flesh at their juncture that felt vulnerable and potent all at once. His thighs tensed as she rolled them in her hand. She startled as his cock jumped on his clenching stomach, reacting to her caress. Aidoneus exhaled sharply as her fingers trailed up the ridge of his shaft, then groaned when her hand wrapped around its base. She stroked upward, lifting it off his stomach as he shut his eyes. Her fingers circled his girth, her thumb barely meeting her middle finger over the pronounced vein pulsing along its length. The skin was softer than she imagined, almost delicate, a surprising contrast with the powerful hardness underneath. She gently pulled it back, then stroked her hand up its length and heard him sigh, his back arching forward. She recognized that reaction, and wanted so badly to give him the same pleasure he had just given her. She ran her thumb over the head and felt the drop at its tip slick over the crown's uneven edges, smiling in delight when he moaned once more. Another clear drop welled up and replaced it, filling her with an irrepressible urge to taste him.

Persephone brought her lips down. Aidoneus felt himself straining closer to her waiting mouth. She smiled and stopped for a moment, faintly remembering something Hecate had said just after she arrived, and looked up at him with a playful glint in her eyes. "Aidon?"

"Yes, love?" he said, his own eyelids heavy with passion.

"I won't be trapped here, will I?"

"What?" His forehead was etched in lines of strained confusion. "What do you mean?"

She gave him a half smile. "Well, if you eat the fruits of the Underworld…"

"But, sweet one, 'fruits of the Underworld' are the asphodel roots out in th—" He stopped as a smile curved his mouth upward, understanding her meaning. The laugh started deep in his throat, his entire body shaking forward. He brought his hand up to his forehead and smoothed his hair back. His laugh sounded unnatural yet beautiful to her, as though such a sound never before existed.

"What?" she said in mock innocence.

"No, sweet one," he laughed, "I don't think *that* counts."

She watched his chest and stomach clench again in another laugh, his eyes squinting against his smile. He stopped and breathed a sigh, looking up at her tenderly.

"You've never laughed like that before," she said quietly.

"No," he breathed, "I don't think I've laughed like that in my entire life."

She returned his smile. "Really?"

"I never had cause to," he said softly, sitting up and staring into her eyes. He looked to where her hand still rested.

She squeezed him, and his eyes glazed over once more. Persephone stroked upward again while he rested back on his wrists and tipped his head forward to watch her. She licked her lips and placed them against the tip, feeling him tense. Aidon moaned as she descended to taste the salt and warm spice of his flesh. Persephone felt his hand reach softly into her hair as she enveloped him with her hot mouth. With her hand, she gripped the shaft below her lips and felt him fight to keep from thrusting into her throat. She tightened her grasp as he strained, his breath coming in ragged bursts when she darted her tongue across the crown. Out of the corner of her eye, she could see the fabric of the bed sheets crumpling in his other fist and smiled, knowing that she was bestowing the same gift of pleasure on him that he had just given her.

Aidon was dying. Every sensation in his body pulled him toward her tongue circling the head of his cock. Rational thought left him when her hand closed around him, then her lips, then her tongue, then the hot touch of the back of her throat. He moaned. Her lips dragged upward with straining pressure before descending once more, enveloping him in the soft wet heat of her mouth. Her rhythm reflected his when he made love to her, each pull upward making him feel twice as hard as before. The feel of her loving him with her mouth became all consuming, pressure building up in the head, ready to burst. He felt himself hurtling toward the precipice.

"Stop, stop! Persephone, please…"

"Did I hurt you?" She looked at him, her face falling. "Did I do something wrong?"

"No! No, *far* from it. I just—" he ached for her, veins throbbing under his skin, pulsing his desire for her. He needed to look into her eyes once more. "I need to be inside you, my love. Please…"

She sat up and moved over him as he tilted upward. Her body crashed against his chest and she brought her legs over his hips to straddle his lap. This wasn't how he'd planned to take her, but her advances were very welcome, nonetheless. He felt heat pouring from her center. Aidon drew her into his embrace, his tongue searching hers out in a kiss, his hands tangling in her hair. He reached under her and lifted her up, crossing his legs in front of him while she wrapped hers behind his back. He had dreamed of making love to her this way since they first met in Eleusis, but in the three weeks he'd spent coupling with her in near silence, he wouldn't have even known how to suggest it.

Persephone reached between them and gripped his shaft, guiding him to her entrance. With a swift thrust, Aidoneus was inside her. He broke off their kiss and kept his eyes open, face to face with her, watching her gasp, feeling her shudder in his arms as her channel stretched to hold him. Aidon held her hips steady so he could guide their lovemaking. His movements became slow and stilled when her eyes opened to his again. If he went any faster it would be over too soon. He needed this to last as long as possible, to experience the love he knew she felt but still could not voice to him. He needed to show her that it was safe to open up to him fully. Persephone shifted in his arms, needing to feel the sweet friction of him plunging into her, frustrated and mewling for him to go faster.

"Aidon—"

"Not yet…" he whispered.

"—please…"

"Shh… Persephone…"

He ran his hands across her back, soothing her until she calmed and came back to him. Persephone felt their union, deep within her and beyond their joined flesh, surrounded and surrounding, supported, blissful. She looked into his eyes as he withdrew. He pushed upward, watching her shudder as he filled her again. Aidon took his time, trailing his lips over her skin, one arm wrapped around her waist as the other wound its way through her hair at the nape of her neck. The last barriers she held against his full possession of her seemed almost strange now, and she could feel herself edging closer to those three fateful words that he longed to hear from her. He pushed into her in a slow rhythm, feeling her grasp and release him with each thrust.

She started to crane her head back in pleasure as he leaned forward and latched his mouth onto her breast. Her hands rested on his shoulders and wound their way into his hair, pulling him forward. He held her between her shoulder blades and sped up, their foreheads tilted together, eye to eye, breathing in unison, feeling every pulse through and around each other. Every sinew in her body from the arches of her feet to the back of her neck tightened once again, the now familiar sign that told her she was at the edge of climax. His own peak drew near and he grew impossibly hard within her. She tilted her head back in pleasure.

"I want to look into your eyes when you come," Hades rasped, gently pulling on the roots of her hair to guide Persephone's gaze back to his. "Let me see you."

She felt her face then her entire body clench as she struggled to keep her eyes open for him, seeing the image of her own ecstasy in the strain on his face. A vein coursed over his forehead under beads of sweat, and his face flushed with pleasure. He gasped his completion staring directly at her. Arching forward, she cried out as he cried out, her lips parted wordlessly as his were, face to face, staring into each other. When the intensity overwhelmed them, they fell against each other, their arms and legs wrapped tightly around each other, breathing in unison. Aidon stroked the long waves of hair matted to her back and stayed inside her as she brought her knees back to the side of his hips and fell limp against his chest.

He tilted their spent bodies back and fell against the pillows, still intimately locked together as they stretched their legs out. He softened and her tight channel slowly released him. In the absence of her most intimate embrace, Aidoneus brought his arms tightly around Persephone, holding her on top of his chest and kissing the top of her head.

He raised his shaking hand and doused the lights. His eyes closed and he draped his wrist across her back. He held her to him, and stroked her hair. "I love you, sweet one. I love you… My Persephone, I love you. I love you, I love you…"

Her eyes stayed open, listening to him whisper the words over and over. They faded and slurred as he drifted off, his chest rising and falling under her head. Hades's words rang in her ears while he fell into a sleep deeper than he'd had in aeons. His breathing was peaceful and measured. Hers was not. Persephone lay awake, her mind repeating his susurrations endlessly— words that she still could not say to him, no matter how badly she wanted to. Exhaustion and the rhythm of his heartbeat finally lulled her into sleep and dreams.

They burst. Wound against one another, tangled and embraced, they burst in six-pointed flames of red against the life-giving leaves. Their forms were gentle: delicate and temporary. Each petal opened against the air, vulnerable and tender. Their centers unfurled. They waited.

13.

I*T COULD BE LIKE THIS,* SHE THOUGHT, WAKING UP IN THE crook of his arm.

Persephone watched the rise and fall of his chest as he slept peacefully. The thoughts were hers, but in her mind, his voice spoke the words. *Open yourself to me— love me— be my wife, and it could be like this for all eternity.*

Aidoneus had found a permanent place in her heart yesterday. Persephone didn't know if it was love, but she longed to say the words she knew he wanted to hear—words that would bind her soul to him forever. She wondered if the mysterious trees in the garden were blooming just as they were in her dream. She nuzzled against Aidon, tempted to wake him and walk with him out to the grove. Perhaps her dream matched his again. The proof would be hundreds of red flowers, their soft petals gilding every branch.

Persephone looked up at his peaceful face. She had never seen him asleep before. He had always waited for her to fall asleep first, and was already gone before she awoke. If he slept as little as he said, she guessed that this was the first time he'd slept through the night in centuries. Aeons, even.

Very carefully, Persephone sat up and looked around, their passion-scattered clothing strewn about the room. She leaned over to pick up one of her sandals by the straps and set it by its mate, then got up and folded her chiton, quietly placing it on the chair next to the table. Persephone saw his himation lying in a heap on the floor and sighed contentedly, remembering when he had placed it over her freezing shoulders in the cypress grove without any hesitation. Its edges were soft in her hands as she stretched her arms wide to unfurl and shake out its long length.

Persephone heard the muffled clink of metal on the floor and glanced at Aidon. He slumbered, undisturbed by the noise. She turned over the fabric. A long gold fibula was fastened and hidden within its folds— a strange place to wear one. She drew out one side and peered closer. Were those quills? Persephone pulled the other end out and held up a golden arrow the length of her forearm.

What you saw wasn't true love, it was just lust.

She clapped her hand over her mouth in disbelief. Why did he have this? Her mind spun between her mother's warnings about men and Aidon's whispered declarations of love from the previous night. She thought about the many sweet things the Eleusinian man had said to his wife in the wedding tent after they coupled. Then about her father's many lovers.

They were pricked by Eros, and their love will die someday.

"Never mind the clothes, Persephone..."

She gasped and turned her head toward his voice.

"Come back to bed, sweet one... I want to make love to you while it's light outside."

Persephone faced him, the arrow behind her back. Aidoneus was lying against the pillows, smiling at her. His hands were folded behind his head and she shuddered as her eyes followed contours of smooth muscle and the line of his hip to the fabric pulled up just above his navel. She saw the unmistakable ridge of his arousal ghosting through the sheet. Unbidden, the coil tightened in her stomach and her thighs squeezed together in response to the warmth that flooded between them. Her response to him was always so sudden and overpowering. Had he pricked her with the arrow?

"What's the matter, my love?"

Persephone brought the golden arrow out from behind her back. Aidon's expression quickly shifted from bliss to his usual mask of solemnity, worry lines deepening on his forehead and his lips pursed together. *Of all times, Fates, why did she find it now?!* he thought, then closed his eyes and smoothed his hand back through his hair, his forehead etched with frustration.

"What is this?" she said quietly.

"Persephone, it's very dangerous. Please—"

"Answer my question! I asked you: 'what is this?!'" she shouted. "How long have you had this? Is this— is this the only reason you—"

"No! It's not," he tried to cajole her. "Please put it down and let me explain—"

"Explain what? This is a golden arrow, Aidoneus. There's only one being who shoots these!"

He sat up and swung his legs over the side of the bed, the sheets still pooled at his groin, covering his diminishing hardness. "Before I came to you the first time, I went to Olympus to speak with your father about taking you as my wife. After he consented, Eros tried to shoot me in the heart, but I caught the arrow before it reached its target."

"I know how these work!" she said angrily. "One only has to be scratched—"

"And I was!" he snapped back at her, momentarily raising his voice to her level. He tried to calm himself and regain his composure. "But it doesn't work like—"

"You pricked me with it last night, didn't you?! To make me fall in love with you!" Her eyes widened in panic once the words left her mouth. Persephone froze.

"Oh?" Aidoneus said quietly. He hadn't even entertained the idea of pricking her with the arrow. After Eros had loosed his bow, he'd kept the cursed thing with him so the emotions that had tortured him ever since wouldn't befall anyone else. But Persephone had just admitted she loved him. Aidon held his breath and waited.

Persephone looked away, unable to breathe as she realized what she had just revealed. Every moment she stood here saying nothing would just confirm his suspicions. She tried to look at anything in the room but the man sitting on her bed.

He watched as she twisted, knotting his forehead. Why couldn't she have just said something, anything, during their tender moments last night? Maybe she was scared and looking for the right moment to tell him. A hopeful, vulnerable smile teased the corner of his mouth. "Is that what you feel for me, then?"

"Just answer my question!"

"The answer is *no*, Persephone!" Her anger sliced through him, and he felt something constrict in his chest. "I thought I'd already made it clear to you by my actions that I would never use trickery to have you." Surely she remembered how he had refused her advances when her memories had been washed away by the Lethe— when the girl that was Kore told him that she loved him…

"Then why were you carrying it this whole time?!"

"Because it's dangerous! Just hand it over."

"You didn't answer my question!"

"I just *did*. You think I carried it with me to bend you to my will? The exact opposite is true! The only reason I kept it close to me is because I didn't want you or *anyone* to be accidentally influenced by its power."

"Then you admit that you only… love me… because of this?"

"No! That's not how it works. It only made me *aware* that I've loved you since…"

"Since when?"

He stayed silent, searching his memory for the moment that he first felt anything for her. Nyx and Hecate may have persuaded him that it was time to claim her on the night of the full moon, reminded him that she'd been a woman for many centuries. But Aidoneus had thought about her, felt *something* for her long before he'd ever visited her dreams in Eleusis. Despite there being a host of nymphs in his kingdom who, thanks to Thanatos's philandering, had proven themselves very willing to take lovers, he'd never so much as glanced at one of them. He had always attributed his avoidance of them to his somber self-control, and to his own pretense that unlike the other gods, he operated above the level of baser instinct. But the truth had always gnawed at him— he was a man with needs as much as anyone else. Leuce, a nymph that once lived amidst the white poplar trees in his garden, had tried to seduce him early in his reign, only to be immediately rebuffed. He could have used her body in a moment of lust, or kept her as companion to ease his self-imposed exile. She had even suggested as much. Yet, he didn't want anything to do with her. Nor any of the others who saw his place in the cosmic order as a prize to be claimed, or regarded his celibacy as a challenge to be conquered.

Aidoneus only dreamed of Persephone. Demeter, joyous in conceiving a child by Zeus, had once grabbed Aidon's hand and placed it on her womb to feel the tiny life move about within her. He remembered drawing back in surprise as a jolt traveled up his arm, filling his mind with an augury of a future he couldn't begin to comprehend and a startling vision of the three Fates pointing at him. Before she was even born, he'd beheaded Iapetos to save her. When he stood in Demeter's home at the end of the war to remind her of their agreement and the infant Kore started crying, he had only wanted to comfort and protect her. He'd felt love for her swell in his chest, though he hadn't known what had struck him so profoundly that day until now. Aidoneus had left his kingdom for the first time since that night to be gawked at by the Olympian gods in order to ask for her.

The string of epiphanies hit him so hard he sat awestruck, almost forgetting that this same woman, whom he had loved and would love forever, was in the room right now. And she was very angry with him.

"You can't even answer me," she scoffed, frustrated by his silence. "All you've done since the beginning is evade my questions."

"The beginning of *what,* exactly?" he said, snapping back into the moment, alarmed. He was losing her…

"The moment I met you! When you came to me in the dream, I asked you who you were. You turned it around and asked me who I *thought* you were. It angered me then and it angers me still!"

"You know I couldn't have told you then, and you know the reason why! Demeter would have hid you from me if you told her, no matter how innocently, that Hades had come for you. I was trying to introduce myself to you slowly. Would you rather I just took you below the earth right then and made myself known to you for the first time once we arrived?"

She stood tall and narrowed her eyes. "Well, isn't that what you ended up doing?"

"That was *not* how I wanted to—"

"But you did! You *did,* Aidoneus! You abducted me from Nysa and took my maidenhead on the way to the Underworld! I don't care how much you wanted it to be different, *that was it!*"

He winced, knowing she was right. He couldn't give back what he had taken from her. And when his thoughts lingered too long on their first time, he didn't want to.

"That's what happened," she continued, fighting back her own memories, "and it stands as another example of how you can't ever speak plainly to me about *why* you did it."

"I *cannot* answer that for you. We've been over this!"

"And why not?"

"Because any answer I give might harm you as much as it will harm our marriage."

"Oh, speak plainly to me, Aidon! I am not Charon; I am not Hecate. I am your *wife!* And I am tired of riddles and partial truths and evaded questions even as you continually ask me to trust you. You make it impossible for me to love you!" She saw his eyes flash with hurt and anger.

"You want me to speak plainly, my lady? Fine! If I didn't take you, and *take* you in every sense of the word, your mother would have eternally rooted you to the earth to keep you from me!" Persephone gaped at him in shock. He paused, but it was too late to take it back, and his voice hitched as he continued. "The only way she could have done it was if you were still a virgin. You would have lived the rest of your days like the nymph Daphne unless I acted. Is that what you wanted to hear?"

She clutched her hands around her naked body, backing away. "My mother would never— you're a liar! I can't believe I ever let you touch me! You're a *liar!*"

"And now you know why I didn't tell you!" he bellowed back at her, matching her volume. Any urge to hold her and comfort her was overridden by anger— anger at Demeter, at his wife's obstinacy, anger at the destruction of any chance he'd ever had to begin their life together peacefully. "Honestly, Persephone! If I was going to fill you with lies, wouldn't it have been easier for me to do so from the start? Instead of suffer through *this?!*" he said gesturing at her.

Persephone's mouth was dry, her eyes wet and aching as though acid were about to spill out instead of tears. She blinked them back again.

"Let me speak plainly to you again." His voice wavered. "I did it because I love you! I've cursed myself every day for how it had to be done. But if I hadn't, you would have been lost to me forever."

Unwanted heat flooded into her again at the memory of him whispering in her ear, her legs twined around him in the dark. She turned her anger at her traitorous body back at him. "If that's the truth, then you weren't afraid of losing *me,* Aidoneus! You were afraid of losing your claim over me. All I am, all I ever was to you is a fulfillment of a contract."

"Listen to me again very carefully, Persephone. *I love you.* Whatever oath I made with your parents has nothing to do with what I feel for you!"

"But you could have had these feelings for *anyone* as long as they were already bound and betrothed to you! The only reason you took me here as your bride was to perpetuate your eternal pissing contest with my mother!"

He gritted his teeth. "You don't know what you're saying."

"Yes I do! And how exactly do you know what *you're* saying anyway? You're still under the golden arrow's spell! Without it you would have never felt anything for me, you wouldn't have fallen in love with me, or… whatever it is you feel right now! Eros needed to shoot you with *this* before you'd even contemplate bedding me, much less loving me," she said, thrusting the arrow before his eyes in her clenched fist.

"How can you even think these things," he shouted at her, his face reddening, "when I bare my soul to you time and again? When you *know* what is in my heart?!"

"*This* was the only thing that ever found its way into your heart!" she screamed back, throwing the arrow at him. It skipped across the floor and spun, coming to a stop at his feet. Aidon threw the sheet off and stood up, stepping over the golden arrow. She shrank toward the columns next to the door.

"Enough of this! I am tired of scraping for your affections, Persephone. What more do I have to say before you will believe me?!" Aidoneus strode toward her quickly and deliberately until he loomed over her. "And tell me this, *wife*— why give half a thought as to whether or not I truly love you in the first place? We wouldn't even be having this argument if you didn't love me! Tell me!"

"Well, *my lord husband,*" she said chewing on the last words, "that's rather presumptuous of you, don't you think?"

He narrowed his eyes and smirked at her. "Now who's evading questions?"

"As you evade mine in the same breath!" she said, balling her fists.

He drew intimately close to her and lowered his voice. "Fine. I do presume, *wife.* I know that you love me, Persephone, because I can *feel* it. I can feel it whenever I'm in your presence. Even now, through your anger, when I look into your eyes— I feel it. I can feel it when I speak to you, when I hold you, when I touch you, when I'm inside you. Deny it all you want, but if you felt nothing, then you wouldn't have shown me such tenderness last night."

"It's not as if I feel *nothing* for you," she said under her breath, averting her eyes as he came within inches of her. She felt her body shudder at his closeness, her heart beating fast.

"Then what do you feel? Look at me." He lifted her chin roughly. "Look at me! Look into my eyes and tell me you don't love me!"

Her blue gray eyes met his, then filled with tears. She turned away from him.

"That's what I thought," he sneered and stepped back.

"How could you ever expect me to love you?!" she spat back at him. "You've kept me prisoner here and you'll never treat me as anything more than your bedmate! You say you 'lay all you rule at my feet' but they're just *words*! Sweet, condescending words to keep me pliant!"

"I meant every word of what I said to you! And at this point I'll do anything to convince you! What is it that you *want* from me, Persephone? Name it!"

She took a deep breath. "I am She Who Destroys the Light and I want to know why the Hundred Handed Ones knew me by name."

He closed his eyes, realizing too late that he'd walked right into this one. She was about to trap him with the one thing he could not give her. Aidoneus glared at her again and pursed his lips, knowing full well where this was going.

"I want to know why the pathway I opened to the ether was surrounded by the Phlegethon. I want to know what I am and why I am here! *I want you to take me to Tartarus!*"

He stood in front of her silently. Unnerved, Persephone inched up to sit on the column relief as far from him as she could get without bolting from the room. Aidoneus closed those same few inches with another step forward, his body magnetically pulled toward hers. He stayed there until she met his eyes then spoke slowly, his voice rasping in anger. "You have no idea what you ask of me. You think that

Tartarus is just another new place to wander into, and that I'll be able to casually rescue you if you get into trouble as I did when you ran into the Lethe. I assure you— it's not."

"Why not let me see that for myself?"

"Why?! To see how fatally perilous it is even for gods?! I'm not taking you there!" he shouted at her, watching her flinch in fear.

"Then you've proven me right, Aidoneus," she shot back at him. "Your pretty words mean *nothing*! All you want is to dress me up to look like a queen, without any power or consequence whatsoever, and lock me away in your palace!"

"If that were in any way true," he fumed, trying to control his anger, "then why for Fates sake would I have spent yesterday showing you our realm from the Styx? Why would I have gone out of my way to take you to Nysa last night"

"You gave me a taste of what I could be, what I am supposed be, and then pulled it away from me! For that, you're worse than Demeter!" She saw his eyes widen in shock as she compared him to his enemy. For that's what her mother was, Persephone realized, if his accusations against her held any truth. She looked up at his clenched jaw, the stone column cold and unyielding against her back, his body looming over hers. And she felt pulled toward him, and knew he felt the same thing. She shivered. Her voice faltered as she continued. "At least my mother had the decency to keep me *completely* unaware."

Hades gritted his teeth and slammed his hand against the column, the smack of his palm echoing through the room. He narrowed his eyes at her and stilled for a moment before he spoke low, struggling to abate his anger. "Your mother kept you an ignorant girl because she needed the eternal devotion your father could never give her. And once she knew for certain that I had come to you— that she would lose you to me— she decided to obliterate everything that made you what you were. I saved you; I gave you freedom and knowledge, and made you into a woman when I took you here to be my queen. Don't make me regret that."

"You don't want a queen, you want a *whore!* All you want is for me to lie on my back and spread my legs for you!"

Once she said it, they became acutely aware of their proximity to each other. Persephone looked down at his hips parting her knees. Her breath hitched. Aidoneus looked away, biting his lip in anger, his body responding to her closeness. The air hummed around them, the space between them alive and closing. She saw his muscles tense as he fought to restrain himself. Persephone shuddered, heard him grinding his teeth together as he stood over her, and felt the heat of his cock pressing against her trembling thigh. She was unable to back away any further— and didn't want to. All either could hear was the other's shallow breathing. He stood there cursing himself, cursing her, every fiber of his being screaming to be inside her.

Aidoneus closed the gap between them and grasped her by the nape of her neck, tilting her head up, his fingers catching and lacing through her hair. Coiled lust made him tighten his grip, and a short cry from deep in her throat nearly undid him. He stopped an inch from her face, eye to eye with his wife. He tried to ignore the sensation of her thighs trembling and twitching around his hips, the infernal heat pouring from between her legs, and the scent of opening lilies rising from her skin. His breath came out in pants against his ragged words. "I should never have brought you here. My life was ordered; it made sense before you threw it into pandemonium. And when you do spread your legs for me, Persephone, when you welcome me inside your body, you turn me into a fool— an idiot— that thinks you are capable of loving me."

Persephone watched him shiver with a barely restrained need that mirrored her own. She brought her hand up to lightly trace along the straining muscles of his arm. He brushed his other hand over her hair, cupping the back of her head. Her lips moved against his with a whisper. "Hades…"

He crushed his lips against hers so hard it flattened her against the column behind her. The shock of the freezing marble against her bare back made her shriek and arch toward him. She heard him grunt into her mouth as his knuckles grated on the stone behind her head. Persephone raked her fingernails down the solid wall of his chest, leaving a trail of raw lines on his skin. Their tongues battled for dominance as he possessively mauled and bruised her lips. When Persephone caught his bottom lip between her teeth and pulled back, he hissed in pain. He broke away with a feral stare and ran his tongue over his lip, tasting blood.

Aidoneus whispered her name and pressed his body against hers, tension humming between them. His hand knotted in her hair, pulling her mouth up again to accept his. She locked her legs around his waist, tasting him. He dipped down to her exposed throat, then nipped at the flesh on her neck and shoulder, leaving a trail of rose blotches as he went. Persephone cried out and felt his hand squeeze at her breast, her nipple beading against his open palm. She squirmed and trailed her foot along the back of his leg. When his lips found her puckered areola, she tightened her thighs around him. He lightly pulled at the tip with his teeth, delighting in her sharp intake of breath.

Her fingernails bit hard into his skin, leaving reddened marks across his lower back. Filled equally with fury and delight, she whispered around punctuated gasps. "Better an idiot than the whore you've made out of me."

Aidoneus released her breast and narrowed his eyes at her again. He locked his lips to hers to silence and taste her. Persephone moaned around his darting tongue. Her hand found an opening between their bodies and he groaned in surprise when she wrapped her fingers around his cock, her thumb swiping the gathered liquid across the crown before stroking him, squeezing and pulling the silken skin away from the head and over the hardness underneath.

The pleasure forced him away from her red, swollen lips. His eyes squeezed shut as he tilted his head back and gasped. She relished his reaction to her. His hips involuntarily thrust toward her hand and he rested his head on her shoulder. She gripped him tighter, and he tensed. Aidon's breath poured hot over her breast, his voice just above a whisper. "Do not forget who you toy with. I am the eldest of the gods and I will not be made into a fool. Especially not by a mere slip of a girl."

"You're *my* fool," she whispered into his ear, guiding him to her entrance.

He pulled back her hair and bit at her collarbone, angry and undone, feeling her undulate against him. "*And you are my whore,*" Hades growled.

She pulled him into her, the first inch sliding in effortlessly until he took over and slammed his hips into hers. His head leaned on her shoulder once they were fully joined and he gritted his teeth, groaning from low in his throat. Persephone lurched forward upon his withdrawal, and cried out when he pushed deep into her again. She wrapped her legs tightly around him, locking her ankles, trapping him inside her.

He looked down at her, desperate to move again within her. His nostrils flared at her challenge once he realized he was caught. Aidoneus glared at her, unsure of her intent until he felt her inner muscles close in around his cock, shooting pleasure up his spine. He gasped. She tensed every part of her body and squeezed around him in waves, orchestrating his bliss.

Aidon's eyes rolled back in his head and a strained moan forced its way from his throat. Desperate, he squirmed from side to side within the tangle of her legs, stirring her insides until she felt lightheaded. It was difficult enough to close around his fullness when he was still, let alone thrashing about. With all her will, she focused and contracted around him again. Each squeeze sent a burst of pleasure through her while it buried him in waves of slick heat, and Aidon was unsure if he wanted her to release him, or to never let him go. Persephone bit her lip, realizing she could not sustain this much longer.

She wanted to send him crashing into his peak before he could prove his mastery over her body. Aidoneus read the determination in her face, and his eyes danced at the challenge. He brought his left forearm across her body, grabbing her breast and pinning her back against the column.

Her eyes opened wide as he drew his thumb downward to the newly accessible thatch of curls above where they were joined, drawing her sensitive nub out from under its fleshy hood. Persephone arched hard against his restraining arm and cried out as she struggled against the pleasure he gave her. Hades curled his lip triumphantly, watching her writhe. He grasped her mound and ran his thumb in circles across the small ridge of flesh, the intensity shooting straight to her core. Between sharp breaths, she wondered how often that look of wild victory had crossed his face during the war.

Unwilling to relent, Persephone fought against the cruel ecstasy and squeezed around him, bearing down as hard as she could. She watched with satisfaction as he threw his head back with a gasp and broke the contact of his thumb against her clitoris. His efforts had at least loosened the grip of her legs around his hips. When his senses returned, he withdrew and thrust forward with all his might, finally breaking her hold when she cried out.

Persephone felt his arms wrap around her body, lifting her from the column. She crossed her ankles behind his waist for balance and held onto his shoulders. His fingers dug into her hips. Hades plunged into her, taking her, fucking her in the same position as he had when he initiated her in the dark. As his hips rolled against her thighs, he kissed Persephone hard and savored the hum of their mingled moans, muffled by their intertwining tongues.

With long steps, he took them across the room to the bed and laid Persephone down at the edge, pushing her knees up to her shoulders in one fluid motion. He stood over her and mounted her again, her calves held above her head in his outstretched arms. Pleasure swelled into anger, anger melted into pleasure, forward and back again as they lost themselves in each other.

It took half her energy to resist the ache and tension of her impending climax, and the other half to keep up with his relentless thrusts. She refused to allow Aidoneus to win— to prove that he possessed her body and spirit. She was so close to driving him to ecstasy first as he entered her harder and faster, his rhythm fevered and accelerating, his cock thickening, the telltale vein prominent on his forehead. His face and neck were tinged by the blood pumping under his skin as he hovered at the precipice.

Aidoneus wildly mating with her finally pushed Persephone past the point of no return and she screamed, her back arching toward him. She let the crashing waves carry her, shaking her body as she cried out. Her sheath spasming around him raced him toward his peak, shattering him.

"Persephone!"

Her name tore from his throat, drowning her cries. Lightheaded, he planted a hand beside her to steady himself, not willing to leave her body just yet. They gasped for air as they came back to the room and to each other, their eyes glazed over, their breathing falling into unison. Aidoneus exhaled a long shuddering sigh. Exhausted, his mouth twisted into a satiated smile.

"Well, sweet one," he crooned softly, "I can't think of a better way to forgiv—"

He barely registered the blur of her open palm in the corner of his eye. It cracked against his cheek. Aidon brought his hand over the stinging, reddening mark on his face in shock.

"Get out!" she cried.

Aidon pulled away from her and gaped at Persephone, still holding his cheek as he stepped back.

"*Get out!*" she screamed, sitting up.

He grabbed his himation and wound it loosely around his waist and shoulder. Aidon quickly gathered his effects, the rings and pins clinking in his hand as he swiped his tunic off the floor. She lay on her side crying, her face turned pointedly away from him, sobs muffled. Persephone hugged her knees to her chest, unwilling to even look at him. He felt sick.

The final piece lay at his feet— the golden arrow. He picked it up and threaded it back through the folds of his himation before walking to the door. Aidon turned to her one last time.

"Persephone…"

She didn't answer.

"Persephone, I'm—"

"Please leave," she said quietly around a sob.

It had all been undone. Everything he had shown her, everything they had shared yesterday, was now obliterated.

Maybe he had been fooling himself, thinking that she could love him; maybe he really was a monster after all.

He stood by the door longer than he should have, listening to her cry and waiting in vain for Persephone to change her mind. He should have followed the first suggestion Thanatos had given him and not pursue her any further. It had only brought them heartache and pain. He fought back memories of her kissing him as she pressed her body against his back and caressed the wide scar he had shown to no one else. His eyes and throat stung.

Aidoneus finally shut the door, wondering if he would ever see the inside of this room again.

14.

"OFF WITH YOU, WITCH! WE HAVE NO FOOD HERE."

"I don't need food," the old woman said, "only a hearth to sleep beside."

"As you can see, we don't have that either; and certainly not for one of Demeter's hags."

Demeter glanced down at the telltale sheaves of barley embroidered on her himation, the same pattern worn by her priestesses. Behind the dark bearded man, she could see his household packing their belongings and placing coals in the bronze and hide carrier that would protect their hearth fire, praying to Hestia to spare the small flame from the cold on their journey. If it went out, it would portend death in the family. Death was everywhere these days.

"Where are you going?" Demeter asked.

"Ephyra. And if you have any sense in you, you'll go there too."

"When the Great Lady of the Harvest gets her Kore back from Hades she will—"

The door slammed in her face. Demeter tucked a white lock of hair behind her ear again and rubbed her boney fingers together for warmth. All the gods of Olympus had abandoned her. She had first gone to the depths of the sea to Poseidon's court. The price he had named for helping her was unthinkably lewd, the very idea of it an abomination. Demeter had practically run from his underwater palace, chased by the sound of his derisive laughter, wishing she could retch. She had wandered the frozen wastes of Hellas begging local gods and nymphs to help her get her daughter back, and receiving no assistance. Most were too afraid of Hades to even speak with her.

Eleusis was her last retreat, and her only remaining hope. Surely her most devoted priestesses would come to her aid. But when she had returned to her temple, she had found no offerings but barren straw, and no sacrifices but a fetal lamb that was obviously dead long before it found its way to her altar. She stood by as the people of Eleusis escaped to Athens for warmth, or to Thebes for food— wherever the rumors of better circumstances took them. But Demeter had been everywhere. There was nothing left for them, and there wouldn't be until Zeus returned her daughter and ended her grief.

Everywhere she had gone she'd seen priests bleeding black sheep over open pits, averting their eyes as they did so. They made offerings to the Underworld, all of them begging the hard-hearted King of the Dead to return Kore to the earth, to end the famine and cold. They didn't bother to appeal to Demeter anymore.

Empty temples were something she could live with. She had suffered through empty temples when the people of Attica went to war, burning each other's fields a few centuries past and nearly razing Eleusis to the ground. But soon mortals started dismantling her temples altogether, taking the wood to burn in their homes for warmth. Then they burned her effigies in grief and anger as their children and elders died. How quickly they had turned against her when the food ran out, and without their devotion, Demeter weakened. Hades's abduction of her daughter had turned her hair white with grief. And while she ignored the prayers of Hellas, the sacking of her temples had aged her further, beyond even her own recognition. Her joints were stiff and ached in the cold. Her shoulders were hunched and she leaned heavily on an oak staff.

Demeter at last came to the final refuge that she dared approach. It was also the place she most feared to set foot. Rumors from villages to the east had it that King Celeus would burn Demeter's priestesses alive for what she had done to his people. Immortal though she was, Demeter didn't relish the idea of burning. She was weaker now than ever— weaker than when Kronos spat her out all those aeons ago. It was so very cold. The great palace of Celeus, the Telesterion, loomed large before her; its wooden gates freshly cleared of snowdrifts. It was the only sign that someone still dwelled within. Demeter wrapped her hand around the cold bronze knocker and hammered it against the door three times.

Nothing.

The wind bit at her skin as she waited. She was about to reach for the knocker again when she heard the door begin to creak open, a dusting of snow falling from the cracks in its jamb high above her.

A tired-looking woman dressed in the dark blue of mourning peered out, her gray-faded blonde hair falling loose and matted around her shoulders. She turned to speak to someone behind the door. "One of Demeter's wise women."

Demeter nodded a bow. It had been so long since she had been called anything but a witch. "I am at your service, my lady. I humbly seek shelter and the comfort of your hearth for the night."

"Are you a healer?"

"Yes, my lady."

"What is your name?"

Demeter thinned her lips. "Doso."

The door swung wide. She looked up to see a white bearded man dressed in dark blue standing next to the woman, a circlet of gold framing his balding head. King Celeus.

Demeter fell to her knees. "My lord, please spare me. I am but a humble servant of the Lady of the Harvest."

"Supplication doesn't suit you, Doso," he said grimly. "You have too noble a bearing about you."

"I do come from… a high born family, my lord."

"And where were you born?"

"Crete."

"Rise," he said. "If you are a healer, Doso, my wife and I welcome you."

"Then the tales about you—"

"Burning priestesses?" he scoffed. "You must have traveled here from Athens."

"Yes, my lord. But the rumors…"

"People are saying all sorts of things these days," he said somberly. Celeus motioned her forward. "Come in from the cold, Doso, before we lose what little heat we've managed to keep in the hall."

Demeter leaned on her staff, pulling herself across the threshold. The heavy smell of pennyroyal and parsley wafted from a censer, and she knew at once that illness had plagued their household. Wisps of fragrant smoke hung in the air, illuminated by the great fire in the hearth, and warmed her skin. Its heat so inviting that she would have blissfully fallen asleep had she sat down. Ancient tapestries, pulled from around the palace in a desperate attempt to seal the heat into this one room, bridged the great hall's marble columns. The household shrine stood at the back of the hall, and Demeter could make out the mitered soot silhouette where her effigy once stood. Though it was barren, she could still feel the offerings that had been made to her. They flowed from the altar and into her bones with a heat that rivaled the hearth fire.

"The countryside is in a panic. It's not safe now, even for the king and queen, to openly keep faith with the Great Lady. So many say she abandoned all mortals to die," the woman said sadly. Demeter recognized her now, though she appeared to have aged ten years in the past month. Queen Metaneira spoke again. "Our servants have long since fled, the people of Eleusis are leaving us, and we're too weak to defend our own home from being sacked. Best to be more subtle, and not incite anyone."

"I understand," Demeter said. "I'm sure the Great Lady would understand as well. Bless you for keeping the faith."

Celeus shook his head. "We're among the last. So many of our friends have left for Argos, Knossos, Ephyra..."

"What is in Ephyra?"

"You haven't heard?"

"As you said, my lord," Demeter replied, "you hear all sorts of things these days."

"King Sisyphus has food there. His infamous greed during the harvests meant that his silos were full when the cold and famine struck. His ships come back laden with gold and slaves from the trade of even small amounts of it."

"Why has your house not joined in the exodus west?"

"Mighty Zeus will strike him down and curse all who dwell in his wicked city," Metaneira said angrily. "Sisyphus demands the worship and devotion of anyone who approaches the walls of Ephyra. And he takes the maiden daughters of noble families. Calls himself a god king. The

Receiver of Many will send him and his acolytes straight to Tartarus for his hubris."

"Metaneira!" Celeus shot at her. "I thought we agreed!" He turned to Demeter. "I apologize, priestess, for mentioning the Unseen One in your presence. We meant no offense."

Demeter smirked at their epithets for Aidoneus. "Why do you admonish your wife to keep He Who Has Many Names nameless, my lord?"

Celeus and Metaneira looked at the ground in silence. Metaneira's voice wavered when she finally spoke. "We were weak; we feared for our lives. We thought to appeal to him in our desperation, and if he wouldn't hear our prayers to return our people's beloved Kore, he would at least save us. Our prayers and sacrifices fell on deaf ears."

Demeter narrowed her eyes. "Trust me now when I tell you that no matter how hard you plead with him, Aid— the Unseen One will never hear you."

"We should never have called on him, Doso. He took so much from us."

"Yes, he did," Demeter said, her eyes stinging. "He will not take any more from you as long as I'm here. You said you needed a healer?"

Metaneira motioned her toward the fire, where a crib was set up and a couch was turned toward the flames. Demeter hobbled over and peered into the crib. An infant boy slept fitfully, murmuring and twisting in the throes of a fever, clearly having been given drops of barley beer to soothe and quiet him. She looked over to the couch and held her breath. A young man lay there, his brow beaded in sweat, dark circles under his eyes, his lips parched and cracked. He slept just as restlessly as the infant. Dusty blonde hair fell across his forehead. Even in his sickness he was strikingly handsome. Demeter felt heaviness creep into her chest. The youth looked so much like Zeus did when she had first met him. When he still loved her.

"My lord husband and I had the fever as children and lived, so it didn't sicken us. But—"

The queen broke down, her words lost as she cried. Celeus wrapped an arm around her. "We'll see them again, my love. Someday."

"My daughters!" Metaneira cried. "Kallithoe... Kleisidike... little Deme... He took them last week! Maidens, all of them... Kallithoe was to marry in two weeks and I had to bury my eldest daughter in her bridal dress! Gods, why?!"

Demeter's mind turned to her Kore, drawing a thistle up from the fertile soil and dancing through the field with the little fiery copper butterfly. And then their world had collapsed around them. No levy could hold back her tears.

"Shhh, wife..." Celeus stroked her hair. He looked to Demeter, his own eyes watering. "Please help us, Doso. We've kept the faith alive in this house. Surely the Great Lady will show us *some* measure of mercy and save my sons?"

"She will," Demeter said, rivulets pouring down her aged face. "Hades stole my daughter as well."

The king and queen shuddered at his name. Celeus spoke low. "Woman, you cannot call on him—"

"I do not fear him—" she said, raising her voice before she remembered that she was Doso, not Demeter, "—m-my lord. And I am through ceding ground to him. He will have no power over your sons; not as long as I'm here. I swear on the Styx they will not pass into his clutches as your daughters did!" She walked over to the youth and swiped his hair from his forehead. "Tend to your altar once more, my lords. My work is done through your offerings to the Great Lady. What are your children's names?"

"The infant is Demophon," Metaneira said, wiping her eyes with the sleeve of her mantle. "And this is Triptolemus. The Prince of Eleusis."

His eyelids fluttered, and Demeter lightly touched his forehead. "Triptolemus…"

He heard his name called and saw light once again. Triptolemus had turned away from it before, but it was so very close this time. Was he finally slipping away toward the realm of the Unseen One? Had Thanatos come to reap his soul and send him to the Other Side? He let out a sigh, wondering if this exhale was his last breath. At least he would see his sisters again. But when Triptolemus looked up, he didn't see a desiccated skeleton looming over him. Instead, a beautiful woman filled his vision, her long hair cascading from her golden diadem in rich waves of spun flax and copper. Her eyes were emerald green, and her chiton a brilliant red, emblazoned with golden barley. The light came from her. He smiled and passed back into unconsciousness as her soft hand stroked his forehead.

* * *

This was her last day as the Maiden. She stood taller, nearly flowered. Hecate could feel the impending shift to the Woman as surely as she had for a hundred aeons. She walked through the garden in her white peplos, her adolescent feet padding over the earth. She sensed the bursts of colorful blossoms at the garden's edge before she could even see them, felt the warmth of breathing life radiating from the six trees. They had taken a little less than a moon's cycle to bloom, their flowers vibrant red against the rich green leaves. Their brilliance stood like a beacon against the pallid grays and midnight-darkened evergreen of the Underworld.

Ducking under the branches, she stood in the middle of the small grove. Hecate walked to one of the flowers and peered at its petals, soft and translucent red, glowing as if the sun shone through them. She reached out and touched the waxy leaves, then drew her hand back in surprise. They were warm, as if they were basking in the daylight of the living world above. The red blossom would be unremarkable if it were growing above ground. But this was Chthonia. This sun didn't shine here. Hecate pulled a single petal from a low hanging flower, examining it in her hand. As she did, the one beside it shook loose and floated to the barren ground below. She rolled the petal in her hand and smelled it, tasted it, closed her eyes and moved the energy of the ether through it, trying to find something, anything, unusual about it. She could find nothing that made these trees any different from those growing in the world above, other than how quickly they grew. Perhaps that was their only miracle.

Hecate tucked the single petal into the neckline of her peplos, and reached for the one that had fallen to the ground. When she picked it up, she cupped her hand to her mouth in shock and stumbled back, falling hard on her rump. She stood again, feeling her heart beating out of her chest, and dusted off the back of her peplos, staring closely at the place from which she'd picked up the fallen blossom. Hecate's fingers feathered over a small tuft of light green grass. It grew in the exact shape, in the exact place of the flower that had fallen to the infertile ground. She leaned over, her breath teasing the fragile blades. "It can't be…"

She stood up again and looked at the trees all around her, breathing shallowly. "It can't be!"

Hecate turned her eyes upward and called out to the mists above. "Nyx! Mother Nyx, you must see this!"

She waited.

"Nyx?"

"Your mother was Asteria— daughter of Phiobe, daughter of Gaia— who pledged you as my acolyte, young one," a lilting voice said behind her. Hecate turned to meet the silver rimmed eyes of her mentor, the Goddess of Night, aged as many centuries as Hecate could count years. Darkness wrapped around the curves of her body like an unbound, thin himation, clinging to her and flowing around her as though she were underwater. Her jet-black hair waved about her weightlessly, and her bare white feet stuck out below the cover of darkness, hovering above the ground. She smiled at Hecate. "And after all these millennia, Hecate, we are more friends now than teacher and student, no?"

"Yes, my lady," she smiled.

"What troubles you, young one?" Nyx looked around at the red flowers and answered her own question. "Is it the trees? They are no doubt the work of your student."

"His hands couldn't grow this orchard. Not his two alone," Hecate said, walking over to the tree and brushing her fingers over the leaves.

"Which is why I first hesitated when you told me you had chosen Aidoneus," she said. "The line of our sacred knowledge has always been passed from goddess to goddess— never to a male."

"And that sacred stream had never flowed to an avowed virgin before me. The world has its seasons, and sometimes we have to change with them. True, there is still much for him to learn. But please trust me, as I have asked and you have done before. *Your* favorite proved herself unworthy, after all," Hecate replied. "Simple passions ruled her, not the call of wisdom. Her decisions may undo us all one day."

"Sooner than you think, young one. My dear son Thanatos walks the earth above too often. The Fates will cut too many threads from the Cloth of Life before this ends. Perhaps it's best for all if we send the little queen back…"

"We cannot, Nyx," Hecate said, returning to where the flower had fallen on the barren ground. "The soil itself tells us why. Look..."

The Goddess of Night tipped forward as though she were swimming through the air, her hair gently waving behind her. The shroud of darkness followed after, falling away from one breast before it rushed up on its own to cover her once more. Nyx leaned down and looked at the tuft of grass. She listened intently to a silent voice above her and moved her hand along the darkness shrouding her body, caressing it and looking lovingly up to where it swept up and faded away from her form. A slow smile spread across her face. "I knew there was a reason my husband liked her so much."

Hecate looked at her, perplexed, before it dawned on her. "I knew they first coupled before they reached the lands below, but I hadn't imagined it could have been while they were—"

"Erebus said he was honored. He told me he bore witness to the Goddess mating with her thrice-chosen Consort in the ancient manner, the way it was done before the Tyrant." Nyx spat the last word, refusing to say Kronos's name. She rose, righting herself. "Chaos mated with the Void in kind to create the cosmos. It was the original *hieros gamos,* before my generation perfected it. The true Sacred Marriage of the gods— not the pantomime your Lampades engage in with the mortals."

"Aidoneus's eyes saw their union differently," Hecate said, ignoring her teacher's slight against her nymph acolytes. "And a mere moon's cycle learning of her thoughts gives me much doubt that Persephone would see it your way either."

"You know better than most that things are not always what they seem," Nyx said as she moved back to the trees. "The narcissus I had Gaia plant in the center of Persephone's sacred grove was what drew her here. When she plucked it, she laid aside her old life and chose us and our ways. She chose him as her mate in that moment, whether she knew or not."

"The divine purpose of that flower is unlikely to bring peace to either of their hearts."

"Our ways are not the ways of the world above. Aidoneus has only begun to realize that. And she will see that one day as well."

"They have not yet performed the Rite. Perhaps then—"

"All in due time. Be patient with them, young one."

"My lady," Hecate said, pointing at the small tuft of grass, "if these blades carry the meaning we suspect, and the true purpose of their union comes to pass— will you join your consort, and become the night as he became the shadow?"

Erebus had not always been the encompassing darkness that separated Chthonia from the world above. Before Kronos enslaved the entire House of Nyx and imprisoned them in the Underworld, all the Protogenoi walked the earth in forms made flesh. Erebus was a tall man with silver hair and midnight blue eyes. Every shadow cast in the daylight stretched forth from his raven black wings— the Lord of Shadows was a fitting consort for his wife, the Goddess of Night. After the war, one by one, they had chosen to fade from their tangible forms into their respective provinces. Hemera grew more luminous until she was the daylight itself, Gaia took root and melded with the earth, and Erebus faded into the darkness. Slowly, others among the old gods followed in their stead, including Hecate's beloved mother. Of the Protogenoi, Nyx was the last to retain her original form.

The Goddess of Night smiled as Hecate ruminated on their fate, which would someday be the fate of all the immortals. "Truth be told, Erebus likes holding me this way," she said, brushing her hand over the wavering shroud of darkness surrounding her. "He says it makes him feel young when he touches me. I'll keep this form for now. If our ambitions are realized— then we'll see. I'm allowed to change my mind."

Hecate sighed. "I thought to sow the seed of our future when we sealed the betrothal of Hades and Persephone at the River so many ages ago," she said, running her fingers along the sun-warmed leaves. "Now, infinitely more hangs in the balance, and their sapling already twists in a storm."

"They will find a way to weather it."

"The aeons have passed us by, and only this and the next remain."

"Patience."

Hecate and Nyx turned simultaneously to see Aidoneus step out through the palace portico, walking slowly toward the grove, arms folded across his chest.

"Do they know?" Nyx asked.

"That these are their creation? Perhaps not. They have both seen how they flourish here. Persephone carried her husband to the grove's heart when she found her own path through the ether, and both are led here in dreams. Aidoneus knows as well as I that creating them is beyond his wisdom, and Persephone is thwarted when she tries to grow even asphodel in the fields of its namesake, much less leaves soaked in sunlight."

"How long since they spoke to each other?"

"Three days," Hecate said, lowering her voice as Aidon approached.

"Have faith in them," Nyx returned.

They silently watched Aidoneus walk into the grove, the gravel crunching under his leather sandals. He touched the warm leaves, then thinned his lips once he realized he was not alone.

"Hecate. Lady Nyx." He nodded grimly to them in acknowledgement.

Nyx floated toward him. "What troubles you, little one?"

It was his least favorite sobriquet, and one she always managed to use when his frustration was greatest. Aidoneus said nothing; the Goddess of Night was a thousand aeons older than he, and with Erebus, had once ruled both the Underworld and the night sky. He was too tired to challenge her anyway, his body and soul weary from lack of sleep.

"You dislike it," Nyx said, effortlessly reading him, "but our other name for you, Liberator, seems to fit poorly right now."

Aidoneus merely circled the grove, his arms crossed behind his back.

"Ever as taciturn as you were before. Before her, at least. This isn't about your new queen, is it?"

He clenched his teeth and looked away from her.

Hecate followed closely behind Nyx, who tried again to draw an answer from him. "Aidoneus, you can greet the rest of your subjects behind a mask of solemnity—"

"—but you can see through it, my lady; I know. I don't wish to talk about it," he paused, glancing at their expectant faces, and scowled before dryly continuing. "But clearly I'm to be pestered by both of you until I say something. I'll be brief: I'm taking Persephone back to Demeter."

Hecate shook her head. "Tilling the shoots under so soon?"

"Soon?!" he flared. "She has been here nearly a month! And as soon as there was a glimmer of hope that this could work, I *destroyed* it. I've ruined everything, Hecate. She will never find it in her heart to love me after what we did—

after what I said. I've agonized over this for three days and I'm just going to do what is best for all."

"And what does she have to say about this?" Nyx said.

"I cannot bring myself to speak to her, nor would she want me to. Not after we—" he walked away from Nyx and looked out above the twined branches of the trees, the waterfall in the distance cascading upward to the world above. "The mortals are suffering in her absence, thanks to her mother. After what happened between us, Persephone cannot possibly still wish to remain with me. We will still be married in name and title. She will live in the world above where she belongs, where she's happiest, and my life can go back to the way it was."

"There is no going back, Aidoneus," Hecate replied, "And neither can she. What was done cannot be undone. You cannot build a new tree with those boards."

"This is *my* marriage!" he said, turning back to them. "It's my decision to make."

"So," Nyx said, "you will leave this realm without a Queen? Or do you have plans to take a concubine? Many of the nymphs who reside here would be willing…"

"No." He felt bile well up in his throat as he contemplated any kind of intimacy with anyone but her.

"Would you stop her if *she* took a lover?"

His jaw and fingers clenched shut and he closed his eyes so Nyx could not see the fire that lit them. For all the nausea he felt at the idea of laying with another woman, the thought of his wife being touched by another man filled him with a rage so potent it could lay waste to the earth. The Olympian men had no qualms about seducing a woman once she was unbound from her vows of chastity. Unbidden images of Persephone's body being dragged underneath Apollo or Ares tore at him until he thought he would scream.

"Did you think you could push her away so easily," Hecate chided with a smirk, her eyes narrowed at him, "when you hold so tight?"

Aidoneus slammed his fist into the trunk of a tree next to him, feeling his skin break open on its rough bark. His wrist smarted at the impact. He looked at his abraded knuckles, then flexed his fingers outward and felt the wounds knit back together. The branches above dropped delicate red petals to the ground all around them.

"Do not presume that I come to this decision lightly." His voice rasped and he forced his anger to subside. He wouldn't let any of them— not Hecate or Nyx, nor his wife— destroy his hard-won peace of mind ever again. It had taken him aeons after the war to bury anything that could touch him. Now the wounds were open again. She needed to go back; he saw no reason why she wouldn't *want* to go back. It was the right thing to do for both of them. Once she was with her mother, he would pay a visit to Olympus with a stern warning for each of the male gods. Their fear of him would keep her safe.

"Look around you, Hades. Our world is dark and deep and hidden— an eternal tangle of flowing rivers that surrounds and protects the souls waiting to be reborn to the world above. This is a realm that needs a Queen. We have been without one for too long." The Goddess of Night moved toward him. "Setting me and my children free, drawing the shortest twig when Lachesis held out those three fateful lots for you and your brothers… Those pale beside the real reason the Fates chose you. The gifts and curses of ruling Chthonia were never meant to be your burden alone."

"I have judiciously ruled this kingdom *alone* for thousands of years. Three and a half weeks are not—"

"And for those thousands of years we waited. We waited for the Queen to find you. To seek you out. And seek you out she did, beckoning you, before you were thrice chosen by her. First when you appeared in her dreams, second when she entered your sacred grove wearing a wreath of laurel and olive, and lastly when she plucked the flower that drew you to her from the depths."

He shook his head. "That's not how it happened, Nyx. I went to her father for permission to take Persephone as my bride, as it is done in the world above. I invaded her dreams; I chased her from her home, I rapt her away in my chariot and took her maidenhead in the dark."

"Thousands of years, and still you think like an Olympian." Hecate said. "Theirs is a different world, and ours are different ways."

"Hecate, if I never hear you say that again, it will be too soon." He turned to leave the grove again. "Please— both of you— just leave me in peace with my decision."

"Hades…" Nyx breathed.

He turned, slowly and deliberately, to face her. Aidoneus watched as she raised her hand and looked at the ground. Nyx splayed out her fingers and turned her palm upward. The red flowers lifted, hovering in midair as languidly as she did. They circled her and spiraled into a tight ball hovering weightless above her outstretched palm before bursting into flames, the embers shining like stars before vanishing into the darkness that shrouded her.

"Tell me, little one…" she said to him, "at what point should *these* be factored into your decision?"

Aidon looked down to where Nyx pointed her long fingers. On the gray, lifeless soil were scattered tufts of vibrant green, lying in the exact places the petals had been knocked to the ground. Making sure not to step on any of them, he walked carefully over to one, and crouched low to examine it. Aidon squinted at it and gingerly brushed his fingers along the soft blades of grass. "What in Tartarus…?" he whispered under his breath.

Hecate met his confusion with her placid gaze. "You are not the first lovers to quarrel, Aidoneus. But you are the first to create anything like this."

"I did not… I *cannot*—"

"No, you cannot," Hecate said. "Not you alone."

"How are Persephone and I able to do this?" he said, his eyes wide with confusion.

Nyx and Hecate looked at each other. The Goddess of Night spoke. "My son said you came to him seeking an answer— that you've seen these in your dreams, and she as well…"

"Morpheus knew nothing about these," he said. "They don't appear in the dream world."

"When you first went to Persephone, my son brought you together," Nyx said. "To dream of another or ask that another dream of you is one thing…"

Aidoneus thought about their first meeting. How full of confusion he had been when he discovered himself pressed against her skin. How natural it felt to be with her.

"…But to bring two together in the same dream, to unite them— has only ever been asked of my son once."

"Remember how you appeared to each other in the dream," Hecate said. "And consider that it was *her* dream."

He looked at Hecate, dumbfounded.

"Is it so hard to believe, Aidoneus?" she continued. "You dreamed you met her in her own shrine, and so did she. She dreamed of her future husband that night, the night you walked into her dream to announce your betrothal. How you appeared to her was *her* idea. Your name a mystery, your realm unknown to her, she still grew your sacred bloom from the earth where she slept and dreamed of you."

"You are her chosen Consort. And just as was done in that first dream, you, Aidoneus, provided the seed to create these. Together you have dreamed these pomegranate trees into existence, little one," Nyx said, softly motioning to the leaves and flowers hanging above them.

"But what does it mean?"

"That is knowledge I cannot pass to you," Hecate said.

"Of course it isn't!" he said sarcastically. "Because the day I get a straight answer out of either of you, the Styx will flow backwards!"

Hecate and Nyx stared back at him. Aidoneus turned once more to leave.

"I don't think you understand Hecate's meaning," Nyx began, stopping him. "We cannot pass this knowledge onto you because *we* don't know what these mean. There are possibilities, but that is all they are."

He looked at them somberly. "A shame they will remain just that, then."

"Aidon," Hecate said, "do you love her?"

"You know that I do," he said softly.

"You fought each other with hard words— and you both chose how to end that fight," she said, folding her arms. "Neither could have happened unless she loved you just as fiercely. You believe your love compels you to send her back, and you are willing to sacrifice your every desire for her happiness, Aidoneus. But one more offering is required— your pride. Go to her."

He loved her. Throughout all this, he loved her terribly, achingly— his passion undiminished. Since their argument he'd barely slept, not even spending time in his own bedroom, instead electing to nod off in the evening for an hour or so, slumped on his throne between the increasing number of judgments. He swiped a hand over his unshaven face. It was a marvelous contradiction. Thoughts of her tormented his waking moments relentlessly, yet he couldn't be at peace unless she was with him. His knew his needs, but what of her? Nyx, as she was wont to do, spoke of the metaphysical, the unsubstantiated. Her revelations were about a kind of love that Persephone wouldn't understand— Aidon could barely wrap his mind around the imagery Nyx used, most of its meaning lost to the ages.

But he knew from the moment Persephone started tracing the scars of his past, healing him far deeper than the shallow marks on his skin, that she loved him as well. For that one sublime act, Aidon was eager to spend eternity returning that affection to her. How much would they miss, how many more perfect moments would lie cold and dormant if he released her back to Demeter? He stood at the precipice, fear flooding back into him. What if his wife wanted to leave him, and this was all for naught? Could he convince her to stay?

Aidoneus plucked a single red flower, cradling it in his hand. It was bright and warm. He nodded and carefully tucked its red petals into the folds of his himation. Pointing at solemn Nyx and a wide-grinning Hecate, he said, "I'm not doing this for either of you," and purposefully turned on his heels to leave the grove. "Or whatever you think may come of these."

"We should be the least of your concerns. All you see here is mutable and inconsequential," Nyx said, sweeping her hands out at the trees. She spoke quietly to herself as Aidon walked back toward the palace. "But your beloved queen is not, Liberator. Nearly anything can be forgiven, if one is willing to open their heart completely."

15.

THE WARM RUSH OF DIVINITY FLOWED BACK INTO Demeter— beating in her heart, coursing through her veins. She could feel the Telesterion's altar nourishing her. When Demeter placed just a few drops of ambrosia on his tongue, Triptolemus's fever broke immediately.

The infant Demophon was far more difficult.

She rocked the restive babe against her breast, feeling utterly alone in the cosmos. Zeus had abandoned her long ago, and had now betrayed their daughter. Poseidon was only ever loyal to his accursed brothers, and had made a disgusting mockery of her grief. Hades— she couldn't even *think* his name without whipping up a wind that would shake the stone foundations of the great hall. Her daughter was trapped in the Underworld, dead by any mortal definition. The people of Hellas had abandoned her. The gods and nymphs cared nothing for her. Even loyal Minthe was nowhere to be found.

But the House of Celeus cared for her, had restored her life as surely as she would heal both their sons. She could have saved their daughters from Hades's grasp if only she had arrived sooner. Maybe after she finished with

Demophon, she would make them all immortal— a new family to replace the family that had betrayed her.

There were other curatives for the boy, but those required the earth to be healthy and fruitful, which it most certainly was not. Only bestowing immortality on the child would save him. It was the least she could do for the last of her worshippers. She placed the sleeping Demophon back in his crib. The sacraments granting him deathlessness were almost finished, though the last would be the most difficult. It would be unwise to do so in daylight— not when she was in the constant presence of mortals.

"My Lady…" A warm tenor voice echoed through the cold hall.

Demeter turned, suppressing a smile, and nodded to the young man. "You look well today, my Prince. But I'm just a humble old priestess. Addressing me as 'my Lady' is unnecessary," she said, retrieving a piece of kindling from the hearth.

Triptolemus wore a gold circlet on his head, similar to his father's. He was dressed in indigo to mourn his sisters, the wool himation wrapped tightly around him. Recovery had been quick. The dark circles under his eyes were fading. His skin was golden and flushed with from a childhood spent in the sun. He smiled at her. "Whatever you say… my Lady."

Demeter looked back at him, the heavy crow's feet around her eyes giving away her amusement.

"And that's not entirely true, is it Doso?" Triptolemus said. Demeter placed the glowing ember in the censer and wafted the vapors of dried parsley over Demophon's crib. "My mother said that you come from a noble family on Crete."

The glamour of advanced age fell away for a moment, her hair flashing radiant gold and copper instead of brittle white. Anyone else would have missed it. While Demeter was healing him, Triptolemus had seen her youthful face many times through the delirium of his breaking fever.

"That was a long time ago," Demeter said. "Before you were born."

Aeons before I was born— isn't that right, my Lady? he thought, but said nothing. He had never even met a nymph before, much less a goddess. Triptolemus had known from the moment her hand stroked his forehead at the height of his illness that Doso was none other than their lost and mourning Great Lady of the Harvest. Her skin and hair and clothes were haggard. But her gait was lighter than a crone's should be. Her eyes were free of jaundice or cataracts and sparkled a deep green. "What made you leave?"

She looked up at him, unsure of how to answer. Her tyrannical father, the deposed King of the Gods, had *swallowed* her as an infant. Her mother the Queen had let him. How could she compose a half-truth from that?

"An oracle once told my father that one of his children would violently overthrow and imprison him. My mother resolved that she would never go to his bed, and thereby have no children by him, thus saving him from the oracle's prophecy. But my lord father lusted after my lady mother relentlessly, and one night, he took her against her will. The eldest of us was begotten that way. After he was born, after he was… hidden… she acquiesced to give my father his husbandly rights, her spirit broken. I was the last born girl."

"Doso, if you don't want to continue, I won't make you. I was just curious." He knew his hymns. He knew that Kronos had swallowed nearly all his children— lastly her. Triptolemus placed a hand on her shoulder, forgetting for a moment that he was touching a goddess. Through her glamour as the healing priestess and beyond the true nature she hid, he looked deeper into her and saw Demeter, the woman.

Demeter shivered, though the palm of his hand was warm and soothing. If he were any other mortal, she would have turned him into a lizard for daring to touch her, but his presence was comforting and welcome. "No, my Prince, it's all right. No one's ever asked these questions about my past before. Well, one did before, but the answers would have been too harmful…"

"He must have tried to kill all of you. Where were you hidden from him?"

"Everywhere," she answered. She thought about Hecate, her former teacher, for the first time in a long while. Demeter remembered the three of them leaving the protection of the ether each night, always emerging somewhere new. Aidoneus would build a fire and she would tend to it while he sharpened his sword in long strokes beside the flames. One night on Samothrace, when she was still a virgin, Hecate had taken her aside, away from the rhythmic scrape of whetstone against bronze. Amidst the chirping cicadas, the Titaness had whispered cryptic words to her, and explained Demeter's eventual part in the *hieros gamos.* Those were bloody, dangerous, and simple times. "And nowhere all at once."

"Was your father overthrown?"

"Yes. Eventually."

"What happened to your brothers and sisters?"

"I don't speak to them anymore," she said, looking down.

Triptolemus could now see through the glamour Demeter had cast over herself. His hand rested on a shoulder whose joints were not swollen or bowed with age, but smooth and straight as though she were no more than thirty years old. The dusky himation she'd wrapped around herself was truly a bright red peplos held by fibulae in the shape of barley. He gingerly touched his thumb to her collarbone and her awareness came back, returning her form to wise old Doso. Triptolemus spoke to her. "If you can spare a moment from my baby brother, I have something you might like to see."

Demeter wrinkled her forehead and looked back up at him.

He stood and offered her his hand. She smiled and accepted, allowing him to help her up. Her joints had stopped aching days ago, but she tried to rise slowly nonetheless. She had to keep this appearance at least until she was done curing the infant. Otherwise, there would be too much to explain. She let Triptolemus support her at the small of her back and leaned into his strong hand.

They walked to the end of the main hall adjacent to Demeter's shrine. Triptolemus pulled back a tapestry that hung across one of the great oak doors. He cracked it open and motioned for her to step through.

The room beyond smelled like plants and growth—living, breathing things with their own green heartbeats. A pulse drummed from them, a rhythm that she had felt so completely before her Kore was taken from her. In raised wooden boxes of rich peat and soil, dozens of small plants grew green and healthy, all carefully arranged in tight rows. She peered closely at them. Oat. Barley. Wheat. Rye. Millet. All had pregnant sheaves fuller and longer than anything she'd ever seen on a mortal plant in the fields. The corns were ripe to near bursting. Demeter looked up to see a sloped plane of clear quartz held aloft by the stone walls and columns. A great iron pot filled with water hung over a brazier of coals and boiled away in the corner, flooding the room with heat and thickening the air with steam.

"What is all this?" Demeter said in awe, touching one of the sheaves, its velvety kernels sliding through her fingers. "How did you do this?"

"It started as something to pass the time. I called this place a greenhouse when I first started experimenting three years ago. The crops in here stayed green and grew a few weeks longer, while the sun outside turned the plants to brown," Triptolemus said. "That was the marvel that turned this from a pastime into the project that has consumed me ever since."

Demeter looked up at the sun filtering in through the polished stone above them.

"That was the hardest thing to procure," he said, following her gaze. "Truth be told, it is a good thing that the ice and snow hid the walls and ceiling of the greenhouse when the food started running out. Otherwise this would have been overrun and destroyed within days. I've always been fascinated with the gifts the Great Lady of the Harvest gave us mortals. Each time I harvested, I offered a third of the fruits of my work to Demeter on her altar and thanked her for her generosity. I was so afraid when I fell ill that these plants would all die." He tentatively took Demeter's hand and looked into her eyes, afraid. "Doso, does the Great Lady of the Harvest think that I am full of hubris for what I do? That I overstep my bounds as her worshipper? What would she say to me if she saw this?"

Demeter looked at him in mild shock and placed her free hand on his shoulder. "She would commend you, my child. How did you do all this?"

"This is the seventh time I've planted. After each harvest I experiment further, culling the weaker stock and crossing the strongest seeds to create better ones. The Great Lady's priestess said I had a gift given to me when I was born, that I would somehow be given great honors and my works taught to all. I don't aspire to that. I only want to take care of my plants and let them take care of my family. My sisters used to help. With prayer and luck, mixing the right soil, and keeping the heat steady in here, I've been able to create wheat sheaves twice as long as any found in Eleusis. Helios does the rest," he said, pointing at the sun shining through the snow-dusted quartz roof above.

"I can tell you now that the Great Lady Demeter would be touched by your offerings. Her heart would be glad." For the first time in nearly a month, she smiled. For the first time since the morning she fell to her knees to rip Hades's profane asphodel flowers out of her daughter's shrine, Demeter felt joy. She cupped a warm hand to the young man's face and he smiled back at her.

Triptolemus leaned down and quickly kissed her next to her ear. "Thank you, Doso."

Demeter shivered at the warm touch of his lips against her cheek. "Sh-She would tell you to go into the world and teach this to all the mortals of Hellas once the cold ends—once Hades gives Kore back to the Lady of the Harvest. This *needs* to be shared."

"Everyone in Hellas?" he said with a smile. "My Lady, that would take longer than a lifetime."

"Yes," Demeter said, looking at the perfect rows of grain. "Yes, it would."

"My Lady, before I fell ill, and after I recovered, I prayed day and night for Kore's return from the halls of the Unseen One. We all miss her greatly. I know that as her priestess you feel her loss, more acutely than most. My mother said that you once had a daughter," he said, realizing even as he did that he might be tempting the Fates and incurring the anger of a powerful goddess. *Trust me,* he thought. *Let me help heal you as you healed me. I know who you are…*

Demeter turned from him, her eyes watering. "Yes. We were traveling to… Thorikos," she spun. "My daughter and I were driven from our familiar shores, hunted by a pirate, a thief of the seas who lusted for my daughter. I entrusted her to two warriors whom I thought would protect her, but they were in league with him. When he finally found her and carried her away, there was a mighty storm and she was dragged down to Hades."

The tale was creative, and one she'd probably told a few times on her journeys around Hellas. But Triptolemus knew that only the last part was true. "You saved me from the journey to the Other Side, Doso. I wish there were some way, any way at all that I could help return your daughter to you."

Demeter nodded to him, and then pondered her situation. The warmth and vital humidity of the room drifted around her, soaking into her skin. She was struck with realization. They stood in the last place on earth were food grew, and the bounty was all hers. The only sacrifices that could be made, the only honors left for any of the gods, weren't for Zeus. They were for her. She straightened her elderly frame and looked up at him. "I saved you from Hades, and I swore to your mother that he would not have you. I will continue to be true to my word," she said, sweeping her eyes across the garden Triptolemus had dedicated to her, "and I would do so forever."

"My Lady?" His mouth went dry. *Surely she didn't mean...*

"Triptolemus, what if I told you there was a way? A way that I could ensure that you would live, that you would be young, that you could share your gift with all once Kore is returned and the winter ends? A way that I am using to save your baby brother Demophon even now?"

"If I understand you, my Lady," he said slowly, remembering to whom he was truly speaking, "Then I would be favoring one god and angering another. The Unseen One does not like to be cheated out of souls. I'm only a man; I know my time is fleeting. I was ready to be reaped not three days ago when you arrived. If I try to escape my mortal fate and fail, I might burn in Tartarus forever."

"Only if your soul were still mortal. You must share your gift with all of Hellas one day. The Great Lady commands it," she said imperiously, lifting her chin.

"Are—" he swallowed, "are you saying that you would make me im-immortal?"

"You would need to trust me, my Prince. Wholly and completely."

Triptolemus thought about his mother and father, his friends. He imagined watching them wither and die, as he remained evergreen. He had thought to outlive his mother and father and rule Eleusis one day, but to outlive cities and kingdoms, to outlive forests and mountains… The fruitful crops surrounding them— were possibly the last in the entire world. What if something happened to him? Three days ago he nearly died from a fever, and years of careful work would have followed him to the grave. His parents thought his plants were a miracle, but they didn't know how to tend them or teach his methods. His sisters had only learned the most essential secrets, and now they were all gone to Hades, wandering as shades among the asphodel beneath the earth, with no memory. To live forever would be lonely; but could he risk letting every mortal mouth go unfed?

He looked Doso— Demeter— in the eye, slowly inhaling to calm his racing heartbeat. "I trust you."

She nodded. "It will not be easy, and you will feel the change. It will require fire and water, earth and air, and most importantly, this." Doso pulled the leather satchel she always wore around her neck from the folds of her himation and opened its string closure. Triptolemus peered inside and gasped. A golden glow grew from within, and warmth that eclipsed the balmy air of his indoor garden poured out. It smelled sweeter than warm honey. Was this truly ambrosia?

"What do you need me to do?"

"I require olive oil; enough to coat your skin. You will need to find me pennyroyal and honey to mix into *kykeon.* The barley mead *must* be free of all impurities, especially ergot," Demeter looked at him sternly as she said the last word.

Triptolemus nodded and shoved through the door of the greenhouse, running for the kitchen.

* * *

Whenever he decided to seduce a woman in the world above, it took concentration not to appear as a wraith. He needed to focus every bit of himself to keep his face, his hands, his very flesh warm and corporeal. One careless moment imagining what she looked like underneath her clothing, and he was once again a skeletal shadow cloaked in a heavy himation. Here, he was Death. The end. The hooded man in black with the bony fingers and the fearsome blade.

Thanatos didn't need to think about these things when he was with Eris. His conscious self could disappear. Whether she saw his angelic or skeletal aspect mattered little; if she ever did see his shadowy self, Eris never let on that she cared. Perhaps, he thought, she enjoyed it— the chaotic transition between vitality and death, youth and desiccation.

But whichever side of him Eris preferred, Thanatos knew exactly what state he was in at that moment. The hard smack of his hips against her inner thighs, skin on skin, was buried in the chaos of the smoking Chalcidian battlement where she'd found him. With thin black wings outstretched, Eris had swooped on him like a falcon, demanding her fulfillment. It was a habit of hers when she discovered him walking the killing fields, searching for those who had died honorably.

They'd had more trysts in these situations than he cared to admit— surrounded by the smell of freshly spilt blood, the screams of city folk and horses mingled with the cold puncture of bronze spears, the black smoke of olive oil burning in store rooms. For ages the mortal blood had soaked into the ground while they coupled, the dust of men returning to the earth, seeping through the rich soil and falling toward his home in the Underworld, rejoining his family and his king.

But now the blood stood fresh and red on the snow, frozen in time, bodies and souls trapped in the cold unnatural waste of the living world. It troubled him. But her high-pitched cries drowned out thoughts of the disastrous imbalance plaguing the world above and of his wearying role. Her velvety heat made him forget where he was, who he was, what he was each time he slipped into her.

Thanatos let their surroundings vanish from his thoughts and tried to find warmth within her, fighting against the cold that chilled his bones. Heat she had in abundance, but no warmth existed in Eris. It had always been that way with her, even when the world was fresh and green. Eris gripped his right arm, fingernails digging half moons into his wrist, and pulled his sickle dangerously closer to her throat with each flex of his hips. She stared at him with dark irises, light freckles framing a twisted smile. Just as he was about to question whether or not the Goddess of Discord could feel anything at all, he got his answer.

She gasped and opened her eyes wide, digging her slender fingers into the mortar cracks behind her, arching away from where he was joined to her. Thanatos dropped the sickle into the snow and grabbed her hips, quickening his thrusts. Eris screamed and laughed as she undid him. A groan forced its way out of his lungs and through his gritted teeth, and he felt a heat flash through his body that could have melted all the snow in the world above.

Stepping away from her, Thanatos picked up his sickle and himation, shaking the fallen snow from his cast off cloak. She leaned against the stone with her legs still spread open, a sated grin on her lips and her skirts were hitched up around her waist. Eris whooped in gratification and triumph, then leapt off the masonry ledge and twirled in a circle. Death wrapped the heavy black wool around his slender frame while she sang to herself and danced about. She ran her tongue along her teeth when she came to a stop in front of him. Thanatos smirked.

"I needed that," she said, exhaling and sighing contentedly, her wings fanning behind her. Eris smoothed her tattered peplos over her hips, paying no heed to the remains of their tryst meandering down her inner thigh. She snatched his sickle out of his hand and cut off a lock of her black hair, casting it over the edge of the stone battlement. It floated on the breeze, drifting in front of the last line of the Chalcidian phalanx defending the city. She bit her bottom lip and smiled, standing on tiptoe to see what would happen.

A panicked cry went up when the lock settled to the ground and the soldiers broke their lines, the Thracian army plowing through them, slaughtering as they went, and battering down the wooden gates. They swarmed hungrily toward the precious grain stores the Chalcidians had struggled the whole of the afternoon to defend. The air was filled with the death cries of livestock, the pleading screams of women, and the acrid smell of thatch rooftops burning.

Eris stretched her arm toward him, sickle in hand, her lip caught in her teeth. She looked perfectly coquettish— a mockery of the innocence she'd abandoned long before he'd first come to her.

Thanatos grabbed his instrument from her roughly. He shook his head, still recovering, his voice harsh. "Foolish woman…"

"Foolish how? To live up to my name? To engage in my divine role?" She sauntered closer to Thanatos and scored his flesh from the hollow of his neck to the underside of his chin with a sharp fingernail. "To enjoy fucking Death?"

"You know what this sickle really is, don't you? That blade I press to your fragile neck at your insistence? You're aware of what it could do to you?"

"So why don't you do it?" she said, tracing the tip of her tongue over the rosy line left by her fingernail. Her lips brushed across his abraded alabaster skin. "Slip one of these days. Cut my throat as you fuck me."

He didn't know if it was a dare, a request, or a taunt. Thanatos remained silent and stepped back, looking at her askance, before he gave up trying to guess her intent. Wrapping his himation around his shoulders, he saw her grin in triumph.

"Oh, Thanatos, you care so much about my well-being," she said, then clasped her hands to her chest in mock realization. "You *do* love me! I always knew you did! After all, I'm the only woman whose bed you've ever returned to."

"I've only seen your *bed* once."

She laughed again and danced in a circle around him. "Coy as ever, my delectable little murderer of souls, but you know what I mean. I've lost count of how many times you've put your magnificent prick in me."

"The thing I like the most about you, Eris," Thanatos said, hissing her name through his teeth, "is that it's like fucking a different woman every time."

She narrowed her eyes at him, the leering smile still decorating her face as she came to a stop in front of him. They heard heavy buskin boots crunching through the snow, growing louder. "So why are you here, anyway?"

"I need to speak with your... associate."

"Oh, you mean my *brother.*"

"I've told you a thousand times, Eris," a deep voice said, "don't call me that."

Thanatos drew his hood back over his head against the bite of the wind and turned to face Ares. The red cloaked God of War and Bloodshed stood with spear in hand, his Chalcidian helmet squarely framing his jaw and pasting the fiery red ringlets of his hair to his forehead and neck.

"Would you rather I called you *daddy*?" Eris said with a wicked grin, sidling up to him and leaning against his shoulder. Ares pursed his lips and looked sick. Thanatos understood from the expression on the Olympian's face that Ares had recently made the same mistake he continued to make with the Goddess of Discord.

Death grinned. Eris had no parents. No discernable ones at any rate. Most didn't know where she came from, and she always gave a different answer whenever anyone was foolish enough to ask her.

"Leave us be, woman," Ares sneered at her. "The men need to talk."

"Men," she snickered, clutching roughly at her breasts. "Oh! So if I grew a prick, I could join you? Because it really wouldn't take much to grow one like *yours,* brother."

"Get out of my sight!" Ares bellowed, his face turning as red as his bloodstained cloak.

Thanatos bit his lips together and thanked the Fates that his hood currently hid his face from the angry god's view. Eris laughed and walked between Thanatos and Ares, her hands outstretched and pointedly brushing past both of their groins. She spread her wings and spun around, her path through the ether opening behind her, its edges wavering and bending as though all of existence were collapsing within it.

"I'll see you soon, *lover,*" she said, blowing an indiscriminate kiss into the air. Eris snickered again and vanished.

"Intolerable, insulting wench…" Ares muttered, his anger abating. "I don't know how you can stand her."

Thanatos shrugged. Black ink outlines of an eight-pointed sun and horses dancing along a meandros of waves decorated Ares's forearms. He cocked his head to the side to examine them. "Those are new."

"I'm siding with Thrace today," Ares said with a smile.

"And yet your helm would suggest otherwise."

"That was from yesterday," he replied, "We'll see how it goes. If Thrace continues to please me, I'll change it, too."

"Well, that's part of the matter I came to speak with you about. You *do* realize what's happening all over Hellas and beyond, don't you?"

Ares snorted. "You mean Demeter refusing to tend the earth? Or can we call a spear a spear and attribute this to your dread lord and lady?"

"This has nothing to do with our king," Thanatos said quietly. "And even less to do with our queen. Wanton destruction is the domain of the Olympians; not us."

"Ha! One would think Hades would be pleased with all this. Isn't he? More souls for his kingdom, after all."

Thanatos looked at him with a cold smile. "You're a fool, young one."

"Oh? How so, Death? If I were unlucky enough to draw the lot for the Underworld, I would redouble my efforts to make sure that my third of the cosmos was the best share."

Thanatos raised his eyebrows at that. "Well then, I'll be sure to thank the Fates every day that you will never set foot in the greatest of the three realms."

"Greatest?!" Ares laughed long and loud, the slice of swords through flesh crescendoing around them in answer. "Gods above, I'd rather be a slave to the poorest mortal alive than lord over all those who have perished. I *meant* that it would be great under *my* guidance! You're funny, Death— I always knew I liked you for a reason. Greatest, indeed…"

Thanatos absently twirled his sickle and wrapped his himation tightly around him, the bite of the wind chilling him to his core. He gave the red-cloaked god a toothy smile. Death took a menacing step closer to Ares. His cheeks sunk in until the taut flesh split and pulled away into the gaps between his pale bones. Hollow sockets stared into the war god's eyes. "Keep telling yourself that, Ares."

The grin left the Olympian's face and he paled, almost losing his balance on the icy slush underfoot.

Coward, Thanatos thought. *You wouldn't last a day on the Other Side.* His bony fingers clutched at the hood hanging over his skull so it wouldn't be pulled back by the bitter wind. "I've been busy enough, God of War. Stop exploiting the famine. Your thirst for bloodshed can wait until Demeter has finished her… grieving. And if you do not grant me that simple request, then someday I just might fail to show up and give your worshippers a noble death."

"You wouldn't," Ares bristled.

"Try me. Would you rather deal with my sisters?"

Ares swallowed and slid his right foot backward.

"I thought not." Thanatos spread his black wings and took flight above the killing fields. "End this ridiculous war today, Ares, or next time your honored dead will be visited by the Keres. Consider yourself lucky that I'm leaving you with the choice."

16.

THE ROOM, IMMENSE UPON HER ARRIVAL, NOW FELT small and cloistered. But she didn't dare leave it. Three days had passed, and still no Aidoneus. The first night she was glad to be alone. Each subsequent night, loneliness and fear grew steadily in her heart and the walls shrank around her. She had steeled herself, waiting for him to come to her, for what purpose or to what end she knew not.

Do not forget who you toy with. I am the eldest of the gods. . .

When she was a child in Nysa, Persephone had heard how the queen of Olympus grew angry with her husband, continuously shamed and humiliated by Zeus' endless infidelities and the fruit they produced. One night, Hera chained him to their bed and convinced several of the other immortals to rebel against him. Demeter wisely chose to stay out of it. Artemis ran to Persephone the next day to tell her their father had been freed— that a monstrous, many-armed creature had climbed Olympus in the middle of the night to subdue the rebels and break the chains that bound the King of the Gods.

Her mother had crowed when she'd learned that Zeus had chained Hera in the sky for a year for her impudence.

Demeter had taken Persephone on her only memorable visit to Olympus, and could barely restrain her triumphant glee when she swore her and her daughter's undiminished fealty to Persephone's father. Then joy reverted to spite, and her mother cursed Zeus' name when he took Hera back. She cursed him further still when he went years without taking a woman to bed other than his wife.

Persephone hadn't chained Aidoneus— by striking him in anger, she'd done worse. The shock on his face before she'd screamed at him to leave was the last she'd seen of him. She feared his response, and the waiting only made it more terrifying. She was no fool— by every law she knew, Hades could still demand his rights to her body as her husband. But he hadn't come to her to demand anything, and Persephone now worried that his ardent declarations of love had faded into despondency, or worse— hatred.

I should never have brought you here.

She knew enough about what happened among the mortals— Demeter had at least educated her on that. Insolent wives were punished all the time in the world above. The gods did the same, as Zeus had when Hera defied him. Though Aidoneus had let down his guard, had told her he loved her and thereby left himself raw and exposed to her the night before their fight, she knew that his affection toward her might quickly turn to hostility. Who knew what retribution he had in store for her? He was the master of Tartarus, after all. He'd been separated from the other deathless ones for aeons— from the end of the Titanomachy to the day he came to Olympus claim her as his wife. And at his core, he was a hardened warrior.

She'd had an intimate, deliciously forbidden taste of that part of Hades after their fight, or during their fight— she wasn't sure which was which. The line dividing anger from lust had melted in the heat of coupling. Persephone loved it and hated it equally — she desired the way he had taken her, and loathed herself for desiring it at all. Aidoneus had seemed so pleased and effortlessly in control once they were both sated— so very different from the emotions he'd awakened in her.

"Do you think this room is your only sanctuary?"

Persephone looked up from her cupped hands, her eyes red. "What are you doing here?"

"Seeing to my queen." Hecate sat beside her. "As I was when you first arrived, I am now: at your service."

"Did he send you?"

"No."

"But you're his agent nonetheless," she scoffed.

"Look more closely at our roles. The waves roar, but do they command the sea?"

"So you have told him to stay away?"

"There was no need." Hecate fought back a smile. "You had already done so, my queen."

Persephone stood and paced across the room, her arms folded over her chest. "It's not your concern."

"But it is." She stood. "The wellbeing of this realm is my absolute concern."

"You have your own to attend. The ether."

"Rivers run through each other. Much as they do here."

"Stop… stop with your riddles! I am tired," she said, tears welling in her eyes. "I am so *very* tired of not having any answers. Who am I, Hecate? *What* am I?"

"It will take two sets of oars to reach those unknown shores. You know who holds the other pair."

Persephone clenched her teeth. "Why am I even here? Why not someone else? I am nothing here."

"If you so believe." Hecate stood. "Do you wish to return?"

"I…" Of course she had considered it. She could leave this place behind her and go home, to a place she knew well… back by Demeter's side. Charon would row her to the other side. He could not refuse her because she was… Queen. Her hands dropped to her sides. *All* of them, from the least of the shades to her great husband, saw her as Queen. Hecate smiled.

"Do you wish to return?" she asked again. "To a world where you know you are nothing as the crow knows it can fly? Where you were a caterpillar and could be a happy little caterpillar and would only be told that butterflies existed somewhere?"

Persephone thought about her poor mother, grieving in the world above, and the recent victims of the famine. She missed Demeter, in truth, but a great chasm stretched between her life as Kore and her place here as Persephone. There was no going back. She swallowed, her answer barely audible. "No."

"Then you must cast off childish raiment for the garb of a queen."

She scowled at Hecate. "Have I not already done just that? Or rather, was it not done to me? My *lord husband* made certain that I'd 'cast off my raiment' when he brought me here!"

"You are maiden no more." Hecate grinned. "But a broken maidenhead does not a woman make."

"I have…" Persephone glanced at herself in the mirror. "I have changed, though."

"Your journey has begun. No more than that." She tittered and swept her red hair back from her shoulder. "Would that it were so simple: a man lays with you and you rise from the bed a woman, full and formed!"

"Of course I don't believe that," Persephone mumbled, her cheeks flushing at Hecate's snickering.

"Don't you?"

"Only a *fool* would believe that!"

"Should I count you among them?"

"No!"

"Then leave this room."

She teared up again. "I... I can't. You don't understand."

"Are you afraid, child?" Hecate spoke the word pointedly, but her voice was tender.

Persephone leaned against the column, then flinched, realizing it was the one where she'd started her last fateful encounter with Aidoneus. She walked away, pacing near the door.

"Why do you flee him?"

"I don't..." She balled her fists. "This is *my room*. I'm not running away from anything. If he cares to, he will come."

"Why do you think he stays away?"

Persephone bit at her cheek and felt her throat close. "Because he hates me now."

"No, not 'hate,' I think."

"Then what? Anger? Indifference?"

"Something far deeper. Fear."

She shook her head. "Why would Hades, the Lord of the Underworld, ever fear *me*?"

"Because you are the Queen."

"That means *nothing*."

"Then you should tell Alekto, and relieve her of her duties."

Persephone tilted her head to the side. "Alekto?"

"One of the Erinyes. She awaits you on your balcony. Hypnos already left, but—"

Ice ran down her back. "Oh Fates! Merope... I'd nearly forgotten." Persephone paced, wringing her hands. "What should I do? About Alekto, about..."

"You should do what Alekto expects of the Queen."

"Do *what?* What must I do?"

"Rule."

Persephone looked up, but the Goddess of the Crossroads was gone. She swallowed the lump in her throat and paused. She'd never met a daimon before. She'd heard frightful things about them in passing from nymphs and mortals.

But she was their Queen. Persephone pulled at the great bronze ring on the door. Her heart hammered as she took one careful step, then another into the amethyst antechamber.

A nymph lay on the divan, naked and shivering. Persephone gasped, then ran back to her room and fetched a blanket from her bed, returning quickly to spread it over the sleeping Merope. The light dimmed, blocked by a great pair of golden wings. Persephone turned to look. The woman who stretched them was terrifyingly beautiful, her long figure clothed in a white chiton, her hair arranged in coils that moved like snakes. She brandished a bronze-tipped scourge and for a moment, Persephone's heart stopped, fearing that Hades had sent this woman to punish her— that Hecate had coaxed her from her room to meet her fate.

The beautiful daimon bowed low, her scourge at her side. "Praxidike. Mother Queen."

Persephone nodded to her. "Alekto?"

"One and the same." When she grinned up at Persephone, her dark lips revealed rows of pointed teeth. Alekto righted herself and folded back her wings. "She's been shaking like that since we pulled her from the Pit."

"Do they all do that?"

Alekto shrugged. "I don't know. We've never removed someone from the Pit before."

"How did you find her?"

She smirked. "We have our ways."

"Thank you," Persephone said solemnly. Her hand shook at her side. She would not be afraid…

"No need to thank me." Her irises flashed gold— a sharp contrast to her dark eyelids, heavily rimmed with kohl. "My sisters and I shall enjoy it very much when you find the man who should be there in her place. Consider the *real* Sisyphus payment. With interest."

Persephone tried to jostle the nymph awake. She pushed at her shoulder, but the woman lay there stiffly, shaking still. The Queen gingerly lifted the nymph's eyelid. Her pupil was dilated and scanning this way and that, but Merope saw nothing. Persephone flinched back. "Why won't she awaken?"

The winged daimon rolled her eyes. "The girl wouldn't stop screaming. Not once the entire way up here. I had to call for Hypnos. She would have driven us all mad, including herself. And it wasn't just a soft slumber he had to use to quell her. She's in a stupor."

"And still she shakes like that?"

Alekto nodded.

Persephone's jaw tightened and fire coursed through her. "Sisyphus will pay for what he did. I promise you that."

Alekto smiled, showing all her teeth again, and folded her arms in front of her. "I like you. You, me, my sisters… We'll get along just fine."

"I… I should hope so," Persephone said, raising a questioning eyebrow.

Alekto laughed. "Ah, I see it now!"

"What is that?"

"Why he's so madly in love with you." She clapped her knee. "Gods, you two are so alike, it slays me!" Alekto's throaty laugh continued, echoing into the antechamber. The nymph stirred but stayed asleep.

Persephone remained quiet. *Alike?* She pursed her lips. How were they alike? She was from the world of the living and he… She scowled, her teeth clenched, and Alekto stopped.

The frightful daimon cast her eyes to the ground. "My apologies, Praxidike."

"No, it's… Think nothing of it." Persephone managed a brief smile. "We'll have to see each other again."

"Yes. And soon, I hope. Don't let that dusty bag of bones you call your husband keep you up here forever."

The Queen guffawed before composing herself and giggling behind clasped hands. Alekto fought off laughter again and brandished her bronze scourge in the manner she had when Persephone had first sighted her.

Alekto gave an exaggerated curtsy, to Persephone's amusement. Her wings spread and with a few beats she rose into the cool air. Her voice faded into the mists as she flew toward the Phlegethon. "Until next time, Praxidike. Perhaps in Tartarus?"

* * *

It was finished by sunset. Demeter was impressed by how the Prince had remained serene and obedient throughout the ritual. She glanced behind her at Triptolemus, who was sleeping peacefully on the couch near the hearth. His parents were unable to see the change, and the Prince had wisely said nothing. But she could see what they could not. A faint luminescence under his skin shimmered back and forth, his body adjusting to being one of the deathless ones. Now that Triptolemus was immortal, the house of Celeus wouldn't die of starvation. He could work his magic with the plants, teach the secrets to his house, and teach all of Eleusis, all of Attica, and then all of Hellas one day.

It had been quicker for him than for Demophon. She had spent three days coaxing the baby to drink the *kykeon* and ambrosia, the infant fussing and twisting every time she tried to feed him. Demeter remembered how her infant daughter would suck the sweet liquid off her fingers. Kore had been such an easy baby.

Demeter thought about the uncertain days of Kore's infancy. Eleusis was just a handful of wood and straw houses back then, and though her mortal neighbors left offerings at her nearby temple, none spoke to her, or even recognized who she really was. The effigies of her were crude back then— big breasted clay women with fertile wombs and comically large hips that the villagers would heap with sheaves of barley, millet and wheat— the crops her lady mother Rhea had created for the humans.

Aidoneus's promise to steal Kore away to his sunless kingdom once she came of age had haunted her since the night he came to her home. From the moment he left, she lived in fear that he would return any day to rip Kore away from her, keep her as his ward until she came of age, or let Hecate or even frightful Nyx raise her daughter to distrust or despise her. On one of Demeter's rare visits to Olympus, Hestia had told her that his awful promise to her was the last he had spoken to any of them. He would shun the company of the Olympians in order to abide by Demeter's hasty oath and one day take her daughter. Demeter was left to guess when that would be.

Half a year after that fateful night at the end of the war, a farmer named Iasion heard Demeter weeping for her loneliness and her daughter's immutable destiny. She had startled when he appeared in her doorway, and asked what could make such a lovely young mother cry, and wondered if she had lost her husband during the war. He sang Kore to sleep. Demeter had only leaned on his shoulder and continued her tears. The next day Iasion brought fresh milk and sweet figs. He mashed up the figs and laughed as Kore happily gummed the fruit from his fingers. The day after, he popped a pomegranate seed into Demeter's mouth and surprised her with a quick kiss and tender words. Iasion still visited Demeter even after she told him the truth— that she was one of the immortals whose long war had ravaged the earth and its people, and had turned Iasion into a childless widower. He took Demeter to see the plowshare he'd made from melted down shields and spears, and the even rows he used to organize each plant in his field, so different from the clumps of wind blown seed in the villager's fields.

Demeter had loved him for the short time they had. She remembered listening to the crickets chirp all night as the mortal farmer's calloused hand wrapped around her arm and cupped her breast. She remembered the lullabies he taught her to soothe Kore back to sleep. She remembered the thick blond stubble on his chin and the laugh lines around his turquoise eyes. She remembered refusing to make him immortal. She remembered when he died. They had been lying hand in hand under the open sky in one of his freshly tilled wheat fields, blissful and exhausted from lovemaking. The king of the gods still harbored jealousy for Demeter, and with a single sudden bolt of lightning, he destroyed her brief happiness. In grief, she took Kore from Eleusis and fled to Nysa before the first green shoots of wheat broke the soil.

She grew sad thinking about how she had almost forgotten him, even though she knew Iasion had long ago drunk from the Lethe in the Underworld and forgotten her. No doubt his soul had been reborn and then died again many times by now, crossing back and forth between this side and the Other. How proud he would be of Triptolemus, who took the fruits of the land that Iasion had once organized into neat rows and transformed them into something even greater. She looked back at the sleeping Prince again and felt her heart beat faster. From the questions he had asked, she suspected that Triptolemus knew who she was, and perhaps could even see through her aged disguise. The Prince had tried so hard today to please her and offer her comfort. He had the passionate idealism of young Zeus and the mature strength of her lost Iasion. And now that he was one of the deathless ones, neither the King of the Gods nor the Lord of the Dead would be able to harm him.

Triptolemus had stripped for her in his greenhouse. She had rubbed the ambrosia-infused olive oil into every inch of his skin and hair, admiring his form in the soft light and tamping down wayward thoughts about his crystal blue eyes and the sinews and muscles under his golden skin as she concentrated on her task. He hadn't flinched at her hands once, not even when she had massaged the oil onto his most intimate parts. Triptolemus simply stood there, calmly breathing through his nose, smiling softly and following her lead as he accepted each of the five sacraments that would grant him immortality. The last part was the most difficult.

Demeter now faced this same difficult task as she fed the *kykeon* to baby Demophon. He was quiet, murmuring only once when she lifted him out of the crib. She had just enough ambrosia left to complete the ritual for the babe. This time the infant was relaxed, accepting the liquid from the ceramic feeding cup that dry-breasted Metaneira had used to feed the child goat's milk since his birth. Demeter stood up and gathered Demophon in her arms. As she slowly unwrapped the swaddling clothes and brought the loose end of her himation around his body to warm him, she bounced him on her knee and softly patted his back to keep him quiet and break up any gas. If he was too cold or uncomfortable, he might cry out and wake his family. Demeter had rubbed ambrosia oil into Demophon's infant skin yesterday. He glowed in the light of the hearth fire, his nascent immortality begging to be loosed from its mortal bonds. She knelt down with the babe in her arms, and blew on the coals.

And now to separate the chaff from the corn, she thought. She pulled the end of her himation over her head to improve her concentration.

Demeter waved her hand over the coals and watched them flame to life in a ring, an empty space created in their midst. She brought her right hand over the flame, the fire swirling now into a circle around her extended palm. She felt its heat radiating through her. Three days ago it would have burned her skin, but after the House of Celeus started placing sacrifices on her altar, all she could feel from the fire was the gentle lick of heat under her palm. She splayed out her fingers and swept her hand in a circle at the wrist. The fire responded in kind; its flames swirled like water in a basin. A circle of protection for the infant formed in their midst. It wouldn't take but an hour— there was plenty of coal in the hearth for the time she required.

She lifted the infant's ear to her lips and whispered the words she had said to Triptolemus before he stood atop the coals spilled from the brazier in his greenhouse. "Initiate to the holiest of mysteries, behold the final sacrament. Now we cast aside your mortal life to be sacrificed in the fire. As the corn must shed the chaff, so too immortality must free itself of the dust of the earth. Accept this final purgation and join the sacred deathless ones."

The baby murmured and looked up at Demeter, his limbs moving languidly as she placed him on the coals. He hiccupped once but otherwise remained quiet. Demeter kept winding her right hand over the fire as she drew his mortality out of him with her left. Embers flared around Demophon, who lay unburnt within the circle of fire, the essence of his mortal life consumed… just a little while longer…

Metaneira awoke when the flame started to flicker. She looked over at Doso hunched in front of the hearth. *That kind old priestess… stoking the fire so late at night. May the Great Lady bless her.*

She glanced at Demophon's crib. Empty. Her breath caught in her throat as a gurgle came from near the hearth. Metaneira stood slowly, her bare feet padding across the freezing stone floor. A loud hiss from the flames stopped her for a moment and lit the shadows as a drip of sap from a fresh log flared and fizzled. It calmed. Her heart beat faster. She neared the hearth and the shrouded Doso, who fanned the fire with her breath and drew tendrils of gray smoke from it by the tips of her raised fingers. A golden glow shone just in front of her. Metaneira heard a cooing murmur and peered over the oblivious priestess's shoulder.

"My baby!"

The queen screamed and heaved Doso away from the hearth fire, where she landed hard on her elbows. Demeter spun back as Metaneira dove forward into the fire and gathered the startled infant from the flames. She batted away the embers that clung to the sleeves of her mantle while Demophon wailed.

"Celeus! Celeus! Wake up, Celeus!"

"Quiet! Put him back, you foolish woman!" Demeter rasped, pleading with the hysterical queen. "It's not finished yet!"

"Witch!" Metaneira screamed over her. Demeter watched helplessly as the fire closed back in on itself and dissipated. "She's a witch!"

"Metaneira! What is the meaning of this?!" Celeus threw off his wool blanket and sat up from the divan to see Metaneira drop Demophon into his cradle and furiously grab the old crone's hair. Doso cried out in pain.

"Celeus! She was trying to kill our baby! She's a witch! A servant of Hecate! We must *stone her!*" she said, still gripping a clump of Doso's hair. Triptolemus startled awake and stood up from his bed.

"Let her go!"

Metaneira spun around as Triptolemus slowly advanced on her.

"Mother, let her go. Doso wasn't harming him."

"I know what I saw! And I saw a *witch burning my son!*"

"How dare you say that about her! She's not who you think she is—"

"She's poisoned you, Triptolemus!" Metaneira pointed back at her son, tears stinging her eyes. She roughly wrenched Doso away, the old woman's body splaying across the stone floor.

"Mother, if you could calm yourself long enough to let me explain—"

"No! Stay back! You are under her spell!"

Demeter got up on one elbow and looked Triptolemus in the eye. She was certain now— he knew.

Metaneira spat in Doso's direction and leveled a quivering finger at her. "I curse you, witch! Murderous she-hound of Hades! I curse you with all the fires of Tartarus! I call upon the Queen of Curses, Persephone Praxidike Chthonios, to—"

A blast of heat rolled through the room, nearly knocking everyone off their feet. Doso rose above them to the rafters, her clothes became flame and ash, her naked form shone with blinding golden light and flaming sheaves of barley. A warm wind blew from the altar and wrapped around her. From the empty air, a golden peplos took shape and draped itself around her. Wrinkled skin smoothed and tightened from the worry lines in her forehead to her crooked and callused toes, and color flushed her furious cheeks. Fragile white hair thickened into coppery blonde curls lifted and coiffed around a golden diadem. Her green irises burned with rims of gold.

"Ignorant humans!" Demeter's voice resounded throughout the room. Triptolemus and King Celeus immediately dropped to their knees and bowed their heads low. Metaneira staggered and fell to hers. A red mantle with a gold barley border draped around Demeter's body. "Heedless and stupid! Unable to recognize good fortune from bad! You have made a mistake without remedy."

Metaneira bowed her head and cried, clasping her hands, preparing to be immolated by the goddess and her golden fire. "Forgive me, Demeter Anesidora, Goddess of the Harvest, bringer of many gifts! Holy daughter of Great Mother Rhea, I—"

"Silence!" She alighted on the ground, the air around her still flaming with gold. "Foolish woman, you would cast me out as a witch when I saved your children? Then think to curse me with the very name Hades raped onto my stolen daughter's body?!"

"Please, Great Lady of the Harvest, forgive your humble servant's ignorant words! I could not have known it was you!" Metaneira's pleading grew unintelligible, her tongue thickened by her sobbing.

"I swear by the Styx, Metaneira, I would have made your precious son immortal and young all the days of his life. I was not trying to burn him! Not after you had shown me such kindness." She calmed, the fires around her abating as she watched this woman cry and cower before her, much as she had cried and cowered before Zeus in Nysa the night her Kore was taken. She remembered supplicating uselessly to the god she thought had once loved her; the god who betrayed her and her daughter. "Demophon was too far gone with the fever, otherwise I would never have attempted such. Now there is no way to save him from death."

"Please, no!"

"And yet you force me to find a way," Demeter rasped, pacing the floor, "because I swore an oath to you on the Styx that I would not let Hades have him."

"Great Lady," Celeus said, his voice soft and measured, "just name what it is you want us to do— anything at all— and we'll do it. My sons would be dead right now were it not for your kindness and wisdom. I will do anything I can to repay you."

She stilled and the room calmed. In the background Demeter could hear the baby Demophon bawling in his cradle. She slowly walked to the crib and leaned down, picking the infant up in her arms. "Sh-sh shh… they didn't mean to scare you, *glyko agoraki.*"

"My Lady—" he started again.

"You will refashion your home, the Telesterion, as my temple. Propitiations from the fruitful earth are the only thing that will save your boy," she said without looking up. Demophon started to calm as Demeter bounced him in her arms. "There, there, precious little one…"

"Fruitful earth? B-but how—"

"I will restore fertility to Eleusis. Only to Eleusis. The crops will call your people home from Ephyra, Thebes and Athens." She walked over to trembling Metaneira and knelt down to her, the baby still in cradled in her other arm. Demeter grabbed her roughly by her chin. "Swear yourself to me," she rasped. "Swear to never call on the servants of the One who stole your daughters and mine *ever again.*"

"I swear myself to you and only you, Great Lady," she said, tears still streaming down her face. Demeter put her calmed babe into her arms. "You are wise and merciful."

Let Zeus come to her. If he would not listen, if Aidoneus would not listen, if the other gods would betray her and if lowly tricksters like the sorcerer king of Ephyra would make a mockery of all the deathless ones, then she would restore order. The fertility of the earth was hers. The mortals needed her gifts more than they would ever need thunder and lightning.

You are the mother of the fertile fields. The earth's people will be your children for all eternity.

Let the people of the earth come to her, until all her children cried out to the heavens in one voice to bring her Kore home. Let Zeus hear them. Let her reign as Queen of the Earth and the Harvest start here.

She walked over to Triptolemus, his head still bowed. "Your son, who believed in me." She let a smile lift a corner of her mouth. "I made him immortal this afternoon. His honor is greatest among you, Celeus, and he will show your people all they need to know to restore your kingdom. Rise, Triptolemus."

Triptolemus felt her hand, warm and comforting on his shoulder. He lifted his head to look upon her true form for the first time. She was radiant. Beautiful. Powerful. A Goddess. Just as he'd seen her in his visions, when her glamour would fade in front of him, allowing him to see her for what she was. He rose to his feet and stood next to her unbowed body, only half a head taller than her now. She smelled like sunshine and freshly threshed fields. "How may I serve you?"

"Well, my Prince," she said with a thin smile. "Your priestess was right all those years ago; you are to become a great teacher of men, after all. And your gifts to them will bring back my Kore."

17.

DUSK LIT THE STYX IN A BRILLIANT FIRE OF PURPLE and gold, reflecting them back into the mists that hung over the palace. Hypnos had arrived that afternoon, if the latter part of light in the Underworld could be called that, to wake Merope from the deep sleep that had healed her mind enough to restore her to coherency.

At Persephone's request, he would be returning with his brother this evening— after she had questioned the wife of Sisyphus. Persephone had changed her lightly colored chiton to a burgundy peplos earlier and tied her hair back with a simple matching ribbon. Dressing simply but with the air of a queen, she thought, might give her more of a measure of authority to ask the nymph questions. She lingered on the balcony, listening to Merope shake like a leaf behind her, her breath shuddering. The traumatized nymph quaked as Persephone turned to face her and walk back into the torchlit amethyst room.

Persephone hadn't been someone who would have even been respected, much less feared. She had only ever been Kore— a child woman, living in Demeter's shadow. It was the outside world that was to be feared, a world where venturing from the shelter of Eleusis was forbidden. Now Merope lay in her antechamber, and the emotion that most frequented the nymph's face when she looked at Persephone was terror.

The rescued nymph hadn't stopped shivering since her arrival, and had remained silent since Hypnos had awoken her. Persephone had paced for an hour from her chamber to the amethyst room and back, wondering if her husband knew that their guest had arrived, fearing and anticipating his return and his pronouncements of what should be done.

She sighed. It could wait no longer.

Merope's eyes tracked her as she approached. Her berry lips looked cracked and raw, the only mar on her otherwise flawless olive-complected skin.

"Please…" Merope said quietly as Persephone stood over her. "Please don't send me back, my queen."

Persephone knelt down next to her. The nymph cowered, shrinking further beneath the blanket. She gave Merope a dry, reassuring smile. "I wouldn't dream of sending you to Tartarus again."

The nymph winced from a pain in her side, and Persephone wished that she had poppies to help ease her discomfort. But, she remembered, the nymph before her was dead; and the pain she felt existed only in her mind— in the consciousness of her shade. It would have been far worse without the deep stupor provided by Hypnos when she'd exited Tartarus.

Persephone started. Merope had spoken to her— and all the other shades she had ever encountered were mute to her ears! "Why can I hear you?"

Merope looked up at her, wondering if this was a trick question. "I… I did not drink the waters of the Lethe, my queen. My voice, my memories, are still my own."

The Queen bristled at the idea that a prisoner of Tartarus knew more about how these things worked than she did. Aidoneus could hear the shades. When they had walked to the Styx, he had heard a little girl running across their path and held Persephone back to let her pass before she could even be seen. She shook her head. In the course of her stay, there had only ever been two days worth of meaningful conversation between her and her husband about the workings of his kingdom. One of those days was her ill-fated attempt to run across the River of Forgetfulness.

"How long were you in Tartarus?" Persephone began, silently wondering what she was doing. Who was she to ask these questions anyway, and how would she even know what to ask?

"It's hard to tell. There is no day or night in Tartarus, and every day seems to last… a lifetime. The only light is the glow of Ixion's Wheel. The others said the only way to mark time was the Keres leaving for the world above each year when mortals celebrate Anthesteria."

"Who are these *others*?"

Merope looked at her curiously and swallowed. "The damned."

Persephone kept a mental note to ask her husband about Ixion's Wheel and who the Keres were when she next saw him— if she ever saw him. A month of lifetimes in Tartarus. She stroked the nymph's forehead, brushing back tight curls of hair from her face. "I'm so sorry. You'll never have to suffer through that again."

Merope squinted at her. "Kore?"

Persephone drew her hand back as if from a flame.

"Kore, my lady, is that you?"

Her mouth went dry. "H-how do you know me by that name?"

"We played together in Nysa. You and I, and Leucippe, and Ianthe… We were all so young back then— aeons ago, it seems. Your mother asked us to watch over you, and we would keep Apollo and Hermes away. My sisters were there too; Alcyon and Celaeno…"

She looked down, remembering those innocent days of her adolescence amidst the valleys and groves of the gods. Demeter had surrounded her with nymphs, thinking they would provide ample protection from the Olympian men. And, Persephone realized belatedly, they would warn her mother if Hades ever dared to visit her. There were five or six nymphs with her at any given time, cycling throughout her life, their faces and voices interchangeable. She scarcely remembered their names. "Merope, I'm sorry. I— there were so many of us back then…"

The nymph nodded with a smile. "It's all right; I wasn't there for long. Maybe a decade. I wove flowers into your hair a few times."

One of the Oceanid nymphs— she hadn't figured out which— got with child by Poseidon, and that promptly ended Demeter's experiment in keeping Kore innocent of the ways of the world. Her rotating troupe of nymphs was disbanded to be replaced with Demeter herself, and less frequently Cyane, Demeter's faithful servant before she retired and dissipated into a favorite spring. After that, constant Minthe would watch her when Demeter was called to Olympus. Just a year after the *nymphae* left, Kore had her first flow of moon blood and her mother promptly moved them to Eleusis— the place of her birth.

Persephone continued with a new question. "What happened after you left Nysa?"

"I went back to my mother's home in Thessaly. We lived in a very small village by the sea called Antikera. I watched two of my sisters bear Poseidon's children. Three more attracted the attentions of Zeus and bore his children. I did not want to follow in their footsteps. One day, about twenty years ago, I saw a man riding a horse along the beach near my mother's home. He stopped when he saw me. To me, he was very handsome; not in the usual way, but he was charismatic. Eyes as blue as the Aegean. I ran away from him the first time I saw him, thinking that he would try to force me in the same manner Zeus took my elder sister, Taygete. He called out after me, but I was already gone."

"Go on…" Persephone sat on the divan at Merope's slender feet.

"The next day I saw him again, this time staring out at the sea toward the place Ephyra would one day stand. He asked me for my name and I gave it to him, almost without thinking. I was enraptured. He told me his name—Aeolides, son of Aeolus who was king of all Thessaly. He was gentle to me and gave me a polite nod when I refused his kiss. He came to my mother's house asking after me. Not just to take me as a fleeting companion as the gods would, but to make me his wife. I was overjoyed, needless to say. I knew that I would outlive him— he was only mortal after all— but I didn't care. I'm a nymph; our likely lot is to be loved for the length of an afternoon. With Aeolides, I could be loved for thirty or forty years, if the Fates were kind. I could be happy at least for a time.

"For the first few years, our lives were beautiful. Aeolides traveled south with many of the slaves his father captured in wartime. We built our beautiful city of Ephyra where farmers had once herded pigs. Aeolus fell into disgrace, so my husband renamed himself Sisyphus, King of Ephyra, to distance himself from his father's legacy. Our ports were full of gold and saffron, ebony and date plums, and the tax on them made us wealthy beyond my wildest dreams. It seemed like every week he would give me one marvelous trinket or another. One day, Sisyphus woke me by dangling an emerald over me the size of a ripened fig. And so we continued. I happily gave him sons and remained blissfully ignorant of what he was doing."

"What was he doing?" Persephone asked, enrapt with Merope's story. She suddenly felt embarrassed by her innocent isolation all the aeons of her life— the nymph's tale standing in stark relief with her pastoral, sheltered existence.

"Sisyphus was well learned. He had a keen interest in studying things that were a bit more… esoteric. Scrolls arrived with his guests, and the scrolls remained with him. Later I found out that the guests who brought them didn't leave either— at least, not alive. He aged more slowly than other men, but watched me stay evergreen, and would often comment on that fact. When I finally confronted him about our missing guests, and how he had acquired the Book of Tantalus from one of them, he very carefully said that he was devising a means by which he could live with and love me forever. He said that his methods were necessary— if anyone knew of the library of arcane scrolls he had spent years procuring, it would make us vulnerable. Naturally, I trusted him. To my eternal shame, I trusted him."

"Forgive me," Persephone said, "but what is the Book of Tantalus?"

"It was a set of five clay tablets. Written down by Tantalus himself in the old tongue. They explained his philosophies, and buried within his writings were the directions for creating ambrosia and the rituals that grant immortality— closely guarded secrets that only the six Children of Kronos were supposed to possess. He was once a trusted friend of the Olympians, helped them during the Gigantomachy, but he secretly despised them. He fed them the flesh of his own son and tried to share the secrets of the gods with all mankind. The book my husband had was the last copy in existence. Sisyphus shared some of its secrets with me, assuring me he trusted me implicitly and said that if I loved him, I should likewise trust him in all things. But he didn't love me. He never loved me. I was a means to an end. A nymph consort for a king who wanted to be a god and hold sway over life and death. It wasn't until I realized that he was trying to bring down the gods themselves that I saw him for what he truly was."

Persephone shuddered. "How can a mortal bring down the gods?" she thought out loud.

Your parents are Olympians, Hecate's voice rang in her head, *so you won't ever die, as long as there are mortals who worship you. . .*

"I may have ended up in Tartarus just the same as him for what I was taught— what forbidden knowledge and heresies I came to believe. . ."

"It cannot be as bad as all that."

"Sisyphus taught me one truth that mortals aren't supposed to know— that the gods need mankind far more than mankind need the gods. The cosmos is a paradox. Gods created the mortals, and mortals created the gods."

The Queen of the Underworld was silent.

"Please don't send me to Tartarus for saying that," she said meekly.

Persephone shook her head. "I can't. In some ways, what you say is true. Not for all gods, but those in the world above need the worship of mortals. And if souls were sent to Tartarus simply because of what they *thought,* then surely the Pit would overflow. So please do not worry. I would never hold against you the things you tell me about Sisyphus." Persephone wondered if these things were also true of her and her husband. She contemplated the idea of existing in a world without mortals and knew she would regret her next question. "Which gods did he speak of?"

"All of them. Ephyra is a busy port; its overland waterway straddles the Isthmus. We had traders sailing through with spices from half the world away. Jewelry. Linen. And they brought their stories with them. There are other lands outside Hellas where the gods have other names. Sisyphus taught me that all are one and the same. Before you came here, the Arcadians and Thracians didn't call you Kore. They called you Despoina. In the easternmost islands of Hellas and the lands of Phrygia your name isn't Persephone— it's Perephatta. Beyond Phrygia, in the crescent land of the two rivers, you are called Ereshkigal. And in the desert sands, across the water to the distant south, you are called Nephthys and also Isis. The stories they tell about you are different, but The Lady Beneath the Earth is one and the same. The same divine role; and in the end, the same destiny..."

Persephone blanched. "But I haven't even been here a month..." she said quietly.

"Is it really so strange, when you are already known in Tartarus?" Merope said. "Where their name for you is Praxidike? When your husband Hades Aidoneus Chthonios— Isodetes, Plouton, Euboleus, Polydegmon, second only to Zeus, an immortal with a hundred names— rules the place of his namesake?"

She walked to the portico columns leading out to the terrace and stared into the darkness of Hades... Chthonia... Erebus... her realm... her home. All beyond the balcony was oblivion but for the torches and braziers of the palace reflecting in the still waters of the bottomless river Styx.

"Merope, how did you end up on a pyre?" Persephone said, her voice small and shaking as she tried to change the subject.

"Tyro."

"Who...?" Persephone trailed off, coming back into the soft light of the amethyst room.

"The daughter of Salmoneus; who was Sisyphus's brother. My husband wanted to destroy his brother and expand his kingdom, so he lay with Tyro. Unbeknownst to me, he raped two sons onto her who were prophesied to kill Salmoneus and claim his throne for Sisyphus. She murdered them when they were born, then ended her own life, knowing even as she did it that she would be sent to Tartarus as a kinslayer. My lord husband kept his hands clean because he knew the laws of the gods above— what would incite their wrath and what would not. And he knew that even if Tyro did kill their children, his actions would destroy his brother all the same. After I learned of this, I went to his library. He didn't deserve immortality. He didn't deserve to live another wretched day. I destroyed the Book of Tantalus— the tablets that would render him deathless— before he could finish deciphering them."

"And he burned you for it," Persephone said darkly.

"No. He kept me alive— terrified and alive. He threatened that he would kill our youngest son, Glaucus, if I ever questioned him or went into his library again. For years after I destroyed the tablets, I lived in abject fear. I was forced to obey his every whim, fulfill his every need, was to always appear to the public as his dutiful wife and doting queen, the immortal nymph whose sisters had borne the progeny of the gods. I appeared less with him in public and he isolated me further still— from our guests, our servants—" her voice hitched. "—Our children.

"When statues of him started appearing in the temples in place of Almighty Zeus, I finally understood what he was doing. All his arcane texts, marrying me, then keeping me alive after I betrayed him, his plans had been set in motion long ago. Because he had committed offenses against Zeus himself before he met me, Sisyphus already knew he was bound for Tartarus. He was, he is, terrified of death. If he wasn't able to find a way to make his own soul immortal, he would just use mine instead. Sisyphus wasn't happy just being a king. He wanted to become a god.

"One night he woke up with a great pain in his jaw and thrashed about in bed, howling. The court physician said that the worm had come after one of his teeth and the infection had spread too far to save him. He had that doctor thrown into the sea, and then asked for a second opinion. Our apothecary said that he should make preparations before the illness clouded his mind and told me to leave the room so he could speak to Sisyphus alone. He lived and was appointed the new court physician. At the time, I didn't know why."

The nymph's face contorted in pain and Persephone knelt down once more beside her, stroking her forehead. "I'm sorry I'm forcing you to relive this, Merope. I heard what you screamed out when you were in Tartarus, but you *need* to have courage and tell me. It's the only way Hades and I can make sure justice is done."

An awareness of her husband, foreboding and familiar, filled Persephone as she invoked his name. She didn't know where he was, but knew he was close by. Her heart thudded, wondering what purpose brought him close to her room. She could sense sadness and longing, not so very different from the way she could sense him before their argument. Persephone wondered if the other immortals could perceive their mate as clearly as she could hers.

"Merope?" Persephone said again, turning her attention back to her guest. Tears ran down the nymph's sun-kissed face.

Aidoneus listened to their conversation echoing down the hallway, basking in the sound of his wife's voice and her nearness to him. He leaned his cheek against the stone, knowing that Persephone stood on the other side of it. She had referred to both of them together— not by the name he preferred that she called him, but by the name the deceased nymph would know him best. Persephone was acting as Queen of the Underworld— his counterpart in judging souls.

All day he had struggled with what he could say to her, trying to find anything that would keep her here. If she wanted to return to the world above, he would let her. But Aidoneus couldn't just send her back to Demeter. To do so would rob her of her divine role just as her mother had done over the aeons she kept Persephone ignorant of who she really was. This was her home— her realm— as much as it was his. This was her birthright— her place beside him. And listening to her, he finally understood what he needed to say. Inspiration supplanted the fear that had plagued him for days. Aidon's heart swelled at the idea of her embracing her role, embracing his realm, and the faint chance that she would embrace him again.

Persephone cupped Merope's hand between her own and heard a rustle of wings from the terrace. "You need to tell me what he did to you…"

"He drugged me with black henbane and broke my legs so I couldn't escape or cry out. They built me into a pyre in the center of the *agora,* hidden from the view of all. There were rumors that Sisyphus was near death and he wanted all of Ephyra to witness his supposed resurrection. After that, it was as I told you. We burned— *I burned.* He used all the knowledge he had spent his life gathering to steal my immortality and make it his, then placed a glamour on me to fool the judges. I— I died. I was once immortal and *I died.* The illusion lifted only after I took my place— his place—

in the Pit, but I was only a faceless shadow at that point, like all the shades in Tartarus."

"It's over now," a soft male voice said. "He'll never touch you again."

Persephone turned to look behind her and saw a young man in a black chlamys leaning against one of the portico columns. He bowed his head to Persephone and brushed his silver hair away from his dark eyes as he met her gaze again. In his hand he carried a long stalk ending in a poppy bulb dripping with sap. She stood and greeted him with a quick nod. "Hypnos."

"My queen. How is she?" He folded his silver wings back and stepped forward. "Does she need to sleep again?"

"No!" Merope yelped. "Please no; you'll bring the nightmares back! I don't need to sleep again, I swear!"

"Ah, I don't think you recognize me, lady. Dreams are the domain of my elder brother. I will merely give you peaceful sleep. And don't trouble yourself. I'll talk to Morpheus. Nightmares won't bother you anymore," he said with a smile. "But you know that in the end, only one thing will give you peace."

"What would that be?" Merope said wearily.

"The waters of the Lethe," Aidoneus said quietly from the doorway.

18.

All eyes turned in Hades's direction. The shadow of a beard covered his face and neck, and a few more of his curls than usual had escaped their bonds. The arm left uncovered by his himation tensed visibly when she looked at him.

Persephone paled, slowly rising to her feet as Hypnos nodded to his king. Her heart beat so loudly she could barely hear anything else. Aidoneus's face was unreadable, and the wall she'd built around herself in his absence immediately rose again. Her only other choice was to cower in fear.

Aidoneus watched hopeful surprise fade from his wife's face and resolve into cold solemnity. He tightened his lips. There was so much damage to be undone. "Hypnos, take Merope to one of the rooms downstairs. I need to speak with my queen alone."

"No," Persephone said, then swallowed hard as his eyes widened. She felt needles poking her stomach and her legs going soft underneath her, but willed her voice to remain steady and strong. "Merope needs to recover, Hades. She endured enough when she was wrongfully imprisoned in

Tartarus. I'd at least like to offer my guest the comfort of my antechamber."

She stood tall as Aidoneus took a step closer to her. *The voice of a natural ruler.* He bit the side of his mouth to keep it from twisting into a smile. "Very well…"

The nymph tried to sit up and formally greet the Lord of the Underworld, but grimaced in pain. "Please. Remain where you are," Aidoneus said, crouching down to where she lay. "You are Merope?"

"Yes, my lord."

"I want to offer you my sincerest apologies. I cannot give you back the nine and twenty days you spent in Tartarus. But I come asking for your forgiveness nonetheless, and to offer you a gift."

"Please, my lord, I do not seek your apology," Merope said, lowering her eyes since she could not bow her head to him. She blinked and looked up at Hades. "What gift?"

"I want to offer you what I give to all whom I receive: peace. Morpheus can stave off the nightmares of your mortal life while you sleep, but there is only one way that you will be rid of the suffering you endured in the world above. Allow yourself the privilege of letting go and forgetting."

Persephone listened with her hands clasped in front of her to keep from shaking. His mood and motives were still a mystery to her; his two-word response to her defiance could mean anything. She stood back as Aidoneus tried to reason with the deceased nymph. She knew Aidon as her lover and husband, but here she was seeing Hades the King. It struck Persephone that while nearly all saw him this way, this solemn face he presented was her first glimpse into his divine role. It also saddened her to think that this cold, rational, emotionless part of him might be the only one he would expose to her ever again.

"My lord, please don't make me drink from the Lethe," Merope begged. "I don't want to let go of my name, my voice, my very form. My sisters, my mother—"

His voice was monotone but gentle. "Without it, I cannot let you roam free in Asphodel, nor can I let your soul return some day to the world above. As you are, you are trapped. Why do you cling to your mortality?"

"Because, my lord, there is so much I simply don't *want* to forget. The last twenty years— the span of a lifetime for so many mortals— I would gladly drink the waters to escape. But I was immortal once— one of the Pleiades. I've lived for aeons, my lord. I attended to my lady, the Queen, when she was younger."

Aidoneus glanced back and made eye contact with Persephone. She merely nodded at him. Her heart thudded in her chest as he rose and moved away from the nymph. Persephone could feel the air sparking between her and her husband as he walked to stand beside her. The final scorching minutes of their last encounter played out in her head in inescapable detail, and frissons of longing and fear coursed through her when his hand accidentally brushed her arm. She was certain Aidon felt her shudder.

"If you drink from the Lethe," he said to the nymph, "you won't be utterly obliterated. Part of who you were will *always* remain— the parts that give you the most peace. But the pain will be gone."

"Merope," Persephone said, "What is it that you want? If you will not join the souls in Asphodel, what would you have us do?"

"I don't want to forget everything about Sisyphus until I know that justice has been done."

Persephone looked to Aidoneus. He tilted his head toward her. At least for now, she was able to read his face: he was telling her to do what she willed. Merope continued to resist drinking from the Lethe— was there a way to spare her that fearful loss? She inhaled and sighed a long breath before reaching her decision. "You attended to me in life and served as a companion for me. When you fully recover, I will gladly have you as my maidservant."

The nymph smiled and tears of relief welled in her eyes. "Thank you, my queen."

"And I will understand if you change your mind— *when* you change your mind," Persephone continued. "Because eternity in the Underworld is a long time to hold onto your memories of the world above."

Aidoneus winced as though a needle had been driven through his center, wondering if that was directed at him. He closed his eyes for a moment, out of view from her. He would let Persephone go if she asked. If she wanted to return to the world above, if that was her sincere wish, he was willing to do it for her happiness. Nyx and Hecate be damned. He would still protect her. It didn't take much to imagine himself wearing the Helm of Darkness and visiting the world above to watch over her from afar, much as it would pain him to do so. Hades was certain that fear of his wrath would keep her safe from the appetites of the Olympian gods.

Merope looked to the balcony as a black-winged man carrying a curved sickle alighted and walked in from the terrace. Her breath hitched. Thanatos felt her fear and followed her eyes to the blade in his hand. He leaned down and placed it against the wall. All eyes came to rest on him as he readjusted the pin of his chlamys to sit high on his right shoulder.

"You must be Thanatos." Persephone smiled, noting the resemblance between the brothers.

"I am. And forgive me, my queen," he said falling to one knee, his wings spread low, his head bowed. "My duties in the mortal world delayed me."

Hypnos went to stand next to Thanatos as he straightened, then glared at him. He hated it when his twin was late. Thanatos nodded at his brother with a serious glance that let him know his reasons were genuine this time. *Mostly genuine,* he thought. Eris had been an unforeseen detour.

Persephone found the resemblance uncanny. They were identical but for the opposite coloring of their hair, eyes and wings. Even their subtle mannerisms mimicked one another.

"Thanatos," Merope said, curiously. A smile curled his lips. "*You* are Death? But I remember seeing you the night you reaped me from the fire. You don't look now as you did then."

"To be fair, my lady," Thanatos said, folding his arms across the front of his chlamys and cocking his eyebrow at her, "neither do you."

They smiled at each other in silence. Thanatos admired her curves under the blanket, taking her in from head to toe, leering as one of his wings lifted.

Aidoneus cleared his throat and narrowed his eyes at him.

"What?" he said, wide-eyed, folding the wing back again.

"Nothing," Aidoneus said grimly. "Try to make sure it stays that way."

Thanatos rolled his eyes.

"You are *such* a whore," Hypnos said under his breath as he grinned.

"Oh, you're one to talk." Thanatos said aloud, clicking his teeth together. "What was your plan to find Sisyphus again? Your... *connections* with the stable master or the keeper of the andron? Or was it the cook's nephew?"

"We'll see when we get there," he replied, his grin turning sheepish.

"Thanatos," Persephone said with her arms folded across her chest. She could feel Aidoneus's eyes boring into the back of her head. "I assume you and Hypnos had a chance to form a plan?"

"Well, my queen," he said with an uncharacteristically warm smile, "I think that my brother and I, if my queen will permit it, should stay here and question your honored guest. There are whisperings that Sisyphus can now travel short distances through the ether. If he can, we will need to work fast. Hopefully, we can take him by surprise."

"I need you to bring Sisyphus to judgment. Quickly," Persephone said, stepping toward him. "Without harming any mortals, if at all possible. Find him and bring him before us so he can answer for his crimes against Merope and his sins against my husband."

Aidon swelled with pride and felt a faint flicker of hope— the first he'd felt in days.

"We'll find him, my queen. He's made quite a spectacle of himself already. Our best hope is that he won't even see us coming. Because if he does, he could be halfway to Illyria before we can catch up with him again," Hypnos responded. He leaned down to Merope. "Are you rested enough to answer a few more questions?"

The nymph nodded, still mesmerized by Thanatos as he smiled at her. The three were soon embroiled in a conversation about the palace's hidden passageways.

"Persephone?"

Persephone turned around to face Aidon. His demeanor was taciturn, his lack of expression completely hiding his intent from her. "Yes?"

"May I still speak with you in private?"

She bit her upper lip and glanced back at the double doors leading to her bedroom.

"Not there," he said. *And certainly not with these three on the other side of the door.* No matter how this resolved, he didn't want a spectacle made of it— especially not in front of their new guest. Looking around the antechamber gave him an idea as to where they should go instead. Aidoneus offered her his arm. "Would you care to walk with me?"

Persephone gingerly took it. Both of them nodded to Hypnos and Thanatos as they left the room. She swallowed hard and tried to keep her hand from shaking as it rested in the crook of his elbow. It was the first time she had touched him since her hand connected with the side of his face three days ago. He remained silent. She guessed that he was either as apprehensive about seeing her as she was him, or he was quietly devising an appropriate punishment for her and wanted to have Persephone alone to carry it out. Perhaps he thought she would make a scene. Nothing she could guess was much comfort, and the uncertain silence between them made it worse.

Her eyes were cast down and followed the mosaic tile on the floor to where it ended at the threshold. They stepped through an open doorway and heard the drumming of the falls. A long, open hallway stretching across the cliffside, its columns pristinely carved from the granite itself. Torches flared along its length and Persephone could hear the waterfall on the other side of the palace grow louder. The normally dead air become more lively as they approached the rushing water and the breeze that blew across her face was soothing and reminded her of a cool evening in the world above. But there were no stars here. The darkness beyond the hallway was all encompassing.

"Where are we going?" she said, already knowing the answer. She had felt him approach her room from this hallway many times and guessed that his chambers must be at the other end.

"To the antechamber outside my bedroom." He stopped. "Is that alright with you?"

She paused for a moment, trying to read his inscrutable face in the flickering torchlight.

His eyes darted away from her. "If that's too much to ask right now—"

"No, it's— it would be good to have some privacy," she said. "Can we stay here for a minute? I've seen this hallway from my room, but I've never walked it."

"Of course."

They both leaned against the stone ledge, side by side in silence. He stole a glance at her every so often. The jeweled fibulae he'd given her weren't there neither was her necklace or her girdle. Instead, she wore simple golden pins to hold up her peplos, and had tied it at the waist with a simple sash, both a rich burgundy. No asphodel flowers crowned her head. Instead, she'd braided her hair back and wound it into a chignon with a simple ribbon that matched her dress. Even so plainly adorned, she was the most beautiful creature he'd ever seen. He ran his hand over his rough face and thought about what a frightful vision his sleep-deprived, neglected person must be to her.

Finally Aidon could stand their silence no longer. "I have something I want to show you."

She held her breath and turned to him. Aidoneus withdrew a single pomegranate blossom from the folds of his himation and held it out for her examination. The center was a mass of tiny golden anthers and its petals bloomed in a brilliant shade of red, even in the low light. She gently took it from him and turned it over in her hand, her thumb tracing the edges of each of the six waxy points that lay behind the soft petals. "Is this what I think it is?"

"Yes."

"So they *did* flower." She let a smile spread across her face. For a brief moment, her fear was forgotten. She thought about Aidon holding her in the grove the first time they recognized the trees for what they were.

"And you were right about them," he said, cautiously smiling at her reaction. "We grew pomegranate trees in the Underworld."

"We—" She startled and looked up at him slowly. "Wait; Aidon, we only… We're just dreaming about these, aren't we?"

He stared back at her, his face softening as he shook his head, "No. We didn't *just* dream about them."

"But how…" She said, her stomach fluttering in shock and delight that this was even possible.

"I don't know. No one knows. Not Morpheus, not Hecate— even Lady Nyx had no idea why this happened when I brought you here," he said quietly. He had to ask, to confirm his suspicions. "Do you still see them in your dreams?"

"Infrequently. For only—"

"—an hour at a time or so?"

She paled. "How did you know?"

"Because I've barely been able to stay asleep for that long since—" he looked away from her, not wanting to bring up their fight just yet. He hoped this distraction from *that* inevitable conversation could continue just a bit longer. "When I did sleep, I always dreamed of them."

"This is impossible. I can't grow anything down here, and believe me, I've tried."

He cupped her hand from underneath, holding it and the blossom aloft. "This is proof that you did; that we did. For me to do such a thing on my own is impossible— here *or* in the world above."

"But..." she started, "that's not true. After you came to me in Eleusis, my shrine was covered in asphodel. You left the flowers for me when I awoke."

He smiled. "As much as I would have loved to have done that for you, I wasn't the one who grew them. It was you."

She looked up at him in disbelief.

"Persephone, my intention that night was to introduce myself to you as your betrothed husband. I didn't anticipate, much less plan on, arriving in the dream already embracing you. And from your reaction, I don't think you expected to see me that way either."

That's not necessarily true, she thought, chewing on her lip. Persephone drew her hand away from his and felt heat wash over her from her stomach to her face. "Aidon, I visited a mortal wedding that day in Eleusis. It was the first time I'd ever witnessed... what happens between men and women. That night I had gone to sleep thinking about it, wishing to dream about what it would be like with— with *my* husband."

He fought to suppress a smile. She *had* brought them together intimately. But in truth, he had too, though the desire had been buried in his heart, disconnected from his conscious mind. "When we came together that night, something happened. Something... unexpected and beautiful, honestly— and it carried itself with you when I brought you here as my wife. The pomegranate grove should not be possible. Those trees are alive— well and truly alive, and every other thing growing in the Underworld is not."

"How do you know?"

"Early this morning I went to the grove, and underneath a fallen petal I discovered living soil, new shoots of grasses— things that haven't existed in the Underworld since Chaos formed it. I don't know what to make of it, but—" He turned away from her again and stared out into the darkness.

"I honestly hope to reconcile with you, and maybe we can find those answers together."

His clumsy earnestness finally revealed to her what she had been seeking behind the mask he'd worn all evening. Her fingers tapped on the ledge once more before she leaned away from it and stepped back from him. "Th-that is my hope as well. Maybe it would be wise for us to speak in private?"

Aidon turned and offered his arm once more. "Our destination is… acceptable to you?"

"Well, what could be more private than your own antechamber?" she said quietly as she held the flower in her hand. "I haven't even seen your quarters."

"No," he said with a brief smile. "You haven't."

She placed her arm within his and walked, thinking about the first dream they shared. *When we have each other, it should be in the proper place— in my own bed, after I've claimed you.* His last words to her the night they met suddenly felt like ice in her stomach. Perhaps he was going to assert his rights to her after all. Maybe that was what Aidoneus meant by wanting to reconcile with her. And here she was encouraging him.

He pushed open one side of a heavy ebony double door. The wood surfaces were intricately inlaid with gold in the shape of the great poplar tree that stood at the palace entrance. A stylized meandros of sapphire and lapis lazuli flowed like a river at the base of the door underneath the poplar tree. They walked into the dimly lit room and Aidon closed it behind him. Persephone shuddered, trying to let her eyes adjust as the latch clicked into place. The same elaborate design was inlaid on the other side of the door.

He licked his suddenly dry lips, looking up at the design as he took the Key of Hades off his left hand. Aidon wanted to be alone with her— without the constant throng of voices from Asphodel and Tartarus. He spoke quietly. "I've had a lot of materials to work with over the aeons and created most of the palace myself, but I'm not half the craftsman that Hephaestus is when it comes to shaping metal. He gifted these doors to me a few centuries ago when I—"

"I don't want to have sex with you tonight."

He flinched and stood there for a long moment before he turned to her. "Excuse me?"

"I—" she looked down at her clasped hands, fearing that she was treading on very dangerous ground. "If that's why you originally thought to bring me here. I know you are m-my lord husband, but…"

Idiot! he thought to himself. *Of course she would think that all you wanted to do was bed her. You hauled her straight to your private rooms, for Fate's sake…*

He turned away so she couldn't mistake his annoyance with himself for anger at her. Aidon clinked the heavy rings together, rolling them in his hand before setting them on the ledge next to the door.

"I think I gave you the wrong impression, Persephone. The only thing I wanted tonight was to finally speak with you again. Sex is the furthest thing from my mind, right now." *Liar,* he thought. *When is making love to her ever far from your mind?*

With a flick of his wrist, the torches on the wall flared to life one by one and illuminated the room. She smelled ignited pitch and the faint hint of date plums and olive oil. On the floor of the antechamber, black, blue and white marble formed a mosaic that mapped out the rivers and marshes, the palace, the fields and groves of Chthonia, their names marked in ancient glyphic letters that she didn't recognize.

The borders of the ceiling were low and hewn in white marble, but a central dome swept high overhead in a deep black obsidian. Bits of gold and small polished diamonds studded it here and there, flickering in the torchlight like stars. When she saw the constellations of the Hunter and the Bear, Persephone realized that Aidon had set each one of them in the exact arrangement of the sky in the world above. She peered at it with a mix of wonder and unease. She tried to imagine how long it must have taken to place each diamond star in the obsidian heavens above them, and to perfectly recreate them from memory. Behind a set of sheer indigo curtains, the room opened to an outside terrace where she could hear the falls and feel their cool mist even where she stood. Two ebony divans sat facing each other, covered with soft black sheepskins, their backs draped in fine indigo-dyed linen. Her version of this room was smaller and meant for one, furnished with a single couch, and she gathered that these quarters were not meant for Aidoneus alone.

He stayed quiet as Persephone timidly took in her surroundings. "How can I trust that you didn't bring me to your room for that? For… sex?"

"You can't," he said without even a hint of emotion in his voice. "As you have said, I am full of riddles, and partial truths, and evaded questions, no? I've given you no cause to trust me."

She wasn't expecting that, and looked at him wide eyed. His face remained calm; hers burned at his bold words. Persephone walked into the center of the room and stood near one of the divans, her face the same color as the red flower in her hand. She stared down at it, not wanting to lift her gaze, to answer his indirect accusation, or address her embarrassing one. "Y-you created our rooms rather far apart when you made them. The hallway we walked through was almost as long as the palace."

"That wasn't meant to be your room forever."

"What do you mean?"

"When I built it, my intention was to make sure there was a place in the palace for you to call your own when you came here to be my queen. Somewhere for you to stay as long as you needed until you were ready. That is, until you were comfortable enough to come to me of your own accord. At least that was my plan." He looked at her warily then shook his head. "Obviously, the Fates have never had much use for my plans."

"So, right now, we are in our… yours and my…"

"Yes." She sat down and folded her hands in her lap, carefully holding the blossom so she wouldn't fidget. He remained standing— restraining the urge to pace about. "I didn't take you here to cajole you into staying in this room, either. If we cannot reconcile what happened and fix this tonight, then I'll gladly walk you back. Or you can go alone; whichever pleases you. Even if we do find a way to mend this, and you're still uncomfortable in my presence…"

"How can we even begin to mend this, Aidon?"

"You can start by trusting me," he said. She opened her mouth to speak again, but he held his hand up and silenced her with his next sentence. "Wait. I *know* that you don't trust me; I know *why* you don't trust me. So if my evasiveness has harmed you, harmed us, then please allow me to put an end to it for you. Forever."

"How?"

"Ask me anything."

19.

"ANYTHING?"

"Persephone I promise that— No..." He straightened his shoulders and looked her in the eye. "Persephone, I swear to you on the great River Styx that I, Hades Aidoneus Chthonios, firstborn son of Kronos, will answer plainly and truthfully anything you ask of me from this moment forth."

Persephone raised her eyebrows. "Anything..."

"Yes."

"Why did you abduct me?" she started without preamble.

He knew she must be full of questions, but was taken aback by the suddenness of her asking. When he considered how many questions she must have built up within her all this time, fears started to well up. Aidoneus silenced them. He loved her. He'd sworn an oath to her. He was ready to answer anything for her. "I spoke precipitously when we fought but the reasons I gave for taking you here were the absolute truth. I didn't want to lose you; not when I was... when I was falling for you. If I had arrived too late, or if we hadn't consummated our marriage as soon as I had you with me, then I would have only been able to sit under the shade of your branches and mourn you forever."

She looked down, "So what you told me— what my mother was going to do to keep me with her…?"

"I'm so sorry."

She clenched her jaw and turned away from him. Aidoneus took one step toward her, then drew back. He let Persephone feel her anger and sadness, own it, strengthen from passing through it, and didn't move to comfort her just yet. There would be time enough for that.

"Your mother was coming for you, and I needed to reach you first, before she did something all of us would regret for eternity. Hecate warned me of the danger. She knows everything that transpires within the ether, and when she heard Demeter's wail of grief at losing you, she knew your mother's reason had been overtaken, and Hecate cried out in pain from the shock of it. I'd never seen her respond so acutely to a vision as she did that day. She wrenched me away from you at my grove in Nysa when I wanted so badly to stay— because I had to save you."

She sat silently for a moment and forced the tears back. Could his words be true? Aidoneus had sworn an unbreakable oath on the Styx that he would tell her the truth. It must be true. "Then, are we actually married, Aidon? Or did you just… have me… and later call me your wife?"

"Your father, the King of the Gods, said that I should find you and bring you to my home, that you were already my wife in all but deed. He told me this before I came to you in Eleusis. We were husband and wife by the word of Olympus before I even laid eyes on you."

"Why was there no ceremony?"

He shrugged at her, incredulously. "We're gods. We need no ceremony. To whom would we swear ourselves?"

"But what about Aphrodite and Hephaestus?"

He snorted. "Empty pageantry. And everyone knows how well *that* arrangement has turned out. The Blacksmith is one of the few Olympians I actually respect. But that poor man's been shamed and cuckolded so many times by that wife of his, I fear I'm the only one left who does."

"Is there any ceremony that we *could* have had?"

"I know of none. Zeus came to Hera in the guise of an injured bird and simply claimed her. And as for the traditions of the mortals— you *did* come to my sacred grove with a bridal wreath of laurels in your hair. But I wasn't about to grab you by the wrist and drag you like a sack of grain from your father's *oikos* to my bedroom the way the city folk do." He smiled wryly and paced across the room as he thought. "Those who work the land still respect the old ways, but you and I are not peasants. As for the immortals, there is one… ritual. It's not necessarily a marriage *ceremony,* though. And— it's not for us. At least not right now."

"What is it and why can't we have it, then?"

"It's called the *hieros gamos,*" Aidoneus said. Persephone carefully cradled the pomegranate flower in front of her as he continued. "The great rite of sexual and spiritual union between our kind. It's a creation act that very few have participated in, and even fewer have practiced it for its intended purpose. That first night we all met on Olympus, it was your mother and father's participation in that ritual that created you. I know the *foundations* of the rite, but I've not been made entirely aware of its particulars— something about twin souls, opposites working as one, conjunction and transcendence. Those are Hecate's words, not mine. You'd have to ask her if you wanted to know more. But I do know that for the ritual to work as originally intended, for it to be as transformative is it claims, it requires that we love each other, wholly and completely."

She swallowed and looked away from him again. "Do you love me, Aidoneus?"

"Yes," he said without hesitation.

"Why?"

"I could give you a hundred answers about your beauty, your wit and curiosity, your strength, and any number of other things, Persephone, but the simplest one I have is that you make me feel alive. And as I'm sure you can guess from seeing the realm I've called my home all these aeons… that's not an easy thing to do."

"Do you love me because of the golden arrow?"

"No. I loved you far before that."

"Then why did Eros shoot you with it?"

He bristled. "Zeus told that little *kakodaimonos* to do it. I think your father thought, in his own way, that it would help me court you."

"Had you ever courted another woman?"

"No. I had never sought out nor coupled with a woman before you." He paused, knowing full well that if he withheld anything from her, it could destroy their fragile peace. "There was one who pursued me. But nothing came of it."

Her mouth went dry and she was filled with a strange brew of curiosity and white hot jealousy. Persephone was so confused by her reaction that she barely managed to voice her question. "Who?"

"A nymph of the Acheron from long ago. I spurned her affections. Bluntly. After that no one else dared. I was already bound to you, as far as I was concerned. Taking another would have dishonored and betrayed you."

"That's… I…" Persephone stared at Aidoneus incredulously. "All my life, all I knew was that the gods can't remain faithful to the women they married, let alone are betrothed to. I've never even heard of such a thing."

"Which is probably why Zeus thought it would be a good idea to shoot me," he chortled. "Truthfully, I've wondered what would have happened if he hadn't. I fear I would have been a rather cold husband to you. I often worry that I still am."

"I don't think you are," she said softly, shaking her head. They smiled thinly at each other. She remembered how confidently he had spoken to Merope, and how vulnerable he seemed with her now. She was perhaps the only being in the cosmos to truly know Hades for who he was. "What did the arrow do to you then, if it didn't make you love me?"

"It unlocked something within me— lust, certainly— and also the *capacity* to love, perhaps?" He paused for a moment and thought on this, remembering the revelations that had struck him so profoundly during their fight. "I had already made up my mind to finally take you as my wife. I wanted you with me after I knew you'd reached majority, and spent millennia wondering how I should go about courting you. I didn't know what it was that I felt. I had no way to recognize it until after I caught the arrow. When I did, I felt this… fire… rush through my veins. It smoldered and became an obsession. I thought that seeing you in the safety of the dream world would resolve it. It didn't, and what I felt after I held you bordered on madness. I couldn't think of anything else but having you in my arms again. And that fire burned unabated until I finally joined with you."

She shivered and felt her skin start to prickle. Persephone dropped the pomegranate flower in her lap and brought her hands around her arms reflexively, as though she were trying to warm the rest of her body until it matched the heat burning low in her belly. "I… I almost wish that I had been shot with it. Maybe it would be easier for me to—"

"I wouldn't have wished that sudden insanity on anyone. Least of all you. The golden arrow is a *weapon*. And one that

I thought too potent to risk anyone finding or using, especially down here. It's why I kept it on my person. I consider myself lucky that I saw it coming before it pierced my heart. The potency of the arrow striking true would have driven me to… couple with you immediately."

She blushed at her own thoughts, hoping he didn't notice the heat seeping into every part of her body. Persephone pictured Hades rampant and priapic, out of his mind with need, searching all over Hellas for her and pulling her away from the Eleusinian wedding without a single word. She imagined him carrying her off over his shoulder and laying her down in a field of soft grass and poppies, his lips trailing across every inch of her. Her fingers tensed, as though they were digging into the sinews of his sun-warmed shoulder blades, the cool grass on her back, the breeze fanning their burning skin. Aidoneus cradled her neck with one strong hand, locked her legs around his waist with the other, and made her his— slipping in and out of her in a rhythm as old as time, until narcissus, crocuses and larkspur blossomed all around them. While that would have frightened her unimaginably that day, the fantasy set her aflame and drenched her in liquid heat. Persephone shifted uncomfortably on the divan. It had been three days since he last touched her.

"You said you loved me before you were shot," she said, desperately trying to push those thoughts from her mind. "How long?"

He sighed. "There's no easy way to answer that. I was often and *correctly* referred to as cold and hard-hearted for most of my life. I buried the need to experience love, and with it every other emotion, so I could survive— so *all of us* could survive. And that instinct didn't leave me once my imprisonment and the war were ended. But throughout the aeons it took to accept the lot I received, I would often reflect on who you would one day become— and how very much you would mean to me. I often thought about you. I even… I dreamed about you sometimes. If that was… as close as I could come to feeling love, then…" He trailed off and looked down. He'd swore on the Styx to tell her.

"How long?" she whispered.

"Persephone…" Aidoneus waited, made sure his wife's eyes met his, that he had her full attention before he dared to say it. "Persephone, I have loved you and only you for forty thousand years. And I will love you and only you until the stars are shaken out of the sky."

She took in the full weight of what he said and blinked back tears, wondering how someone who called himself cold and hard-hearted could say that— or feel that. Hades had loved her since she was born. Since before she was born— since the moment she, Persephone, came into existence. "Aidon," her voice finally cracked from her dry throat, "I don't know what I can say to that. I mean, what *can* I say? Compared to how long you've… loved me, I've only known you for the blink of an eye. Do you think me cold?"

"No," he said, pacing away from her and looking at the floor. "Maybe. I can be patient, though. I've waited this long, haven't I?" he said with a pained smile. "With every fiber of my being, I already know what you feel. But I should never have demanded that you voice it; that's for you to decide when you're ready. It was arrogant and presumptuous of me to force it from you. For that, I'm sorry."

"I'm sorry I slapped you; and I'm sorry for the things I said to you in anger," she blurted out in return. Aidon cautiously sat down on the divan across from her and leaned forward.

"Well, I wasn't too happy about you striking me," he said, eyebrows raised, "but I'm quite sure that what I said in the heat of the moment was *unpardonable.* Believe me, for your part you're forgiven."

"No, Aidon, it wasn't… unpardonable. I mean, you *were* repeating my words." She relaxed, her worst fears unfounded and dissolved. She looked down at the pomegranate blossom and nervously picked it up again. "I was so afraid of you after I struck you. That's why I screamed for you to leave."

"Why were you afraid of me?" he said softly.

"Because of how you could have punished me."

"Punish—" He drew back in disgust. "I would never do such a thing. As for the slap and what I said to earn it, I honestly mistook our… ahhh… *way of resolving* our argument for forgiveness. I was caught up in lust, and didn't realize you were still upset at me," he said. Aidon closed his eyes. "I acted like a beast."

"Did… did you enjoy it?" she said meekly.

Gods above, I'm only male, he thought. *Of course I enjoyed it.* "Persephone, I—" Aidoneus pinched the bridge of his nose with his fingers before running his hand back through his hair. "Listen, I'm not going to bend my oath to you any further than this, but could you *please* grant me one favor?"

"Yes?"

"Can you answer that question before I do?" he said, visibly wincing.

"I…" Her cheeks flushed a deep pink and she worried her bottom lip between her teeth. It was all the answer Aidon needed. They shyly looked away from each other, both aflame with the memory of it.

He spoke first. "Obviously not the circumstances, but I enjoyed the passion of it."

Persephone nodded, still avoiding his gaze. "Same for me," she muttered under her breath. "But… I feel like I shouldn't have."

He cleared his throat and folded his hands in front of him. "Well, this is *our* marriage. I'm fairly sure that *we* get to decide what things we should and shouldn't enjoy together."

"That's not how it works, you know."

He looked up at her, confused. "How so?"

"The husband decides the workings of the marriage." She swallowed. "I mean, I was actually surprised that you didn't come to my bed these past three days. You were within your rights to—"

"This is not the world above," he raised his voice pointedly, interrupting her with an irritated scowl, then shook his head. "The scales have been tipped so far out of balance, and my realm deals with the *consequences* of that disparity daily. Females are chattel up there, and it's getting worse every century. I would betray every principle I ever held if I consigned you to that lot," he said.

"My mother, and the rest of the gods, they don't see it your way."

"The Olympians see the souls for a few fleeting years. I spend aeons dealing with their problems when they come here, and trust me, the mortals' lives are a mess."

"I know nothing else, though, and I don't understand why you are so convinced that things should be different."

"Because I'm not like the other gods, Persephone."

"But Aidon, you do realize that I would expect you to say something *exactly* like that to try and win me over?"

He pursed his lips. It was natural for her to mistrust him. "I'll spend all the aeons this world has left proving you otherwise."

"You are not the only god who has tried to win over his wife with lofty promises. The Oceanids told me that when Poseidon courted Amphitrite, she refused him, saying that he couldn't remain faithful to her. He spent *centuries* pursuing her. He said he would swear off all else, and would make her his consort. She eventually relented and married him. But she was a nymph of the sea and after the challenge of winning her was over, he tired of her and moved on. I know I'm not a nymph, but my divine role before I met you was so minor I might as well have been. What is to say that you won't tire of me?"

"Impossible. And to lay your fears to rest, let me assure you Persephone, you occupy no minor position in my life. You are my equal."

She blinked at him, wondering if she'd heard him correctly. "I cannot be your equal, Aidoneus. Three gods rule the cosmos. You, my father, and Poseidon. I hold no significance at all."

"Up there, perhaps. But you are with me, and the ways of the world above do not hold any sway down here. Persephone, everything I can possibly share with you is yours. In your own right, you are a goddess of the earth. But as long as you are with me, you will be queen of everything that lives and moves about, and you will have the greatest honor in the company of the immortals. Hera herself does not have one *iota* of what I wish to share with you."

She looked away from Aidoneus, shaking her head and set the flower beside her on the divan before she bruised its petals any more than she already had.

"Sweet one, I do not want your place here to be ceremonial or merely as my bedmate. I want you to rule *with* me."

"It's just not how it's done..."

"This is how it *was* done. It is the old way— the way things were before my father's tyranny. And we rule a kingdom populated by old gods— far older than the Olympians. But by virtue of us being here, you and I are not Olympians anymore. You were born for this. The Underworld is *our* kingdom. Its rules are whatever *we* say they are, and it needs a Queen that sits as an equal to its King."

She felt her mouth go dry.

"I forget these things sometimes; I let the ways of the world above, the way I spent the first half of my life, influence me too greatly. I should have told you the whole truth the moment I swept you into my chariot. I should have trusted you. You are not a little girl that needs to be sheltered— that much is plain and evident by the strength you possess and the responsibilities you've placed on your shoulders of your own accord. Doubting you, underestimating you, was my gravest mistake."

"So your solution to my… insignificance— and before you say anything, that's honestly what I am compared to you, if you asked anyone in the world above— your solution is to *make* me your equal?"

"I don't have to *make* you anything," he said, taking her hands in his. "What I'm saying, Persephone, is that you already *are* my equal."

She laughed nervously, wondering if he was truly out of his mind, driven to madness by his long years of isolation from the world above. She looked above them at the intricately arranged diamonds overhead.

"Is it really so strange for you to hear? You and I know what *they* said to you." His voice grew low and serious.

She shuddered, remembering the Hundred Handed Ones, the many voices of the one called Kottos calling her full name from the Pit— calling her their queen. She thought about everything Merope had told her. "You really do see me as more than just your consort?"

"Why shouldn't I?" He gingerly ran his thumb across her knuckles, tracing each soft rise and depression, searching Persephone's face as he spoke to see if this small display of affection would be acceptable to her. He would understand if it were not. "Only the Queen of the Underworld could have commanded the Hundred Handed Ones as you did. Only a true ruler of Chthonia could have comforted a misplaced soul. And only Persephone, She Who Destroys the Light, is brave enough to tell Thanatos, Death himself, upon meeting him for the first time, what his orders were and the speed at which he should carry them out for her," he said with a playfully wolfish grin.

"You want me to rule beside you as an equal, even if it means that you must give up—"

"Sweet one, I'm not giving up anything. I have my place and always will. Your place was waiting for you. This realm *needs* a Queen— needs *you* as its Queen. And you, Persephone, have started stepping into your role with very little help on my part and in so much less time than it took me to embrace who I was fated to be. You've accomplished in less than a month what stubbornly took me aeons," he said. Aidon squeezed her hands lightly, his thumbs now winding circles around the base of each of her fingers. "You are not the screaming Kore I pulled into my chariot."

It felt strange to hear that name pass through his lips, and the newness of it sent a thrill through her. Not because she wanted him to call her that, but because she knew he never did and never would. Kore was not who she was anymore. He had seen that from the first. Aidoneus was the only being in existence who didn't see her as a child. His rough thumbs traced the contours of her hands. Here he sat across from her, the Lord of the Underworld, rightful ruler of one third of the cosmos, treating her as his queen— no— as his mate and his equal. In all the time spent growing up and the millennia she walked the earth as the Maiden of the Flowers, she had never embraced her role in the world above with nearly as much passion as she had down here. She was Persephone Praxidike Chthonios. The Queen of the Underworld. And, she thought with a delighted quiver, the Queen of Hades, her husband.

Maiden no more.

Persephone stood up in front of Aidoneus and put her hands on his shoulders. He looked up at her from where he sat, not moving, not even breathing. She could easily read the fear in her husband's face. He thought he'd said something wrong, had touched her too much, that she was getting up to leave, and would never enter this room or his private life again. The fear of losing Persephone forever was written in his eyes and across his forehead, though he was trying so very hard to mask it. And she knew just how to dispel those fears.

Taking a step away from him, she reached behind her back and started untying the sash that girded her waist. Aidoneus didn't believe what he was seeing at first. "Persephone..."

Her heart raced for him, and it didn't stem from any acquiescence or submission to him, nor any seduction. She desired Aidoneus completely and wanted to claim him as hers. He stared up at her, confused. She said nothing and let the girdle fall to the floor.

"Persephone, what are you..."

His breath hitched when she pulled the fibulae away from her shoulders and let the entire length of her peplos fall to her feet. She flung the pins out in either direction, hearing each one bounce across the stone floor on either side of the room. Her husband sat in stunned silence. She looked down at him. His breathing was shallow, his eyes squeezed shut. Persephone stood there, watching as his brow furrowed, his knees shook.

"Aidon..." she whispered, "open your eyes."

This is a test, he thought. *She's testing my restraint... Fates, help me, I've gone too long without her...* Aidoneus tilted his head up before he looked, hoping that what met his gaze would be his wife's face, and not the curve of her hips or, Gods help him, her breasts. It made little difference anyway— her scent enveloped him. He stared directly into her eyes and whispered back to her. "What are you doing?"

"I am your wife, am I not?" she said softly and moved one knee onto the divan beside his hip, then brought up her other leg until she straddled him and settled in his lap.

"You are," his voice ground out, trying desperately to ignore the heat of her body pressing against his stomach. "But—"

She wrapped her arms around his neck and kissed him softly on the lips.

"—Persephone—"

She kissed him again.

"—you said—"

She kissed his neck.

"Persephone, stop! Please…" His voice rose to an anguished peak, his face contorted and unsure. He was still too afraid to look anywhere but at her face.

She pulled back and looked into his eyes, unnerved by the fresh tension in his body and voice. "Yes?"

"What are you doing?" he repeated, his tone tempered but still strained. "You told me *very clearly* that you didn't want to have sex with me tonight. I'm bound to honor that, but… I…"

"My sweet Aidoneus," she said, brushing her hand across his worried forehead. She stroked her fingers over his scalp until they reached the clasp holding back his raven black curls. She pulled it loose and heard it hit the floor twice and roll away. "I don't want to have sex with you."

Frustration licked through him. "Then *why* are you—"

"I want to make love to you." She silenced him, and watched his eyes go wide. "And, and I want to…" Persephone swallowed hard and looked away, embarrassed, before leaning closer to his ear with a fevered whisper. "And I want to fuck you."

He felt lightheaded. Blood rushed from every part of his body to his loins so quickly he might have collapsed if he wasn't already leaning back into the cushion of the divan. That word had never sounded so innocent or full of promise as when she whispered it. His fingers dug and twisted into the fiber of the sheepskin fleece underneath him. He refused to touch her just yet, instead enjoying the return of her soft lips to his, the taste of her tongue as she explored his mouth. Her hands caressed the sides of his face and brushed over the stubble on his cheeks and neck. She threaded her fingers through his hair, tilting his head back. Aidon shrank away from her. "Wait."

Persephone cupped his face in her hands. "My husband… it's alright. In case there was any doubt in your mind, I forgive you for everything you said… everything we did. Do you forgive me?"

"Of course I forgive you. But why now, Persephone? Why are you doing this?"

"Because I can trust you now. Do you want me in your bed tonight?"

"I would be lying if I said 'no'."

"Aidon." She moved to kiss him again, but kissed the bridge of his nose as he leaned away at the last moment. "Aidon, I want this. Please. You are the only person I've ever had in my life who has treated me as anything other than a child. I can see it in your eyes— when you look at me, you see a woman. You love me; you *actually* love me. And not as your bedmate, or your queen consort even, but as your… your… your…"

"Goddess," he finished.

She ran her fingers through his hair. "I would never toy with your heart. But until I truly understand what I feel," she said, her voice cracking, "can I at least *try* to love you the best way I know how? If you don't want this, if this is too much for you…"

He stared into her pleading eyes, then let go of the fleece covering the divan. His hands moved slowly over her thighs, and almost shook when they reached her hips, before finally encircling her waist. Persephone kissed him again, and Aidoneus met her with equal fervor this time, embracing her, his fingers tracing the ridges of her spine. She scraped her fingernails over his scalp and let them tangle at the nape of his neck once more to tilt his head back. She leaned over him as his arms locked around her bare skin and pressed her to his chest. Her lips came away from his and he whispered softly to her. "What way would you have me, my queen?"

She pulled away and looked down at him, his eyes heavily lidded. "In your room—"

"Our room."

"In our room," she said, smiling. "Laying on *our* bed."

She pulled away from him, so he could stand up. He looked down at her and took her hand, bringing it up to his lips and kissing the back of her fingers before leading her to the carved ebony door on the opposite end of his— *their* antechamber.

He pushed open the door and Persephone felt warmth flood out from inside. Unlike her room, or even the soaring vault of his antechamber, the ceiling was lower here— more intimate. It and the walls were embedded with innumerable large chunks of resinous amber, each piece a captured portrait of seeds and ferns, insects and leaves, and other once-living things now preserved forever in time. Their trapped figures danced and flickered in the light of a low fire burning on a raised obsidian hearth in the center of the room. The bedroom smelled of ancient evergreens, cypress, cedars, musk and spices that were all at once masculine and foreign. She shivered, feeling enveloped by aeons of his presence here. The fire consumed no fuel, but Persephone didn't have to ask him how it burned. After the freezing night they spent in Nysa, she would recognize those orange flames anywhere. It was a small piece of the river of fire, the Phlegethon.

His bed lay hidden behind a wide curtain, built into a niche on the opposite wall. She walked across the room as naked as she entered it, feeling her husband's gaze rest heavy on her movements as she reached up to pull back the thick black curtain. She drew in a breath. When she had first awakened in her bed nearly a month ago, it had made her feel small. His was even more grand— an inviting mattress raised up on a dais behind the curtain, a black sea of soft spun wool bed clothes, pillows and fleeces arranged haphazardly. It could have comfortably slept eight. She remembered him talking about how restlessly he slept, and wondered if he had needed the space in case he thrashed about and needed the utter darkness of the curtain to stay asleep.

She also thought about how easily they could get tangled up in these sheets together. A shiver of delight traveled through her as she turned back to see him standing next to the hearth fire, his himation already in a heap at his feet and his hands deftly working to remove his belt.

"It's warm in here," she finally said.

"It was cold without you all these aeons," he returned. The belt fell to the floor. Aidon lifted a sleeve of his tunic over his head and shrugged out the open side, then untied his loincloth to stand naked before her, unmoving. The glow of the fire and the light from the amber walls and ceiling played against the hard contours of his frame, almost making him look kissed by the sun. With his unshaven face and golden skin, she thought he must look very much like the warrior who had loved her even before the Fates consigned him to rule the Underworld. "Does it not please you?"

She was mesmerized by him, her mouth gone dry. "No," she finally said. He smiled, noticing that she visibly lusted for him. "The fire pleases me greatly." She walked over to him and took his rough hands within hers, gently pulling him forward as she walked backward toward the bed.

"Would you like me to lay down?"

"Yes."

"Would you like me to draw the curtain?"

"No."

Aidoneus smiled at her and scooted backward on the bed until his head was propped up against the pillows, then watched the dark silhouette of his wife against the flames, moving toward him, her hands and knees pressing into the mattress as she crawled forward, then rose over him. He didn't touch her, no matter where or how boldly she touched him. Instead, Aidon let her seduce him, still aware of how new and fragile their forgiveness was. With his unmoving limbs splayed out on his bed like this and her shadow cast over him, he thought, he must look like some sort of sacrifice. The idea amused him, then disappeared completely as her hot mouth enveloped his flesh, his body rising and falling to meet her careful ministrations.

"Sweet wife," Aidon finally ground out when he could take no more. "It's been a few days too long… So if your intention tonight was to fuck me," he said hoarsely, "sooner would be better."

Persephone stopped when she heard the word she'd shyly used and looked up at him with a coy grin. She licked the hint of salt from her lips. He shivered at her absence and saw her rise over his body, her thighs splayed over his hips. Aidoneus tilted his head forward. The light of the fire burned vibrant and sanguine, shining through the space where they were about to join.

"Strange," his voice slurred around a ragged breath as he looked back up at her. "To think my plan was to seduce *you* here one day."

"Well, dear husband," she said, lightly drawing him closer to her waiting heat, "you did say the Fates had very little use for your plans."

He laughed, then shuddered and rocked his hips forward as she slowly lowered herself onto him. The light between them disappeared, the fire eclipsed. He closed his eyes in pleasure.

"And maybe that's not a bad thing," she said, her voice deeply affected as she felt him stir inside her. Persephone watched a contemplative smile light up his face as he took in her words.

"I love you," he moaned.

She responded the best way she knew how, by starting her movements slowly and deliberately, drawing his pleasure out of him, taking her pleasure upon him. Aidoneus still kept his limbs spread away from her, his palms gripping the sheets. She quickened her pace, tearing a harsh groan from his throat. Her limbs started to shake; her motions grew fevered and she started to falter.

"Aidon, please…" she cried and whispered. "Please hold me!"

He sat up and caught her in his arms, steadying her, then carried their rhythm himself as she cried out and dug her fingers into his shoulders. The waves rolling through her crashed down on him. He tightened his embrace and violently rocked forward, his ecstatic shout muffled against her breast.

They collapsed, out of breath, and she lay on her back beside him, staring up at the black linen canopy draped over the bed. He held her hand once his senses returned and gazed at her before drawing her back into his arms, their legs tangling together. She placed a hand on his chest and he occupied his with undoing the braid and ribbon that held her chignon in place. Aidoneus wound her locks around his fingers as he gently pulled at them and discarded the ribbon, then massaged her scalp and spread the cool waves of her hair across his shoulder. He closed his eyes blissfully, his mind and body intent on reclaiming the sleep he'd denied himself the past three days.

"Aidon?"

"Yes, my love…"

She tensed for a moment. "This is important to me. You want me to be your queen and your equal, but you know what that means. Where you need to take me."

He opened his eyes again and took a long breath before answering. "Tartarus."

"I need to speak with them, Aidon. I need to know why they call me their queen."

He separated from her embrace and turned to her, watching fear wash over her face, no doubt remembering the forcefulness of his last refusal. He smiled at her, then nodded his head. "Alright. I will."

She relaxed forward and he tilted her chin up until she looked into his eyes.

"But…" he said firmly, "it means that we're getting up at dawn tomorrow, and you will do so with me every day until we go."

"Why?"

"Because I have to prepare you," Aidon answered. He kissed her on the forehead. "I'm not sending you down there defenseless."

Persephone moved closer and kissed him again, feeling Aidon's arms gently wrap around her and his fingers trail over her hips. They languorously tasted and touched each other. It was careful and comforting at first, the fire in their blood building slowly. She felt him quicken.

"At dawn," he said, rolling Persephone onto her back and leaning over her.

"At dawn," she whispered in agreement.

"No matter how late we stay up."

"I take it we're not going to sleep yet?" she said breathlessly.

"No," he said, lying astride of her. "Not yet. Not even close."

Then he was within her. Having denied himself when she rode atop him, he touched and kissed Persephone everywhere he could reach without breaking their intimate contact. When they finally stilled, Aidoneus drew her against him and held her around the waist. He buried himself in the scent of her hair as they both drifted into a deep and peaceful sleep.

Their softness, their heralding purpose, was now ended. Knowing they were needed elsewhere, they fell, resting against the cold earth and one another. Life rose up to greet them. High above, the six-pointed stars they left remembered their hallowed purpose. In a triumphant sign of union and completion as old as the cosmos itself, they drew inward upon themselves and started to grow.

20.

BRONZE AGAINST BRONZE, THEIR SWORDS CLASHED. The echoes rang off the walls of the courtyard atrium. Gray morning mist and the golden poplar tree hung overhead. Aidoneus fought her back until she retreated, panting. They stared intently at each other. He gave her the signal to advance and held his sword aloft, coiling back and light on his feet as she swept her blade at him.

He swung his sword down in a hard arc as he spun aside, knocking the weapon from her hand. It skittered across the cobblestones. Persephone stumbled forward and Aidon swept gracefully around her, capturing her from behind with his arm. He held Persephone by the silver cuirass that bound a short tunic to her body. The edge of his blade sang through the air, stopping a safe distance from her neck. They held there, motionless.

"How did I beat you?"

"I forgot my footing," she said, feeling his chest rise and fall behind her. He relaxed his blade back to his side, but his left arm still bound her to him intimately. She felt his breath against the back of her ear, her hairs standing on end.

"And what was one of the first lessons I taught you a month ago?" he said, his fingers sliding up her neck over the slick sheen of sweat until he felt her pulse fluttering under his touch.

"You're distracting me," she whispered.

"What did I teach you?" he breathed back into her ear, gently nipping at her earlobe.

"That footing is everything," Persephone finally answered.

He broke away from her and her body rocked backward at his absence. She watched him walk over to her sword. Aidoneus picked it up by the blade and tossed it to her. "Again."

Persephone caught the handle and sighed. "We've spent two hours on this today."

"And you're getting better. Again!"

She wrinkled her nose at him.

"You're adorable when you give me that look," he said with a smirk.

She rolled her eyes at him. "Aidon, truly, I'm tired. How long did you practice when you started learning?"

"I trained with Prometheus for ten hours a day, every day, for four years before I ever swung a sword in battle."

"What?!"

"Don't worry, my love— only another war among the gods could force you to learn as I did," he said. Their swordplay in the courtyard was a peacetime dance, a game— basic defensive movements and nothing more. He prayed she would never hear a warrior boast of his courage at dawn, then plead for his life before noon. He prayed she would never see the sun set on a battlefield blackened by crows.

"Could I defend myself in Tartarus?"

"You could defend yourself if we were momentarily separated, or if the Keres don't recognize you."

"What if a shade got loose?"

"The shades in Tartarus aren't chained. Their minds are their prisons; their eternal punishments are their bonds."

"What about one of the Titans?"

"Then we would both be in danger. No matter how many thousands of years I've spent mastering this," he said, flourishing his blade, "it would take all the immortals above and below to stop them."

"Then everything you have taught me, though I'm glad to have learned it, and to have you as my teacher," she said with a shy smile, "is completely futile."

"It's not futile, sweet one. And worry not. The world itself would break apart before the Titans' chains came loose. I'm teaching you to make sure you're not defenseless down there. I held no expectations that you would master this within a month."

"Someday," she said.

"Perhaps," he grinned.

Persephone knew her movements were still clumsy and slow. He'd begun by teaching her to reshape her peplos into armor, and the silver cuirass she'd chosen now hung heavily on her shoulders by its leather straps. She bent over and exhaled, trying to roll her spine as she came up, feeling tension in her arms and the back of her legs. After a month of practicing, she now knew why her husband had such perfectly sculpted calves and thighs.

"Come; one last time for today, Persephone. Afterward I'll show you something."

"Show me what?" she said, rotating her shoulders to stretch out the kinks in her back. Persephone fell into the sidelong stance he'd taught her.

His smirk grew deeper, his eyes echoing the feral look he got when they were in the midst of sparring… and other times. "It's a surprise."

She bit the corner of her lip and smiled, trying to read his face. "I wouldn't call *that* a *surprise* anymore, Aidon. A month ago, yes, but—"

"It's not what you think," he said in mock innocence. "But I certainly won't complain if it turns into that."

She sighed, happily defeated. "Last time?"

"I promise. Come, wife."

Persephone rocked from her heels to the balls of her feet, determined to keep her footing this time. Her legs corded against the straps of her sandals and she advanced. He knocked her sword aside. She sidestepped and ducked backward to avoid his riposte.

"Good!" He called out, returning to his stance.

She circled him this time, locking her eyes to his as she waited for his attack.

"Remember what I told you. Look to the shoulders and the chest to gauge movement; never the eyes. Eyes can lie; sinews do not," he said, pushing forward. She met his sword and pushed it away, knowing that his movements were slowed so she could learn, his true strength held in check so she wouldn't be injured.

"But your shoulders and chest, husband..." she said, stabbing at him, "...tend to distract."

He laughed and parried, locking the hilt of his sword against hers and pushing her away. Persephone rolled back and came up on one knee, blocking his downward swing, the blades scraping together loudly. She wheeled around and swung at him with her riposte. His eyes widened as he retreated from her barrage of swift strokes, blocking one after another, until she accidentally left her left side open to him.

His sword curved over her, its tip angling down toward her shoulder as he stopped his retreat. Neither moved. They stood close enough that the heat of her breath left a trail of mist on his armor, and she could feel him panting hard against the intricate coronet of braids Merope had piled on top of her head that morning.

"How did I beat you this time?"

She smiled up at him, glad that Aidoneus never just let her win and took this as seriously as she did. But he'd forgotten where her sword lay.

"You didn't," she said. "How did *I* beat *you*?"

He raised an eyebrow. "Well, wife, that's a… curious question. Considering that the next move from this sword would be through your neck."

"Indeed, husband," she breathed. "But my blade would have cut into your leg before you had a chance to bring yours down on me."

Aidoneus looked at her quizzically, then lowered his sword and leaned away from her. Sure enough, the flat of her blade lay against the interior of his thigh. If they were mortal, her cut would have sliced tendons and opened veins and collapsed him to the ground before he'd even begun his swing. She'd used her stature to her advantage.

A smile slowly decorated Hades's face. His sword clattered to the ground, and she carefully withdrew hers. He stepped toward her as her blade followed his onto the stone floor. When his hand cupped the nape of her neck, their clothing started to shift, the armor softening around them. By the time his lips met hers, they were once again draped in their familiar spun wool robes. He led her all the way to the courtyard gate. When she felt the cold press of the stone wall at her back and her husband's warm body in front of her, she wished there was no cloth barrier there at all.

"My fierce little warrior wife," he whispered against her lips.

She had to laugh. "Oh, now you're just having fun at my expense! You make it look so easy, you move so slowly to accommodate me and here I am hacking away…"

"How else will you learn?"

"Well, how did you learn? Did someone go easy on you?"

Aidoneus looked away, his mind on remote Thera and his first violent lessons with Prometheus. He scanned the courtyard.

"Aidon?" Persephone said, shaking him out of his memory. He blinked, then focused on her inquisitive face and smiling thinly, trying to remember her question.

"No, sweet one, he never went easy on me," he finally answered. "But those were different times." He smiled at Persephone and trapped her within his arms again, kissing her neck. His head bent lower and he felt her wince. Aidon stepped away from her. "I'm not hurting you, am I?"

She rolled her neck. "No, I'm just sore."

He smiled. "Well, then this might be the perfect time to unveil the surprise I promised you."

Persephone looked at him skeptically as Aidon took her by the hand. They walked through a long hallway level with the palace courtyard, then descended stairs lined with lapis lazuli and aquamarine. Persephone could hear the muffled drumming of the waterfall through the thick wall, along with a persistent echoing drip. The staircase twisted around and grew darker, all light now behind them. Aidoneus held her arm tighter, but she still bumped into him until the stairway ended and they took a few steps forward into utter darkness. This room was warm, the air heavy.

"Ready?"

"I can't see a thing."

"Not yet," Aidon said. She could hear the smile in his voice and feel his lips trailing on her cheek as he searched for her mouth in the dark. Persephone turned to meet him, closing her eyes as he kissed her. He raised his hand and light filtered in from behind her closed eyelids. She caught the sharp scent of pitch igniting.

When he let her go, she opened her eyes, and her lips parted in wonder. A rectangular pool dominated the center of the room, its tranquil surface reflecting the light of sapphires and diamonds that that hung high above in the domed ceiling. The precious stones were set in a tight mosaic, a stunning display of wealth that humbled even their ornate royal bedroom. Persephone smiled, remembering that Aidoneus held dominion over all the riches of the earth—the stones' value in the world above had little meaning here.

The diamonds reflected the light of the torches, diffusing the steamy room with watery light. Blue-gray limestone tiles covered the floor, the fossilized outlines of ancient sea creatures trapped in the stone. Near them sat a raised divan covered in a thick pad of folded wool.

"Why had you never shown this to me before?" she asked.

"Honestly, I'd forgotten it was here until yesterday afternoon."

"For—"she looked at him, shaking her head. "How can you forget about a place like this?!"

"Sweet one, I created *hundreds* of rooms during the millennia I've lived here," he shrugged. "I only keep to a handful of them. I think I made this one sometime… ahh… five thousand years ago, perhaps? I forgot I had."

"I wish you hadn't," she said with a laugh. "This place would have been a wonderful retreat after practice."

"To be fair," he said with a sly grin, "a tour of the palace seldom crosses my mind after practice. Or yours, for that matter."

He folded his arms and watched her blush. The first few times they'd entered the courtyard, their movements had been like a slow, sensual dance. He had held her hand and weapon from behind and angled her slow thrusts, his other palm splayed across her belly to guide her into each new position. On the second day, they couldn't return to their bedroom fast enough. Aidoneus had forgone the stairs and hallways, instead carrying her through the ether to their bedroom and pinning her to the wall. Later he had taken great care with her, soaking a sponge in warm water and sweet scented tallow soap and running it along her limbs, cleansing her body of the sweat from their exertions.

It had become a daily ritual for them. She would lie on their bed languidly and watch him go about his morning routine, roughly scrubbing himself with tallow and pumice and warm water from the basin before taking a short razor and olive oil to his face, keeping his beard meticulously trimmed.

A quick kiss on the cheek snapped Persephone's drifting attention back to the room.

"Do you like it?" he said.

"I love it!" she said. "How deep is the pool?"

"About eight pechys, I think," he said. She was untying her girdle before he got the third word out.

"Perfect!"

She cast her unbound peplos to the floor and ran naked to the water's edge, much to Aidon's amusement. Persephone jumped and tucked her legs against her chest, landing in the center with a mighty splash. He stepped clear of the rebounding water just in time. The pool stilled, the last dark ripple bouncing off the stone edges. The water calmed.

Aidon scanned its murky surface. "Persephone?"

She breached the surface with a happy shriek, and looked up at him through the water falling from her hair. "It's so warm!"

He relaxed, admiring her. "The water's from the falls; the heat's from the Phlegethon."

"Well?" she said, wiping a hand across her face. "What are you waiting for?"

Aidoneus neatly folded her discarded peplos, placing it on the divan. He took his himation off his shoulder and did the same with it. He turned back to her and was met by a wave of water that hit him crisply in the face. He cursed and sputtered, blinking away the rivulets and staring down at the soaked front of his tunic in open-mouthed shock. Persephone doubled over laughing, the joyous sound filling the room, warming him. He wiped the water from his face with a mischievous grin and a low growl. "You'll pay for that."

She treaded water and drew in a halted breath, wondering for a moment if he was serious. Aidon cast the rest of his wet clothing to the floor and walked to the end of the pool farthest from her, his wife's eyes following him all the while. He dove in gracefully, almost silently, to the bottom of the pool, until his shadow was lost in the dark water.

A hand wrapped around her ankle and she yelped. She heard her own voice, broken and muffled by the water rushing over her head. By the time she regained the surface, gasping, he was already in front of her. His hair was slicked back by the water, his smile toothy and mirthful.

She sputtered again. "Was that how you planned to make me pay?"

He laughed. "Oh, certainly not," he said, treading closer toward her. "When I do, you'll know."

She bit her lip and swam away from him. He followed her closely until she was backed up against the opposite end of the pool.

He grinned at her. "Aren't you the experienced little swimmer..."

"I'd better be," Persephone answered as he planted his hands on the pool's edge on either side of her, ensnaring her within his embrace. Before he could move in to kiss her, she disappeared underwater, diving to the bottom. He looked around for her, then heard a small splash and giggling behind him. "After all," she said as he turned to face her, "I grew up with water nymphs."

She drifted toward him and rested her hands on his shoulders, her nose rubbing against his before she kissed him. She pulled his face closer to hers, tasting him, her hands tangling in the coarse waves of his wet hair. Aidon closed his eyes and pictured her swimming in the sunlight, the grass her carpet, the sky her ceiling, the trees her columns, the pools and rivers filled with her laughter. He smiled as he kissed her; he could taste the living world on her lips and wanted more. "Tell me about your life when you were Kore."

She tensed and turned away. He immediately regretted saying it. This conversation might end with him taking her back to Demeter. She looked down, filled with memory, then up at him again, almost perplexed. "What is there to tell?"

Her reaction pained him, but Aidon was relieved that she wasn't upset at him. "Everything," he breathed. "Anything. I want to know all of you."

"I have no idea what to tell you, Aidon. Nothing I say could be as exciting as the life you've lived."

He threw his head back with a short guffaw. "Exciting? Look around you, sweet one. Granted, I enjoyed working upon it, but spending millennia creating hundreds of rooms I never use was hardly *exciting.*"

"You fought a war, you've been the king of this realm for aeons... and..."

"And you're my queen." He leaned forward, giving her a peck on the nose. "And you always were."

"But— the people you met, the things you saw… You knew Prometheus. And Metis. "

He remembered the Titaness; gray eyed Metis, graceful and frighteningly intelligent— now gone forever. When he'd glimpsed Athena out of the corner of his eye at Olympus, he'd almost startled. It was like seeing her mother's ghost.

"What about Prometheus?"

"He was my teacher. Prometheus made me into a man, honestly. Once I was free, all I wanted was blind and bloody vengeance, careless of all else. If I had pursued it without his teaching or Hecate's counsel…"

"Did he still teach you after the war?"

"No; after several years he said I surpassed him, and we fought side by side. Prometheus was my friend, my brother— and one of the very few who would visit me in the Underworld afterward. He even named his daughter Aidos after me. He never understood why I quietly accepted this lot."

"Why did you?"

"Because I abide by *ananke,* the will of the Fates. Not everything I've ever *wanted* has come to fruition, but as I recall you saying," he said with a smile, "that's not a bad thing. *Ananke* has been the guiding principle of my life— as it *should* be with all the deathless ones," he said, narrowing his eyes, slightly. The edge in his voice was not lost on her.

"Did Prometheus not believe that?"

"No, he did. He just thought I deserved more and advocated on my behalf, though I never asked it of him."

"Is that why Zeus took issue with him?"

"It certainly didn't help matters. Prometheus did manage to find *every way possible* to undermine Olympus after the war, especially in defense of the mortals he created."

"So when he was to be punished for giving the humans fire—"

"I supported him." He shook his head. "It was contemptible. They needed fire. Too many were needlessly waiting on the banks of the Styx. When Zeus condemned him, I stood against your father. He wanted to send Prometheus to Tartarus, but I told Zeus that I would set him free."

"He chained him, anyway. My mother sided with Zeus."

He grunted in acknowledgement.

"And Athena defended Prometheus too."

"She did. In retrospect, I should have kept my mouth shut. Zeus never comes down here. Prometheus could have been my honored guest, with no one the wiser. He wouldn't have lacked company; the Underworld is full of old gods."

"See? I told you your life was more exciting than mine ever was."

"The Titanomachy was not as thrilling or heroic as I seem to have led you to believe. There's nothing exciting about killing, Persephone."

"But it was *something*. Your strategies, your plans, a history I had never known."

"My plans…" he snorted. "The Fates were never kind to my plans. I had ten *years* in the sun. You had *aeons*…"

"Why did you never come to the living world in all that time? Didn't you want to see me?"

It was Persephone's turn to wonder whether or not her questions reached too far. Aidon looked away from her, his face turned solemn before his eyes met hers again with a sad smile. "My reasons were twofold, my love. First, I needed to acquaint myself with every facet of Chthonia and truly become its lord. Paying constant visits to the surface would have… impeded that. And second, and most important, it was part of my own bargain with Demeter in order to have you as my wife."

She knit her brow, thinking about what might have been if her mother had approved of their match. Persephone would have known about Aidoneus her whole life— maybe she would have visited him and seen the Land of the Dead she would one day rule with him. She saddened slightly. Maybe it was better this way.

"What do you miss the most about the world above?"

"After ruling here and seeing all the beauty this kingdom has to offer, not much…" For a moment, his eyes wandered upward while he pondered her question. "The stars. The forests. I loved walking through the forests on a moonlit night. Even though it was still, if you listened you could hear everything moving. Living. And sometimes you could hear things dying so that other things might live. I loved the solitude of gathering wood, building a fire to keep the darkness away. The world was so uncertain then. That was the only thing I felt I had any control over."

"I rarely ventured into the forests, and never at night. My mother was worried about satyrs. I mostly kept to the wide-open fields. I liked the smell of the ocean air—"

"So did I."

"—the warmth of sunlight on my shoulders, small lakes as bright as the sapphires you used to decorate this room…"

"Tell me more," he whispered.

"There was a field of barley near Eleusis that had the most beautiful little fiery copper butterflies, but they only drank from thistles, so I would put one or two at the borders of the field and give them a home…" She trailed off and looked at him quizzically. "Aidon, this can't be anything you'd *ever* care about."

"And why not?" He stroked her cheek.

"What about barley fields and butterflies could possibly hold your interest?"

"Everything. I rarely saw them."

"You were in Thessaly and Lacedaemon and on Crete. Surely if we had them in Eleusis..."

"The open fields I knew were... razed. No place held much life once war touched it. And everywhere the war went, so did I." He swam away and circled around her as she backed against the edge of the pool once more. He closed the distance between them. "But you, sweet one, you've only known life..." he said with a kiss, "sunlight," he kissed her again, "innocence..." he said with another.

She laughed. "That last one's not *entirely* true. Of course, I never saw anything until the day you came to me, but I at least knew about how babies are made. I spent my adolescence around nymphs, after all."

For a fleeting moment, he cringed. "Nymphs like Merope?"

"Only briefly. Each was only there for a short time." She looked down. "I had my mother, but I was... I think I was very lonely most of the time."

Aidoneus smiled at her— in loneliness, they had a common companion. He kneaded her shoulders with his fingers and she relaxed back against him, sighing while he deftly worked the knots out of her neck and arms, then taking each of her hands within his and pressing into her palms with his strong thumbs. He drifted behind her, one hand spread across her belly for support, and gently kneaded along her spine from her neck to her tailbone. She hummed in appreciation and fell limp against his encircling arm. Her bottom rhythmically ground against him with each dig of his fingers into her knotted back. Soon he was twitching hotly to life, the muscles of his abdomen tensing. Aidon exhaled harshly and swam to her side, leaning on the edge of the pool, then carefully pulled the wet strands of her braids free. Fumbling with her tresses, he grunted in frustration. Persephone failed to restrain her smile.

"I swear she makes this more complicated every day just to vex me," he muttered while he smoothed out the last bound lock. Her warmth and scent started consuming him.

"And yet you insist on taking it down every day after practice and before we…"

He returned her half smile. "It gives me pleasure— not to mention another part of you to hold on to."

She worried her bottom lip with her teeth as he closed in on her again, his intent clear on his face and in the tension knotting the muscles of his arms. "If it were up to you, my hair would always be unbound, wouldn't it, my lord?"

"My lady, if it were up to me, your hair wouldn't be the only thing going unbound at all times." He gave her a wild grin that left Persephone blushing. He sank under the warm water, still holding her sides.

Persephone held on to the pool's edge as he kissed a quick line down her stomach underwater. She cried out in surprise, then again in pleasure when his tongue rasped against her core. Submerged, he wrapped his arms around her below her hips, tasting her. Her eyes widened and her palms flattened against the limestone as he slowly exhaled, bubbles rippling against her, the sensation taking her breath away. He rose in front of her, breathing hard once he broke the surface.

She questioned him with wordless gasps, her eyes lidded, her head swimming. He grinned back at her, rivulets of water falling down his face. "Now… *there's* your payment for splashing me."

"I… I'll be sure to do so more often."

He quickly lifted her out of the water by her hips and placed her on the edge of the pool. Aidoneus separated her knees with his shoulders, his arms pinioning her legs, his hands gripping her thighs and pulling them apart, his tongue warm.

"Aidon…" she cried, struggling to stay upright and needing to touch him. "Please…"

He ignored her, deciding that she would pardon him for doing so. She grasped his head, attempting to stay upright. Her fingers threaded into his hair, torn between pushing him away and pulling him closer. Finally, Aidoneus removed his lips from Persephone's and he hoisted himself out of the pool to sit beside her. She stared at him, passion wrestling with frustration, her eyes darting down the curved length of his body to the column of his flesh standing rigid and begging to be touched. "Forgive me, sweet one, I didn't *want* to stop," he nuzzled against her neck. "I still don't want to…"

"What do you suggest?"

He stood and offered her his hand. She took it, her whole body trembling, and Aidon meandered with her around the pool, toward the divan on the opposite side. Midway there, Persephone quickly spun and crouched low, his member grasped in her hand. Surprised, Aidon stopped, and she pulled him into her waiting mouth. The soft heat enveloping his cock drew the air from his lungs. His knees faltered, her hands and tongue drawing him deliciously off balance. Aidon grabbed her hair and gently pulled her away so he could stare directly into her eyes. "Perhaps something to both our liking," he rasped. She kept stroking him until he thrust into her clasping fingers.

He tamped the powerful, instinctual desire to bear her down against the floor, to push his knees and her back into the unyielding limestone again and again until both achieved a bruising, shattering release. She read his want easily, his expression set dangerously on edge while she goaded him into taking her. But he did not, and clearly had something else in mind. Curious, Persephone released him and stood with a smirk. He took one look at her and pulled her with him.

When they reached their destination, he roughly brushed their clothes to the floor and sat her down, kissing her as he positioned his leg behind her on the divan. Aidon leaned in and nipped at her neck and breasts while he scooted away from her, and lifted one of her legs. She looked at him inquisitively, but followed his lead. He trailed his lips across her stomach and guided her down next to him until they lay on their sides, facing one another, toward yet opposite on another. She laid her head against the side of his leg, face to face with what she had been so eager to enjoy beside to the pool, tracing her finger up its length. He sighed at her caress and focused on his own prize.

He darted his tongue into her slick folds, lapping up her essence, his head cradled against her thigh. The closeness and intensity made Persephone gasp. It was new, exotic, sublime. And even better, this angle made possible her full descent onto him. He rolled his eyes back and groaned, breaking contact with her momentarily, fearing he would burst as her throat closed around him.

Aidon hadn't wanted to let her fully taste him when she'd first suggested it. He felt it would demean her, but she had insisted, voicing her desire, reminding him that he'd brought her to completion without feeling demeaned. He'd agreed with that, at least. Persephone had quietly coaxed it from him one night, when the light of the full moon shone through the Styx and turned the Underworld silver. They had been on the terrace outside their bedroom, unseen by all. She had pressed herself against his chest with a kiss, leaning him back onto the corner railing, the rush of the falls drumming in his ears. When she'd knelt before him, he'd gripped the stone ledge so hard he thought it would crumble like chalk in his hands. Moonlight pooled in the movements of her hair and lips and fingers, and at the end Aidoneus was certain that his shout had awoken every soul in Asphodel. It was him, his essence distilled, all earth and roots and salt, which she drank eagerly and triumphantly that night.

Persephone sought that taste once more, curled up against him on the couch. Their bodies raced each other, ecstasy building, giving and taking in a symmetry of raw need. She pulled back and sucked at the crown, her hand tightening around his shaft with each stroke. Driving him toward his peak, she felt him breathing hard through his nose, fire licking into her beyond the heat of his mouth. His tongue danced through her folds, briefly descending to spear inside her before spiraling upward when his fingers replaced his tongue. He teased the spongy ridges within her, and closed his lips again, sucking at the little bundle of nerves, the pressure making her writhe uncontrollably. Her moans vibrated along his length, sharpening his pleasure and echoing hers. They hovered together at the precipice.

Lips locked against her flesh, Aidon's arms tensed, cradling her waist and hips, anchoring him against her to keep from thrashing about. His eyes squeezed shut and a punctuated groan burst from his throat, rippling through her core, pushing Persephone to her own ecstatic peak. As she threw her head back and cried out, the last waves of his release landed hot across her neck and cheek. She moaned and swiped a finger over its warm path, drawing his essence back to her mouth.

She felt sticky, blissfully drowsy, replete. Persephone opened her eyes to his lustful admiration as she hungrily licked his seed from her fingers and lips. They relaxed, breathing shallowly, heads pillowed against each other's inner thighs. Aidoneus reached out and took his wife's hand, utterly spent, smiling at her with dark, heavily lidded eyes. "Persephone…"

She looked up and turned white in horror. Persephone scrambled back to cover herself and almost kicked Aidoneus in the head before she screamed. Alarmed, his eyes followed her wide-eyed stare and saw the rim of a golden hat dart in a blur of motion around the corner of the stairwell.

"Apologies, my lord! I had no idea—" the voice rang from the top of the stairs.

"*Hermes!*" Cursing, Hades reached down and grabbed his himation, throwing it around the shoulders of his cowering wife. He held her close and spoke low into her ear. "My love, I'm so sorry, I don't even know what to say. Go now; I'll meet you in our room," he said softly before he snarled in anger. "I will deal with this."

Persephone turned her head up to him, her cheeks still hot. He looked at her gently and contritely once more, then kissed her on top of her head.

"Sweet one—"

"I'm alright," she muttered just above a whisper. Drawing from the Phlegethon, she created a gateway of fire and stepped through, traveling back to their room. Persephone looked back at him as it shut behind her.

His jaw clenched. Aidoneus grabbed his tunic, still wet from when Persephone had playfully splashed him, and wrapped it around his waist. With a sweep of his hand, it dried instantly. Hades sat upright and narrowed his eyes, seething anew when Hermes landed at the bottom of the stairs. The Messenger fell to one knee just outside the doorway.

"Enter," he rumbled.

"My lord, I humbly apologize," he said, taking his golden petasos off his head and holding it in front of him. "You're usually alone when I—"

"Well, in case you hadn't heard, Hermes Psychopompos, I'm married now!" He stood, towering over Hermes.

"Lord Hades, if you forgive my saying so, the entire cosmos knows you're married."

"What's that supposed to mean?" he growled.

"N-nothing," he said, tousling his short brown hair. "My lord, surely you've noticed the number of souls crossing the River is—"

"Yes, I know! Why hasn't Zeus stopped Demeter's foolishness?" Aidoneus grumbled and swiped his belt off the floor. He unwound the tunic from his waist, shaking the black fabric out to put it back on properly. Hermes startled, blinking, then averted his eyes.

"Uncle, please…"

"Do not call me that, boy! I was Lord of the Underworld *ten thousand years* before you were deposited in Maia's womb! And spare me your shamefacedness. I know what you do in your private life…"

"A warning would have been—"

"Like the warning you gave my queen when you disgraced her just now?!" Hades exclaimed, wide-eyed. He snorted sarcastically and reached for his cast-off fibulae, then pinned up one shoulder of his tunic. "I can only hope that my lack of warning will be branded clearly in your memory. Maybe next time you'll remember that before you think to enter a room where I am alone with my wife."

"Aidoneus, I'm sorry, truly. I had no idea that I'd find both of you… here… in the middle of… It doesn't take me but a minute to go through the entire palace, and I usually just fly about until I find you. It's what I did the last time I was here. And the time before that…"

Aidon sighed as he pinned up the other shoulder and tied his belt low on his waist, pulling at the fabric until it draped to his satisfaction. His legs were still bare from just below the knee and he remembered that Persephone had taken his himation with her. His thoughts turned to how he would apologize to his wife. "Just don't barge in on us again, Hermes," he said calmly. "Things are different now."

He nodded, chastened, biting back a smile at how true Hades's words were. The Messenger had come to know Aidoneus better than most Olympians dared— or could, for that matter. When the Lord of the Underworld announced his impending union with Demeter's daughter, Hermes had assumed that the stern and prudish god would merely do the deed once to make his marriage official and that would be the end of it. Hermes had never seen a lick of emotion from Aidoneus in all the aeons he'd known him, and would likewise never have guessed that he would feel so passionately for his bride. He certainly didn't expect to see… he squeezed his eyes shut and shook the image from his head.

"So why hasn't Zeus reigned in Demeter?"

"The… um, the earth isn't his domain," Hermes said weakly. "It doesn't belong to any of the gods. So we—"

"I don't need a lecture on how the cosmos is arranged, thank you. What is being done to fix this?"

"He's sent almost all the others to see her, to beg her to stop. She even turned Iris away."

"Where is she?"

"Eleusis, my lord. They've built a temple to her."

Hades almost laughed. "Demeter freezes and starves the mortals, and they build her a temple. I make sure the dead don't return to haunt the living, and they fear to speak my name." He ran his hand back through his wet hair, thinking about what horrors would befall the earth if he shirked his duties. "Why hasn't Zeus himself gone to her?"

"He's… I…" He swallowed and hushed his voice. "Aidoneus, between you and me, I think that his pride won't let him. He can't honor her wishes, obviously, and so he'd have to beg her to—"

"Damn his pride!" Aidoneus shouted, pacing the floor. "Go tell Zeus that I say he should go to her himself! Let him *remind* Demeter that their daughter isn't some vapid virginal flower nymph. She is the Queen of the Underworld. *My* queen! And if Deme's so intent on forever clinging to one of Zeus's offspring, he can go ahead and beget another one on her while he's at it!"

Hermes chuckled, his hand over his mouth, trying hard to keep quiet.

Aidoneus cocked his head to the side. "Mortals are *dying in droves* because of her. What do you find so amusing?"

"Nothing… It's just hard to imagine. I mean, with *Demeter.*"

Aidon thinned his lips. He'd known them. It wasn't hard for him to imagine. "Besides delivering bad news, what else brings you here? Did you finally accomplish the task I gave you?"

"Oh, yes… that's right…" Hermes said, reaching into his bag. "With all that just happened, and my apologies again—"

"You're forgiven."

"—I'd almost forgotten why I came down here." He handed it to Aidon. "Brontes and Steropes asked me to congratulate you on your marriage, by the way."

* * *

After Hermes left, Aidoneus walked up the twisting stairs and passageways to his antechamber. He paused for a moment outside the ebony doors, took a deep breath, and traced a finger over the gold inlay of a poplar leaf. "Persephone?"

"These are *your* rooms, Aidoneus," she said through the door. "You don't have to ask to come in."

"Our rooms, my love. And under the circumstances—"

"Are you alone?"

"Yes, sweet one. Hermes is likely already back on Olympus by now."

She groaned.

"Persephone?"

"Come in," she mumbled.

Aidon slowly opened the door and shut it silently behind him, one hand held behind his back. She sat with her knees curled up to her chest on the divan, still wrapped in his himation, her toes sticking out from under one edge and her wet hair matted to her back underneath it. He shook his head. "I cannot apologize to you enough—"

"Aidon, it's alright. I'm just... embarrassed."

"I promise you that it will never happen again," he said. "I believe I put the fear of Tartarus into Hermes, and besides a rare visit from Hephaestus, he's the only one who comes down here."

She dropped her face into the folds of his himation again. "Hermes knowing is enough, isn't it?"

"Knowing what?"

"What... what we were *doing* together."

"Are you ashamed of what we enjoy together?" He remembered the fear and shame on her face after the first time he'd carried her to bed. Aidon grew quiet and cast his eyes to the floor. "Are you ashamed of me?"

"No! No, absolutely not! How could I be?" She rested her chin on her knees. "I just... word is going to spread all over Olympus and—"

He chortled and shook his head, "We could have been making love hanging upside down from the rafters, wife, and

I doubt a single one of those licentious louts would care one way or another if they heard of it."

"Perhaps not, but word will still get back to my mother," she said.

"If it makes you feel any better, Demeter has ensconced herself at Eleusis and she's not admitting anyone. I don't think she'll learn of it."

She shook her head. "Why is she still doing this?"

"I don't know, sweet one. But there isn't anything you or I can do about the misfortunes in the world above. Zeus will speak with her directly; find a way to sort her out, and put an end this nonsense. I tasked the Messenger with telling him as much."

"And in the meantime, more will die."

"Everything dies, Persephone. They will come here, their suffering will be ended, and they will be reborn to the world above once this famine ends."

She found cold comfort in this. Persephone looked out to the terrace in the direction of the Styx and the throngs that were now a daily presence on its far shore.

"Before we were so rudely interrupted, I had planned to tell you something." He sat down across from her and placed a silver helm next to him.

She looked at the black horsehair crest, its long tail falling away next to it. Shifting her feet to the floor, she leaned closer. The last time she had seen something like this was when he had pulled her into his chariot. His was cast in gold. Persephone inhaled sharply and looked back up at him.

He gave her a soft smile. "You're ready."

"Ready…" Her eyes widened. "You mean—"

"I wish he had just stayed in the main hall and waited for me, but it's not in Hermes's nature to wait for anything. Two weeks ago, I had him visit the Cyclopes; they owe me a few favors. I asked them to make a replica of my helm for you; Hermes just delivered it."

"But—" Her mouth fell open. "Aidoneus, you *cannot* do this! The three gifts they originally gave were only for—"

"Those who rule the cosmos?" Hades said, stopping her. "I told you that you were my equal, no?"

She reached forward, the himation still wrapped over her shoulders, and ran her fingers through the soft brush of the plume.

"And you will need this for Tartarus."

She looked up at him and sat back. "When are we going?"

"Tomorrow, if you wish it." He picked up the helm and held it out to her. "Go ahead. Put it on."

Persephone touched the cold sides and lifted its weight into her hands. She stared at the faceplate, its eye slits almond shaped. The nose bridge dipped down into a diamond point and the cheeks' flat planes angled forward to let the head move easily from side to side. "I'm surprised you never used your helm to visit me."

"Helm or not, Demeter would have sensed my presence. The original six of us are bound that way," he said, then smiled. "Also, it would have made it very difficult for me to kiss you."

"So how does this work?"

"Just think about being invisible to me— or being invisible to all. Anything more complex would be useless in the heat of battle."

Persephone turned the helm over in her hands and raised it above her head. She lowered it, her scalp and face tingling and electric as they came in contact with its magic. She looked down, expecting to see nothing at all, but saw her hands and the himation wrapped around her. "Aidon, I don't think it works for me. I can still see myself."

"That sounds about right." His gaze fell beyond where she stood, but he still inclined his ear in her direction.

"So you can't see me?"

"Right now? No. But I can hear you." *More so, I can feel you, my love,* he thought.

"So… do I look like a robe hovering in the air?"

Aidon laughed. "No, sweet one. Anything on your person is also invisible. What— did you think I fought the war naked?"

He heard her titter at that. "Now there's a thought."

Aidoneus smiled in the direction of her voice, then opened his eyes wide as his himation suddenly appeared and flew away in front of him before settling in a heap on the floor. He listened carefully and heard her breathing lightly against the silver faceplate as she came closer. The touch of a warm thigh settled on one side of him, and a soft hand gripped his shoulder. She sank gently into his lap, her stomach pressed against his tunic, her warmth surrounding him. His breath caught as she lifted the helm off her head, her breasts appearing and filling his vision. Aidoneus looked up at her.

"You're right," she said, setting it aside. "It would be hard to kiss you wearing that."

Aidoneus met Persephone's lips, her fingers raking through his damp hair. As his arms wrapped around her waist, he silently wondered what in the name of the Fates he'd ever done to deserve her.

21.

"AS THE BASKET COMES, GREET IT YOU WOMEN, AND say 'Demeter, greatly hail. Lady of much bounty, of many measures of corn.'" Triptolemus held the large bread-basket aloft before the assembly.

"Demeter, greatly hail!" The women cried out and fell to their knees. "Lady of much bounty! Of many measures of corn!"

They pulled their indigo veils over their hair to mourn the lost Maiden, then rose in lines to receive their daily bread. The room was warm, almost stifling from the hundreds of milling bodies and the crackling iron braziers lining the walls. The air hung thick with rare frankincense and common pennyroyal. The dark-robed Mother sat where her altar once stood in the Telesterion, a great oak throne on a nine-stepped dais constructed by the first Eleusinians returning from Athens. Demeter looked serenely out over the assembled women and back to Triptolemus, who descended the steps in front of her. The women formed a line and bowed in front of the Queen of the Earth. Each lay a sheaf of wheat, millet, or barley at her feet, murmuring quietly 'Bless you, holy mother' with their eyes cast down. Triptolemus gave each of the congregation a piece of flatbread from the basket before they returned to their rows.

Demeter wore indigo, the borders of her chiton and himation framed in a gold meandros of wheat. A dark linen veil covered her hair, draped from her golden diadem, and her long robes pooled at her feet, covering the first few steps of the dais. The baby Demophon slept peacefully, cradled in Demeter's arms. Metaneira, now the Lady of the Harvest's high priestess, stood on her left holding a great golden cup filled with *kykeon.* Celeus stood on her right, the hierophant *archon basileus* of Eleusis— king no more, though he still wore his circlet crown. He swung a heavy bronze censer between the worshippers and Demeter, the perfumed smoke rising like a screen.

Before the women broke the bread, Demeter stood before them, young and old, rich and poor, slave and freeborn, from Attica and Peloponnesus, Thrace and Illyria. "You maidens and mothers," she called out to them, "You have traveled far and stand all of you together. Equal. Loved and cherished. My children of the earth."

"The children of the earth give thanks for your mercy," they responded. Demeter sat back down and handed Demophon to Celeus, who exited through the halls to put his son back in his crib. Not long after his mother had interrupted the rites that would grant him immortality, the babe grew sickly again and Demeter had worried that he would be lost, her oath to Celeus and Metaneira broken. But rumors swirled throughout Hellas that the Lady of the Harvest and her bountiful crops had returned. The people came back to Eleusis and as they did, the infant's health began to improve. He even started to smile, his eyes twinkling pale blue gray, his cheeks and limbs soft and fat, flushed with vitality. The infant's every happy gurgle made her heart ache.

Her memories of little Kore were stirred every time she heard Demophon cooing and saw him staring up at her with his wide, trusting eyes, the shade of his irises so close to that of her daughter's. Though she wanted to, Demeter could not make the babe immortal as she had done for Triptolemus. The last of her ambrosia was gone. The means to create more were there, supplied by the prayers and offerings of the Eleusinians. But Demeter knew that the final process to create ambrosia, distilling it through the water of the Styx, was ultimately cut off from her. Perhaps permanently. She didn't dare go to the shores of the Underworld and risk facing her daughter's captor or any of his servants.

"By this sacrament, I am your Mother. You hold in your hands the fruitful bounty of the earth. Go out into the world, you maidens and mothers. And as you give this bread to your elders, to your menfolk, to your children, pray only for the return of my Kore from the halls of the Unseen One."

"Of Demeter, of corn-rich Eleusis, and of the violet-garlanded Kore we sing!" the women said in response, and broke the bread in half as a promise to share it with the masses that had made the pilgrimage to Eleusis.

A heavily-veiled girl rang a *koudounia* at the back of the room, its copper chimes signaling the women to leave. The indigo throngs slowly moved toward the doors. Metaneira drew her himation over her head and greeted each of the women with a sip from the blessed cup of *kykeon* as they exited, then followed after them, leaving Demeter alone. The room felt colder, and Demeter's slightest movement echoed through the lonely hall. She looked around for Triptolemus, then remembered that he had gone into the greenhouse to meet with his two new students, Diocles and Eumolpus.

No matter how many people she surrounded herself with, no matter how many praises and prayers, heartfelt thanks and supplications she received, she was still without her Kore. Her poor trapped Kore. She must be scared, alone, surrounded by the frightful House of Nyx if she were allowed to meet anyone at all. Demeter knew Aidoneus— his selfishness, his inexorability, his violence. He had most likely locked Kore away, greedily isolating her from anyone's eyes. She wondered how desperately her daughter must have searched for a way out, how many times Kore must have injured herself trying to escape him.

Her throat started to tighten, remembering the asphodel growing in Kore's sacred shrine the morning before Hades stole her. Aidoneus had come to her daughter, had seen her sleeping there peaceful and innocent. He'd touched her that night and she'd let him— Demeter knew it. The defiance in Kore's gait, the shame and guilt of discovery on her face that morning had said it all. It was the same flushed look she'd had on her face when she was young, and imperious Hecate had questioned her, arms crossed, about the evening she stolen away to Crete to be kissed and caressed by Zeus, two years before their *hieros gamos* on Olympus. He had used all manner of tender words and heated touch to persuade Demeter, but ultimately respected her wishes to remain a virgin that night. Demeter had no such assurances about Hades.

He had sweetly tempted Kore, lured and seduced her to convince Demeter that her daughter had given consent. With the asphodel he'd planted to mark the place where they'd lain, Aidoneus had made it clear to Demeter what he wanted, what he would have, what he would take. He couldn't have left Kore alone and unspoiled this whole time. She thought about the great tear in the earth, the breached and ruined grove in Nysa where his chariot had sprung forth to abduct her Kore. Hot tears stung her eyes. When she pictured Hades dragging her to his bed and pinning her struggling, crying daughter under his body, they blurred her vision. When Demeter imagined her taken unwillingly, screaming in pain as the dark god moved upon her without pity or remorse to turn Kore into Persephone, her tears finally spilled over.

He would have broken her spirit by now, just as surely as he would have ruined her innocence. Demeter cupped her hand to her mouth to muffle her crying and drew the veil down to hide her face. No one should hear her. Her throat made hitching, choking noises around wrenching shudders that refused to go away no matter how much she willed herself to do so. Kore no more. The cold wind howled outside, the foundations of the Telesterion shuddering, its wooden rafters moaning. The braziers in the hallway guttered for a moment, dimming the room. Aidoneus had made good on the prophetic name that Zeus and the Fates had given to her daughter. She Who Destroys the Light.

The door to the greenhouse behind her throne banged open and she sat upright, pinching her arm, biting her lips together, anything to force herself back to serene silence.

"...And we'll terrace them on the hillside when Kore is returned. The ground will be warm enough," a nasal voice said.

"But remember, Diocles, you cannot fill them with the dry dust you find in the field," Triptolemus answered. "The soil needs to be thoroughly alive. Living soil, living harvests. All the crossing in the world won't help you unless it is. Do you believe I grew wheat like that from any random scoop of dirt?"

"No, my lord."

"But what about the water?" Eumolpus asked.

"From the springs. Grow near them or carry water from there," Triptolemus drifted away in thought for a moment. "We need to devise a way to convey it... build cisterns to store it… Maybe we can build one before we have to focus on the planting when Kore is returned…"

"My lord, I know. But those springs come from… under the ground. Aren't they the domain of—"

"It matters not," Triptolemus interrupted. His voice grew low. "And do *not* mention his name or any epithet he answers to while you are in this sanctuary or in my presence. Thanks to *his* greed, my sisters are gone. To say nothing of our Lady's precious Kore."

"Apologies, my lord," Eumolpus muttered.

One student had been the son of a mighty king from a great city state, the other the spawn of a nymph. Both were now leveled from their lofty positions, students of newly immortal Triptolemus, once the humble prince of simple farmers. Diocles and Eumolpus walked around to the front of the throne and spied Demeter. Each immediately fell to one knee. "Queen of the Earth," they said in unison.

Demeter stood slowly, still veiled, the stream of tears hidden. She curtsied to them slowly and walked down the dais in silence, the sheaves scattered at her feet clinging to the base of her robes, strewn behind her as she walked. Demeter entered the greenhouse door they had just exited. The smell of freshly tilled earth greeted her, but barely calmed her tortured mind.

She swished her robes away from the door and closed it behind her, leaning back against it. A loud sob burst out of her throat, and she walked over to a bed of soil. The wheat had been harvested, milled, turned to bread, and now the loam lay thrice plowed, waiting for new seeds to be planted. She sat down and buried her face in her hands, wishing more than anything to escape the echoing loneliness of her own gasping breaths, her wretched tears. How was she supposed to lead these poor people if she couldn't even gain control of her own emotions?

She heard the creak of the door opening and stilled, facing away.

"My lady?"

Demeter lifted the veil over her head and wiped her eyes and nose with the back of her hand, pasting a smile on her face for Triptolemus. "My prince."

The title had no meaning for him anymore, now that he was one of the deathless ones, but she still used it with him. Triptolemus closed the door behind him. "My lady, is something wrong?"

Demeter looked down, her voice wavering. "I'm fine."

"I'm sorry that *he* even came to mention in the temple, my lady. If Eumolpus said anything that upset you—"

"No, my prince, it wasn't him. I already was…"

Triptolemus saw her shudder again and turn her head away. He cautiously took one step forward, then another, finally sitting down beside Demeter on the fresh bed. Cautiously, he reached a hand out toward her shoulder. Before he touched her he drew it back. "Do you wish to be alone?"

She crumpled toward him, her shoulder leaning against his chest, her body shuddering as she cried quietly. She said nothing. He brought his hands up once more, forgoing his usual caution, embracing her. Triptolemus could always see through her disguise. But it had been easier to talk to her when she was Doso. He could at least pretend that she was a gentle crone, a humble wise woman. The barriers of decorum he would have normally kept with her were so much easier to cast aside before. Now here she was, a beautiful goddess, one of the most venerated beings in all creation, weeping softly in his arms. He stayed still for long moments before rocking her slowly in his embrace. She sniffled once, calming down.

He hummed, then started softly singing a lullaby he had heard long ago, or in a fever dream. He couldn't remember. As he reached the next verse, she stiffened and turned to look up at him in astonishment.

"Where did you hear that?" she whispered.

"I—" he thought for a moment. "I've always known it."

She stared into his eyes, not breathing. She had been taught that same lullaby long ago. Aeons ago. By a man who held her just like this— a kind farmer. She'd sung it to Kore throughout her childhood.

"Should I not sing it?"

"No, it's..." Demeter trailed off. It couldn't be. These poor mayfly mortals. Prometheus had created their bodies from the dust of the earth and the blood of the Golden Men— forms that couldn't hold their immortal souls for long. They passed between worlds, from the verdant to the chthonic, taken apart and put back together, lost to oblivion each time they crossed the Lethe. But the obliteration of who they were was never absolute. There were distant memories, ancestral dreams...

Demeter would never know for sure. Names and details were lost forever on the Other Side. It could just have been coincidence— in her despair she was wishing for something familiar, wishing to be comforted. But to hear a song she hadn't heard in aeons, a song taught to her by Iasion, her lover, that she in turn had sung for Kore... Her eyes watered again.

"Forgive me. I won't cause you any further distress. I'll go."

"No, don't!" She leaned again on his chest and cried, her face red, tears streaming down her hot cheeks, finally letting go and sobbing aloud. Grieving. "Triptolemus..."

"Shh... I'm here. I'm here," he whispered, stroking her lovely hair. She was a woman. In this moment, she was just a woman. Demeter. He petted her hair, holding her close. She smelled of wheat and barley, the sun, fresh cut grass. He was struck with an image of holding her and comforting her like this before, but he'd never been this close to her, nor would he ever dare to be so intimate with the goddess of his people. But right now, she was a woman— a soft, vulnerable, disconsolate woman who needed him.

And he was a man.

Triptolemus leaned down and tilted her chin up, stroking her face. He tilted his head and kissed her. She brought her hand up to his neck and returned it. Her lips were so soft and warm, and a fire burst to life within him. But he dared not take it further. She shut her eyes, her breath catching around a sob.

Her little mewling sound made his heart freeze in his chest. He pulled away in fear. "My lady, I'm sorry!"

Triptolemus stood up and backed away from her. Demeter touched her lips, still tingling from his kiss, the first she'd had in aeons. "For what? What's wrong?"

"Forgive me. You're… you're the Lady of the Harvest and I'm only… Gods above, what was I thinking?"

"Please stop calling me 'My Lady'; I asked you before—"

"That was when you were Doso. I have no right to that familiarity. You'll anger at me later for taking these liberties with you."

"Liberties, what—" she shook her head, the corner of her mouth twisting up. "Triptolemus, I'm fully aware of my choices. I enjoyed your kiss; truly. There's no harm, here."

"There is when you're grieved and I'm *comforting* you, my lady. I'm taking advantage of you."

"Please, just call me Deme."

"Deme was my baby sister's name."

"Then Demeter. Call me Demeter."

He took another step away from her. "I have no right…"

"No, no please… come back," she reached out to him.

Triptolemus just shook his head.

"Why not?" she said, knitting her brow.

"Because I have no right to love you!" He swallowed, the words finally out.

She raised her eyebrows at that. "You…?"

"Isn't it obvious? Everything I've ever done…" He thinned his lips. "Even when you were Doso I knew who you were and loved you. I thought Death had come for me, but you were there. You stopped him. And I knew instantly who you really were. I've tried my best to love you from a distance, but…"

Demeter's mouth twitched up at this. She had quietly admired her prince since she arrived, not daring to think that he harbored anything for her other than respect for the wise woman Doso or reverence for the Lady of the Harvest. She secretly looked forward to accidental brushes of skin, or a glance from his bright blue eyes. This past month, Demeter had tried in vain to forget the warmth that flooded through her when she'd touched him. She remembered the hard lines of his body, the slight thickening of his phallus when she had him undress for the rites that gave him immortality. She would never have guessed that he had feelings for her, or that this handsome young man might even want to…

She blushed and looked away.

"I adore you, my la— Demeter. I would never presume, but I cannot help what I feel. And what I feel for you seems to have always been— even before you arrived," he said glancing around them at the greenhouse. "What do you think all this was for? I've had this passion lit in me my whole life. And it feels like a continuation of sorts. A progression. I know I was delirious, but it all seemed so clear when I had the fever. I saw you— us— in my dreams."

Demeter opened her eyes wide and drew closer to him. "What did you see?"

He drew back, wary of her intensity. "N-nothing… they never made any sense."

"They're dreams! They're not supposed to make sense to you." She stood, tilting her head to look up at him. "But I can understand dreams. I'm a goddess, aren't I?" Demeter said, smiling gently to reassure Triptolemus.

He sighed and looked away. "Which is why I shouldn't have kissed you."

"Just tell me," she said softly, running her hand along his cheek. Her heart was beating fast. The first time she'd felt it truly beat in aeons. She had spent so long being a scorned lover, a mother, a protector, a goddess. She'd forgotten how intoxicating it was to be a woman. Not since…

"It was a shield with strange symbols I couldn't read— nothing I've ever seen before. And I saw sparks and a ceramic mould and the shield melted into a plow. I opened a pomegranate with you. You were so very beautiful, just as you are now. I gave you a seed and kissed you. You told me who you really were, and you were afraid to do so— afraid I would hate you. But I didn't and I…"

"Tell me," she whispered.

He looked down, his face reddening. "I made love to you. Many times. One time, we were in the sunlight in an open field and you held my hand and smiled at me. But the sky darkened and everything disappeared. There was a man taking an obol from my hand and asking me to sing for him. Then an endless field of white flowers under gray mist. Someone unseen, wrapped in shadows, asked me many questions about you, about my life, about your Kore, and called me by a name that isn't mine."

Demeter's eyes watered and she breathed in sharply, almost staggering back from him.

Triptolemus looked at her and blinked, fearing he'd said something terrible. "Is something wrong?"

"It's…" a tear rolled down her face again, "It's too complicated to explain. I can't—" She ran her fingers under his jaw and kissed him, and he returned it hesitantly.

Demeter pulled away, her lips thinning. It would happen again. This was infatuation— at best, an echo of who he once was; at worst, only a feeling of obligation to her. She had saved his life and granted him immortality— and Triptolemus now felt that he owed her whatever she wanted. She admonished herself. Here *he* was, worrying about taking advantage of her. She was a Child of Kronos, deathless for millennia, and he had only been immortal for a month. The blink of an eye. And since Triptolemus was one of the deathless ones, he would tire of her eventually, just as Zeus had. Mortals could love for twenty or thirty years if they were lucky. Gods, deathless and free of consequence, for even less time. To expect a being to love another for thousands of years was impossible. She had come to terms with that long ago.

"My prince, you could have your pick of any maiden here."

"I don't want them," he smiled. "And please call me Triptolemus."

"But so many noble families have come to Eleusis. Fathers and brothers have gone to your family without demanding bride prices. They've even offered *dowries* that would make Midas blush."

"Riches mean nothing here, and nothing to me."

"They will again, when my daughter is returned."

"I see none but you."

"I'm *old,* Triptolemus. I was *ancient* as Doso, but even now—"

"Not to me."

"If we were mortal, I would appear ten years your senior. It's been a long time since I looked like a flower in bloom."

He wiped a tear off her face with his thumb. "We're not mortals, Demeter. I know I haven't witnessed the aeons you have, but I'm here to stay. I don't want some girl that just wandered into Eleusis for food."

She drew closer to him, trembling. His thumb traveled across the curve of her bottom lip, still swollen from his kiss.

"I want the most beautiful woman I've ever seen," he threaded his fingers into her hair and pulled her close, slanting his mouth against hers. Demeter melted into him. It had been too long.

Triptolemus held her close and deepened their kiss. To her, he tasted of mild sweetness, like honeyed bread. She was filled with an irrepressible urge to touch his skin again, just as she had when she'd massaged the ambrosia and oil into his limbs. Her fingers pushed his himation off his shoulder and started pulling at the fibulae of his tunic. Triptolemus wrapped his hands around her wrists.

"Demeter…"

She looked up at him.

"Is this what you want?"

"I wouldn't have started this if it wasn't. If it's too s—"

Her words were swallowed up in a kiss. They moved nervously, shaking in delight, in the sacred space he had built to honor her. She felt innocent and unsure with him, and it only took a short time for Demeter to understand that Triptolemus was not untried. He had probably been taken to the home of a *hetaera* by his father when he first became a man, as was tradition among the nobility. By his innate knowledge of her, she guessed that he had done this far more recently than she had. Demeter nearly laughed out loud at that idea. Civilizations had risen and fallen since she was last touched.

Wrapped in the warmth of the room, they slowly removed one piece of draped wool after another, her low-slung girdle, his leather sandals. Their heat outpaced the fires warming the room. Triptolemus spread his himation out on the fresh loam with her in the center, the soft tilled earth cradling their intertwining bodies.

Demeter could forget about Zeus, about Hades, about her grief, about the cold, hungry mortals milling around outside the Telesterion. She remembered when Iasion curled up behind her and kissed her neck, and when Zeus playfully swatted her rump each time she rose from their bed. Neither of them worshipped her in quite the same way as Triptolemus. He traced her ample curves reverently, watching her every reaction as his hands moved over her skin, followed by his lips.

Triptolemus drew it out, unsure if this intimacy would be allowed tomorrow. He wanted to drink her in— prolong this. She might not allow him this close to her ever again. The time finally came when he could hold back no longer. Triptolemus covered her body with his, slipping into her in ardent strokes while her legs and arms tangled around him, holding him closer, urging him onward. Demeter's entire body tightened and shook when his hand came between them, firmly grasping the blonde thatch covering her mound, massaging her with his fingers and bringing her to the edge. He started to lose his rhythm. The jolt that coursed through her as he came with her arched her back and shuddered her entire body. Their locked lips muffled their ecstasy.

Demeter held his trembling, collapsed body to hers, twining her fingers through his damp hair. His breath landed hot on her neck. Triptolemus whispered to her that he loved her and only her, that he would never leave her side. She only nodded, believing him, tears streaking from the corners of her eyes and lost in the tangle of her copper curls.

The thrice plowed field. She'd lost one lover to the jealousy of another on a thrice plowed field.

She wouldn't lose him again.

22.

TYPHOEUS WAS GONE. AIDONEUS RESTED ON THE southern face of Mount Aitne and watched the sunset bathe the shores of Sikelia and the sea beyond in brilliant gold. In this light, the island didn't show the deep scars of their last battle. Beside him sat the sword he'd pushed into the earth. The salt and sea breezes whip past him and he closed his eyes, breathing in the clean air.

The war was finally over. All that was left was the final meeting with Lachesis tomorrow. She was the apportioner of lots, and what each of them drew would divide their father's dominion between them. Poseidon had already told Zeus and Aidoneus that no matter how it went tomorrow, he wanted the seas. His allies were already there. The Oceanids, Tethys, even ancient Thalassa and her children had already sworn their fealty to him. Poseidon was drawing up plans for how he would organize the long-neglected waters and build his kingdom below the waves, and had confided in Aidon that he already knew whom among the nymphs he wished to take as his wife.

"Liberator," he heard a familiar voice behind him.

Aidoneus stood up, then bowed to one knee. "Lady Nyx. I wasn't expecting you above ground."

"It's been a long time since I was able to properly oversee the coming of night in the world above," the goddess said. She was suspended in the air, as

always, her husband's protection and dark essence swirling about her. "Too long."

"The war is over. You're free now, my lady," he said, standing and looking up at her.

"I heard from Hecate that the cosmos will be divided tomorrow. You were wise to suggest it to Zeus. Absolute power is dangerous. Gods have gone mad from it."

"Gods like my father, you mean. . ."

"In ways you mercifully never witnessed, Liberator. Not directly at least."

"I was aware the entire time," he said with a shiver. "We all were."

Now he would never need concern himself with his father again. Kronos was forever locked in Tartarus. Tomorrow, Aidoneus would be granted his birthright. The kingship of the gods, the mastery of the heavens. He would build a new home for the Children of Kronos. Olympus was a good fortress but seemed too lofty, too high above the mortals. Perhaps he would choose an island such as this for the home of the gods— somewhere between the earth, the sea and the sky. The sharp cliff sides of Thera stirred his imagination.

"When I am King, Lady Nyx, the Underworld will be yours to rule once more. I won't allow anyone to take it from you. Lachesis will tell us tomorrow exactly how the lots will be divided, but the sky, the earth and the sea seem likely. That's what Poseidon thinks, at least."

"Do not make assumptions about the nature of the Fates, my lord. My family learned that lesson through hardship."

"I will keep my word to you, regardless. Our victory would have been impossible without you and your children."

"Ruling Chthonia," she said, using her people's name for the Underworld, "was only one of Erebus's and my tasks. Now that my consort has become the darkness itself, we will leave that realm to younger gods. Whoever draws the lot for it will be its Lord."

He smiled thinly. "I received word from Eleusis. The nymph Cyane left the side of her mistress to let me know that my betrothed was born yesterday."

"So we heard. Congratulations, my lord."

"I will not dishonor my oath to Demeter and Zeus. Zeus can do what he will, and he's perfectly suited to draw the lot for the earth." He narrowed his eyes and thought about poor, abandoned Deme. "His… lust for life is great, but his ways are not mine. I'll take no other before my queen."

Nyx smiled, though her next words were solemn. "Do not assume you know more than the Fates, Aidoneus. The more we attempt to control our destiny, the less it bends to our liking." He acknowledged her call to humility with a polite nod. Nyx straightened, her smile spreading across her face. "But there are things destined, and there are things earned. You set my house free, Liberator. For that, I will give you what is yours by right: the Key."

"The what?"

"No matter who draws which lot, I only trust one of the Olympians with the task of forever binding the Titans and demons of the old order to Tartarus. That one is you. The sigil of my house will be remade as yours— the Key of Hades."

Her words made the corner of his mouth twist up. Aidoneus had long been under the impression that Nyx knew more about the will of the Fates than she ever let on. The Weavers were unmoved by the prayers or desires of any god or mortal. But they still lived in Nyx's realm; she must know that the first lot, and with it rulership over all, would go to him. Why else would she give him something of such importance? He knelt again. "You honor me, my lady."

Nyx leaned down weightlessly as if she were swimming through the air. The Goddess of Night placed her palms on his temples, her fingers wrapping around either side of his head. The darkness that was Erebus swirled about her then blocked out the last rays of the sun. He felt a burning cold, a shivering warmth seep into him, and shuddered. Nyx spoke. "And you honor us, Aidoneus…" she said. Beyond her fingers, her reach extended into him like molten fire and twisting vertigo. Aidon's eyes grew wide. He spasmed and gasped before she leaned down to whisper into his ear. "…fated Consort of the Queen."

He jerked forward and the ground rose up to meet him. All went white. His vision went black.

When Aidoneus awoke the sun was rising. He lay prone, his cheek pressed against the cold ground, and the wind whipped across the mountain-side, making him shiver. He opened his eyes. His blade stood where he had left it, its tip buried in the earth beside him. On his left hand sat three rings. The Key. His honor. His reward. Aidoneus smiled. He would be King of the Gods. This sign from Nyx proved it.

Voices began singularly and quietly, but grew in number. 'Pater... Theos... Sotir... Pater... Anax...' they said. He startled at what they called him. God. Savior. Father. King. The mortals spoke through the Key, praying, calling to him. They were quieter than he imagined they would be— soft whispers, one nearly indistinguishable from the other. He concentrated, trying to pick out individual voices above the din. They asked after the families they left behind, asked about when they would go back, asked after things that confused him. Did they fight in the war and were asking for a way home? Some were in pain, asking for forgiveness and cursing their fates, begging for a way out of where they were. Were they trapped? They sounded anguished and angry. Aidoneus shook the individual voices from his conscious mind, but they persisted in the background, growing fainter as he raised his head from where he lay.

Aidon would consult with Hecate later and sort out what all this meant. He had an eternity to figure out what the mortals wanted— forever to interpret their strange prayers. It was his birthright, and they were his responsibility now. The more immediate task at hand was meeting the others on Crete and deciding how everything else was to be divided. He stood slowly and dusted himself off.

"Hades..." his father's voice growled at him.

Aidoneus sat up in bed abruptly, sweat beading on his forehead, his breathing heavy. Persephone laid next him, her eyes blinking open at his disturbance. He crashed back down onto his pillow, shaking, his skin prickling.

"Aidon?"

Her hand came to rest over his drumming heart and she laid her head in the crook of his outstretched arm. Aidoneus looked down at Persephone, disoriented, before pulling her tightly into his arms. He held her close and shut his eyes, his hand trembling and his fingers digging into her shoulder blade. She shivered, both from the caged strength he'd momentarily let slip from his control, and from the distress rolling through him that tightened his embrace.

"What's wrong?"

"Nothing," he said around a gulp of air, then relaxed his grip on her. "Nothing."

"Are you alright?"

"Yes, my love." They lay there for a long moment. She ran her hand over his chest, his heartbeat slowing, his breath lengthening as she did.

"Husband, you don't have to worry about me," she said quietly. "I'll be safe and protected when we're down there."

Aidon wiped the sweat from his brow and leaned on his side, watching a flicker of light from a split in the curtain dance across her curves. He smiled and languidly traced a finger over the path it made on her skin. "I know you will, sweet one."

She sighed and he felt her body rise to meet him when he doubled back with the palm of his hand, his caress intentional and insistent this time. Aidoneus leaned down to kiss Persephone before he moved over her, desperate to lose himself in her comfort. He'd lived here for millennia. Right now, he needed to feel like he was home.

Persephone awoke late, blinking as cool light filtered in through the open bedroom door, mingling with the warmth of the fire. During their training, she'd become accustomed to waking at dawn and was sad to have missed the first light of the Styx cascading in from their terrace. Merope must have seen the bedroom door closed this morning and decided not to disturb them. Persephone heard the rush of the falls outside, and looked around for Aidon, who was crouched in the corner of their room.

She heard him roughly scrubbing at his skin, the pumice turning it as raw as the little half moons her fingernails had dug into his back last night. He must have been up for at least an hour. Aidoneus stood and dropped the stone on the ebony table. He quickly splashed himself with warm water from the basin in front of him before drying off. Aidon exhaled and turned to her with a short smile, then grabbed a small ceramic jar of olive oil and his razor.

"So fastidious," she giggled, lying on her side, her head propped up against a pillow.

"Well, I didn't get much of a chance to do so the first half of my life," he said. Upon being freed from Kronos, his beard hung down past his waist and his hair to the back of his knees, both matted and snarled. He'd looked more like a creature than a man. Disoriented and blind the day he was disgorged, he'd groped around for the first sharp blade he could lay his hands on and dispatched every bit of it. Hecate had found him not long after. He was shivering under the cover of a small outcropping of rocks a day's walk from his father's home, naked, bloody, and too weak to stand on his own. She'd fed him his first real taste of ambrosia, wrapped him in a heavy wool cloak, and led him away from Delphi.

"Doesn't it hurt?"

"What? The razor?"

He saw her reflection in the mirror as she nodded back at him. The corner of his mouth lifted slightly, realizing that as Demeter's sheltered daughter, seeing a man was rare, speaking to one nearly impossible. Her experience with their day-to-day lives was non-existent.

"Not unless I slip, and I haven't in a long time. On the battlefield, I used the edge of a knife and did it without the luxury of a mirror."

"Why? Wouldn't it have been easier to just grow it out?"

"I would've looked too much like my father if I had."

She caught his eye in the mirror looking back at her. The wide scar carved across his back was enough to stop her from teasing him further.

* * *

"Hypnos." With a slight push of his hand, the door cracked open just a little further, swinging loudly on its bronze hinges. Two figures lay sound asleep on the wide cot. "Hypnos!"

"Mmmhuh?"

"Wake up! If we take much longer he'll move on. And this time *you* will get to explain to them why he slipped through our fingers," the winged shadow in the doorway whispered angrily.

Hypnos shifted under the thick layer of bedclothes and fleeces, his form shimmering silver and translucent as it always did in the world above. Next to him laid broad-shouldered Argyros, son of the magistrate of Chios— a hilly island on the far eastern side of the Aegean. The man's thick arm was wrapped over one of Hypnos's folded wings. Thanatos bit his cheek. His conquests in the world above would be so much easier if his shadowy self even remotely resembled his brother's. Fates, he'd be buried in willing women. If he didn't appear as a bony wraith, he could have a lady warm him all night the same way Hypnos slept entangled with this young man. Thanatos thought about that for a moment and grimaced at the idea of having to deal with her the morning after. No, he decided, it was better this way.

"Just give me a moment," Hypnos whispered back and swung his legs over the bed.

"A moment might be all we have. Knowing him." Thanatos heard his brother's bedmate stir and gasp when he saw Death in the pale light of the oil lamp he carried.

"Peace, boy." Thanatos said, "I'm not here for *you.*" As he moved the lamp closer to his face, he concentrated, shifting his form to angelic youth. The beautiful idiot might scream, otherwise, and ruin everything. "Where is he?"

"With the Canaanite woman, I'd imagine. That's what he was going on about over dinner, at least. Something about the moon being right…" Argyros swallowed, then chewed on his lip, glancing from Sleep to Death and back again. "Gods! You two *are* twins."

Death watched Argyros's mouth twist up into a lustful half smile. It was a wonder this guileless youth got Hypnos *this* far. Thanatos looked him over thoroughly. "Tempting, but no. We're here on business."

Hypnos wrapped his himation around his shoulders. Death walked past his brother and grabbed the chains from the corner of the room, each link tightly wound in strips of linen to muffle their sound. That had been done at Aidoneus's suggestion. Quieting the chains, after all, was the way he had crept up on the Tyrant. Thanatos slung their cold weight over his shoulder.

"Well *one of us* is."

Hypnos shook his head at him. "You know, this would be a whole lot easier if you could set aside this aeons-old nonsense and just *talk* to her."

"Why? She has no desire to speak with me."

"Hecate could have helped us *find* him! Or even denied him a path through the ether. Instead we've gone from Ephyra to Crete, Illyria, Libya—"

"Yes, yes. And if you don't hurry, he'll take us all the way to the damned Euphrates!" Death said impatiently. He turned to Argyros. "Take us to the home of the *kedeshah*."

The magistrate's son led them through the streets. The horns of the crescent moon lay on the horizon, shining pale gold and reflecting in the snow. Cold wind from the sea whipped past them as they walked. In the distance, they heard ice floes squeezing a trireme into splinters, its sailless mast groaning and crashing down on the frozen surface of the harbor as the remains of the mighty warship sank into the depths. It had become a daily occurrence on Chios. Thanatos extinguished the lamp in a snowdrift so they could move in perfect darkness. While his eyes adjusted, he let his other senses guide him. On the wind, he heard hushed voices. The scent of frankincense and female wafted from a doorway up ahead. How he loved that combination. He imagined that was what Merope's hair must have smelled like when she lived in the world above.

Argyros motioned them into the courtyard, and then ran back the way they'd come, the cold too much for him. Thanatos suspected that betraying his father's enigmatic guest was too much for him as well. Death didn't blame him—Argyros had good cause to fear this man. Hypnos and Thanatos stood outside. Within, they heard the woman's strange tongue as the *kedeshah's* preparations for the ceremony reached their culmination. She implored her gods to guide the rites between her and her consort, to restore fertility and warmth to the earth. A male voice answered in her own language, his accent perfected by study, his words echoing hers.

"That's the real reason, isn't it?" Hypnos nodded toward the doorway as the priestess grew quiet.

"Why we despise each other? No, it's more complicated than that."

"What Hecate's doing isn't all bad. If our ways ever die out, they might be the only ones left who honor them."

"I'd hardly called what the mortals do 'honoring' our ways. And Mother agrees with *me*, anyway."

"Hecate doesn't care what Mother thinks about her work. And she wouldn't care one way or another about *your* opinions if you could just refrain from fucking the Lampades nymphs for—"

"Well, where's the fun in that, brother? Of course I leave them alone when they're intact, but beyond that I don't hold sacred anything she teaches them. Also, there are very few ways I can get under the white witch's skin," Thanatos said as they walked through the courtyard, "since she's a sworn virgin."

A gold-painted statue of a goddess with perfect waves of hair and the crescent moon crowning her head stood where Hestia's altar would have been if the *kedeshah* were from Hellas. He gazed up at the flawless folds of linen carved to drape over the relief of her perfect marble bust. Throughout Hellas, this goddess was called Aphrodite. But in this aspect, and to the priestess who owned this house, her name was Astarte. Gasps and the rhythmic groaning of the floorboards could be heard from the bedroom upstairs. The ritual coition had begun.

"It doesn't mean that you have to turn the *only one* who could have helped capture him against us!" Hypnos whispered sharply. "If you weren't so busy with your amusements we wouldn't have been wandering the frozen wastes for—"

"Shh," Thanatos quieted him. "It's time."

Thanatos cast a glamour of invisibility over himself. It would have made no difference to the sight of a deathless one— only Hades's helm could do that— but his mortal quarry wouldn't see him until it was too late. Their preoccupation with the rite would aid Hypnos and Thanatos; it was why they chose this night. The *hieros gamos* in progress above them was a pantomime, a play-acting of the divine rite of the gods. Thanatos remembered long ago when he had scoffed at Hecate and her decision to teach the nymphs and mortal priestesses a rite in which she herself could not engage. The words she had shot back were painfully true, intended to wound him, and would have if he hadn't already long passed beyond the point of caring what his mother's strange little student thought about him.

He forgot about the white witch and focused on their current impediment. The ladder leading up to the bedroom above would squeak. Flying in would rustle wings and disturb the air. Their quarry could be gone through the ether before they even caught sight of him. Thanatos listened to the hard push against the floorboards just above their head, and smiled. He glanced back at Hypnos and softly tapped on a rung of the ladder, his finger moving in time with the rhythm of the rutting above them. His brother nodded in agreement. They placed one foot after another in time with the grinding of the boards, the squeak of the rungs masked.

When Thanatos reached the top of the ladder, he bit back an amused laugh at the scene before him and shook his head. The Canaanite priestess lay sprawled beneath her consort, her body covered from head to toe in gold dust. Her eyes were heavily lined with black kohl, the tips of her breasts and her lips stained red with ochre. A golden moon headdress, much like the statue in the courtyard, was precariously perched atop her head. It shook with each rock of her consort's hips into her painted thighs.

If her costume for this farce was garish, her partner's was obscene. The man was likewise dusted in gold but his head was covered with the heavy gold mask of a bull decorated with carved ebony horns. Death imagined that he must look a bit like Asterion, the fearsome creature one of Minos's forebears put in the labyrinthine tunnels underneath Crete. Thanatos had never seen the beast, but had collected his share of mortal souls from the sacrifices made to it. For all the abomination the very existence of Asterion was, it didn't fairly compare to what he witnessed now. Thanatos ground his teeth at the sacred symbol of the Protogenoi drawn into the floor with gold dust and herbs. His grotesque quarry profaned it with every flex of his hips.

Hypnos climbed the last steps next to him and raised his eyebrows at the scene before him before glancing up at his brother. Thanatos tilted his head toward them and motioned Hypnos to join him. Both unwound the chain from around Thanatos's shoulder. They stepped carefully on the floorboards, but the mortals' wild mating was too frenzied now for any rhythm to be necessary. Death felt blood coursing through him in anticipation, as alive as he usually felt when he was with Eris. He wondered as they drew out the long chain if this was how Aidoneus felt when he silently stole upon and garroted the sleeping Tyrant with the Chains of Tartarus. No, he thought. This was different. Kronos had destroyed everything Thanatos had ever cared about—forced his mother and father into exile, ruined and enslaved his family. This pithy mortal that thought himself a god, his attention diverted by the wealth of sensations overtaking his body, was no threat to them.

It was nearly time; they were close. The woman's moans were contrived. Thanatos had had enough women to know that for certain. So many of them were so used to putting on a show that they'd forgotten how to come, or worse, had to ignore their pleasure under the guise of ladylike respectability, lying still as their husbands used them. He took particular delight in helping them remember, or teaching them, before he took them. What little he'd seen of Merope's olive skin flashed through his mind before he shook himself of his distraction and focused again. The priestess's body arched too dramatically. Thanatos wondered if her cries were for the benefit of the man pumping away on top of her or the gods she served, or the neighborhood for that matter. The series of grunts from under the metal mask became ragged and his hips lost their tempo. Hypnos and Thanatos quietly looped another length of chain under and one length around the bull-headed man, careful not to touch him just yet. Hypnos took position on the other side of the pair and waited for Thanatos's signal. He waited. He nodded.

With all their might, they pulled. The chains stretched taut, the brothers straining to secure him in its bonds. They lifted him, uncoupling him from the woman at his moment of climax. His penis was violently pulled out of her, ropes of his seed landing on her gold painted stomach. Her squeals of feigned ecstasy turned to silent confusion as he convulsed against the invisible chain above the *kedeshah's* supine body.

"*Now!*" Thanatos yelled. Linen burned off into flying embers and the binding potency of Tartarus surged through the iron chain. The brothers let go of the ends. Suspended in the air, the links rattled and whipped around the *kedeshah's* consort, ensnaring him. The Canaanite priestess lay on the floor, shielding herself. Her eyes grew wide as the Chains of Tartarus, Hypnos, and Thanatos appeared before her.

She opened her mouth as far as she could, her blood-curdling scream echoing through the room and courtyard below. Hypnos swept his silvery hand through the air to guide the chain around the bull-headed consort. The man's feet lifted off the ground, kicking fruitlessly in the air as it wound around his legs. Thanatos mimicked his brother, then closed his bony fist. The chains responded, binding the consort's arms to his sides. Finally, the loose ends wrapped themselves around a wood beam above his head, suspending him from the rafters.

The *kedeshah* scrambled on her palms and feet, backing up against the wall. A smear of gold was left in her wake; the six-pointed symbol she and her consort had laid in moments before was broken and distorted. When she couldn't retreat any further, she started a new round of piercing screams, the back of her head smacking the wall.

"Will you shut her up?!" Thanatos yelled over his shoulder.

Hypnos brushed his palm over the dripping poppy he kept in the folds of his himation. He walked to the priestess and lightly pushed on her forehead with two sticky fingers. She slumped against the wall and fell to one side, unconscious and unmoving.

"I said 'shut her up', not send her into an opium stupor!"

"What did you expect me to do, Thanatos? Besides—now she won't remember anything beyond getting fucked and passing out."

"Is she still breathing? The last thing I need tonight is to come all the way back here and harvest her shade."

Hypnos walked over to the *kedeshah* and lifted her wrist off the ground.

"If I have to come back to this godsforsaken place, so help me, I'm dragging you back here with me!"

"Quiet!" Hypnos pressed his thumb into her glittering flesh until he felt her pulse. "She's alive."

A loop of the chains smacked the ground behind them as the man struggled and writhed one last time, testing the Chains of Tartarus. Thanatos pulled his sickle from his belt, and walked to within an inch of the bucking golden bullhead. Looking at the dangling man, he smirked, then pushed him with the blunt metal curve until he swung forward and back. His struggles waned.

Thanatos chortled. "Those chains were crafted to bind Titans, you fool."

The bull mask slumped to his chest once he realized, humiliated, that any more struggles were in vain.

"Well," Hypnos smiled, "you almost made this look easy."

"I couldn't have done it without you, brother." Thanatos concentrated and appeared angelic once more, having heard enough screaming for one night. He raised his voice in melodic glee to speak to their prey. "Now— who have we here?"

He pulled off the heavy mask by one of the dark horns and threw it aside, the gold nose of the bull denting in as it hit the floor with a hollow clang and rolled away behind them. Thanatos raised the mortal's chin with the flat edge of his sickle. He was met with fear and fury and eyes as blue as the Aegean.

"Sisyphus, I presume?"

23.

THE FIRST THING PERSEPHONE REALIZED WAS THAT Aidoneus would prefer to avoid the Pit unless duty called him there. From the tension in his face and shoulders all morning, and the way he'd clung to her body last night, she guessed that he hadn't been called there in quite some time. The second thing, and the very clear memory she tried to force from her mind as they made their way to the Phlegethon, was that she was standing on the very spot she had lost her innocence to him.

He wore the same gauntlets and greaves they'd trained in the past month, the same cuirass she'd clung to as they plunged through the bowels of the earth, the same cloak he'd wrapped around her after he pierced her maidenhead. Kore had descended into Hades and burned away with her flimsy chiton. Persephone stood tall in her place, her silver cuirass binding a black peplos to her body. The helm Aidoneus gave her yesterday was raised and pulled back, set on her head like a crown. Her sword was slung across her left hip. Aidoneus wore his on his back in the way he had during the Titanomachy, saying it made for a quieter and quicker draw. He'd spent the last month teaching her the classical stances, and said that he would show her his own variations one day. When she had pressed him to learn his way, he'd smiled at Persephone and told her that she needed to know how to walk before she could learn how to run.

The chariot rocked gently, flying over the vast river lands and marshes of Acheron, then turning to follow the snaking red rivulet of the Cocytus. Not a single one of the shades that lined its shore looked up to watch them pass overhead. His arms were on either side of her, tugging the reins every so often to guide the black steeds— and to keep them from spooking as they neared their destination.

"You're very quiet," he said. Aidon had been silent himself before he said it, and she suspected that he was trying to ease his own trepidation as much as hers. She wondered if their last journey in this chariot played as prominently in his mind as it did in hers.

"Just taking in everything." She looked back at him with a forced smile that she hoped was reassuring. His eyes regarded her softly, though the rest of his countenance remained set in stone, his hair tightly pulled back from his face. His helm rested between her feet. She thought of the crack of his staff when he had hammered it into the center of the courtyard not an hour ago. Persephone had stood next to him as the beasts and chariot sprang out of the crumbling ground with a billow of smoke, so very much like her last day in the sunlight. The girl that was Kore reached upward for the sun even as the chariot descended, knowing that where they were headed she would be even further removed from its warmth. Even the woman that was Persephone shifted back and forth, knowing that the meager light that reached them through the Styx would be absent in Tartarus. She swallowed, imagining the possibility of never escaping, trapping her in crushing darkness, then shook the thought from her head. "Where do the horses live?"

"*Living* might not be the right word. They are creatures of the ether— bound to my will. Each of the Children of Kronos had a chariot during the war. Gifts from Helios and Selene." He smiled playfully, trying to lighten the mood. "Your mother's chariot was drawn by a pair of flying serpents."

Persephone looked back at him in surprised delight. "Really? What happened to them?"

"I wish I knew," he shrugged. The mists started glowing with fire as they got closer, and the smile faded from Aidon's face. "If you wouldn't mind picking up my helm for me…"

Persephone turned to him, watching him smooth back the couple loose curls of his hair that never seemed to obey his comb. He bent down to her height and she slid the Helm of Darkness over his head. Aidoneus straightened and looked down at her, only his bearded chin and mouth visible underneath the golden faceplate.

Hold on!

She froze, remembering the first words Aidoneus had said to her when she saw him— touched him— real and in the flesh, in all his dark glory, his arm closing around her waist and her fists bruising against his armor. It was yesterday; it was an aeon ago. The same hidden face of the Lord of the Underworld looked back at her now. He didn't smile, but brought his hand up and trailed the back of his fingers across her cheek to reassure her, though both knew that there was no comfort where they were going.

Persephone faced forward once more and steeled herself. She saw the great fiery ring of the Phlegethon at last. She'd created a likeness of it each time she traveled through the ether, and woke up every morning in Aidon's arms feeling the steady warmth of the River of Fire emanating from the hearth. The River Phlegethon was new yet familiar, its orange fires licking and swirling above a gyre of molten stone. A vortex of flame from its edges swirled toward the center, covering the entrance to the Pit of Tartarus. The coursers started to snort and pull on their reins, their feet skipping rhythm. Persephone felt her heart beat faster as the chariot angled down, and tried to stay calm so she wouldn't further spook the horses. She felt her husband's arm protectively circle around her waist, holding her fast against him.

"Do you remember Nysa?"

She shivered. "Wh-which time?"

He sighed, and held her closer. He should have phrased it differently. "The last time; at night in the grove. The thing that I… reacted to… was the change that Tartarus made in your appearance. In the same way that Chthonia changed us when we became its rulers, Tartarus changes you when you descend into the abyss. When it happens, don't be afraid."

Don't be afraid, sweet one… We're only passing through Erebus… the light will return…

Where they were headed there was no light. *Except Ixion's Wheel,* she thought, remembering the mysterious things Merope spoke of. She looked back at Aidoneus, whose face was fixed and solemn, his persistent barrier returning, so strong it blocked out even her. "How do we get through to the Pit?"

"The Phlegethon will part for us, and only us," Aidon said.

"They call me Praxidike down there. What do they call you?"

He was silent for a moment, his breathing measured, before he spoke again. "I have many names in Asphodel and in the world above. But in Tartarus, I'm only known as The Unseen One."

The Unseen One. *Hades.*

Hades held her against him, the heat of the fire below warming her face. As he said it would, the vortex spun a narrow, dark eye into its center, just large enough for the passage of the chariot and nothing more. The winding River of Fire circled deafeningly about them, then above them. Persephone pulled her shoulders back and drew in long breaths through her nose, not willing to let any fear crowd into her mind. If it did, she would be lost. She remembered why she was here— to speak to the Hundred Handed Ones. To see the darker half of her realm. To know who she was; *why* she was. A rail of light from above pierced the darkness, lighting their way before the fiery seal over Tartarus lensed shut. The rusty, wavering glow of the Phlegethon fire was now their only illumination.

The chariot leveled, and she felt lighter, as though the whole thing were falling in slow motion. It took Persephone a moment to realize that falling was exactly what they were doing. Filled with a sense of vertigo, she turned around to face her husband and get her bearings. The passageway to the Pit yawned on every side of them, a hollow cylinder of jagged obsidian that stretch forever into the abyss. Holding Hades's arm, she looked over the edge of the chariot. A circle of sharp white teeth stretched out from the walls, their points framing the entire passageway.

"What is *that*?"

"The Ouroboros of Kampe," he said. "The true boundary between Asphodel and Tartarus."

They descended further, the teeth growing larger in their view. It wasn't until they got closer that she could see that they weren't in fact teeth, but the protruding edges of an immeasurable serpentine ribcage, glowing in the dimmed light of the Phlegethon fathoms above them. The bleached skeleton was coiled around the entire passageway, each rib larger than the one before it. The spine ended in a horned skull with teeth as long and as sharp as the sword at her side. Stuck along the length of the Ouroboros were bronze and iron spears. Its neck was broken and pinioned to the rock by a heavy iron bident, and its tail sat lightly clasped in its jaw.

"She once guarded Tartarus. Kronos sealed the Cyclopes and Hundred Handed Ones here for nearly all the aeons of his rule, so your father, Poseidon, and I had to destroy Kampe to free them and make them our allies. But the barrier between Tartarus and the rest of the cosmos was still bound up within her, just as it is now," he said as they passed level with the vanquished serpent's spine.

Persephone watched his armor tarnish and dull to charcoal black, unreflective, as though the light itself was trying to escape him. Hades's skin paled further than his usual pallor, appearing bone white, any vestiges of the few years he spent in the sun obliterated. Behind the slits of his helm, each of his dark irises lit up with a rim of orange fire. Persephone shuddered, knowing at once that this was what he saw in her when she reached through the ether in Nysa. She looked down, her silver armor also turning black and dulled, her skin looking as lifeless as his, shadowy veins wending their way across her wrists. When his jaw clenched minutely, she knew it was because her eyes were cast in the same fire as his.

"Below the dark of Erebus, there are no Olympians," he said solemnly. "Below the Ouroboros, there are no gods."

"No gods…" she repeated. Persephone looked up at the Ouroboros, its bones silhouetted against the vanishing light of the Phlegethon. The River of Fire reflected in their eyes became the only available light and the passage widened immeasurably. The obsidian walls on either side of them faded into the encompassing black.

"The Hundred Handed Ones and the Erinyes aren't gods, but they preside over the Pit of Tartarus," Hades reached to the side of the chariot and raised a long metallic torch. "You may want to avert your eyes when I light this."

Persephone squeezed her eyes shut, then blinked them open, tears welling in response to a light so harsh it was like gazing into the sun. The torch flared hot white, blindingly bright against the darkness. Hades squinted as well while their eyes adjusted. "I've never seen light like that before."

"White *magnes.* This is the only way to produce light in Tartarus." He held it aloft, but its glow touched nothing but them. Persephone didn't know if the walls were absorbing all light or if they were so far away that even the blinding torch couldn't reach them. "Any other flame burns black down here."

She saw twisted stalagmites of razor-sharp obsidian and hexagonal columns of basalt appear below, like great jagged teeth threatening to snap shut around them and trap them here forever. The chariot jarred to a stop as it touched the ground. Their horses whinnied quietly and nervously, one of them stamping their feet. All else was silent.

"Keep close and stay behind me," he said in a hushed voice as he jumped down from the back of the chariot. He offered her his hand. Persephone lifted the skirt of her peplos and set one sandaled foot, then the other in Tartarus.

She had imagined that it would be unbearably hot. 'May you forever burn in Tartarus' was always the curse mortals made against their enemies. However, it wasn't scorching flames and acrid smoke that greeted her but… absence. No light, no sound, nothing to touch. Isolation.

It was cold, save for a prickly electric vibration that shot through her, making her shiver. She wondered if that came from the Pit, or from the fear she felt. She wondered if there was a difference. A jaundiced glow emanated from far away in the wide caverns, twisting around the rocks, too faint to produce shadows. The metal torch Hades held in his left hand lit their way.

They walked on in utter silence. Persephone could hear her breath and her husband's near-silent footfall. Her heel slipped on some small rocks, and the stones bounced off the side of a precipice beside the pathway. She hadn't noticed the steep drop, and listened closely, but didn't hear the pebbles land anywhere.

"Careful," he whispered, and lowered the torch to their feet so she could comprehend how precarious their journey was. They were on a stone path no wider than the hallway outside their private rooms. As her eyes adjusted, she saw it meandering labyrinthine through the immense cavern, either side of it dropping sharply into the darkness. The path they had already walked also angled and swerved in a pattern that made no sense, but she hadn't remembered them turning in any direction as they'd walked it. Its edges wavered, as if it were a sandy road baked by the midday sun. Looking at it made her eyes hurt.

"What is below us?"

"Nothing," Hades said pointedly.

Persephone shivered. She followed him to the center of the stone bridge— if it could be called that— and stopped when he did. He tensed, his heels digging into the ground, alert. Then she heard it— a soft hissing and staccato shallow breathing. They looked up at a crack in the ceiling far above and saw pupilless white eyes set in a shadowy gaunt face staring back at them. The creature clung to the rocks with wiry limbs, its black leathery wings fanning out, beating without flight. Its head was turned completely around like an owl's. The daimon stopped breathing and stared right at her.

"Persephone..." Hades took a step back to shield her. She stared up, as transfixed and frozen as the creature, then startled when it skittered into the crack, its claws loosening gravel that pelted the pathway ahead of them.

"Th—" Her mouth went dry. "That was—"

"One of the Keres," Hades finished. "Daughters of Nyx. The daimones of violent death."

A whistled shriek tore through the cavern, echoing off the walls, lost in the nothingness below them. They heard it answered by another wail from ahead, and a third from behind them. Then they stopped. All fell silent again.

A high-pitched ping sounded against her helm, then a steady rain of dust and small pebbles fell from above. Hades and Persephone looked up, the ceiling alive, crawling, running, from every crevice a mass of thin wings, whispered hisses, and tapping claws.

"Persephone, get back and lower your helm."

She stood frozen as he quickly pulled his sword off his back and held it ready, the torch in his other hand. Silence. The Keres had stopped moving.

A shrill in a thousand voices— an earsplitting chorus— filled the cavern. The daimones peeled off the walls and ceiling, flapping madly toward the light of the torch.

"*Lower your helm!*" Hades yelled back at her.

She pulled it down and stumbled back from him, watching her husband disappear into the darkness with the light of the torch. Everything around her moved and swirled dark and chaotic, the Keres' shrill cries unbearable. A wail sounded behind her, getting closer. Persephone dropped to the ground as it flew past where her head had been moments before, the Ker sailing, claws outstretched, in the direction of where Hades stood invisible. She backed up and lay prone against the cold rocks. Screams and trills filled the darkness, punctuated by the nauseating wet slice of a sword cutting through flesh and bone.

Persephone heard him yell and saw the flash of torchlight appear again. A Ker chewed on his arm above the gauntlet, and he appeared, his ability to remain invisible momentarily lost amidst the pain. With gritted teeth and wild eyes, he pushed his blade through the daimon's skull, shaking its body off of his sword and casting it into the abyss. On the backstroke, Hades sliced clean through the wings of another, then slashed in wide circular arcs as the black mass of Keres swarmed around him, eclipsing the torchlight. He disappeared again and all went darker than before, her night sight ruined by the white torch. But it was too late. The Unseen One had been seen.

Persephone blinked hard as the burning light trailed across her vision again. She muffled a shriek with the back of her hand as a Ker grasped at Hades's helm and threw it clear of his head. It landed on its side and rolled next to her, the empty faceplate and eye slits staring at her accusingly. *You did this,* it said to her. *You wanted this.*

The daimones attached themselves to Hades like iron to a lodestone. Their talons scratched at his head and arms, tearing his cloak. He used the torch in concert with his blade to beat them off of him. Its lit end swung through the air and shattered a Ker's face. Against the burning white light, he turned and she finally saw him. Bites and gashes lacerated his arms. A dark scratch stretched from his eyebrow to his jaw leaking a stream of gold-flecked blood down his neck. Ichor. She stopped breathing.

Gods above, what have I done? Why didn't I listen? Persephone panicked. *We should never have come here. I shouldn't be here... Aidoneus, my love, what have I done?*

She was about to draw her sword and rush in to help him, heedless of falling into nothingness or being slashed to ribbons by either the Keres talons or her husband's blade. Hades fell to one knee and Persephone watched helplessly as he fought them back and rose to his feet again.

Praxidike?

"Who's there?" She looked around her, seeing no one.

Not so loud, Praxidike, the many voices said in unison. *They should not hear you before they see you.*

"Make them stop!" she whispered. "Make them stop hurting him!"

They do not hold allegiance to us. Or to him, Praxidike.

"What do you mean?! Hades is their—"

The Keres do not recognize him. He bears the likeness of the Enemy.

"...Kottos?"

No, Praxidike, I am Gyges. Kottos is my brother. He's the pretty one. The many-voiced one chuckled at his own remark.

Hades bellowed in fierce determination, fighting his way above the twisting fray of black limbs and wings. He swung his sword overhand, cleaving through the daimones, separating wings, arms, a foot, a neck as it sliced down. The torch fell from his other hand and rolled away.

"This isn't funny," she whispered to Gyges. "Do something!"

I cannot. Only you can. You are their queen, after all...

"What?!" Persephone said in disbelief. *Their queen?* "What do I do?"

Stand. Take off your helm. Let them see you.

"Are you mad?!"

Not so loud, Praxidike. Please trust me, my queen; they saw you disappear and thought he was to blame.

"Run! Persephone, *run! Ruuu—*" her husband screamed out into the cavern. His words turned into a cry of pain as a Ker buried its claws into his neck.

Gyges spoke gently, if such a thing were possible for the many-voices that personified the abyss. *It is the only way to save your consort, Persephone. They will recognize you.*

Tears formed in her eyes. She watched Hades fall to his knees once more, faced away from her. He didn't rise. The Keres dove in over him, their mass pushing him closer to the drop off. There was no time. Persephone stood tall and pulled her helm off her head.

"Stop this instant!" she yelled out over the fray. "I command you to stop!"

They ceased and stilled, as though she had bid time itself to halt instead of these creatures. A thousand pairs of eyes turned in her direction. She held her breath as they cleared away from the path. All fell silent. She heard Hades breathing hard, his body shaking; his sword paused in mid air before it clanged at his side, his arm no longer able to hold it aloft. She took a step forward and watched the Keres retreat in kind. They scattered away and formed a wide circle around her as she made her way toward her husband. He crumpled forward.

"Aidon!" Persephone ran the last few steps and fell to her knees in front of Hades, catching him. She cradled him in her arms, his form slumping forward onto her shoulder. His hand came up and smacked against her cuirass, trailing a crooked smear of blood down the breastplate.

"No… run…" he quietly slurred against her neck between pants, disoriented. " 'S-sephone, run…"

Her fingers ran through his disheveled, bloody hair as she held him close. "Aidon, it's over," she whispered in his ear. "It's over. Look."

Still trying to catch his breath, he weakly brought his head up and looked cautiously from side to side. The Keres held their positions, almost motionless, soundless, waiting. He brought his eyes back to his wife's face. She was safe, unmarked by the violence, so very beautiful, so very worried for him. Hades smiled at her. "Persephone…"

"My sweet Aidoneus, I'm so sorry!" she said, shaking, tears welling up in her eyes again. "Please forgive me, I should never have asked you to—"

"No, no, it's not your fault. I'll be fine. Here, see?" he said, holding a shaking hand up. The cuts from their talons and the punctures from their teeth were already closing. The angry gash across his cheek, precariously close to his right eye, quickly knit itself shut until the only evidence it even existed was a thin trail of blood left in its wake. She wiped it away with her thumb, crying in relief as Hades gave her a weary half smile. "There are… many benefits… to being one of the most powerful gods in the cosmos."

She just held him and wept, kissing him on top of his head, her lips staining with traces of his blood.

"Not many benefits *today*, but some," Hades said, his face somewhere between a wince and a grin. Persephone dried her eyes with the edge of her peplos and stood him up slowly. The frenetic terror of fighting the Keres still raced through his veins. She picked up the fallen torch and held his hand within hers. He looked around again, disbelieving his own eyes: creatures that had been slicing into him without provocation a moment ago were standing back in… reverence. "Why did they stop?"

"I…" she began, meekly, "I told them to."

He stared at her, his lips parted in shock. A whisper went up, filled with ancient words from dead languages.

"*Wanakt-ja!*" the hollow voice of a Ker called out above the others. The word echoed in whispers through the throngs of daimones.

"What did it just say?" Persephone whispered.

"Queen," Hades replied. Persephone stood tall, her stomach turning in circles, her skin prickling, blood thrumming in her ears. Kore no more. She was Queen of the Underworld.

"Listen to me!" she called out to the Keres. "I am She Who Destroys the Light!" They ceased their chatter. "I am

Persephone Praxidike Chthonios, your undoubted Queen, and you will heed my words!"

"*Wanakt-ja! Praxidike!*" the Keres chanted in high-pitched unison, "*Wanakt-ja! Wanakt-ja! Wanakt-ja!*"

They nearly drowned out what she said next. "The man before you is my husband, Hades Aidoneus Chthonios, Polydegmon; your king! You will give him the same respect you give to me!" Persephone held his hand up in hers, watching the Keres retreat to the walls of the cavern. Their parchment-thin wings flapped and they soared in a wide circle around Hades and Persephone. Blank eyes flashed from the weaving mass, glinting in the torchlight.

Hades just looked at her dumbstruck, fearing he'd gone mad. He wondered whether or not he'd actually fallen off the bottom of the cosmos into oblivion, that his mind was lost to reality and simply cajoling him. If he had fallen, he would fall forever into nothingness just as Menoetios, one of Iapetos's sons, had— as near a thing to death an immortal could ever achieve. He blinked again. This was no illusion. His wife stood next to him. The Queen— no— the *Goddess* of Tartarus.

"*Wanakt-ja! Wanakt-ja! Wanakt-ja!*"

A deep rumbling laugh sounded from the hallway ahead of them and echoed in her head. Persephone shuddered.

Heartfelt and sweet, my queen. But they do not speak Theoi. They only needed see you to recognize that you are Praxidike. But, fear not. They know that they mustn't attack your consort anymore.

Theoi. The language of the gods. *Below the Ouroboros, there are no gods,* her husband had said. She doubled back and collected their helms; delivering his first before angling hers to balance and tip back once more on top of her head.

"That one speaking is Gyges..." Hades quietly told her, under the continuing chant of the Keres.

"I know," she answered him with a nod.

Come toward the light, my Queen. We have much to show you.

Persephone looked to her husband. His eyes said everything. She would lead the way from here. One of her hands clasped tightly around Hades's fingers, the other held the torch.

As they walked on, he muttered under his breath. "All this time…"

"What's the matter?" she whispered to him.

"Nothing, sweet one." Hades gave her a strained smile. He had journeyed here many times throughout the aeons of his reign. Each time, he had lived up to the name Tartarus and its denizens called him— The Unseen One. An attack like this had happened only once before, not long after he had arrived in the Underworld as its new ruler. The Keres had mistaken him for Kronos. He'd learned well from that experience, and had taken the Helm of Darkness with him to Tartarus ever since.

Hades dominion over this realm was total and unquestioned— this was his third of the cosmos, after all. Still, he couldn't shake the churning in his stomach right now, and knew it had little to do with being attacked by the Keres. He stayed silent, not having been this ill at ease since the moment he stepped off Charon's boat aeons ago.

Persephone walked beside him, the wan light of the passageway getting closer, brightening and dimming in waves. The sustained scream of a man oscillated in time with each pulse of the light. She could barely hear him over the continuing chants of the Keres.

"*Wanakt-ja! Wanakt-ja!*"

The daimones' voices faded back into the cavern as Hades and Persephone made their way toward the light and the many-voiced Hundred Handed Ones.

"What do the Keres speak if not Theoi?"

They speak the tongues of the dead. Of the ancients of Crete and the bloodline of Minos, of fallen Mycenae, of farther lands and places lost... To them and to the mortals whose languages they speak, my brothers and I are known as the Hekatonkheires.

"Where are you now?"

Not much further, my Queen.

"And then I will finally see you, Gyges?"

We will see you soon. His voices changed to an almost sing-song tone. *Just a bit closer, my queen.*

She swallowed hard as Gyges chuckled again. Hades and Persephone rounded the corner. The pulse of light wasn't her imagination. Set high above them was a burning disk, its fire yellow, but far more dim than either the sun or any light emanating from the Styx.

"Ixion's Wheel," Hades replied solemnly to her unspoken question.

"And the man pinned to it?"

"That... is Ixion."

She looked up in horror at the tortured, faceless shade, his arms and legs stretched across the disk, its spin sending him round with the regularity of a heartbeat.

"Do not feel too badly for this one. I thought it would be a fitting punishment for a man who tried to violate the Queen of Heaven while he was a guest of Olympus." Hades darkened. "I would do far worse to anyone who even *contemplated* such with you."

She listened to Ixion scream out as he looped around the burning wheel, his cries rising and falling with mesmerizing regularity until they became noise in the background. Persephone couldn't see the Hundred Handed Ones yet. To their left lay an open plain of obsidian. Faceless shadows of souls endlessly repeated their actions like cranks and pulleys in a macabre mill. One shadow knelt to scoop up water that wasn't there and bit in the air at a twisted shard of stone that for a moment looked like grapes hanging in a bunch from a vine. Another walked in circles, screaming, his hands plastered over his ears, begging the gods to make the thunder stop. Still more repeated their mechanical theatre, their minds transfixed for eternity on their punishments, unable to be freed, unable to sense or comprehend that Hades and Persephone were even there.

"Who are they?"

"I think Merope may have told you about the two who are closest to us. The one who hungers and thirsts for all eternity is Tantalus, who hungered and thirsted after the power of the gods. He fed the Olympians his own son and tried to steal the secrets of immortality itself. Your father told me what he did, and asked me to devise something... appropriate. Obsession was what drove him in life, and obsession is what drives him now to taste fruit he cannot eat and sip water he cannot drink. The one next to him is Salmoneus, brother of Sisyphus."

"What did *he* do?"

"Before Sisyphus lay with his daughter and drove him to the brink of madness, Salmoneus would ride around in a chariot built onto a raised wooden platform, throwing silver javelins at his subjects and claiming that he was the king of the gods."

Her mouth twisted upward, incredulously. "He did this *before* he went mad?"

"Yes, relatively speaking. Zeus insisted that he wander the fields with thunder echoing in his head for eternity. I believe that I could have come up with something a bit more elegant," he said, his mouth twisting into a dark grin, "but who am I to argue with the King of the Gods?"

They stood, watching the faceless shadows around them. Persephone shifted uncomfortably from one foot to the other before Hades placed his hand on her arm to comfort and steady her.

"I don't send many shades here, sweet one. Only the ones who *must* be in Tartarus are here. Why put an end to the journey of a soul if I don't have to?"

Persephone silently looked below at the burning maw stretched out before them, swirling like water. Dark silhouettes of mortal shades rolled in their wake, filling the lake with the wails of the condemned.

"I'd much rather they gain understanding and do better the next time. It serves all of us far better for them to learn from their mistakes, no?"

She nodded quietly, his calm words balanced against the torment all around them. The smell of brimstone made her eyes hurt. She thought about poor Merope, whirling about in the fires, battered over and over against the jagged edges and felt sick. She thinned her lips and thought about Sisyphus.

"We filled these pits with our enemies during the war. Then mortals who spent their lives destroying the lives of others arrived, and I had to do something with them. Asphodel is a place of peace. I certainly couldn't send them to wander through the Fields with their victims."

She cringed for a moment as a faceless shade screamed and clawed at the sides of the gyre before it was swept away, its shadowy form smashing against the rocks as it went around.

"Do not pity them, Persephone," he said, squeezing her shoulder firmly. "Every single one earned their place here. Without hope for recourse— Tartarus is reserved for those who unrepentantly murdered, those who violated children, those who were kinslayers, and those who dined on human flesh."

"What other sins place someone in the Pit?"

"A few, mostly related to circumstance. If we sent mortals to Tartarus using the litany of sins the priests and hierophants in the world above have created, then there wouldn't be a soul left for Asphodel," he said, shaking his head.

"But why are those ones set aside?" Persephone said, pointing to the gross repetition of the few not bound to the fires. "Were their crimes different?"

"Those condemned to the Field of Punishment are the ones that the gods want to make an example of to the living. Each of them is a warning, of sorts. They did no better or worse in life than the ones who burn."

Suddenly, the flames opened and spread away from the center just as the Phlegethon had when they entered Tartarus. They circled around the edges of the Pit. Out of their midst rose the hairless crown of a head, then another, fifty each, then the innumerable— or one hundred, she knew— arms of the beings known as Kottos and Gyges. They lifted out of the Pit, the flames and the condemned rolling away from them, not touching the Hundred Handed Ones.

Their dark skin cracked like dry earth across their broad chests. Their fifty heads housed fifty pairs of eyes shining pale white without irises, yet all focused unequivocally on her. Kore, the girl she had been less than two months ago, screamed and clawed at Persephone's insides and told her to run as fast and far as she could, but the Queen stayed where she was, swallowed, breathed through her nose, and willed herself to look upon the jailers of the Pit. Instead of running and screaming, the woman that was Persephone contented herself with squeezing her lover's hand.

The Hundred Handed Ones bowed to her. Their fifty heads fell in supplication like an avalanche. One of Kottos's hands pressed to the pathway, reaching out toward her. The sharp iron nail of his smallest finger was as long as one of her feet. Kottos lifted one head and she could make out the barest of pinprick black pupils gazing back at her.

"Persephone Praxidike Chthonios," he said, "She Who Destroys the Light. We are your servants, mighty Queen."

His multitudinous voice was as deep and grinding as a gristmill. Her spine, her viscera shook at its register. Persephone stood tall and curtsied in response, then watched his body, a mass of limbs and heads attached to his thick torso, rise upright once again. The formalities were done. She stood now before those who could subdue gods and Titans; the ones who had helped her father destroy Typhoeus.

24.

"WE ARE SURPRISED TO SEE YOU HERE," GYGES said, fifty smiles showing flashes of teeth. "Especially so soon after your consort received you."

Received? she thought. Persephone inhaled slowly, her knees shaking under her long peplos. "I came because I have questions for you and your brothers."

"Of why you are here? Of why we call you our queen? Of why we know you even though you took up your mantle such a short time ago?"

Her thought was to nod meekly in response, but she caught herself and stood tall.

"Yes," she said, answering firmly.

Kottos grinned at her. The maelstrom of shadows and black flame still whirled about the brothers. "Look to your beloved consort beside you."

Aidoneus, my love... She debated whether or not the Hundred Handed Ones could hear her thoughts. They wouldn't be the first beings in the Underworld who could. And if they spoke to her through their thoughts, it would explain how she could have heard them over the cacophony of the Keres. She inclined her head to meet her husband's eyes. He stayed solemn. Even despite their eyes being lit by the Phlegethon, she could tell that he was looking at her in a way he never had, as though he were studying her distantly. His placid gaze and the contemplation behind it unsettled her.

I'm just worried that you don't want me, as your consort, to be able to just create something like that my first time out. That what I did would somehow make you feel... emasculated... and that you wouldn't want me afterward, Persephone had said to him. She grew flushed when she remembered his demonstration otherwise.

Did he see her differently now? Perhaps her fears were unfounded. Then again, he didn't know the extent of her power, her dominion over this realm, that day. The path through the ether she had opened in Nysa was a theatre trick compared to what they had seen so far in Tartarus.

The Hundred Handed One continued. "He was given this lot, Praxidike. You, however, were born to rule it. Hades has believed this throughout his reign, at least in part. He knows its full meaning now."

Her eyes remained fixed on Hades as Kottos spoke. She thought back to when they were first traveling on the river, and he had silently warned Charon when the boatman asked Persephone about the Phlegethon and the riddle of her own name. She remembered Aidon's reaction in Nysa when she had opened the ring of fire, and his heartfelt words when they had reconciled after their fight. He had declared her as his equal. Aidoneus knew. Not to what extent, but he knew.

Persephone turned back to Kottos. "Why me?"

"For all the aeons of the Tyrant's rule, the Fates told us we would receive a queen, and that she would govern the hosts of Tartarus. That one is you, Praxidike."

"Why do you call me that?" she asked. "I've known since I was young that my birth name was Persephone. I didn't know what it meant in the old tongue until a month ago, but I do know that no one, not even my husband, called me

Praxidike before you did. So how do you know that this prophesied Iron Queen is *me*? What if it is someone else?"

Gyges laughed at this, his voice shaking the Pit itself. "My queen, you made yourself known to us as soon as you opened a pathway directly to the Pit of Tartarus."

"W-what do you mean?"

"None of the other deathless ones have been able to do that since order was restored at the end of the war. Your father, the King of the Gods, cannot. Your husband, the Lord of Souls, cannot. Even the Lady of the Crossroads, Hecate herself, cannot *truly* bridge the ethereal reach in the way that you can. When we saw you standing in Nysa, speaking softly to one of the shadows in the Pit as though no boundary between the worlds existed, we knew at once that it was you."

Kottos spoke. "So, Iron Queen, when I asked who you were, I was wondering if *you* know who you really are. You had questions then as you do now, and we have answers for you. You are Praxidike. Before you even took hold in Demeter's womb, you were prophesied to rule here. The first-born daughter of the Children of Kronos was fated to be our queen. You drank from the Styx before you were born. Because of all these truths, you became Praxidike. The Iron Queen. Aristi Chthonia."

"Aristi…?"

"In the old tongue, it means 'the greatest of us below the earth'. Why do you think the House of Nyx calls this realm such? After your title? It is because all of this is yours, in truth. The mortals call this place *Hadou,* the House of Hades, but it was never really his, alone."

She stared up at Kottos as he continued.

"On the contrary, in truth. Hades received this lot because he was sealed to you at the River Styx," the Hundred Handed One said, watching both King and Queen hold their breath. "Because you were already our queen, the Fates decided that Chthonia should be given to him. Through you alone, Persephone, Hades became its Lord."

Aidoneus felt like the air had been knocked out of his lungs. She was their Queen. More so than he ever had claim over the Underworld, she truly ruled here— and not just Tartarus, but all of the Underworld. He tried to hide his shock from Persephone, but it was fruitless. Aidon knew his wife could feel every emotion he had, or would ever have. From the moment he brought her here, the moment he joined with her— Fates, before she was even born, before he was born for that matter, their souls were intertwined. He remembered Charon refusing her coin at the River. To think he'd always been here as little more than a regent, a surrogate. That Tartarus, the Hundred Handed Ones, the Fields of Asphodel, the entire house of Nyx dwelling above and below the Phlegethon, the very palace he himself built... were never truly his. They were hers.

But you love her, his heart said, *you would have made them hers, regardless.*

What Kottos said struck Persephone, and she grew anxious about how her husband must feel. Every conversation she ever had with Aidon up until now repeated in her head— his brief time in the world above, how long it took him to accept rulership of the Underworld, how he came to love this realm, albeit slowly. And now to find out that it was only because of her that he was here in the first place. Persephone wondered just how thoroughly Aidoneus must resent her for condemning him here.

But hidden under the layers of his unreadable solemnity, there was warmth for her in his eyes. Then, for a moment only as long as was admissible in Tartarus, he smiled at her. What was said in forgetfulness by the shores of the Lethe, what she felt every time he held her, and what she thought in distress when they were attacked by the Keres rushed back to her. It filled her with a peaceful joy she hadn't felt since she last saw the sun.

She loved him.

Persephone loved Aidoneus. She knew it for certain now. Then she panicked, wondering if he had just smiled to cajole her— that it meant nothing more. She feared she was too late and worried that he might cool to her knowing that she, a little girl dancing through the fields of Eleusis mere weeks ago, had stolen his birthright— that he was denied rulership over all, thanks to her.

"Why was I chosen?" she asked Kottos when words finally returned to her. "There are so many far greater than I. I'm only Kore, a shadow of Demeter."

"You are Demeter's daughter, but you were never her shadow. You are the firstborn of your generation, my queen. Your husband, firstborn of his. Charon the ferryman of the souls, is the firstborn of Nyx who herself was the eldest child of Chaos. My brothers and I were the first children birthed by Gaia and Ouranos. One wonders, Praxidike, about all of us who are here by birthright, here by the will of the Fates. And we wonder, what is the *true* inheritance in the division of the cosmos?" Kottos asked with fifty smiles. "The Fates know more than we. If you will pardon your humble servant saying so, your mother and father, their siblings and yours, are fools for thinking that Zeus controls the greatest lot and calls himself the God of Gods. For the only god of gods is *ananke,* the will of the Fates, and *ananke* has brought those who truly rule the cosmos here— to what the frail deathless ones above *amusingly* call the Underworld."

"K-Kottos, I thank you for your allegiance to me and to my husband, but you should not speak such things," Persephone said, her mind now filled with more questions than she had answers. She was still vaguely aware of Hades's hand grasped within hers, unmoving.

"Forgive my brother's forwardness," Gyges said, "but there is a grain of truth in what he said. This is the eternal realm. The mortal world is temporary. Its people live there for but a moment. This place is their true home and birthplace. The gods above are as fleeting as the mortals over which they preside. You and your consort are eternal. The Olympians depend on the mortals who worship them. One day, they too will be forgotten as surely as all the tongues the mortals once spoke and the cities they first built. But you and your consort will endure."

"More so," Kottos continued, "your realm keeps the world above alive and renewing itself. All waking life is but a thin film upon the surface of this world. A balance has existed here for all the years you've been alive, Praxidike. You are the one who transcends and connects the worlds. *You* are the embodiment of balance— born at the war's end."

"Why is that important?"

"With your birth, the boundary between the worlds was made fixed and immutable. No one can cross over to Tartarus except by way of the Phlegethon, as you and your consort did. Your role, your fate, is bound to those who reside here. Including the Titans. The world above would not, could not survive the Tyrant or his servants being released."

"Where are the Titans?"

Hades gripped her hand almost painfully, forcing her to look up at him. His eyes opened wide and he shook his head at her.

"Aidon," she whispered to him. "Please. I've come this far."

Hades swallowed. It wasn't as if he could stop her anyway. He sighed and looked up at Kottos. "Is Briareos there?"

"Yes, my lord."

He turned to Persephone, his face cold and unreadable. "You *know* who is held in the deepest part of Tartarus. Please trust me when I say this, my love." Hades took her free hand in both of his. "You have no idea how dangerous he is. Do not listen to him or believe a word he says. His mind is eternally bent on escaping his bonds and he will tell you— promise you *anything,* Persephone."

My love, she thought. Was it to be said to her after all this as only a forced endearment, now that he knew it was her fault that he was here in the first place? She stared into his eyes. *My love.* "Are you coming with me?"

"I would never leave you alone with them. I don't care whose fated Queen you are."

Persephone handed him the torch. He led once more, the path sloping downward into a perfectly round pit, its edges lined with obsidian bricks. Narrow stairs ringed the great circular chamber with an immense basalt column dominating the center. Ixion's Wheel was far above them now, and Hades's white torch provided most of the light.

The stone path ended half way to the bottom and Persephone felt a heaviness like lead in her chest, as though everything were slowed here. Her feet were weighted down. Her body ached. Once they arrived at the last step, Hades handed the torch back to Persephone, her other hand firmly grasped within his. When he glanced at her to see if she was all right, she saw the hardship of descending into this place written across his entire body. Half his life he had been trapped in pain and darkness, then reborn into the long, bloody war fought to imprison those who were bound here.

Hades's left hand pressed hard into the stone, and he closed his eyes to concentrate on his task. Slabs cracked apart, grinding loudly as shards of obsidian burst from the wall, their surfaces smoothing into the shape of stairs. He walked forward once again, guiding her down. Their pathway appeared before them as they went, a new set of stairs created a few steps ahead of where their feet landed. At the bottom, the pathway circled about a column and Persephone held the torch aloft.

The column was ringed with pitted recesses, heavy chains hanging down to secure the arms of the Titans above their heads. In a dark alcove, a giant of a man covered only by a loincloth, his body as still as stone, hung by his wrists. When the torch flared in front of his face, his baleful eyes opened and narrowed. He looked down at Persephone and cracked a threatening grin. It was then that she saw the thick scar ringing his neck.

"Demeter's daughter..." he rasped in a barely audible whisper before showing her his teeth, yellowed by aeons spent as a prisoner of Tartarus.

Iapetos. Hades glared up at him, and Persephone took a step back.

"Not as shapely as her mother..." The chained Titan laughed dryly. His whispered voice was hoarse and broken, painful sounding, when he tried to shout. "Kreios! Hyperion! Wake up! Demeter's daughter is here..."

Hades clenched his jaw, saying nothing. Persephone heard the rattle of chains from the other side of the column as the Titans stirred.

"Well, Hades," Iapetos sneered, "after all this time you finally claimed your reward for separating my head from my body. And what a reward she is! To think I nearly impaled her in the womb... though now I can think of a spear far better to—"

"*Silence!*" Fifty voices shook dust from the alcoves, booming and echoing across the chamber. She watched as the chains pulled tighter around Iapetos, his head slamming against the rocks behind him, the links pressing into his throat. Persephone felt heavy footfall shake the ground, then cease.

"Come," Hades said quietly, his face transfixed and emotionless. They walked away from Iapetos, a wide grin on the Titan's face, his shoulders shaking in a silent laugh.

Immense hands with thick iron fingernails came into view, flattened against the stone floor. As they walked, she saw another hand, then another, then the fifty heads of Briareos already bowed low to her. He rose. Though she could barely tell Gyges and Kottos apart, their eldest triplet was unmistakable— darker, taller, more strongly built, if such a thing were possible. "Forgive me, my queen… my lord."

She curtsied to him. "For what?"

"For allowing him to speak." His voices rumbling in unison made her nauseous, just as when his brother Kottos spoke to her through the ether in Nysa.

"There is no need to apologize, Briareos. I've come here to see them— and to speak with them, if I must," she said quietly. "To know even the lowest parts of the realm I rule with my husband."

"Very well," Briareos said.

She nervously cleared her throat. "Where is he?"

"Persephone, please…" her husband whispered.

"Hades, I must," she said quietly, using the only name he went by in Tartarus. "How else can I understand what you've endured all these years?"

Any other way, he thought. He thinned his lips and closed his eyes. She ran her thumb over his knuckle until he loosened his iron grip on her hand. It had to be done, he thought; otherwise why come all this way? And he had said that she was his equal. Though for Aidoneus, the very idea that he had any say in her position was laughable now, after what Kottos had told them.

"I will stay nearby, Praxidike," Briareos said solemnly, moving beside the alcove next to them. She stood no taller than the bone in his ankle. Persephone walked with Hades around the corner, staring at the heavy chains extending upward, wrapped around the base. "If you need anything, my queen…"

"Thank you, Briareos," she said. Her husband's steps became heavier and she could feel every sinew in his hand tighten as he held hers. They rounded the corner of the alcove. Piercing dark eyes stared at her from under black brows and she almost shook, unnerved.

He was at least a hand's span taller than his son, his height exaggerated by his elevated place chained to the rocks. His arms were looped above him like the others. His features were sharper. Harder. More strongly set, at least from what she could see under his gray-streaked beard. His hair was shoulder length, waves of black tinged with gray at the temples. But his eyes, the set of his jaw, his neck, his shoulders, were unsettlingly familiar— no— *identical* to those of her husband.

"My favorite son." His voice dripped with honey. "How long has it been since you last honored me with your presence? Ten, maybe twelve thousand years?"

Aidoneus remained silent.

"No greeting for me, then? Not even an introduction to our newly descended Queen of the Underworld?"

"Kronos," Persephone said quietly.

"There, you see, Hades? She can manage it— how hard is it to be civil?" Kronos turned his attentions back to Persephone and dipped his head in as much of a bow as the chains would let him, but kept his eyes locked with hers, like an eagle eyeing its next meal. "You are very welcome here, Queen Persephone. Demeter's daughter by Zeus, if I'm not mistaken?"

"I am," she said. Even in the lowest part of Tartarus he carried a regal air, as though he were receiving Persephone in his own court. He spoke as though the chains wrapped around his torso, legs and arms weren't there, or that he somehow *meant* for them to bind him, and could shrug the irons off at any moment.

"And what a fantastic mess Demeter is making. My poor sweet mother, Gaia. You Olympians are proving to be poor stewards of creation. It's a wonder you've lasted this long."

"I am no longer an Olympian," Persephone said calmly, "and my mother will end this soon enough."

He smirked. "Of course you're not. My apologies. But that doesn't exempt you or your husband from your shared fate. And your choice of wording is… interesting."

"What do you mean by that?"

He stretched and sighed pleasurably, closing his eyes. "I can feel them weakening. The Chains draw all their strength from those who rule the cosmos. And thanks to you, dear Queen, they will break soon enough."

"She has nothing to do with this," Hades hissed, stepping forward.

"Ah, he speaks! For a moment I thought you were Iapetos's son instead of mine," Kronos said with a grin, ignoring Iapetos's shifting chains on the opposite side of the column. "Somehow, I think the Fates *knew* of my return to power when they left the earth without anyone to rule it directly. Nature abhors a vacuum, after all. And who knew poor Demeter would exploit this weakness to hold the earth hostage, hmm? I suppose that you only have as good an earth as the goddess you put in charge of its bounty— and how well you treat her. And you, Hades, as well as your brothers, have treated her poorly. My wife took good care of the earth. Unlike Zeus, I only forsook my marriage the one time. No more. I treated Rhea well."

"My very existence is proof that you did not," Hades said quietly. Persephone turned to him, shocked. She realized quickly what he meant and faced Kronos again, trying to regain her composure.

"Unsurprising that you didn't tell her about the manner of your making," the deposed king said. "I wonder what else you've hidden from her."

"Hades is sworn to tell me the truth," she blurted out, unnerved. She immediately regretted the outburst, angry with herself that she'd given him leverage over her. She felt her defenses crumbling, a hum of sharp energy permeating her.

"Of course he is, if you know which questions to ask," he grinned, "sweet one."

Her heart dropped into her stomach when he used Aidoneus's favorite endearment for her. Kronos looked her up and down. The lascivious trail of his eyes on her skin didn't escape Hades and she felt rage start to overflow from him. Her stomach roiled as she thought about how much she loved that same look on her husband's face, about how similar the Titan's face and voice were to his. That familiar gaze looked twisted, predatory, and unsettling on Kronos.

"I loved my wife. And of my children I suppose I liked you the best, Hades, because you were the instrument by which Rhea finally surrendered to me. At least until she betrayed me. But I knew that was coming. It was fixed by fate…"

They remained silent, and Persephone was overcome with the same electric prickling she felt when they first arrived in Tartarus, stronger this time. She held tight to Hades's hand, running her thumb over his shaking fingers.

"But back to this business in the world above…" Kronos said dispassionately. "Now that you're face to face with me, my queen, I can finally speak honestly with you. I may be chained down here, but I'm still a Titan— one of the gods of time and prophecy whose task it was to safeguard the cosmos. I suppose that's why the usurpers kept us alive."

He threw a glance at Hades, his eyes slitted. Her husband remained unmoved.

"Surely even you can sense that the world has been thrown out of balance. Too much has changed; too many of the mortals these gods above rely upon have perished. It's only a matter of time before I'm free. You might as well embrace it."

"I suppose you want me to free you then, hmm? I imagine you offer all manner of rewards to me if I do?" She said with a smirk.

"I'm sure someone told you at one time that you were very clever, but make no mistake. My escape from these bonds is an inevitability. Truthfully, I'd rather it occurred before these petty gods above destroy the cosmos. And that is where you come in, my dear. The *Hekatonkheires* told you what I also believe to be true. You are both the eldest—rightful rulers of the cosmos. By that right, you and your husband are the only ones who can set me free. And if you do, I will give him his birthright and you yours."

"I highly doubt that." Hades said, calmly. "If memory serves, your desire was for nothing less than absolute power. And my memory serves me *very* well."

"I've had time to reconsider, perhaps even atone, my son. And you've been denied your due long enough, wouldn't you say?" He turned once more to Persephone, smiling. "How would you like to sit the throne of heaven, my queen?"

"There is nothing you could possibly offer that I do not already have. My husband—"

"I can give you what he cannot," Kronos said. The Lord of Souls shifted on his feet, seething, almost ready to lunge at the Titan. His father delighted in the reaction.

The electric hum pulsing through her intensified painfully and Persephone watched Tartarus disappear, melting away. She blinked and looked around, alone, her surroundings white, marble amidst the clouds. She couldn't see Kronos, but felt his presence nonetheless. "This is an illusion."

"Indeed," Kronos's voice intoned, unseen. "But I knew you'd understand that. I would never presume that you were simple."

Persephone blinked again and the scene changed. She sat on a white throne, her body clothed in robes woven so finely that they shown iridescent, their threads heavily dyed with saffron. Her tresses flowed loosely from a gold diadem of stars. Long sheaves of silvery wheat sat in the crook of her elbow, and in her left hand sat a coiled bronze nautilus.

Aidoneus sat next to her, his skin kissed by the sun, his hand wrapped around a staff crested with a golden eagle. A Golden laurel crowned his head, and he leaned over and laid his hand reverently on her rounded belly. She flinched for a moment in surprise, then intertwined her hand with his. Together they smoothed their palms over the hard swell of life underneath, feeling their son kick at her in response…

"Persephone, don't listen to him!" Her husband's voice shouted from far away.

This isn't real…

The hand on her womb tensed in anger. She looked back at the king next to her. His appearance had shifted to that of Kronos, his eyes cruel and clouded with madness. She threw the nautilus and sheaves of wheat to the floor and yanked the starry crown off her head, running down the dais and headlong toward the great open terrace. The land below her burned, fires consuming all from the foothills to the horizon, the scent of death carrying up to where she stood. Kronos, dressed in ancient bronze armor, his sickle in hand, wandered the razed plains of Thessaly standing twelve times taller, plucking Olympian gods out of their war chariots, swallowing them whole, absorbing their strength. Artemis. Hermes. Athena. She put her hand over her mouth and muffled a scream when she saw her thrashing mother disappear past Kronos's teeth. Large hands gripped her shoulders from behind and she stood stock-still.

"Time and prophecy were mine and my brothers' domain— the past, the present, the future. Every harvest and planting and fallow. No matter what chains bind me, they are my domain, still," he said softly, bending forward to speak next to her ear. "I saw the visions of my children overthrowing me as clearly as what you see before you and around you now. I knew I would be here, and I knew I would speak to you. Consider what I am showing you a gift, Persephone. I am giving you the privilege of knowing what will happen if you free me and what will happen if you do not. I would seat you and Aidoneus as the regents of the earth, the seas and the sky. The Olympians will be your vassals; your servants. You will kneel only to me."

She surveyed the scorched earth below, then turned on her heels to face him. "And what of the mortals?"

"The Men of Iron's suffering will be ended for all time. They will return to the peaceful place of their birth in the Underworld and there they will stay, as Chaos first intended. Prometheus's heretical acts will be… set right." He took a step toward her, edging her backward until she stood at the edge of the open terrace, the ground far below. "Under my guidance, the living world will belong once more to those who live forever. You alone, Iron Queen, will decide if the mortals return mercifully or violently. Say the word, Persephone. Let your beloved husband break my chains. The cosmos will be mine once more and peace will be restored. But if you do not—"

Kronos pushed hard at the center of her chest, sending her flying. Persephone tilted heels over head, falling backward off the mountain. The ground and the sky traded places, following one another ever faster, burning Thessaly looming closer with each turn of her body through the air. This was an illusion. She did not cry out. She wouldn't give him the satisfaction. The fall seemed to last forever. Her back hit the ground below and knocked the air out of her before she stood up and dusted herself off. The fine saffron robes and the growing life inside her were gone, replaced with a stained chiton ripped half way down the center. Her hair was matted and dirty. She clasped the tatters of the chiton over her breast and held the open side to cover her nakedness. Embers swirled about her. The bones of women, men, children, and livestock littered the ground amidst charred oak trees hollowed out by fire.

"No!" She heard her husband's scream from behind her and turned toward his voice. "Please, no! Persephone!" Aidon struggled, chained to a slab of rock, just as her father Zeus had bound Prometheus. An eagle circled him and landed, digging its talons into his abdomen. She looked away as its beak tore at his liver, his pain muffled behind gritted teeth. He screamed only her name. "*Persephone!*"

This isn't real. This isn't real...

"—I will destroy all you have ever loved—" Kronos growled.

"*Aidon!*"

Persephone heard her voice, but she wasn't the one who screamed. She saw a vision of herself mere steps away, barely dressed in the same ruined chiton, flailing, caught underneath the Tyrant, his body moving upon her as she screamed for her husband to save her. Her wrists cracked in the grip of his fists. He licked salt tears and sweat from her neck, cheek and breasts.

"—and save him for last," his eyes met hers and he spoke between violent thrusts.

She watched the woman under him, her future self— no, she mustn't think that way— scream and cry, then stare straight at her and go silent. Her eyes became cold and dead, accepting her violation, her mind separating from her body, all hope lost. She stared blankly at Aidoneus in chains as he screamed in anger and struggled in vain to escape and save her, tears streaming down his face at his utter helplessness.

"I will rape you sweetly. Thoroughly— before your lover's eyes. And you will submit, desire and crave me before the end. If you please me, I'll even let you look on him one last time before I devour you." He looked down to the illusory Persephone gone silent underneath him and pushed faster. His sounds were sickening— animalistic as he bit at her shoulder and sucked at the hollow beside her neck. "Mmm, gods… you remind me so much of Rhea, sweet one. When I have you like this, you look just like her. You even taste like her…"

This isn't real. This isn't real. This isn't real…

"Enough!" Persephone shouted.

She blinked and was in Tartarus once more. Her husband's hand gripped hers painfully, shaking. She could feel his anguish and knew at once that he had seen everything Kronos had shown her. His jaw was clenched. His face was a stone mask but in the way he squeezed her fingers, she could feel him screaming as loudly as he had in Kronos's vision. A single tear slid down her cheek as she felt raw dread rolling through him. The Titan king stood chained against the wall once more, his shoulders back, a triumphant smile decorating his face. His features softened.

"Who could blame you for the decision you know you must make?" he said softly. "I can assure you that *he* will not. I know my son better than you, my queen. He will free me if you ask it of him, and later he will cherish and praise you for your courage."

She thought back to this morning, watching Aidon scrub at his skin with pumice, the scar left by his father's cruelty slashed across his back. Her eyes watered for only a moment.

"Have you decided?"

"I have."

Kronos flexed his fingers, yearning to move his arms again for the first time in aeons.

"Briareos," she said, her voice shaking. "The Chains of Tartarus… they are unbreakable, no?"

"Indeed, Praxidike," he said, knowing grins spreading across his fifty faces.

"I don't believe they bite into the Tyrant's skin quite enough." She watched surprise flash across Kronos's face before his expression went cold and filled with anger. She lifted her chin. "Tighten his chains."

She let go of Hades's hand.

"Tighten *all* of their chains!" The Iron Queen stalked past Okeanos and Hyperion, Iapetos, Kreios, and Koios, rounding the column and stopping before Kronos. "Let each of them think of *me* when the links dig into their skin!"

The chains wound around each of the Titans, and Persephone thought she even heard a dry, voiceless whine of protest from Iapetos on the far side of the column. Persephone, the Iron Queen, stood in front of the deposed Tyrant, her eyes narrowed. "I am my father's daughter and the wife of Aidoneus. And I am not afraid of you," she raised her voice and looked past Kronos to Koios and Okeanos. "Nor any of you!"

"A pity," Kronos said, his breathing labored as the chains pulled taut, "that I will have to show you why you should be— as is the manner in which you shall force me to demonstrate it."

25.

THE CHARIOT SWAYED GENTLY IN THE AIR, THEN shook violently once the wheels touched the ground. Aidoneus wrapped an arm around Persephone, his right hand jerking back on the reins to bring them to a stop not far from the pomegranate grove.

Their grove.

She lifted her helm off her head and stepped onto the cool gravel, never more thankful to be back in their gardens. Cerberus bayed from the shores of Acheron, doubtless chasing down a wandering shade. Asphodel rustled in the fields beyond the gate as their subjects peacefully wandered through the ghostly stalks. The air felt crisp and clean against Persephone's cheeks. Inhaling deeply, she relaxed, glad to be home and safe.

She brushed her hands through the leaves of a pomegranate tree, then across the warm underside of a maturing fruit hanging heavy on its bough. The past month had seen them grow day-by-day, far faster than anything like them in the world above. The trees were now filled with the red globes, each one the size of her fist. She twisted a fruit this way and that, looking at its rough surface. Inside, the white sheaths were probably bursting with dark red arils. But it wasn't ripe yet.

Behind her, Aidoneus whispered something in the lead horse's ear. Persephone startled and almost stumbled over a root as the horses and chariot broke apart into black grains of sand and fell through the gravel and bedrock, returning to their home. A last whinny echoed from the ether and broke the silence. She walked to her husband's side. "How did you do that?"

He smiled dryly at her. "I'll show you some day." Aidon took off the heavy golden helm and shook out his hair, smoothing it back. His face was cold, devoid of emotion. She wrinkled her brow at him and he gave her a brief, forced smile. "The first thing Hecate taught me was to move objects through the ether to hide them or keep them safe. Like this."

Aidon held the Helm of Darkness in one hand and passed it to the other, but instead of landing squarely in his other hand, it vanished, leaving behind a trail of black smoke. The corner of her mouth twisted up. "Is it hard to do?"

"You tell me," he said. "You have far more control over the ether than I."

Persephone winced, recalling everything they had been told in Tartarus and the first time she had taken them to this grove. She closed her eyes and put her helm in one hand, then thought about sending it through the paths between worlds. She lightly pitched the helm from one hand to the other, and heard it clang loudly on the ground. Her eyes opened and she looked down, frustrated and embarrassed, the helm's black plume sprawled out on the gravel.

"Here, let me show you," Aidon said gently. He pick up her helm and placed it back in her left hand, standing behind her. "Keep your eyes open. Try to envision your other hand existing in the ether itself, as though you are between worlds."

She followed his direction, then pushed the silver helm into her other hand, watching fire bloom around it for a moment before it disappeared. She let out a pleased sigh.

"You're a fast learner," he said quietly. She looked up at him, trying to find a smile to return. His face was still solemn; distant. Aidon grimaced and walked away into the pomegranate grove. As he went, his armor shifted back to his more familiar garb, the cloak draping back into a himation over his left shoulder. Over the past month, the grove had grown thick with grasses and lichens, moss, patches of fertile topsoil, life springing up everywhere that the red petals had fallen to the ground. Here, more than anywhere else in Chthonia, she was at home. Except for her inability to control how these plants grew, Persephone could have mistaken their lush pomegranate grove for the world above.

"Aidon?" She followed after him, brushing aside low hanging leaves and branches until she saw him. Perhaps he did blame her for being condemned to rule here.

Her mind flashed a searing vision of sitting beside him on her throne, crowned with gold. She shook it from her head. It was falsehood. An illusion. Her armor changed at her will, replaced with a slate blue peplos that matched her eyes. It was covered in his blood just as her armor had been. Glancing at her breast and shoulder, she quickly shifted her peplos to black to hide the stains on her clothes. It did nothing for the stains on her skin. Tinges of ichor clung to her, everywhere. Now that they were back in the light, she could see that her skin was stained where she'd touched him and her fingernails were rimmed with it. Her husband paced furiously, and she tried to keep up with him.

"Aidon, won't you— wait…" she said. It was as if he didn't hear her, and she grew frustrated. "Hades, *please!*"

He turned abruptly on her and she almost crashed into his chest. His forehead was creased with anxiety. "I should have never exposed you to him. I should have said 'no' to at least that and held firm…"

"I *needed* to speak to him, Aidoneus. It was your burden alone for so many—"

"What manner of husband am I that I would *allow* him to—"

"It was all lies! Kronos was trying to get me to sway you any way he knew how so we would turn him loose." She looked up at him expectantly. Those were his very words, after all. He scowled and turned away from her, pacing the grove once more. Persephone followed him closely. "Aidon!" She could feel him burning, her words of comfort lost in his anger. "You said so yourself! He would say anything to be freed."

"I *stood by* as he threatened to rape my wife!" he snarled. "I'll melt the chains into his *teeth* so he can never speak again! I'll—"

Persephone stopped him in his tracks with a kiss. There was nothing Aidoneus could have done to stop the vision. They both knew it, and her lips against his said as much when she realized words would not suffice. His rage melted and he leaned forward, exhausted. They knelt down, holding each other, settling into the soft grasses. She pulled at his shoulders until his head lay in her lap. It was only a few hours ago that he was being torn to pieces by the Keres, surrounding himself with the damned, witnessing the violation of his wife at the hands of the Enemy. Persephone stroked his forehead. "Husband… You know he can't get free. What he said wasn't true."

"I know. It's only… All this drew the contrast between us ever more sharply. And it makes everything so clear…"

"What do you mean?"

"That *you* are able to handle his threats, and I couldn't even…" he stopped and looked away.

"What's wrong?"

"Only my greatest failing as a ruler here."

"You couldn't help the visions he showed us."

He shut his lids and leaned his head into the comforting brush of her fingers across his brow. "No, that's not it. Though I can't help feeling that I failed you today."

"You didn't fail me." She twined a lock of his hair around a finger, and cringed when it left a smear of blood on her hand. She swallowed, thinking about the Keres. *I failed you, husband. I let this happen.*

"It happened a long time ago. I shouldn't trouble you with it…"

"Please trust me, Aidon. Talk to me. Please."

He opened his eyes and stared into hers. "What I'm about to tell you, I've told no one else; not even Hecate."

Aidoneus paused until she nodded and acknowledged the weight of his trust in her, then took a deep breath.

"I've mentioned before how I was… loathe… to accept this lot. My anger boiled fiercely my first decade or so here. Through the Key, I would hear the voices of everyone in this kingdom night and day, destroying my peace of mind. *Especially* the voices from Tartarus. Even if I removed the rings— which I did with the hope that I could finally sleep— sleep never returned. The loudest of those voices was my father's. Every moment I spent dreaming was filled with wild delusions, nightmares planted there by him, luring me to the Pit. I stopped sleeping for weeks at a time. I wanted nothing to do with him. Fates; after the war, I never wanted to see him again. But I started venturing into Tartarus, entranced by what he had shown me, even knowing that everything he said was a lie. That he would tell me *anything.*

"His every conversation with me was bent on convincing me to make war on the Olympians— to claim what was rightfully mine. Kronos told me that he would aid me, and it wasn't long before I believed him. He heaped bitter scorn on their governance. I saw what the world above was becoming in their *capable* hands— rape, murder, disparity and hubris, endless wars, burning cities and homesteads— every calamity a new arrow in his quiver to use against me. I knew they would all come to me. Everything dies. *Ananke,* the will of the Fates, determined that I was to host the decent souls in Asphodel until they returned to the living world, but that I would eternally rule over the damned who would never leave. *Their* numbers would only increase, and their voices would only grow louder. When the first kinslayer finally died and came before me, I decided to take him to Tartarus myself. I was intent on breaking the chains and freeing Kronos, if for no other reason than to silence my doubt of the Fates and bury the jealousy of Zeus that was consuming me like leprosy."

"What stopped you?"

"The man's story. This was long ago, when the mortals were few, and I judged every soul myself. He was the eldest of two brothers and felt that his patron god had dealt him a bad lot. He had tended vast tracts of failing crops while his young brother had inherited their father's livestock and grown rich from it. He slew his brother, ran off from his family in disgrace, and wandered between towns. After hearing him, I was filled with shame. How like that wicked man I was: resentful and consumed. If my envy made me set my father free to destroy the world once again, how was I any better than that murderer?

"Tisiphone took him instead. I visited the deepest levels of Tartarus only a handful of times thereafter, when absolutely necessary, and occupied myself with what I *did* have instead of dwelling on what I thought I'd lost. As atonement for what I'd nearly done, I ate the asphodel roots in the fields to eternally bind myself here and took the name Chthonios. I started marking the time from my last temptation. I had Nyx teach me how to better control the Key, and how to separate my thoughts from the voices of the Pit. To mark each century that went by, I would build a new room for the palace— I looked forward to making each one. I started to make the Underworld my home. I began to appreciate this place. There were the colorful stories brought to me by the shades in all their different tongues. I grew to deeply value the serenity of the Underworld, and the separation from the petty behavior of the Olympians. And I had the promise of one day having you."

"It was just after the war." She ran her hand over his forehead once again. "Hadn't you only been free— hadn't you only *truly* lived for ten short years when you first got here?"

"Yes."

"Then why are you so hard on yourself, Aidoneus?"

"Because allowing him to exploit my weaknesses nearly destroyed the world."

She paused for a moment, contemplating his words. "Am I a weakness for you? Is that why he thought that I could convince you to free him?"

"No, sweet one," he said. "Quite the opposite. You have no idea how much peace you've brought me in the short time you've been here. After aeons of witnessing the caprices of the others, I thought that my taciturn nature was a strength. I was wrong; I had no idea how easily that could have been twisted… exploited. I was cold and my thoughts unknown, even to me. Even the promise of warmth…" He tensed his forehead. "Zeus had *no idea* what he was doing when he allowed me to be shot with that arrow. He didn't know my thoughts; what I might have done, what other... *ambitions* could have been awakened."

She traced her fingers down his bearded jaw line to his neck, her hand finally resting on the center of his chest. He shut his eyes, willing away the burning fields of Thessaly from the vision.

"For them the war ended forty thousand years ago. They have forgotten. They forgot that I hold the Key to the destruction of everything they know. Their children never knew what horrors we saw. The Olympians have *no idea* what they could have done," he said, a single tear trailing into his temple, lost in his hair. "But with you... with you, through you, I know myself. I am a better man because of you, sweet one."

She pulled away from him when he said the words Kronos had used against her, her heart dropping into her stomach as it had in Tartarus. "Why did he know to call me that? How did he..."

"Even chained, Kronos is... He was king for aeons longer than any of us have ruled. Or lived. There is a good reason why he came to be such, and there is a reason why I am restless— why it's difficult for me to sleep through the night, even now. The voices of Tartarus I can ignore with concentration. But other than removing the rings, I've found no way to stop myself from listening to *his* voice. And sometimes," he said, opening his eyes to her once more, "he listens back."

* * *

Hecate sat against her favorite column in the throne room, her eyes closed. Her tranquil contemplation was disturbed only by the buzzing suggestion that perhaps she should come back later.

They were on the path toward her— and had emerged from the Pit over an hour ago. She could feel their movements, and their return had created gentle, soothing ripples in the too-still pond that was Chthonia. She knew they were in their pomegranate grove: it intensified their unity, and she focused on the balance they had brought into each other's lives, delighting in how they had intertwined with one another like the branches of the trees their union had brought into being. Hecate remembered how distraught she was a month ago when they were in tumult, distant, deeply afraid of one another.

Now their happiness blossomed. Hecate only hoped that it could continue, that the visions assailing her night and day would not come to pass. Ensuring that they did not was what brought her to this room to speak with them as soon as they returned. Her singular, meditative focus on Aidoneus and Persephone also quelled her annoyance with the other occupant of the great chamber.

Thanatos wandered blithely about, humming to himself. He paused to wipe his finger over the black marble base of a column, rubbing the small bit of dust between two digits before he slowly moved to the next and did the same. He strolled past Hecate, and looked out to the terrace and the masses of the newly deceased on the other side of the Styx. In all the ages Death had existed, he couldn't remember a busier time than the past month. He tapped his heel against the floor. He should be celebrating right now; and since all the wine and *kykeon* in the world above was either drunk away, frozen solid or in the hands of that Eleusinian sow, he needed to find something warm and giving. The corner of his mouth ticked up just thinking about her.

He glanced at Hecate, her eyes closed, meditating on Fates knows what. He leaned against the other side of her column, then whistled the same tune loudly, his sandals scraping the floor. The white witch shifted and glared at him, her concentration broken. He resumed his slow walk and looked back at her with a wink, stretching his wings.

She wondered briefly what Thanatos was so pleased about. His failure to capture the Ephyrean had reached even her ears. Hecate knew Sisyphus would be caught eventually— a prize buck could only frolic so long while the hunters ranged. The sorcerer king's end in Tartarus was fixed by fate, and every day Thanatos was away from the Underworld was another day he wasn't *distracting* her nymphs. Still— and she suspected it was on purpose— he stoked her curiosity with every pass. Almost unconsciously, Hecate slipped into his thoughts. Her delving unearthed only a single name. Merope.

Thanatos stopped in his tracks. He folded his wings back and spun to face her, his eyes slitted, his mouth twisted into a leer. "I thought you and I had an agreement."

"Your thoughts are normally as subtle as a hungry goat," she said softly, "and I made no such vow."

"We made no *direct* promise, you and I, because you said my mind was… aberrant? Degenerate, if I recall your words? Refresh my memory."

"If my imagined words are lost in the brambles of your memory, Thanatos, you may search among the thorns yourself. And why so merry? Did you defy the Fates and do something right?"

"Well, my dear little witch, if you must know," he said, reclining on the last step of the dais, his black wings spread out behind him. "We have Sisyphus. No thanks to you, of course."

"You never asked."

"You speak as if you would have actually helped me." Thanatos glared at Hecate. It was her turn now. He saw the white witch flinch as he deftly repaid her trespass into his thoughts, scooping out the first bit of information he could find before she closed herself off to him. He cocked his head and ran his tongue along an incisor. "As for your grand schemes, I hope that sow of an earth goddess listens to you. She's making my job harder every day."

When he tried to dive in again for specifics, Hecate practically shoved him out of her mind. She took a calm breath and plaited her fingers in her lap. "So, Thanatos, why do your thoughts swirl around Merope?"

"None of your business. This time at least."

"I doubt the Iron Queen would be delighted by the thought of her handmaiden and friend in Death's bed."

"By all means, Hecate, give me an alternative. One of yours, perhaps? I seem to be running out of Lampades nymphs to fuck." He smiled as she clenched her jaw.

"Intriguing that her name shines above all others like a star in the heavens! How rare and impressive that you can pluck that from among your self-indulgent conquests."

"We always want what we cannot have," he said, shifting on his elbows. "Is that not so?"

"Ah, *cannot*? So Aidoneus *has* named a forbidden fruit in your favorite orchard..."

"That's between him and me," Thanatos said. "And I think it burns you that it isn't any of your concern this time."

"This realm is entirely my garden to tend."

"No more so than it is mine," he said, slinking over to her. Hecate darted her eyes to either side, letting her guard down for an instant that he was only too glad to seize. "Oh, come now, Hecate. We've been feuding since before the war, you and I. How many more millennia are we going to continue this? We have precious few left..."

She glared up at him as he drew closer. "You would ask the hound to make peace with a wildcat?"

"Think of it more as… a requiting." Thanatos sighed pleasurably and licked his lips. His wings spreading wider with each step he took to close the distance between them. "All this tension between us… and you with no way to release it."

Hecate lifted her chin. "I am not drunk on the desires that besot you, Thanatos. Nor will I ever be."

"Mmm. Like blazing Tartarus you aren't," he rasped. "What a waste of talent! You've spent your life concerning yourself with the… channeling… of those *desires* even as you stand aloof from them. A master who cannot demonstrate for the apprentice— who ever heard of such a thing? And yet, you still have not taught the Rite to the one student who could truly affect anything in this godsforsaken cosmos."

"Their time is not yet come, and my ways are no concern of yours."

"They are entirely my concern, *young one,* and became even more so when those trees sprouted up in Chthonia, growing in the very arrangement that the Protogenoi have always held sacred. My mother entrusts her wisdom to you and you squander it."

She bristled at his diminutive for her. "Then try her interest in discussing the matter, Son of Nyx. I have none."

"And this brings us back to my far better idea… acolyte," he said with a smile. "Why don't you and I resolve this ourselves, hmm? Together. In the ancient way… Communicate what words cannot…"

She gave him an indignant laugh. "Do you sing these crooked notes to every woman you seduce? Did you soil the ancient ways to have Phaedra? Elektra, Voleta, Lyra, Philinnia? Or any of the other women whose names you've misplaced?"

"Hardly. My words and intentions are for you alone, Hecate," he said, his palm resting on the column above her head. His gaze was hungry, but refused to peruse her body, instead staring straight into the shifting colors of her eyes. Thanatos quieted his voice as he leaned in to her. "What say you?"

They had played this game before, and Hecate had learned over the aeons that the only successful move with Thanatos was one that led to a stalemate. If she flinched he would crow triumphantly. If she showed anger, he would delight in her reaction. If she left the room, he would claim victory. His wings spread and curved over his shoulders, blocking the light around them, until he surrounded her. Death licked his lips. Hecate gave him nothing. She straightened against the column and raised her eyebrows. "We both know that sacred vows bind me," she hissed at him, "and we both know better still that I detest you as the living flame does the howling gale… what pushes your fevered mind into this fantastical abyss?"

Thanatos chose that moment to trail his eyes down her taut, maiden body, its form echoing the waxing moon. He lingered on her peaked breasts and the flare of her hips. He breathed in her scent of morning fog and aconite. She was ever in control of her reactions, yet her heart beat just a little faster. The corner of his mouth lifted. Close enough to disturb the red curls of her hair, he whispered close to her ear, "We always want what we cannot have."

The door opened, and Persephone stepped through, followed closely by her husband. Hecate immediately stood, Thanatos straightened, and both bowed to their sovereigns. Aidoneus looked from one to the other and scowled, bracing himself for an exhaustive litany of whatever they'd been arguing over this time.

"I bring no quarrel, my lords," Hecate said quickly.

"Neither do I." Thanatos folded his arms and looking at his fingernails.

Aidon thinned his lips. They were always quarrelling. He could feel the tension in the room and made his way up the dais with Persephone at his side. Once he reached the top, Aidoneus sat down and immediately regretted doing so, watching his wife fidget for a moment before standing tall beside his ebony throne. There was nowhere for her to sit and he chewed on his lower lip, inwardly berating himself. She should be sitting here and he should be standing. If he stood to offer it to her now, she'd refuse. Instead he sat looking like a barbarian conqueror with his nubile woman draped over the arm of his throne. He put it out of his head for now and focused on the pair standing before him. "What brings *both* of you here, then?"

"Separate concerns," Thanatos said, smiling warmly at Persephone.

"Who arrived first?" Persephone asked, perplexed. She had heard briefly about their feud, thinking that it had been blown out of proportion by Hypnos. But their barely disguised hostility combined with her husband's exasperation spoke volumes.

"She did," Thanatos said, glancing back at Hecate.

"By all means, Thanatos," Hecate said, motioning him to say his piece first. She smirked as he walked forward and folded her arms across her chest. "Wisdom never stands in the way of a fool."

"Warming up to the idea of yielding to me, are you?" he shot back with a smile.

"Enough!" Aidoneus snapped, raising his voice and startling all. "I've had a *long* and *trying* day and I have no patience to listen to you two bickering like children! So if you don't mind, I'd like to at least have *some* peace here before I retire with my wife for the evening." He pinched the bridge of his nose. "Hecate?"

"I beg your forgiveness, my lord." She stepped forward and took a deep breath. "You need no reminder of the suffering beyond your realm. The Corn Mother shuns all of Olympus. But perhaps she will see me. The future is as a broad delta flowing from the river we now row. Some tributaries end in the frightful auguries you have already seen," she said, pausing to look pointedly at Persephone, "and others could lead to far worse. The waters run swift, and they are deceptive. Following one stream will stop the suffering in the world above and stem the flood of mortals to your gates. I intend to teach Demeter to read the currents."

"Are you asking our permission?" Persephone asked.

"Yes, my queen."

She sighed, thinking about her mother, about her life as Kore and the things Demeter was willing to do to keep her in the world above. Her eyes stung for a moment. Despite all that she knew now, all the ignorance of her true identity that had been forced upon her throughout her life, all the needless cosseting, Persephone loved her. She missed her. Her heart wrenched for a moment as she tried to recall her mother's soft arms circling around her, her comforting smell of barley and sunlight. The kind, peculiar goddess standing before her was her only link to her mother right now. "I… sincerely hope that she will listen to you, Hecate."

Aidoneus shifted. "I am in accord with the Queen. Go with our blessing. I give you permission to speak on our behalf if you must."

Hecate nodded to them and shifted her familiar crimson robes to a darker hue. Indigo. Persephone knitted her brow, realizing that Hecate did so to blend in. Her richly clad mother who always dressed in gold and green and red had donned the colors one would wear to a funeral and forced all of brightly dressed Eleusis to do the same.

The Goddess of the Crossroads pulled up the hood of her himation, readying herself for the cold, and walked toward the ebony double doors, fading and vanishing before she reached them. Thanatos watched her go, admonishing himself for inwardly wishing her well. He was certain she could hear his thoughts from the ether.

"Thanatos?"

He turned and stood up straight. "We have him."

Settling back in his throne, Aidoneus rested his chin on the back of his knuckles. "Good. My suggestion was useful, then?"

"Wrapping the Chains worked flawlessly. Do you plan to send him to Tartarus right away?"

"No. Sisyphus spent enough time mocking the rules of this realm and thinks himself a god. He'll wait the customary three days like every mortal. He will have a judgment, and will come before me like all the other kings of men," he said, thinking. "But unlike the others, keep him bound."

"If you wish it. Isn't he more Alekto's and Tisiphone's concern, at this point?"

"The Erinyes have no shortage of other tasks." He put his hand up before Death could say anything in response. "I know *you* have been busy, as well; we all have. But I'm charging you and your brother with detaining Sisyphus."

He nodded. "Any reason to keep him chained and guarded?"

"He robbed Merope of her immortality and is clearly ageless, possibly deathless, now. That's never been done before; not even by Tantalus. As such, my friend, I don't want to take any chances. You are the Minister of Death. If he tries anything, I trust that you will stop him."

"So done. Anything else?"

"Yes. Do *not* go to his wife, Thanatos." He watched Death grind his teeth for a moment, then school his expression and nod in acceptance. Hades continued. "I don't want to disturb her by telling her that her tormenter is here. And she will guess as much if she sees you. Once Sisyphus has been escorted past the Phlegethon, you can go to Merope and let her know that justice has been done."

Death raised his eyebrows at this. "Three days, then."

"Three days. Keep Sisyphus chained."

Thanatos nodded and walked across the hall, his sandals clacking against the granite, the room otherwise silent. The door closed loudly behind him and Aidon and Persephone were alone once again.

"I'm sorry."

"For what?" she said. Aidon grabbed her around the waist and twisted her into his lap. She squealed in surprise and smiled wide, until she looked at his face. He gave her an abbreviated grin, then let his face fall back into the muted expression he'd worn before. Her mirth dimmed as she sat in his lap. Persephone looked away and leaned back into him, gazing out at the river lands of Acheron.

Aidoneus regarded her. How did she see him now? Would he now simply be the Fates-consigned lover of the Queen, at her call only when she had need of him? Aidoneus wanted all of her. He wanted to possess her as thoroughly as she possessed him. But with what they had been told, he knew that was impossible now. His place in the this realm was forever changed after today. This wasn't his— this had never been *his*. At the division of the cosmos he had pulled a hollow twig. What did that mean for him? As his mind wandered, his fingers absently brushed her bare skin at the open side of her peplos.

She giggled and her side spasmed at his touch and jerked away from his hand. Her lilting laugh was a pleasant distraction from his thoughts. A smile raised the corner of his mouth and he mischievously teased her again. Persephone shrieked and batted at his encircling arm, his fingers dancing along the inward curve of her waist once more while she writhed in his lap. He stopped and grinned, but it looked strained. "I want you with me in three days."

"Where?"

"Here."

"For the judgment of Sisyphus…"

"Yes."

"In your lap?"

He playfully hesitated. "…Maybe."

"Sitting *right* here?" she wiggled against him, feeling him sigh in response. He held her at either side to still the gyration of her hips.

"I'll think of something," he retorted, speaking through his teeth. His body started rebelling against him, even in its tired state.

"I don't think Hera sits in Zeus's lap at court, does she?" Persephone flirted.

"No. Her throne doesn't even sit on Zeus's dais." He saw her face fall.

"What about Amphitrite?" she said. "Does Poseidon tell her where to sit?"

"Based on the one time I met Amphitrite, I don't think Poseidon can tell her to do much of anything. And if he did, I doubt she'd listen." He thought about his brother's sharp-tongued wife. Persephone would get along with her, he thought. The sea nymph was a famous wit, yet didn't make waves with her husband, even though Poseidon had had countless dalliances. There were even rumors that rulers of the sea kept the peace by sharing lovers.

Hades and Persephone watched a warm magenta tinge the mists above the river, the Styx lighting up at twilight. The colors dimmed to a brilliant orange red. Persephone felt him breathe in, his mouth widening into a yawn. She tucked a wayward curl behind his ear. "You're exhausted, Aidon."

He nodded in acknowledgement and rested his forehead on hers. "You?"

"I'm getting there." She covered her mouth, her eyes squeezing shut as she muffled her answering yawn. Persephone lifted herself from his lap when she felt him shift restlessly underneath her.

"Come. There are a few things you and I must do before we go to sleep tonight."

Her mouth twisted up.

"Important things," he said, dispassionately.

She cast her eyes down and away from him.

"Persephone, I didn't mean it like that," he quickly said, lifting her chin up and studying her face. "But given all that happened with the Keres, this is absolutely necessary."

26.

AIDON WORE THE SAME GRANITE EXPRESSION HE'D had in Tartarus. She kept her eyes fixed on her feet as they walked back to their antechamber, wondering what thoughts played through his head. Persephone worried that those thoughts included a deep resentment of her now that they knew she was ultimately responsible for him drawing the lot for the Underworld. She took his hand as they carefully climbed the slippery last flight of winding stairs behind the falls. They came at last to their chambers, situated high above the throne room, and Aidon shut the heavy doors behind them.

He traced his thumb across the ridges of Persephone's fingers the way he usually did when he was taking her to their bedroom, but his face showed nothing. She watched the last of the twilight fade into blackness as color drained from the Styx. The torches in the antechamber flared to life, highlighting the starry ceiling he'd made so long ago. He would have been the king of the heavens if it were not for her, she thought. Instead of building this palace stone by stone beneath the earth, he would have ruled in the great citadel of Gaia and Ouranos that the Olympians had claimed as their own during the Titanomachy.

Aidon walked out to the terrace with his bronze water thief and dipped the perforated sphere into the catchment beside the falls. He filled it, then capped his thumb over the narrow top, walking it back to their room. She followed him back to the bedroom, stepping around the sporadic drops of water it spilled and stood next to their hearth. At least this moment was a comfort. It was the ritual they partook in after practice that she had come to love and know so well. He stopped up the small drain in the sink and released his thumb, filling the basin with water.

"Blood is a dangerous thing in Asphodel," he said, pulling off his himation. "The shades crave it without knowing that they do. If they drink it— no matter how small the amount— it unravels the effects of the Lethe, sends their minds into turmoil, and makes them relentlessly seek out more. Ichor, immortal blood, is especially dangerous."

He took her hand and drew her close to him, unfastening the fibulae that held up her peplos and setting them in the sink. Her garment hung down her waist, and she could feel her skin tighten against the cool air. He pulled off her girdle and set it aside, letting the cloth fall to the floor. Aidoneus quickly pulled out the pins of his tunic and undressed until he was as naked as she. She heard more metal drop into the sink as he pulled off his rings. He turned back and wrapped up all their clothes into a tight ball around their sandals and walked over to the hearth fire.

"Wait; what are you—"

"Neither the cloth nor the leather will burn," he reassured her calmly, holding their garments within the fire. Their hearth flickered hot, the room growing brighter. Orange Phlegethon flames licked around his hands without burning him or causing him pain. She heard drops and hisses in the fire, like fat falling off spit-roasted lamb. When their clothes stopped sputtering he pulled the bundle back, steam rising from it. "Instead, the River of Fire purifies them."

Persephone sat on the wide edge of the hearth once the fire died back down, her muscles relaxing as its warmth melted the tension in her back. Aidoneus occupied himself with meticulously folding their clothes, saying nothing, then knelt down to scrub roughly at his skin with a sea sponge, the beige mass tinted with the rust of dried blood. She stared into the fire, recounting their day. Persephone shuddered when she thought about the Keres tearing her husband to pieces, his sword flashing in the dark. No marks remained on Aidon's skin. Still, his cries of pain filled her ears as surely as if they were still in the Pit.

She didn't know how long she stared at the fire, but she startled when a wet sponge met her shoulder. Aidoneus rolled it across her back tenderly, his eyes calm and caring, but still distant. He was already clean, his hair wet, having washed the violence of Tartarus from his body while she was meditating upon it. Aidon held out one of her arms and she felt her skin prickle as the cold water washed the remnants of his ichor from her skin. Persephone remembered holding him to her, his body slumped over, injured and exhausted, his palm smearing blood down the front of her cuirass. Her eyes watered when she thought about how she had almost lost him, how they had almost pushed him off the ledge into nothingness. And now that they had returned with the inescapable knowledge that she ruled here, that he was tied here because of her, she wondered if she'd lost him all over again. Her breath hitched and a tear rolled down her face.

"Shh…" was all he replied, then stroked her hair gently and stood her up. He dipped the water thief into the basin and held it over her head, showering her with its cool contents. It soaked her scalp and fell through her coronet of braids, running in rivulets down her body. He paused to loosen her tresses once they were drenched, then took the sponge in his hand again and stroked her back rhythmically, calming her body, but not her mind.

Aidoneus moved to her front and washed her neck and collarbone. The sponge rasped against the tender flesh of her breasts and she sucked in a breath. He held her at the small of her back and knelt in front of her, staring up at her with his serene, dark eyes. When the sponge trailed over her stomach, she shivered, though not from the cold.

Her mind filled with the visions she had received in Tartarus: Aidoneus and Persephone, crowned King and Queen of everything above and below. His hand was upon her swollen belly, his fingers twined with hers. Everything changed to tatters of a ripped chiton and dirt and soot stains, embers flying around her and scorching her matted hair. The perspective in her recollection was different—terrifyingly real and different. Cold stone grated against her back. Her heels kicked against his muscular hips, her efforts to struggle in vain. Above her was Kronos, his eyes flinty and dark as he held her down and violated her.

Persephone sputtered a loud cry, doubling over, unable to hold it in, her face red and her body shaking. His arm wrapped around her hips, holding her up, her knees wobbling. Aidon worked faster, brushing the sponge over her thighs while she balanced her weight on his shoulders. She wrenched forward, tears falling on his head as he knelt before her and washed her calves and feet. Rising quickly, he tossed the tinged sponge into the hearth, and held her fast against him, her cheek resting against his bare chest. Her ragged sobs mingled with the hiss of the flames in one ear, his heart beating against the other.

"It's over. Shh, Persephone, it's over."

Her voice was muffled against the side of his arm, and she choked around another cry before she was able to speak. "Kronos-s," she finally managed to say.

"He cannot harm you," he said. She felt his arms tense and his skin flush with heat. "I'll see the world break before he lays a finger on you." Aidon knew this pain far too well, having struggled to deaden himself to it over the aeons. Her breath hitched as it came out and she gasped in between each cry. "Sweet one, breathe with me, alright?"

His chest rose under her head and he stroked her back until she mimicked him, taking in first large gulps of air, then long inhales through her nose. "It hurts," she exhaled.

"I know." The same agony had washed over him a thousand times, every time he journeyed into the Pit or came face to face with his father. There were ways to remove it, and he could do so for her, if she let him. He brushed his hand over her hair and swayed with her in his arms, calming her. "Do you trust me?"

The pools of her eyes were wet and deep when they met his. "What do you mean?"

"I can help you sort through the pain. Not take it away entirely, but at least help you pass through it. It's an exercise I learned as Hecate's student," he said quietly. "I don't have her gift of foresight, but I can at least help you through this. Can you trust me?"

She nodded silently and cast her eyes down. "What do I have to do?"

He stepped back and bent slightly to rest his forehead on hers. "Open yourself to me."

Persephone shuddered and looked up at him, his eyes dark and fixed on hers.

"Your private thoughts are yours," he whispered. "I will not pry into them or take them. But I can at least help ease your turmoil." Aidoneus waited for her to consent and heard her sniffle before she nodded and closed her eyes.

She felt his fingers thread into her hair beside her temples. Beyond his touch she felt his presence sink in even deeper. Memories and visions were given a place and a name. She exhaled as the one containing the vision of her defilement was unwound and pulled apart, its power over her removed. Her shoulders slumped forward and she rested her support entirely upon him.

"That's it…" he whispered in encouragement, his eyes shut. "Just let it go."

Aidoneus sifted through her thoughts as though they were grains of sand. Within her consciousness, he found scattered yearnings for larkspur and roses, for her mother, the sunlight… and looming large, the well-guarded boundaries of thoughts and feelings tied to him. He couldn't reach all of her pain. Much of it was inextricably tied to places he'd promised not to go. He felt his chest constrict when he realized that the pain was tied to *him*. Aidon scowled for a moment. His place in her thoughts was filled with fear and mistrust. Disquiet and sadness. He didn't venture further. He'd promised her. His heart wanted nothing more than to strip that doubt and pain away from her, to sort through it all and reveal in perfect clarity that she had nothing to fear from him, and show her how much he loved her. But if he were to do that, he might as well have given in and lain with her by the Lethe after she'd temporarily lost her memories. It would be just as much a violation of Persephone as what Kronos had forced her to watch— worse in fact, since she'd put her trust in him.

Persephone felt her breathing match his, slowing, her mind calming. He opened his eyes and she followed suit, feeling him gently retreat from her thoughts. His hands moved from the sides of her head and stroked her cheeks before his arms wrapped around her shoulders, drawing her to his chest. He exhaled and swayed again, rocking her.

"Thank you," she said, her voice small.

"Of course."

"How d-did you— H-how come *you're* so calm after… and I…"

"Practice." He brushed his thumb over the line of tears dried onto her face. "Experience. You witnessed what happened to *me* in the grove— Tartarus doesn't leave me entirely unscathed. I just push most of it to the forefront instead of delaying it."

"I don't know if I can do that, Aidon."

"You'll find your own way. Leaving Tartarus in the Pit, sloughing off its hold, didn't come easily to me at first, either. By the very nature of the place, it's bent on chipping away at you and filling you with fear and grief every time you go down there. I should have prepared you for *that* better. But I was used to it— immune to it— and have been for aeons. You… you'll get used to it too, sweet one."

Her eyes watered again at the tainted endearment.

He looked down and thinned his lips, anger rolling through him at the thought of *him* saying that to his cherished wife. "You want I should call you something else now?"

Persephone bit her lip. "I don't know."

"Maybe a shortened name? I like it when you call me Aidon," he said, smiling. "Sephia, perhaps?"

"Sephia…" A diminutive of Persephone. She wrinkled her nose.

"No?" He chuckled.

"It's pretty, but it's not— I don't want your name for me taken away from us. Especially not by him. I like that you call me 'sweet one'."

"Then I will continue to do so until you tell me not to."

Aidoneus stroked her cheek and kissed the top of her head. This might be the extent of his role now, he considered, in her realm and in her life. To catch her when she fell. To heal her when she hurt. To comfort her when the burden of ruling the Underworld became too great. But he wanted more than that. His need for Persephone, his love for her, demanded it. Perhaps he would grow accustomed to this, just as he'd grown accustomed to the vivid nightmares that preceded and the emptiness that followed any visit to Tartarus. But knowing their relative status in each other's lives, could she ever love him as thoroughly as he loved her? Did she think that his feelings for her were just a causality of the role given to him by the Fates? She had so much sadness attached to him, how could she truly care for him? Aidoneus put it out of his mind for now. Despite their weariness, he wanted to wrap himself up in her— to feel that intimacy with her that had become as necessary as air. Without another word, Aidon supported her around her shoulders and scooped her up by the back of her knees, then carried her across the room to their bed.

Persephone felt calmed by him, curled up against his chest, and comforted when he set her down and lay beside her. His caresses were warm and soothing, and didn't arouse right away. Her body ached. She'd spent too much energy trying to be strong, trying to be Queen. Aidon shaped his hand to her curves, from her hip to her waist and upward. Removed from the heat of the fire, her skin had started to cool; his hand reached the side of her breast, and both their tips peaked. A throb started low in her belly when he traced her thighs from her knee to her hipbone. The palm of his hand was warm, and his touch feathered across her. This was soothing, but it usually set her ablaze, caused her legs to wriggle and her back to arch, and drew her closer to him.

When she tilted her head up to accept his kiss, it was gentle, but distant. Persephone looked into his eyes when she pulled away from his lips. Nothing. She remembered last night, how he'd passionately gripped her shoulders and locked the backs of her knees into the crook of his elbows, his lips devouring hers with insistence as though there weren't enough of her that could possibly satisfy him. It was also a far cry from the tenderness and reverence he'd shown her the night before that. This was detached— almost like he wasn't there. And with that detachment, she feared his resentment.

He lowered his lips to one breast, pulling the peak into his mouth and sucking upward, making it rise to a point before his tongue ran a quick circle around it. This never failed to inflame her; he'd taught her every favorite touch. Even now, her body was responding, and she knew that if she hadn't already shared such a deep connection with him, this would suffice. But intuitively, it didn't. It lacked the bond they had so carefully forged this past month, the connection she craved. Did he resent her enough that this was how it was always to be? Mechanical and reserved?

Aidon traced her curves, his mind a maelstrom, his face a mask. After what they'd learned, he felt there wasn't any reason for her to love him equally, the way he desired. At best, he was her consort, her servant. Her pet. He worried that she merely tolerated his affections and reluctantly surrendered to what cravings he could rouse in her body. Or worse, that this whole time she had only submitted to whatever husbandly rights she assumed he had over her body, and had learned to make it enjoyable, but ultimately he had been taking her against her will. His stomach turned at this. He recalled her puzzlement as to why he didn't assert himself over her after their fight. True, she had initiated sex many times in the last month. But now, Persephone had no reason to need him, or want him. Or love him. The desire for pleasure was there, to be sure, but without love she would tire of his attentions eventually. They would curl up next to one another in listless familiarity and obligation until the awful, inevitable day came when she grew bored and left his private life altogether.

His hand rounded under the curve of her other breast and trailed down her stomach, finally stopping at the contour of her mound. Fingers trailed gently over the soft hair of her outer lips, petting her, stroking her. His touch was wispy and gentle, making her insides ache until she could take the light caress no more and rocked her hips forward into the heat of his hand. A digit sunk into her crease, drawing a long sigh from her. When it delved further into her, her muscles involuntarily clenched and twitched around it.

Persephone felt frissons of pleasure course through her body, her stomach tensing from his touch, curling her forward. When she'd first arrived here, when they had made love in the dark and barely spoke to one another, this was how it felt. They had been so untried and so very unsure of one another, their bodies alone acting in the roles of husband and wife without sharing their thoughts, their passions, their souls. She couldn't go back to that. Aidoneus kissed her neck and moved over her, parting her thighs with his knees. She sighed at the feel of his chest brushing against hers, his weight propped up on one elbow. He reached down and positioned himself to join with her. When she felt the tip press against her folds, she looked up at him, searching for something, anything. His face was still blank, the barrier he'd created around himself impenetrable.

"Wait," she said, pushing her fingers against his forearm. "Stop."

Aidon halted and slowly sat back, his face as empty as when he was touching her. He rested on his knees and said nothing.

"Please, Aidon. Just talk to me," she said.

He moved to sit beside her, covering himself with the sheet. She could read him so easily, he realized. It was foolish to believe that she couldn't see through him when they were so intimate. Aidon mulled over what he was going to say, and how he could say it, chewing on the inside of his lip. He'd sworn on the Styx to tell her the truth. But he had also promised not to force her to put into words the feelings and sensations he felt radiate from every part of her being when he was with her. "This past month, we've been friends and lovers, Persephone."

"And it's been wonderful." She swallowed and hesitated for a moment, remembering the fight that nearly drove them apart. "Hasn't it?"

"In so many ways, yes. I obviously didn't have time during our *brief* courtship to… befriend you. And this time we've had together, where I've come to know you fully, has been the happiest month of my life."

"But…" she said for him.

He stayed silent. The words lay unspoken and heavy between them.

Persephone's eyes grew wide and her next words rushed out all at once, stumbling over each other. "Listen, Aidon… I wanted to tell you when we were in Tartarus, but it didn't seem like the right time."

No, he thought, closing his eyes. *Gods, not pity. Anything but pity.* "Persephone…"

"My feelings for you have only grown—"

"Not now—"

"Aidoneus, I—"

"Persephone, please!" Aidon raised his voice and stopped her abruptly. "Please..."

She curled forward despondently and sat up, pulling a pillow in front of her, shielding herself. His forehead was etched with sadness, and it twisted further when he saw anguish wash over her face, her eyes wet with tears. Aidoneus felt as though a spear were piercing through him, knowing that he was the cause of her pain that this would only add to the hurt he'd seen wrapped up in her consciousness. But worse injury for both of them lay ahead if he allowed her to continue.

"Please do not say anything now, under duress, that you cannot take back later. That you would regret having said."

"How could I regret—"

"Please do it for me. It's all I ask of you."

"Aidon." She thinned her lips, her frustration rising, her heart sinking. "If you're trying to distance yourself from me because of what they said to us in the Pit today, don't tread lightly around me for my sake. Just out and say it: I am the reason you ended up here and you hate me for it now."

"What? How could I—"

"If you want us to," her voice hitched, "live separate lives from now on, don't put the full burden of that decision on me. Please..."

"Why would I desire such a thing?"

"You've treated me, looked at me differently since the moment Kottos said that you were here because of me! I can understand why you would resent me, why you would no longer feel for me as you once did, or question why you felt anything for me at all in the first place. If you're trying to put distance between us without hurting me, I appreciate your kindness, but please don't—"

"Resent..." His eyebrows raised and he tipped his head toward her. "Is that what this is about?"

"Well?" She shifted her feet but still held the pillow to her chest. "Isn't that why you won't hear me say that I—"

"No," he sharply cut her off. "No, sweet one. It's not because of that." Aidon looked away from her. "The reasons I have for stopping you don't come from any waning affection on my part, I promise. I love you, Persephone. This last month, I've let those words slip out when I— at the height of our most intimate moments… but I've *painfully* resisted saying them to you directly. I feared that you would feel forced to answer my feelings, but it doesn't change the fact that I love you. Deeply. No matter what we heard today, that remains undiminished. If you worry that I resent you, that I somehow think that you damned me to rule here, that's just not true."

"Are you sure?"

"What we heard today was… *unexpected*. But know that I would have accepted far less than ruling the Other Side if it meant spending eternity with you."

Her eyes watered at his words, but she still scowled at him and shook her head. "This isn't fair, Aidoneus. If that is how you feel, why not let me say what I feel for you?"

"Because when I first said that I loved you—" He stopped and shut his eyes, briefly praying to the Fates for the right words. "I should have waited to say what I did. It just all came out at once because I had never felt such a thing before. I had been with you for less than a day. I fully meant it when I said it, but you are far dearer to me now than you ever were then. And just *expecting* that you would immediately feel the same for me did us both great harm. You should take some time. Process what we heard. For both of our sakes."

She nodded, and he visibly relaxed as she spoke again. "But what I was about to say… I've known what you wanted to hear from me since the first night we spent together. But now that I can say it to you truthfully, you back away from it, Aidon. From me. Why?"

"Truthfully? Because what am I to you now? My significance to you, to what you truly are, is not what I thought it to be."

"Why should that matter at all to me?"

"You are sovereign here, you rule this realm. At least I had something to *offer you* when I… dragged you down here. But now I have nothing; and you honestly don't need me. Know that. Understand that, first. If you still feel the same after you've had a chance to think on it, then yes; I would *love* to hear it. But if there is any chance, even so slight, that you're saying those words out of pity, because you feel it is what I *want* to hear, and not actually…" He looked up at her, meeting her eyes. "My heart can't take that."

"Are you saying this because you somehow feel *less* than me now? Because of what *they* said to us?"

He turned and lay on his back staring up at the ceiling. "It's not a matter of how I *feel,* lady wife, it just *is.* All I ever was to this world was a regent holding your throne. You are the Queen of the Underworld. Its rightful ruler for longer than either of us has existed. And what am I?" he asked derisively. "Merely your consort, here by your grace."

"Oh?" She leaned over him, stretched out at his side and propped herself up on her arm. A smile raised one corner of her mouth. She pointed a finger toward the canopy above them. "You mean just as they say about me in the world above?"

He looked at her quizzically. Her smile spread into a wide grin at his baffled expression, but his features pinched, thinking she was mocking him. "I've endured enough today, my queen. Don't patronize me."

"I'm not," she said firmly. "Aidon, this is *our* marriage, isn't it? Isn't that what *you* said to me before? The gods above see me as your consort. The gods below see you as my consort. I came from a world that sees my body and soul as *your* property, sold to you by my father."

"And what of it, Persephone? The laws of their world hold very little sway here; you know that. This is— *was* my third of the cosmos," he said through gritted teeth.

"It still is! *Your* third of the cosmos, a place you've called home all this time, is where they exalt me as Queen and relegate you to merely being my destined bedmate after you've tirelessly ruled here for aeons— after you made this place your own. I refuse to accept that."

"That's *good* of you, but it doesn't change anything."

"Nothing has to change. This is all dependent on what *we* make of it. Why not just be King and Queen to each other, Aidoneus, and to Tartarus with what anyone else says?"

Thousands of years, and still you think like an Olympian, Hecate had said. *Theirs is a different world, and ours are different ways.* Aidoneus studied her face. "You would share this realm with me?"

"Only if *you* share it with *me,*" she said, her eyes widening. "I love my place here," she said, winding her finger along his chest. "At your side. As your *equal,* Aidon, which is a far sight better than what my place would be if you asked the Olympians."

"You love it here..." It sounded more like a statement than a question. It had taken him millennia. He worried it would take her even longer. "You love all of this? Even though there is no sun or moon, no roses or larkspur..." He looked away from her expectant gaze. "Even though I took you from your mother?"

Her face fell, lost in thought as he studied her expressions.

"You miss her, don't you?" he muttered under his breath.

"Of course I do. She's my mother, and her love was the only love I'd known for aeons." She kissed him softly. "But I love our world too, Aidon. It's peaceful and freeing, its rivers and fields awe inspiring, and when the first light dawns through the Styx every morning, it's so beautiful I nearly cry with joy every time I see it. If I cannot say and you cannot hear tonight that I love Hades the man, at least know that I truly love Hades the realm. I don't live in the world above anymore. This place is my home. *Our* home. I love it just as much as you do."

He cupped her face in his hand, studying the color of her eyes— gray like mist, encircled with sky blue. Aidon pulled her toward him and captured her lips once more, his previous restraint only a memory. His tongue played with hers, his fingers tensed against her back and his body strained to be closer to her. Their passions rose quickly and met each other equally, finally free of the restraints they'd placed around themselves since Tartarus. He drank her in, leaving both of them breathless. "Persephone…"

"You won't hold back anymore?" she gasped as she broke off their kiss.

"I will not," he answered, his voice rasping. Aidon rolled them on the sheets until she was supine beneath him.

"If that's so, then please, I can't be aah— *Aidon…*"

"Apart any longer?" he finished for her, his voice grating as he fully sheathed himself within her and held there.

Her eyes were closed in ecstasy. She cradled his body with hers, stretched and clenched around his length deliciously, and he couldn't stay still a moment more. He supported her neck in one hand, the other gripping her hip, and drove into her in deep strokes. Her fingernails raked his shoulders and he winced and hissed. The physical wounds from Tartarus had healed, but the pain itself was only dulled and still present. Persephone didn't know that she'd unintentionally hurt him— and when he looked down at the expression on her face, he didn't have any desire to make her aware of that. He loved seeing and feeling the effect he had on her, but decided he'd best let the Queen of the Keres claw at him another day.

He turned with her until he lay on his back, his body never breaking its connection with hers. Her legs straddled his and Aidon held her to his chest. Persephone tried to sit up, but he wrapped his arm around her shoulders and splayed his other hand along the base of her spine, keeping her close to him. The air rushed from her lungs when he thrust up into her at this new angle.

She ground against his pubic bone and her thighs started trembling when he seated himself deeper within her. It only drove her harder against him, the tension building when he gripped her hips. His length rubbed against the secret spot within her, its heat igniting the soft ridges while his groin pressed against the bundle of nerves at the apex of her mound. She felt sparks radiating from the point of their joining to the tips of her fingers and her toes curled tightly. With a sharp cry, Persephone reached the edge and bowed her back, his shaft the fulcrum on which she teetered. He grasped the palms of her hands within his, keeping her steady and balanced. Her expression was transported, her body overwhelmed, and any of Aidon's lingering doubts as to whether or not she needed or wanted him were erased.

In awe, he watched her from below. Usually this interplay of surrender and release would have milked his seed from him and tumbled him with her into completion. But he stayed within her unfinished. Aidon wasn't sure if it was exhaustion from their long day or his unwillingness to end their lovemaking so quickly. When she gazed down at him in sweet, weary surprise it didn't matter.

He enfolded her within his arms and drew her body back to his, then pushed down on her hips, grinding against her, and felt her tense anew. Her legs were shaking. She arched away from him, her eyes squeezed shut, her words unintelligible, her sheath rippling around him as she came again.

This was new.

Aidon tilted his head up to look at her as she recovered, then pitched forward into her, feeling her response, her body quivering and clasping at him. With a whimper, she was undone once more. He waited until she calmed enough to open her eyes, then eagerly repeated his motions, giving her exactly what she— lost in sensation— couldn't ask of him. Push. Grind. Shallow strokes that made her ache. Pushing deep and pulling her closer, until her center was all liquid heat and sweet friction. Her release had her clutching at the sheets, her voice staccatoed as she writhed against his chest. Persephone finally raised her head and looked up at him in dazed disbelief.

"Well, sweet one," he growled hungrily, and filled her to the hilt again. "Let's see how long we can make this last..."

"Please..." she slurred. *Aidon, I love you...*

She shivered against him, aching for more, and he obliged her. Aidon grabbed the cheeks of her rear, spreading her along her seam while he plunged into her. When her next orgasm rolled through her, her little feminine shakes and sobs filled him with masculine triumph at the idea of pushing his wife to such heights of frenzied ecstasy.

His reverie didn't last long. She leaned to the side and snaked her tongue out against his nipple and he groaned in response. A nip of her teeth there made him hiss and quake, his control disintegrating. Persephone delighted in his reaction, feeling his body respond to hers. She goaded him into giving himself over and licked at the flattened peak of flesh again. Holding her tightly, he moved faster within her until he reached a fevered pitch, building her pleasure one last time. Her completion coursed through her, powerfully and suddenly, pulling at him, her cries begging him to join her.

Aidoneus grasped her hips and rammed into her with one last fervent stroke, arching under her, his eyes shut tight, his words broken. "S-seph— my— *I love you!*"

She stilled, her insides warmed by each wave of his release. He collapsed underneath her, his gasps harsh. Persephone lay on his chest, listening to his heart race. Her fingertips danced over his shoulders and neck, feeling his pulse slow, his breathing return to normal.

"I love you, Persephone," he slurred with barely a whisper. "I always will." Exhaustion and replete contentment took him and his hands slowly fell away from her waist.

His body felt heavy with sleep underneath her. She recovered, listening to each measured breath that lifted and lowered her with the movements of his chest. When she knew Aidon had sunk deep enough into slumber that she wouldn't wake him, she pulled herself off of him, limbs numb and aching, to rest at his side. She reached for his hand and twined his unmoving fingers with hers.

"I love you, Aidoneus," she whispered to him. "I love you, my husband… I love you so very much…"

She knew he couldn't hear her. His body was nearly motionless, resting at last. Perhaps he could hear her in sleep and dreams. Nuzzling close to his arm, she took in his scent, cool cypress and warm tilled earth. Persephone smiled, joyful tears welling in her eyes and spilling over her cheeks. She whispered it against his skin.

"Hades, I love you."

She basked in it, raw and natural, like sunlight. She loved him. Persephone loved Aidon, wholly and completely. She would wait. Not too much longer— only until she knew it was time. She knew what she felt— but out of respect for Aidoneus's concerns, she would take time to process this. The time, she realized, would also give him greater reassurance so that when she fully and consciously gave her heart to him, he would accept it without any question or doubt.

It should have been said long before, she thought. Persephone reviewed everything that happened since she first arrived. The happiness that filled her heart was not a new sensation. She had loved him for weeks, she discovered to her delight. Chiding herself for not saying it sooner, she thought about how little time it had taken for her to fall in love with him. Persephone almost lost track of the weeks she'd been here. She'd been here for less than the passing of two months, from full moon to full moon and very soon another would— *Gods above...*

Blood is a dangerous thing in Asphodel.

Oh, Fates... Persephone clapped her hand over her mouth. Her eyes opened wide and she felt a cold shock race down her spine, part of the vision rushing back to her. His hand on her womb...

27.

SHE HADN'T BLED. NOT ONCE WHILE SHE WAS DOWN here, and she had been too distracted by her life being turned on its head to count the time. She thought back, trying to remember. On the new moon… two weeks before she was taken. And two weeks after she came here, nothing. A month after that, nothing. Her heart pounded in her ears. Moving the sheet aside, she looked at her flat belly and ran her hand over the natural contour just below her navel, imagining it swelling with life in coming months. Was she?

She thought back to when she was young, before her first flowering, when her mother had surrounded her with nymphs. *What was her name; what was her name? She had dark brown hair…* Kyrene. Demeter had thought she was the perfect guardian for her daughter. She was tall, wore a spotted leopard pelt on her broad shoulders and told Kore stories about wrestling lions to protect her father's flocks at Mount Pelion. On the longest day of every year she went to the vast lands beyond the desert, with grassy plains as far as the eye could see, to tame the wild striped horses. She would wander the earth looking for one that could defeat her. After one such trip to the great southern lands, she came back smiling, saying she had been happily defeated in the hot sunlight by the golden one, Apollo. Kore had pressed for stories, asking how Apollo could have defeated her, but Kyrene refused.

Not long after, Kyrene said she felt sick, and several mornings in a row had showed evidence of that. She had wandered into the tall grasses to lose the contents of her stomach— something that Kore had never seen before. The stocky nymph had moved more carefully, gracefully, patting her belly lovingly. A few months later, she had excused herself from Kore's company forever without even saying goodbye. When Kore asked her other fleeting companions what happened to Kyrene, they had said she was with child. When Kore pressed them, innocently asking if she had found a baby and was caring for it, they had tittered and whispered amongst themselves, a few of them scampering away.

Kore had hung her head in shame until one of the Oriades took pity on her and admonished the others. The kind tree nymph finally sat down with Kore and told her what had actually happened— that Apollo had stuck that *thing* between his legs inside Kyrene and put his seed in her, and the growing babe was what made her sick. Kore was shocked at the idea of this, horrified as the nymph crudely demonstrated with hand gestures what Apollo had done to get Kyrene with child. Kore had cried when she thought about a man roughly spearing into her friend like that. The nymph hushed her, saying that Kyrene had wanted him to do this to her.

Naturally, curious Kore had gone to her mother to ask more questions about men, and that pleasurable part of them they used for making babies. Demeter was furious and banished all the Oriades from her daughter's company. Finally, with great embarrassment, she admitted that Kyrene had lain with Apollo and had left to spare Kore's innocence.

But, she had said, if Kore ever gave herself to a man it would hurt; she would tear and bleed and no longer be a maiden. No longer Kore. Soon, the rest of the nymphs were gone— after an Oceanid swelled with Poseidon's seed and Demeter grew tired of explaining their antics. Between the Oriad's bumbling gestures and her mother's dire warnings, she had no idea that coitus could be enjoyable until she witnessed the Eleusinian wedding.

Maiden no more. Persephone was a woman now— a wife— and had certainly known the pleasures a man could bring her. She looked at her husband, his head tilted back in sleep, his chest rising and falling. Was the vision in Tartarus foretelling what was to come? Was she carrying Hades's child? She *did* understand enough to know that she was at the apex of her fertility— between the tides as Cyane had once put it— when Aidoneus had first taken her. But other than the stopping of her moon blood, there had been no other sign that she was pregnant. She didn't feel any physical changes, and she knew enough about what happened to women to know that she should have at least felt sick by now. The Oceanid who carried Poseidon's child was nauseous and had complained of soreness and tenderness in her breasts. Persephone gave one an experimental squeeze. Nothing. She hadn't been faint or sick either; neither in the mornings, nor in the face of anything she'd seen today in Tartarus.

What if she was with child? Throughout her existence she had never considered the idea of giving life to anything besides flowers, much less a child sired by the Lord of Souls, in the realm of the dead. Persephone had known only her mother's suffocating protection. Aidoneus had known only his father's cruelty. Their child would know no sunlight, no flowers, and no birds. What sort of parents could they hope to be? What if she was a terrible mother? Should she tell Aidoneus what she suspected?

But what if she told him and he didn't want a child with her? She looked back up at his peaceful face and shook her head, dismissing this almost immediately. Persephone couldn't picture him refusing to create a new life with her. He'd been alone and without love for so long. He'd welcome it. And they could have— and the idea sent chills through her— a family. She imagined a little raven-haired infant boy with blue gray eyes nursing at her breast. And as he grew older, Aidoneus would teach all he knew to their son, his heir. He would be eager to give life to more children with her, and raising them together would be a triumph over their own broken childhoods. And if she turned out not to be pregnant at all? He would be crestfallen if she raised his hopes like that then dashed them.

Perhaps her moon cycle had stopped because of the dangers Aidoneus spoke of— what blood itself could do to the shades. This idea wrinkled her forehead in frustration the more she thought on it. If her blood had stopped because she was in the Underworld, then that would mean they would never get a chance to *have* a family. Not as long as they were down here. Anger set in, and then hot tears, followed sharply by confusion. Now that the possibility was being considered, how badly did she want to have a child?

She felt a pang of guilt. Persephone was just becoming comfortable with Aidoneus, enjoying herself and him, had fallen in love with him, and to add a third entity… Was she strange to even think this way? Shouldn't a child be what a woman *should* want? Wasn't it the natural desire of a wife to provide her husband with children, a lady to provide her lord with heirs? Even if everything was different in Chthonia and the ways of world above were not the ways of the world below, didn't the desire to have children mean anything? To see the love of two merge together in the most elemental of ways and create a new life from it?

Persephone lay on her side and covered her belly with the sheet, her head swimming. Fates; she hadn't even told him she loved him yet! She rolled over, frustrated, needing to know more before she said anything. She would wait before she made any kind of announcement. Until she got a chance to speak with another woman about the possibility of being pregnant she would let it rest. Perhaps Hecate, though she had no children of her own, could shed light on this. Perhaps Merope, who had mortal children in the world above, though it would be difficult to meet with her when Aidon wasn't about. Nyx and Erebus had spawned thousands of children over the numberless aeons of their union. It would make for an awkward first meeting, but maybe the mysterious Lady Nyx would talk to her about having children here…

Feeling some measure of relief, and a full day's worth of exhaustion, her eyes drooped shut. Her mind turned from turmoil to the steady, rhythmic breathing of Aidoneus slumbering beside her. *Soon…* she thought, finally drifting into sleep.

* * *

"You've been here a fortnight," the broad winged shadow said. "You know that, right?"

"Oh, it's you." He groggily stared back at the mouth of the cave. "The murderer of souls. What do you want from me and how soon can you leave?"

"Murderer of souls… hmm. I would wager," Thanatos said, "that your sword cut down more than mine ever did during the war. All of mine were at once— and to great effect, to be sure. But you, Hades… you killed with a purpose. And I should know. My sisters were there to drag every one of them away."

"Yes… all that triumph, and glory," he slurred, "and look where it got me." Hades took another swig from his last amphoriskos of wine— the end of the gross he took with him on his descent into the Underworld. He'd intended to make them last. The news he'd received destroyed that plan, as it had destroyed so many others.

"You shouldn't have spoken to them. Hecate and I agree on very little, but she was right on this— it was foolish of you to go to the Cave of the Moirai so soon. You'd barely stepped off Charon's boat and your first destination was—"

"What's so bad about openly questioning the Fates, I thought? Especially when you've been as fucked by them as I have? But thankfully, they confirmed what I've always known to be true." Hades lifted the small neck of the amphoriskos once more to his lips. "That I've been cursed by them since the moment of my conception."

"A curse for one is a winnowing for another. You should ask my elder brothers some time about what being abandoned by the Fates truly means. Ask my mother, who tried for numberless aeons to birth a goddess that could rule Chthonia, and whose female children were all born daimones. You at least have a realm to rule."

"Is that so?" Hades snorted. "I am the glorified jailer of my father and his minions. I am the host of human souls who will be forbidden to even speak my name in the world above and will ward their homes against my presence now that I've been exiled here. And so far, I've only found one way to drown out the constant voices of Asphodel and Tartarus that echo in my head night and day… or whatever it is you call it down here. So, stin ygeia mas, Death," he said, raising the wine aloft in a grim parody of a toast. "Everything I did was for nothing."

"So what is your plan? To sit in this cave forever?"

"Until my wife comes of age and is given to me for my part in the war, yes." He brought his hand to his temples and shut his eyes against the dim light filtering in. "If she will even have me, once she knows what I know now."

"That's a brilliant idea," Thanatos said, looking around. "After all, what Queen wouldn't want to live at the back of a damp cave next to a

freezing waterfall, doting on a drunken husband who wallows in his own self pity?"

Hades threw the half full amphoriskos at Death's head. Thanatos ducked casually out of its way, and it hurtled by him base over spout. The ceramic shattered against the wall, echoing through the cave and amplifying Hades's headache. Sickly sweet rivulets of wine ran into the cracks, diluting on the dank floor. He sat up and looked at Thanatos, seeing two of him for a moment. "Have you come here only to taunt me, Son of Nyx? What is it that you want from me?"

"You must ask yourself that question, Lord Aidoneus," Thanatos said, folding his arms. "What is it that you want?"

"I want my forests and stars back. How do you suggest I bring them down here?"

"Build them," Thanatos said, looking at his new king's indignant face. "I don't say that to mock you, Aidoneus. Bring your stars here; build a palace around them. You hold dominion over everything beneath the earth— not just over the dead— and could use every ounce of what Chthonia can provide to create as much of the world above as you care to."

"It won't be the same. Even less so for her after a lifetime spent in the living world. Why would she ever willingly choose to be here with me in this gray waste?"

"The price we creatures pay for our immortality is being bound to the will of the Fates. There is no choice in this. For either of you. You drew the lot, but she was born for this. Do you really think, Olympian, that I would have chosen my divine role willingly? I would have much rather been the God of Love— or better yet, the God of Fucking— instead of the God of Death. But here I am; and she will arrive. And you, you are now The Host. The Receiver of Many. Not just of the souls of the dead, but of one day our fated Queen."

Aidoneus looked at the ground, mulling over what Thanatos said. "I am not an Olympian any longer."

"Then stop acting like one," Thanatos said quietly. "If you are no longer numbered among the selfish gods above, then prove it. Prepare yourself and prepare this realm to receive She Who Destroys The Light."

The Lord of the Underworld drew his knees to his chest and swayed, then nodded, aching as he moved to finally get up.

"Oh, and one more thing..." Thanatos said with a smirking smile as he turned to leave, "Clean yourself up. You look like the Tyrant."

Aidoneus woke up gently, blinking his eyes, his breathing measured. Persephone lay next to him, her head turned away in sleep and her arm cast over the edge of the sheet resting at her waist. He slowly rolled away from her and sat up so as not to disturb her, then opened the curtain, only enough to leave their bed.

He stood at the foot, gazing at her, her face peaceful in sleep. Her arm curved under one breast, the nipple smooth and full. The thought of gently waking his wife by rasping his tongue against its softness, until it beaded under his ministrations and woke her to his cravings, crossed his mind and stirred him for a moment, then passed. He smiled. There would be forever for that.

The curtain shut slowly in his hands. He didn't want the scrape of the rungs or the light from the fire to wake her. He needed to be alone. Though there were no windows in their room, he knew that it was still dark outside. Enough fitful, sleepless nights before his beloved's arrival had taught him that no matter how well he'd sequestered this room from the motions of day and night in Chthonia, he couldn't escape the innate knowledge of what time it was in his realm.

In her realm.

He contemplated that for a moment. Quietly, he unfolded his himation and pulled it around his waist, tucking one end in before lifting and draping the rest of it over his shoulder. He reached into the basin and pulled his rings out, placing them back on his fingers.

Theos...

The whispered voices started almost immediately. This one was from Asphodel.

I can feel it. I'm ready.

I know, Hades answered the shade.

Does that mean it is time for me to leave?

I am sorry, he said grimly. *No one is being born right now. But that will change, I promise. Have patience.*

In silent wisps of enveloping black smoke, he left his room through the ether and appeared in the grove. The tree branches were dark, silhouetted against the torches lining the palace walls and the small braziers burning atop the pillars at the garden gates. He could see well enough. Aidon leaned up against one of the trees and opened himself to his subjects in Asphodel, omnisciently listening to them.

Sotir... Anax... I am ready... Pater... She's here! Can we speak to her as we speak to you?... Theos... I wish to stay. I am at peace... Theos... Am I here forever?

Only as long as you need to be, he answered the last voice.

He turned his thoughts to Tartarus.

It wasn't my fault... Anax... I don't belong here!... Punish me?! You should punish her... It was too tempting. I couldn't stop myself... Do you know who I am?! Who I was... Sotir, spare me! Have I not suffered enough?!

You poisoned your father, your uncle and his wife for want of riches, Hades admonished the condemned shade. *No, you have not.*

The voices muted when one rose from the din.

Hades...

"No," he said out loud to his father. Kronos only chuckled at this.

She's strong; I'll give her that.

"More than you can imagine," he said, his voice a dead calm. He learned how to deal with Kronos a long time ago. There was no sense in regressing because of what he had been shown in Tartarus.

It will not save her from me.

"Then I will."

You can't.

"Know that I *will* end existence before I allow you to harm her."

The voice of Kronos was silent for a moment. His son's threat wasn't an empty one. *You wouldn't, Hades. I know you.*

"I am the Receiver of Many," Aidoneus said calmly. "I am very familiar with death, and I don't fear the end quite as much as you do, father."

She'd never forgive you. The last thought you'll have before you are extinguished would be the knowledge that she hates you.

"Considering the choice you gave her," he said, standing up, "Persephone would understand."

Selfish, foolish boy, he said. *You know that giving her back to Demeter would end this, yet you won't even consider it. Not even after you were shown what I will do to both of you when I am free. What manner of husband are you?*

"The destruction in the world above is Deme's doing. This realm *belongs* to my wife. It isn't a matter of me sending her back. And I wouldn't give her up if it were."

You throw the cosmos into peril while you blame each other. No doubt Demeter would say the same of you. Kronos barked a short laugh. *What contemptible fools my offspring have proved themselves to be. Petty, hypocritical tyrants. And you, Hades, are their king…*

Then he was silent. No doubt he'd attracted Briareos's attention by now.

Aidoneus paced the grove, then leaned back against one of the trees he and his wife had unwittingly created here. Perhaps Hecate would be able to dissuade Demeter.

It hadn't always been like this between them. When they were first freed, he had gotten along with Demeter. In the first few years they'd spent developing in Hecate's shadow, he'd even considered making her his queen once the war was over. The thought of coupling with Demeter had intrigued him back then but only in the most detached of ways— what it might feel like, if he could make it enjoyable for her, how it would change them. Now the memory of musings about congress with her put the taste of rotten fruit in his mouth. He had been protective of Demeter, but had never loved her. Then again, he didn't love anything back then. Her irrational heart and his methodical shrewdness had slowly driven a wedge between them. And it had made little difference anyway— her heart always belonged to another.

Zeus. A great ally for him— wily yet charismatic, driven and idealistic, and the target of Demeter's infatuation from the moment she saw him. Hades eventually grew to resent the fact that although he spent half his time protecting Deme from one thing or another, she would do nothing but sing Zeus's praises. When they had returned from destroying Kampe the first question she'd asked Aidoneus, though he'd staggered back covered in burns and gashes, was if Zeus was safe and sound. He'd lost his temper at her then and reduced her to a crying mess, castigating her until Hecate intervened and made him apologize. Zeus had waited for Demeter, albeit impatiently. But it was just weeks after he was given a taste of all the sensual delights a woman's body had to offer that he was pursuing Metis and Themis. Then Hera. Deme wouldn't hear any of it. She'd tearfully called Aidon a heartless liar. She'd refused to believe him, until it was too late, that her bedmate's desire for her wasn't based on love or devotion. On its basest level, it was conquest: once Zeus had her, the thrill of the chase was over. The callousness of his treatment of her had sickened Aidoneus at the time.

He walked back inside the palace and through the halls, passing the tapestries that showed the three of them— the *four* of them— by the river so long ago. Maybe he should go above and talk to Deme himself, and try to reason with her.

He scoffed at the idea, remembering the countless times she hadn't listened to him even when they *had* gotten along. It would be that much worse, now. In taking her daughter, he'd made an enemy of the Harvest Goddess for all time. If she was willing to destroy the world to regain her Kore, nothing he could say to her would matter.

Perhaps he *was* selfish to keep Persephone here. But in all his years below, what had he ever asked of the world above? Just her. Only her. He wandered back to the throne room and out to the terrace. The falls did nothing to soothe him. Though it was dark, he could sense the shades arriving in waves on the banks of the Styx. Aidon could hear their cacophony of confused, distraught voices.

He needed to give Hecate time. She was the only one who could reason with Demeter and make her understand that her daughter had a greater role in this cosmos than making flowers spring out of the earth. Aidoneus turned around and stared up at his chair sitting alone on the olivine dais.

You would share this realm with me?

Only if you share it with me.

Aidoneus smiled and walked back inside. Their roles in each other's lives swirled and twined around one another, reaching upward, like the serpents in a caduceus. He thought on that for a moment, then stood in front of the dais and raised his right hand. With a light flick of his fingers, his ebony throne moved, lurching out of the grooves its feet had worn into the stone in all his aeons sitting upon it, judging the dead. Once it sat where he wanted it, Aidon lowered his arm back to his side.

Sweet one, I do not want your place here to be ceremonial or merely as my consort. I want you to rule with *me.*

How little he'd known when he'd said that. Aidon closed his eyes and thought about her. The flowers she grew where she slept when he made himself known to her. The crown she wore when he first saw her in daylight. The moment that crown burned away in his hand as they plunged through the earth. Her nervous fingers braiding a garland almost unconsciously as they walked through the Fields of Asphodel for the first time. The fire she called forth from a single bloom in Nysa to open a pathway back to her kingdom.

Asphodel.

He knelt down to the ground and pressed his hands firmly to the floor of the throne room. It was cold, but as he focused a warmth seeped into his fingers and palms. The same energy rose through the soles of his feet, prickling his skin, filling his arms and shoulders, his calves and thighs, his loins, his heart. He could hear it beating now, just as he could whenever he communed with his domain.

A peaceful smile widened on his face as he reached through the essence of everything over which he held dominion. His awareness spread throughout the foundations of the earth from his contact with the stone, touching every part of it. The deep molten fires, circling and winding around each other, solidifying, cracking, churning solid minerals into being. The veins of gold, iron, copper and tin intricately woven throughout the rocks. The calm, cold familiarity of granite and basalt, gneiss and marble. The portraits and treasures of the ancient seas etched and embedded in limestone. The occasional and pleasant surprise of a precious stone or crystalline geode.

The Iron Queen.

The ore was pulled out of the earth, its wending veins draining at his will. Above him on the dais, they appeared molten, then solidified, piece by piece, wrought and woven into a pattern as delicate and strong as she was, its frame and shape of equal height and breadth to his own seat. When he finished, he stood up and studied her throne. It had been millennia since he had added anything to his home this way. This was the piece that completed it— the last thing he would need to create to make this place whole and ready for her: Persephone's throne.

Aidoneus pulled at his beard. Hephaestus might have done a better job. But the Blacksmith didn't know his queen the way he did, he thought with a knowing smile. He rubbed his exposed arm. Gooseflesh prickled his skin. It was cold business reaching through the depths of the earth. He turned and left their throne room, ascending the stairs, eager to curl up against his wife in the warmth of their bed.

This tale continues in DESTROYER OF LIGHT.

Acknowledgements

This novel, and the one to follow, *Destroyer of Light,* is the culmination of one of my lifelong goals: to publish a book that people liked. I started posting the first draft of *Receiver of Many* online for free, every Wednesday at midnight in serial format and the reaction I got from my readers blew me away. They, dare I say, *loved it*… And supported me through the entire process from its initial debut in Fall of 2012 to the last posted chapter in Fall of 2014. For those who read this for free and bought it anyway, this book is for you.

I want to thank the folks who patiently took the time to review and provide feedback on each chapter of the first draft, namely, C. Thome and L. Wilder. Next, I want to thank Sophia Kolyva, who was my greatest resource for most of the Greek translations, and helped fix my atrocious Greek grammar. Efharistó polí! And much thanks to fellow authors M. M. Kin, Eris Adderly, Titania Oliver, and several others who provided encouragement and insight.

In January 2015, I launched a successful Kickstarter to publish *Receiver of Many* and *Destroyer of Light,* and it is by the backing and contribution of many, many wonderful people that you are reading this today. A very special thanks to Kathryn B., Astrid Broady, Kenzie Capri, Shannon Cooper, Claire Starrs Daly, Stephanie Gilman, Lizbeth Hevia, Elaine Ho, Rostine J.M., Ivy K., Melanie Beth Keffer, Katherine A. Morgan, Bea Payumo, Sarah Rice, Ben Rico, Victoria Rybnick, Kate S., Alyss Scollard, Jessica Smith, Tran T., Kit Ilanya Turner, Tylar Voss, and Abby Woodworth for their generous support.

I also owe a huge thank you to my dear Kim F. (who you especially have to thank if you're a fan of Thanatos as he appears in my book). A special thanks to the wonderful Asphodelon, who provided artwork for the Kickstarter and for collaborating with me on *Bringer of Spring* and just being an all around amazing artist and friend. And to my darling Elizabeth Crowley, who graciously went through the book, line by line, twice, hunting down type-os before *Receiver of Many* went to press. My eternal gratitude goes to the fantastic Morgan Bondelid who designed the beautiful covers for my books. And last but certainly not least, my dear husband Robert, who started content-editing the book while we were dating, and faithfully carried the editing through the busy times of our engagement and eventual marriage. His dedication is written into every chapter, and he has been my greatest source of support and inspiration.

So thank you, everyone, for making *Receiver of Many* possible. This book and its sequel, *Destroyer of Light,* would not exist without you.

About the Author

Rachel Alexander has been a resident of California all her life and finished her first novel at age 16. She co-wrote a play that won awards from Bill Moyers of PBS and the University of Southern California. She received her Bachelor of Arts degree in English Literature and Literary Criticism from Principia College with an emphasis on creative writing.

When not writing, Rachel can often be found sewing corsets, overstocking her spice cabinet, and petting chickens. She is married and lives in San Carlos, CA with her wonderful husband/editor.

Excerpt from DESTROYER OF LIGHT

The following is an excerpt from the forthcoming novel *Destroyer of Light,* sequel to *Receiver of Many. Destroyer of Light* will be released in Spring 2016.

"You were stolen. Ravished."

Persephone looked up at the shade in shocked silence.

"Weren't you? You wouldn't have abandoned us, would you?"

She stayed silent. "I—"

"But you are going back?"

"Yes."

"You are escaping, then!" Her hand tightened around Persephone's. "Quick! Let me help you! That is why you are on this side of the River, isn't it? I can show you the path back to Eleusis!"

"No, I didn't escape. This is my home now, and I—" the shade wrenched her hands away from Persephone's and took a step back, her eyes growing wide. Persephone felt her mouth go dry as fear washed over the woman's face. Her voice rose, pleading. "You don't understand. I'm going back to see my mother. To reason with her. But I will return here after I do."

"Then you— you *did* abandon us…"

"Hades is my husband. I am his queen."

"But everything is dying without you!"

Persephone swallowed. "I know. But I will set it right again—"

"Destroyer," the woman whispered, shaking her head and backing away. "Destroyer!"

"No, please..." Persephone whispered.

"Destroyer!" another shade wailed as it wandered past. "Destroyer!" "*Katastrofeas!*" she heard in the common tongue. The voices blended together in Theoi, Attic, Thracian, and other languages. "*Despoina, torelle mezenai!*" "Persephone!" "*Ekeini pou katastrefei to fos!*" "Destroyer of Light!" "*Perephatta!*" "She who destroys the light!"

They weren't speaking to her, but around her. It was as though her conversation had rippled outward, affecting the shades. The shoreline became a shrill chorus accented by wailing and sobbing. *Destroyer of light.* Persephone felt ice pour down her spine and doubled over as though the wind were knocked out of her. Her very name and its meaning.

A balance has existed here for all the years you've been alive, Praxidike, Kottos had said. *You are the one who transcends and connects the worlds. You are the embodiment of balance...*

She was caught between her mother and her husband, and the fate of the world was bound up with her, just as the Hundred Handed Ones said it was. *No, please Fates, no... no, no, no...*

"Please, I didn't mean to—"

"My Dimitris was right," the shade hissed. "You weren't there to bless us. You did nothing but curse us!"

Carrier of curses...

"I didn't... this wasn't... Please, you must believe me," Persephone cried, nearly hysterical. "I had no idea that it had become so terrible! It's why I'm going back. I— Please, tell me what I can do to help you; to take away your pain. Please!"

"Take me with you."

She blanched. "I am sorry, I cannot. I cannot."

"I must see Dimitris. He needs me!"

"You cannot ask that of me! You know there's no going back to the world of the living."

"Please, Soteira, take me back!" she cried frantically.

"Do not ask this of me, please..." she said softly, seeing the other souls take notice.

The shades around them began to cry out to her, their voices a cacophony. "Aristi, my children!" "Metra, please, spare me..." "Just once more, Thea, let me see her once more..." "*Soteira, voithiste me! Voithiste me!*" someone cried out in the common tongue.

The shades circled her, begging her to spare them. The Eleusinian woman backed away from her, fading to translucence. "My lady, I cannot cross the River, yet. I'm not ready. I must see Dimitr—"

And with that she was disappeared— a soundless ghost bound for the world above.

Persephone crouched and shut her eyes. She clapped her hands over her ears to block the wandering shades out, crying loudly to drown their voices. They stopped their petitions and started weeping as she was. They milled about, wailing and moaning, their cries incessant as she huddled close to the ground, too distraught to rise.

Caught between her love for her husband and her mother's love for her, she'd forgotten why she existed in the first place— for them. The mortals. To look after their eternal souls, not just when they were here, but during their brief time in the sunlit world. To feed them. To protect them.

"Kore? Persephone?"

It was a high tenor voice, almost lost to her amidst the weeping shades. It sounded so clear and distinct that she thought that it was an illusion.

"Lady Persephone!"

She looked up through her tears to see a young man wrapped in a chlamys, his face hidden by a golden petasos. He descended from above and landed next to her.

"Wh-who…" She knew who he was. Hermes. "Why are you here?"

He lightly took her hand, barely touching her fingers. "You're free."

"What?"

"Persephone, I was sent here by our father to bring you back to your mother, Demeter."

"We never *asked* for you to— what…" she drew in a breath as he grasped at her wrist. She wrenched it away from him. "Let go of me! What do you think you're doing?!"

"You've been freed from Hades's captivity. I'm here to bring you back to your home in the living world."